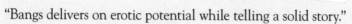
"Bangs delivers on erotic potential while telling a solid story."
—*Publishers Weekly*

"*Wicked Edge* delivers delicious alpha men who are like putty in the hands of their women, and action galore."
—*Fresh Fiction*

Wicked Fantasy

"If you need a good laugh, then grab this one . . . Engaging and fun, filled with surprise twists and turns around every corner. I truly look forward to finding out what trouble the cosmic troublemakers will cause next."
—*The Eternal Night*

"A sensational read full of humor and romance. You'll be burning through the pages while you follow . . . all the hijinks and scorching sex. *Wicked Fantasy* is a great read, and I enjoyed every minute of it. Nina Bangs has created a story with outrageous and hilarious characters, and a romance that will make you wish for your own fantasy at the castle. It goes on my bookshelf as a keeper. Enjoy!"
—*Night Owl Reviews*

Wicked Pleasure

"Wicked fun from start to finish . . . [A] side-splitting, sexy tale that dazzles and delights."
—*The Best Reviews*

"Another terrific Nina Bangs, humorous, action-packed, paranormal romance . . . Readers will enjoy this wicked tale."
—*Midwest Book Review*

"A delightful comedy."
—*The Eternal Night*

continued . . .

Wicked Nights

"Paranormal romance filled with humor and sex . . . and with the right touch of suspense . . . Action packed. Readers will enjoy this wicked tale and look forward to novels starring Eric's siblings, a demon and an immortal warrior, that will surely sparkle with fun." —*Midwest Book Review*

"Intriguing." —*The Eternal Night*

. . . and the novels of Nina Bangs

"Sinfully delicious." —Christina Dodd

"The key to Ms. Bangs's clever . . . novels is the cast never does what the reader expects. [She] combines vampires, time travel, and . . . amusing romance that will lead the audience to read it in one enchanting bite." —*Midwest Book Review*

"Bangs puts a . . . darkly brooding hero together with a stubborn heroine; adds an amusing cast of secondary characters . . . and then mixes in several different paranormal elements and equal measures of passion and humor to create . . . [a] wonderfully creative, utterly unique romance." —*Booklist*

"A witty, charming, sexy read." —Christine Feehan

"Sensuous and funny . . . [A] true winner." —*RT Book Reviews*

"A sizzling story . . . With steamy love scenes and touching characters, Ms. Bangs brings readers into her world and sends them away well satisfied with the power of love." —Karen Steele

"I know I can always count on Nina Bangs for an exceptional read! A pure stroke of genius." —*The Best Reviews*

Wicked Memories

Nina Bangs

BERKLEY SENSATION, NEW YORK

THE BERKLEY PUBLISHING GROUP
Published by the Penguin Group
Penguin Group (USA) Inc.
375 Hudson Street, New York, New York 10014, USA

USA | Canada | UK | Ireland | Australia | New Zealand | India | South Africa | China

Penguin Books Ltd., Registered Offices: 80 Strand, London WC2R 0RL, England
For more information about the Penguin Group, visit penguin.com.

WICKED MEMORIES

This book is an original publication of The Berkley Publishing Group.

Berkley Sensation Books are published by The Berkley Publishing Group.
BERKLEY SENSATION® is a registered trademark of Penguin Group (USA) Inc.
The "B" design is a trademark of Penguin Group (USA) Inc.

Berkley Sensation trade paperback edition ISBN: 978-0-425-25607-7

An application to register this book for cataloging has been submitted to the Library of Congress.

PUBLISHING HISTORY
Berkley Sensation trade paperback edition / June 2013

PRINTED IN THE UNITED STATES OF AMERICA

10 9 8 7 6 5 4 3 2 1

Cover art by Juliana Kolesoba. Hand lettering by Iskra Designs.

For Cindy Hwang.

I truly appreciate all that you've done
to make my books better.
You've shown amazing patience in the face
of talking cats and snarky wizards.
Thanks for being such a wonderful editor.

1

He stood at the end of the pier. A full moon shone over the Gulf of Mexico. How many times had he watched the dance of moonlight on water through the centuries? A thousand? Ten thousand? And each time it triggered the same memory. It never went away, never changed.

On the other hand, some things definitely *did* change. He turned to stare at the amusement rides rising from the long pier behind him. Hard to believe. He owned a freaking amusement park. As weapons of vengeance went, this had to be a first.

He looked beyond his pier to the Castle of Dark Dreams across Seawall Boulevard. Too bad his roller coaster and Ferris wheel blocked Sparkle's view of the water. He smiled and knew it didn't reach his eyes. A view would soon be the least of her problems.

He'd named his park Nirvana. Now he needed a new name for himself. He'd used hundreds of them over the centuries. Names attached you to people, to places. He didn't want attachments. They filled you with all kinds of destructive emotions—love and the need to protect. Been there, failed at that. So when he was ready to move on, he changed his name.

He thought for a moment—about Sparkle, about his revenge—and decided who he'd be in this time and place. Thorn. Because he intended to be a giant thorn in Sparkle Stardust's treacherous ass.

Thorn stopped thinking about Sparkle as he sensed the three men moving up behind him. He might not have felt any aggression coming from them, but they were definitely wary. Not that it mattered. His security chief was nearby. He turned and waited.

They stopped in front of him. No friendly smiles. To be expected. He was the "competition." They'd wonder what game he was playing. No one would guess, though, not even Sparkle, until the end.

"You're the owner?"

Thorn nodded. "Thanks for coming." The speaker had dark hair and eyes that were a distinctive shade of blue. All of the Mackenzie vampires had those eyes. "And you're Eric Mackenzie."

Eric frowned. "You have Mackenzie eyes. Who are you?"

"Thorn Mackenzie."

"I don't know any Thorn Mackenzie. A lot of us have changed our names over time, though. What was your original name?"

Thorn tried to look thoughtful. "I don't remember." Sometimes it was even true.

Eric's snort of disbelief said it all. "I don't know why I took the time to come here."

You came because I phoned and asked you to come. You decided it was a great chance to meet the bastard that Sparkle's been whining about every time she's called you. I planted that suggestion. Thorn would pay for that act of persuasion, but it had been necessary.

"Why'd you send for us?"

Klepoth looked about seventeen. He wasn't. He had blue spiked hair to go with his blue eyes. But Thorn could see the shimmer of red behind the blue. Demons didn't always have the best control when they were excited.

"I want to offer you jobs. Here. With me."

"Why would we want to work for you?"

Thorn studied Zane. Dark hair. Eyes that didn't seem to know whether they were blue or gray. But no matter the color, there was something about those cold, pale eyes that worried Thorn. Sorcerers were unpredictable. And this one was more dangerous than most. Thorn needed him, though.

"I can offer you more of what each of you wants than Sparkle Stardust ever could."

He met their gazes—his vampire, demon, and sorcerer—and told them exactly what he was offering. Thorn infused his words with his power.

When he finished speaking, he waited.

But not for long.

"Wow, count me in." Klepoth's red eyes announced how excited he was about his new job.

Eric didn't hesitate. "I'll give Sparkle my two weeks' notice."

"Finally, a challenge. I can explore my limits." Zane's wicked grin said he didn't believe he had any limits.

Thorn nodded. "Welcome to Nirvana." That might be misleading. He had no way of knowing if they'd discover their own nirvana here. Everyone found their bliss in different ways. Not that he gave a rat's ass about them.

He watched them leave. Thorn wouldn't trust them with his ultimate plans. But that didn't mean they served no purpose. They'd help him create the most spectacular amusements on the planet. And as long as they worked for him, Sparkle wouldn't be able to use their power to destroy Nirvana.

Thorn returned to staring out at the Gulf. They were his. No matter what arguments Sparkle or anyone else threw at them, they wouldn't change their minds. *Couldn't* change their minds.

Because once he "persuaded" someone, they stayed persuaded until he released them. That was his power, and he'd wielded it again after denying it for so many centuries to make sure Sparkle's Castle of Dark Dreams became the Castle of Shattered Dreams.

And if he regretted taking away their free will—because the gods knew he'd experienced the hell of controlling nothing in his own life—he appeased his conscience with a reminder that he'd pay for the power he'd used on the three men. Nothing was free. The monster was awake, and he'd have to starve it into submission. Even after two hundred years, he remembered the agony. But if it meant making peace with his memories, the pain would be worth it.

"When I find the owner of that abomination, I'll shove my heel where it'll do the most good." Sparkle stood at the castle's window with her night-vision binoculars trained on the amusement pier across the street. "Crap. I can't see past that damn Ferris wheel."

Kayla glanced down at Sparkle's tall platform boots with the five-inch stiletto heels and winced. Ouch. She edged away from the other woman. What had Dad gotten her into?

This was her client? A woman named Sparkle Stardust who wore ass-kicking boots, black leather pants, a black corset, and until she'd put it down to pick up the binoculars, had been wielding a whip? Bizarre.

Okay, keep this on a professional level. "Exactly what will I be doing while I'm here, Ms. Stardust?" Her father hadn't told her a thing before sending her to Galveston except to say that this was a test, her first job as a member of the family business, and that she'd have to deal with a difficult client. Kayla took a deep breath. *Love you too, Dad.*

"I've never been a Ms. Stardust. Call me Sparkle. And you'll be helping me get rid of *that*." She took the binoculars from her eyes long enough to spear Kayla with a hard amber stare.

Uh-oh. Kayla didn't need to ask what "that" was, so instead she asked the all-important question. "How?"

Sparkle pushed her dark red hair from her eyes and got back to spying. "I don't know. Be creative. I've used every crooked legal trick Holgarth could come up with to stop construction, but none of them worked. Nirvana opens tomorrow along with that butt-ugly big parking garage the city let them build alongside my theme park."

"Holgarth?"

Sparkle didn't take the binoculars from her eyes. "My lawyer."

"Maybe Mr. Holgarth missed something."

She cast Kayla a puzzled glance. "I doubt it. And Holgarth is his first name."

"Oh." Well, we all dealt with the names we were given. "So why do you think the owner built right there?" Kayla was distracted for a moment as something strange registered. She looked at the big gray cat that stared unblinkingly at her from the couch. Sparkle and the cat had the same shade of amber eyes. A coincidence? Had to be.

Sparkle made an impatient sound. "It's obvious. He, she, or it— could be an evil consortium—wants to leach off the amazing popularity of Live the Fantasy. Of course, Nirvana is nothing more than an ordinary amusement park with boring ho-hum rides that lack any kind of creative brilliance."

"I understand—"

"You understand nothing."

Kayla swallowed her words along with her temper. The client was always right. *Do not tick off the client by telling her to shove her stupid park.* "I'm listening." Besides, Sparkle wasn't the one making her mad. Kayla was aiming all her hostility at her manipulative father.

Her dad's whole life revolved around his work as a P.I., and he'd always assumed his children would join him in the family business. Kayla couldn't convince him that once she earned her law degree she would get her thrills by winning court cases, not sneaking around spying on people. Sending her here was his idea of giving her some field experience. She took a deep calming breath and refocused on Sparkle.

"I built Live the Fantasy because I believed adults would flock to a theme park that allowed them to role-play their innermost fantasies. Even forbidden ones." She smiled. "I was right. The Castle of Dark Dreams is only one of the park's attractions, but it's the only one that's also a hotel. Guests love the whole castle experience." She muttered a few curses aimed at the dirtbag owner of Nirvana. "And part of the experience was the great view. Until *that*."

Evidently "that" was now the code word for Nirvana.

Sparkle lowered the binoculars to look at Kayla. "I assume you've noticed my totally incredible outfit."

"It would be tough to miss." Kayla thought her word choice was ambiguous enough not to offend Sparkle.

Sparkle nodded. "When I finish here, I'll go down to the castle's great hall and become a wicked vampire who enjoys making helpless men her blood slaves. Of course, eventually the fearless vampire slayer shows up to kick my butt and save the slaves." Her smile was filled with sly knowledge. "The slaves rarely thank their savior." She flung her arms wide to encompass the whole park. "And that's just one fantasy. Every attraction in Live the Fantasy has a variety of role-playing opportunities. They last for a half hour and then our customers can move on to another one."

Kayla widened her eyes. Dad had told her this was an adult theme park, but he hadn't elaborated. And he'd loaded her on the plane for Texas before she'd had time to do any research. "What a unique concept. I'm impressed."

Her praise seemed to put Sparkle in a better mood.

"So you understand why I'm so upset that some bastard has built his dull and dreary amusement pier right under my nose." Sparkle put her binoculars up to her eyes again. "In the morning we can talk strategy and . . ."

Kayla waited impatiently for Sparkle to finish her sentence. She had flown into Hobby Airport, hired a taxi to take her to Galveston, and then been whisked to Sparkle's suite in the Castle of Dark Dreams. She was tired. All she wanted to do was go to her room and sleep.

Sparkle never did finish that sentence. Instead she dropped her binoculars and swung to stare at the gray cat, her eyes wide and shocked. "Eric, Klepoth, and Zane just left Nirvana. They're on their way into the castle. What the hell were they doing there?"

Kayla frowned. If Sparkle was waiting for the cat to spout words of wisdom, she'd wait a long time.

Sparkle grabbed Kayla's hand and dragged her toward the door. "Let's go. I want to catch them while they're still together."

"But don't you have a fantasy to do?" Kayla couldn't help it. She was anal when it came to duty and job performance. A weakness.

"Holgarth will find someone else. Now move it." Sparkle sounded as though she was talking through clenched teeth.

Kayla didn't argue. If Sparkle expected her to make Nirvana go away, she'd need every scrap of information she could get. She glanced down to see the cat padding alongside them. Unusual. Cats didn't do much following on command.

They raced down the winding stone steps instead of taking the elevator, ran across the great hall, and reached the hotel lobby in record time. Kayla was still busy congratulating herself on surviving with no broken limbs when Sparkle shouted.

Three men who stood just inside the entrance turned and then strode toward them.

Kayla sucked in her breath. Talk about spectacular. She didn't think of herself as shallow, but wow, just wow.

They stopped in front of Sparkle.

One of them—a man with pale eyes that looked as though they could ice over with a single blink—nodded at Kayla.

"And you are?" His question sounded casual, but something else seemed to flow beneath the surface.

Kayla scooped her jaw off the floor and answered. "Kayla Stanley." She didn't owe him any other explanation. If Sparkle wanted him to know more, she'd tell him.

Sparkle ignored Kayla and moved closer to the man. "What were you doing inside Nirvana, Zane?"

Zane narrowed his eyes at her tone. "Meeting with the owner. He offered me a job, and I accepted. Consider this my two weeks' notice." He didn't wait for Sparkle's mouth to close before walking away.

Well, that was interesting. Kayla looked at the two remaining men.

"Ditto that."

Sparkle stared at the boy who'd spoken, and now that he was closer Kayla could see he really was a boy. About sixteen or seventeen. Beautiful even with the blue spiked hair.

"Why, Klepoth?" They seemed the only words that Sparkle could manage.

"More money, more everything."

Kayla got the feeling that the "everything" was important. She wanted to ask what it was, but decided against calling attention to herself when she saw Sparkle's expression. Kayla worried that Sparkle was about to tug off her boot and go to work on the unsuspecting Klepoth.

But all Sparkle did was glare at him before shifting her attention to the last man. She didn't seem to notice when Klepoth left.

"You were in Chicago. When did you get in? What happened? Talk to me, Eric." Her expression softened a little.

"The owner of Nirvana called. He said he had an offer for me. You'd spent so much time ranting about him that I decided to fly in. Glad I did. I've decided to accept. You'll have to find someone else to take care of things in Chicago. I'll stay on for two weeks before I start working at Nirvana."

Eric didn't sound guilty, he didn't sound anything. He sounded disconnected, distant from the words he spoke. That probably meant something, but Kayla found it hard to concentrate on his words because she was having a tough time looking away from his gorgeous eyes. She didn't think she'd ever seen anyone with eyes that brilliant shade of blue. Once a long time ago she'd visited Moraine Lake in Canada. His eyes were the blue of that lake.

Sparkle tentatively reached out toward Eric and then yanked her hand back. Her expression hardened. "What's his name?"

"Thorn Mackenzie." He turned away.

"Mackenzie?" Sparkle seemed too shocked to call him back.

From the look on Sparkle's face, the name meant something to her.

As Eric walked away, Kayla breathed deeply and refocused on Sparkle. She took an instinctive step back. Sparkle had narrowed her eyes to amber slits. And if Kayla didn't know better, she'd swear they glowed.

Sparkle looked down at the cat who'd planted his ample bottom on the toe of her boot. "Do something, Mede."

Okay, her client had officially lost it. Kayla would call Dad as soon as she got to her room and explain that she couldn't work with the insane.

Her thoughts about where the nearest mental health facility might be were interrupted by the sound of an explosion. She rushed to the glass doors along with Sparkle, the cat, and everyone else in the lobby. Across the street, a small stand right inside the entrance to Nirvana was now nothing more than twisted metal.

"I blew up a refreshment stand. Best I could do, sweetbuns. Made it look like an electrical problem. We don't want the cops opening a major investigation."

Kayla actually felt her heart stop and then start again. *She'd just heard a voice in her head.*

"Give the lady a prize."

A sarcastic voice. Frantically, Kayla scanned the people around her. Maybe *she* needed the mental health facility.

"Your head's fine, babe. Yo, down here. The cat." He sounded impatient with her obvious density. *"Sparkle should've spent less time with her binoculars and more time explaining things to you."* The cat stared at the glass doors and they opened. *"I'm Ganymede."*

Sparkle interrupted the craziness happening in Kayla's head.

"Mackenzie might still be over there, Mede. Find him. Inciner-ate his ass. Or send him into the past, the future . . ." She paused for some teeth grinding. "I don't give a damn as long as he's gone." Then she paused and took a deep breath. "I've changed my mind. Don't kill him. A murder would bring the police around. We don't need them creeping through the castle looking for a killer."

"How about if I pound the crap out of him?" Ganymede looked hopeful.

Sparkle nodded. "Fine."

"There're some undamaged candy bars over there calling my name, honeybunny. I'll fortify myself with a few, and then I'll get right on the beat-down." He padded toward Nirvana, his tail a plumed feline question mark.

Fitting. Kayla curled her hands into fists to stop them from shak-ing. What was Ganymede? Who was Sparkle Stardust really? What had just happened to her sane and ordered world? And how long before she hyperventilated herself into unconsciousness? "Someone better explain things to me right now or else I'm catching a taxi back to Hobby Airport and heading home." Maybe forcefulness would hold the hysteria at bay. *Breathe slowly, breathe deeply.*

"Don't be such a baby." Sparkle sounded annoyed. "I'll explain things later. Right now I have to talk to a few people. Stay with me."

Kayla wanted to run from this place where cats talked in your head and clients had names like Sparkle Stardust. But as she calmed a little, the denials began. She'd imagined the voice. She *wasn't* insane. It was all a giant hoax. *Sparkle* was the crazy one. None of the explanations made her feel better. Then she thought about her father.

He'd made it clear that Sparkle was an important client. And Kayla had made it clear that she didn't want to join the family business. But she did need help with law school expenses. This job would pay well and keep her father off her back for a little while longer. But a freaking voice in her head? Before she bolted, though, she'd get some answers.

"Did your cat just speak to me in my head?" Saying it out loud sounded . . . delusional.

"Yes." Sparkle held up her hand. "Later."

Stay calm. Kayla narrowed her eyes. To hell with later. She asked another question. "How?"

Sparkle waved her hand in an I-don't-have-time-for-this gesture.

Kayla *would* get an answer to one of her questions. "Why are you so important to my father?" *Does he know about the talking cat?*

Sparkle paused to stare at her. "Didn't he tell you? I brought your mother and father together."

"It was *your* fault." And if Kayla sounded outraged, she had a right to her anger. "My parents were a disaster together. Other than the sexual attraction, they never agreed on one thing. They did nothing but fight until the day they divorced. How could you not see how wrong they were for each other?"

Sparkle brightened. "Wrong for each other, but perfect for me. They were one of my success stories."

Kayla glared. "You're a sick woman. And why was my father so determined for me to come here? I have zero experience. Either of my brothers would've done a better job." What had Sparkle meant by one of her success stories?

Sparkle began walking again. "I told your father to send his daughter because I assumed the owner of Nirvana was male."

Kayla couldn't believe what she was hearing. "You want me to use my *sex?*" She said nothing else because if she tried to speak, she'd just sputter. Not a professional response.

Sparkle seemed puzzled. "This is war. We use every weapon we have." A tiny smile tugged at the corner of her lips before disappearing. "And I can make you into a very powerful weapon indeed."

Kayla clenched her fists and kept up with Sparkle. If she decided to stay—and that was a giant neon "if" right now—they'd have to come to an agreement over the terms of Kayla's employment. She had one more question for now. "The name Mackenzie seemed to mean something to you. What?"

Sparkle's heels made angry click-clacks as she crossed the great hall. She didn't bother to look at Kayla.

"It means the owner of Nirvana is a vampire."

Kayla was outta there.

2

Thorn smiled as he continued to stare out at the Gulf. He hadn't done much smiling until a few centuries ago. Smiling had been a waste of time and facial muscles. And for those who thought virtual immortality meant eternal happiness, they needed to walk a thousand years in his soul. When you had the ultimate power of persuasion, everything became too easy. No challenges, just endless boredom.

He'd seen it all, done it all, and there had been nothing left for him. He'd been a solitary creature, so he'd had no friends. He'd seriously considered ending his existence. Not even the thought of raining down revenge on Sparkle's deserving head had seemed to matter.

But salvation had come a few centuries ago in the form of a human he'd met briefly as night was falling. The man had been perched on the edge of a cliff above the sea. He'd attached a pair of ridiculous-looking wings to his back. He'd told Thorn he was going to fly.

That had almost made Thorn smile. Almost. A group of supporters had shouted encouragement to the idiot. Thorn had watched with interest as the man flung himself from the cliff. The pathetic wings had managed a few ineffectual flaps and then the man had plunged into the sea.

Thorn had started to turn away from the cliff and the anguished screams of those who had been watching, but then he'd stopped. Maybe he owed the human for the few entertaining moments he'd provided. Thorn wasn't easily amused anymore.

So against his better judgment, he'd dived into the sea and hauled the drowning dumbass to safety. Once the man had heaved up the water he'd swallowed, he'd gasped his thanks.

Thorn had been vampire for so many years he'd long since forgotten the things that motivated humans. He wasn't quite sure what to say to the man. "Perhaps you weren't meant to fly."

The man gave a hoarse chuckle. "At least not off cliffs that will land me in the sea. I'll choose my spot more wisely next time." He'd glanced at the water that had almost claimed him. "And I'll do it when the sun is still high. I don't want to be in the air when the monsters that wander in darkness are about."

The monster that wandered in darkness who had just saved his stupid ass blinked. Had Thorn heard him correctly? "*Next* time? Why would you put your life in danger again?" Human lives were already wretchedly short. Why would anyone chance chopping any more years from that brief span?

The man met Thorn's gaze. "It's not the flying, it's the thought that I *might* fly. Not this time, but the next, or the next." He shook his head. "I don't know what I would do if I actually did fly. I'd have no more purpose. A man has to have a purpose."

Thorn had stood watching as the man's friends and family climbed down to where he lay and converged on him. They hadn't noticed when Thorn left.

That's when he had his great aha moment. He needed "purposes" in his life. And since his greatest vampire gift, persuasion, made ordinary goals ridiculously easy, he'd stop using it.

He'd paid for his decision. Who knew that using your power every day for centuries would become addictive, worse than any dependence on human drugs. Thorn now knew that the older the vampire, the worse the withdrawal symptoms. He hadn't known how bad it would be back then. A good thing, because if he had, he might not have tried.

The memory of his withdrawal still made him shudder even after all these years. His mind had scurried in circles—confused, panicked. It felt as though some alien creature were trying to claw its way out of his head. The pain pounded at him even during his day sleep. He remembered slamming his head into a wall over and over until blood poured down his face, blinding him. Stomach cramps tore at him, and he spent night after night curled into a fetal position, unable to hunt, to even move. So much pain for a creature who'd known very little of it until then almost took his mind. He now knew why he had never heard of other vampires denying their powers.

But after a month, he'd emerged from his pain-filled hell free of any compulsion to persuade. The agony had been worth it. For the last several hundred years he'd lived as a human would. He solved his problems as a human would. Yes, he still took blood, but that was necessary to survive.

He'd rediscovered his joy in existing, found once again the thrill he'd experienced so long ago when he'd sailed as a Viking. And as an added bonus, he found that people liked him. He usually didn't have to use persuasion to sway them. Of course, their liking would turn to terror if they knew what he was. Once a monster always a monster.

This was the first time he'd used his power to persuade in two hundred years. And he'd done it only because Sparkle was a special "purpose." He wanted to create something so spectacular that it would drive her into a frenzy, and he didn't have time to woo his new employees the human way.

Thorn hoped that since he'd used his power briefly and on only a few people, he wouldn't have to pay the full price when the urge to use it again came calling and he said no. Thorn didn't have a clue how much it would take to form a new addiction.

Because even now, when revenge was so close, he'd still keep his "humanity" unless circumstances forced him to take out the gifts that made him vampire, dust them off, and throw everything he had at the Castle of Dark Dreams and all who stood in his way. And to hell with future pain.

"You're smiling. It looked as though your meeting went well, so I suppose you have a reason to be happy."

Of course, that didn't mean that Thorn wouldn't *hire* the supernaturally gifted. He turned to face his new security chief. "I have three new employees. The power they wield will make Nirvana a success."

"Nirvana opens tomorrow. Will they be here?"

"They mentioned something about a two-weeks notice." He laughed. "Two weeks? More likely two hours. When Sparkle gets really ticked, she doesn't think straight. She'll kick all three out of her castle tonight. They can stay with me until I find them housing."

Grim shook his head. "Hope Ganymede doesn't interfere. He's trouble."

"So are we, Grim. So are we."

Thorn had met Grim Mackenzie in the wilds of Alaska years ago. Thorn had seen what he had once been in the other vampire—a loner, but a *survivor*. So when he'd been considering who he'd put in charge of protecting his pier, he'd thought of Grim. Luckily for him, Grim had grown tired of communing with nature at the same time that Thorn had tracked down Sparkle and thought of the perfect setup for his vengeance. Turned out that Grim had once met Sparkle and Ganymede. An added bonus.

Like all Mackenzies, Grim was tall, muscular, and gifted with the Mackenzie eyes along with a very useful talent.

"The rest of my team will be here in about a half hour." Grim paused.

Thorn sensed that Grim had something to add, so he waited.

"You used your power on those three." Grim met his gaze. "Why didn't you use it on me?"

"How do you know that I didn't?"

"I thought about your offer for days before accepting. Persuasion works faster than that."

Thorn raised one brow. "Would it have worked?"

Grim seemed to consider that. "Yeah, I think it would have. I saw how you controlled them. You didn't even break a sweat." He grinned. "But you never know. I'm a stubborn bastard."

Thorn returned Grim's smile. "I didn't need to persuade you. My money did the persuading for me."

Grim nodded. "There's that. But the money wasn't what sold me on the job." His eyes glittered with anticipation. "It was the thought of matching wits with Sparkle and Ganymede. I haven't had a challenge like that in a long time."

Thorn opened his mouth to answer him . . .

And the refreshment stand near the gate blew up. The boom shook the whole pier as a cloud of smoke billowed into the night air. When the smoke finally cleared, only twisted metal remained along with a scattering of torn snack bags and a few candy bars.

"What the hell!" Grim crouched, lips peeled back and fangs exposed.

"Well, that was fast." Thorn felt a predatory satisfaction. *And so it begins.*

Grim looked confused. "Uh, someone blew up your freaking stand. A little more reaction, please?" He glared across the street at the Castle of Dark Dreams. "Wonder who it could be?"

Thorn narrowed his eyes. "I guess my three new employees gave Sparkle their notice. Maybe I'll go over and see how she's taking the news."

Grim snorted. "Not well. Go over there and they might blow you up too."

Thorn felt a surge of excitement. "They won't know it's me. I've lived a long time as a human. No one will sense my true nature." He glanced at Grim. "What good is revenge if I don't see her expression, feel her rage? If I hurry, I might be in time to catch Sparkle in full fury." What a rush.

"I think you just *did* feel her rage." Grim shook his head. "Better hurry. The cops will be here soon. You don't want to get tied up with them."

Thorn nodded. He strode toward the small windowless building tucked behind the game stands. It didn't take long for him to put on his wig, insert colored contacts, brush a little powder on his brows to lighten them, and pull on his hoodie. He drew the hood far enough forward so that it shadowed his face. Finally, he shoved a few things he'd need into his pocket. Luckily it was a cool spring night in Galveston, so the hoodie wouldn't look out of place.

Then Thorn headed toward the main gate with Grim walking a short distance behind him. He could hear the distant sound of sirens. But he paused for a second to stare at his ruined stand.

Sonofabitch! Sparkle's damn cat, Ganymede—*not a cat, remember that*—crouched in front of the pile of rubble while he chowed down on one of Thorn's candy bars.

Knowing that the cat would be listening as he ate, Thorn shouted back to Grim. "Wow, the boss is gonna be pissed about this. When you call him, tell him I'll be in early to help clean up." That was just in case the cat decided to scope out the pier looking for Nirvana's owner after he finished stuffing his pudgy face. Then Thorn strode past Ganymede, altering his path slightly so that his foot came down squarely on the cat's tail.

With angry feline yowls echoing in his ears, Thorn crossed the street and disappeared into the darkness. When he was sure no one was watching, he scaled the wall separating Live the Fantasy from the street and entered the Castle of Dark Dreams from the door that opened into the great hall rather than the hotel lobby.

Thorn quickly scanned the large room with its towering ceiling, fireplace massive enough to roast a mammoth, and long banquet table that rested on a dais near said fireplace. Authentic-looking weapons and tapestries hung from the walls.

He must've come in right at the end of one fantasy because everyone was running around preparing for the next one. Thorn ignored the actors in their medieval costumes and the customers scurrying to take their places before the fantasy began. He scanned the hall for Sparkle.

"If you'd hoped to join the next fantasy, you'll be disconsolate. All the parts are filled. Even if they weren't, I have a schedule to keep. Not even annoying explosions will interfere with it. I'd suggest you put your name on the list for the one after this. And you might remember that the early bird gets the juiciest parts."

Thorn made his judgment about the speaker even before turning around. Sarcastic, supercilious, and self-important. He could've added snarky, but that would've been one "s" word too many.

Thorn turned . . . and almost laughed in the man's face. Damn, he should've gotten his butt over here sooner. He'd missed out on lots of free entertainment. Thorn was tall enough to almost look down onto the top of the man's head.

This guy took stereotypes to a whole new level—blue robe decorated with shiny suns, moons, and stars; matching tall conical hat that made him seem way taller than he was; the prerequisite magical staff; and a pointed gray beard to go with his narrowed gray eyes.

The wizard drew himself up and puffed himself out. "I sense that I'm amusing you."

Thorn widened his eyes. "Me? No." He tried to look impressed. "Hey, can you really do magic?"

"Cave-dwelling troglodyte."

Well, Thorn had been called worse. "What's your name?"

"I'm Holgarth. And I have no more time to waste on you. If you want to wait for the next fantasy, then wait over there." He waved imperiously to the wall near the door. "If not, I would suggest you leave." His expression said he really hoped that Thorn would just go away.

"I can tell you're a real people person." Thorn throttled back his temper. If he wanted to stay, he'd have to buy a ticket and keep his mouth shut.

"I find that most people aren't worthy of my effort." Holgarth's stare said that Thorn was one of the least worthy. "Now, I must abandon this fascinating conversation to take care of a casting problem."

Bemused, Thorn watched him stride to where a woman was selling tickets to the fantasies. He cut in front of the line.

"We seem to be missing an evil vampire dominatrix. You will have to do for this fantasy. Try to disguise your natural tendency to mewl and cower." Holgarth walked away, leaving the woman with her mouth hanging open. But then she sighed and left the table.

After the line disappeared, Thorn walked over, took a ticket, and left his money on the table. Then he leaned against the wall watching for Sparkle's appearance. If she didn't show in a little while, he'd go hunting elsewhere in the castle. Because wherever she was she'd probably be yelling. And he had great hearing.

Kayla almost trotted to keep up, shedding bits of her sanity along the way. But she didn't have time to stop and pick them up or she'd lose Sparkle. If Kayla was convinced of nothing else, she was convinced that her client held the key to every bizarre event she'd witnessed tonight. And she intended to gather all the evidence she could before fleeing back to Philly and her father's anger.

Sparkle wound her way around the ongoing fantasy, heading toward a man who must be the castle's resident wizard. He was dressed for the part. From his expression, she'd bet that no laugh lines would ever dare crinkle his face. Didn't seem like a friendly type. Sparkle stopped in front of him.

"You are *late*. I had to find a replacement for you." He almost vibrated with righteous anger. "Your replacement is *not* satisfactory. She has no flare for portraying a sexual creature. I'm embarrassed for her." He sniffed, dismissing the woman as a failure. "I have a schedule to maintain, and you should care enough about the castle's reputation for excellence to show up on time."

Sparkle ignored the wizard's outrage. "*Your* traitor son has sold his services to the vampire hell spawn across the street." Her tone hinted that only weak family genes could cause his son to do something that stupid.

The wizard's thin lips thinned even further and his eyes narrowed to slits. Kayla expected laser beams to shoot from them and leave a smoking hole in Sparkle's forehead.

"My son would *never* stoop to working for a . . ." He paused. "Wait. Did you say *vampire*?"

Kayla's thoughts exactly.

"The owner of Nirvana is one of the Mackenzie vampires." She tapped out an impatient rhythm with her toe.

Kayla decided that Sparkle was prepping the toe for upcoming ass-kickings.

The wizard seemed to consider her words for a moment. "I still can't believe he'd agree to work for a mere vampire."

Kayla blinked. He hadn't even paused at the word "vampire." And no matter that her brain was trying to explain everything away as the ravings of a bunch of crazies, *she'd heard the cat speak in her head.*

Don't panic, don't panic. Kayla swallowed hard and glanced away as their argument escalated. She wanted to be a lawyer. A good attorney listened to all the evidence. Before leaving, she'd give Sparkle a chance to tell her side of things. Not that anything her client could say would explain away talking cats and vampires. But until then, she needed to concentrate on something else to calm the mad pounding of her heart, to keep her feet from taking her away from here right now.

Kayla glanced at the people around her. The ongoing fantasy looked like fun. Too bad she wouldn't get a chance to try one. But if she stayed, how would she maintain her professional objectivity without being sucked into the madness surrounding her?

Stop. Think of something else. She scanned the people standing against the wall. They must be waiting to take part in the next fantasy. Ordinary people. She needed a huge dose of ordinary right now.

Her gaze reached the end of the line and froze. A man stood leaning against the wall. Tall with wide shoulders. Nothing unusual about his clothes—jeans, boots, black T-shirt with a hoodie pulled over it. He hadn't bothered to push back his hood. Her father had taught her to notice those kinds of details. And she would swear he was staring right at her.

She shook off the idea. He was probably interested in the wizard and Sparkle. They were getting louder by the minute.

Kayla couldn't seem to drag her attention from him, though. His face was in shadow, and strands of blond hair fell down over his eyes. But her first impression was of a hard beautiful face. You'd think those two words wouldn't go together, but they did. She felt the urge to walk over and pull the hood away from his face so she could get a better look.

Then he smiled at her. At *her*. There was no doubt. The same way there was no doubt that his smile left her gasping. Literally. She took a deep breath.

She should look away. That's what people did when they were caught staring. But she'd grown up in her father's family. One of the first things she'd learned was that looking away was a sign of weakness. You never dropped your gaze from a predator unless you were prepared to turn and run. And on some level she recognized the predator in gorgeous-guy's smile.

Kayla smiled back.

She'd never know where that smile might have led because he turned his head to say something to the couple in front of him in line. But he'd served his purpose. He'd distracted her for the few minutes she needed to achieve some calm.

Kayla looked back at Sparkle and the wizard just in time to see the man with the pale dangerous eyes join them. Zane.

"Traitor." Sparkle ended the word with an angry hiss. "And after all I did for you."

Zane raised one brow. "All you did for *me*? Give me a second to recall *all* you did for me." He paused while Sparkle practically crackled with suppressed fury. Then he shook his head. "Nope. Can't remember anything." His gaze turned hard. "But I haven't forgotten all I did for *you*. So maybe you should lose the attitude just because I found another job."

Kayla silently applauded Zane. He had to be tough not to buckle under Sparkle's death glare.

"Think about what you're doing, son. Yes, you're a powerful sorcerer, but there's still so much I could teach you." The wizard's voice softened.

Kayla could read the subtext: Stay here with me. The wizard had lost his superior expression. She saw real distress in his eyes. Kayla forced herself not to feel too much sympathy. She couldn't afford to get emotionally involved here. Wait. Had he said *sorcerer*?

"Mom is the goddess of magic, Dad. I'll always have someone who'll brainstorm ideas with me." Zane smiled. "And you'll be just across the street. We can meet for lunch, do dinner, spend quality time together whenever you want."

"Goddess of magic?" Kayla spoke without thinking first. She didn't want to be part of this crazy conversation, but Zane's claim had caught her by surprise.

Zane glanced at her. "Isis." Then he returned his attention to his father.

"Of course." After a certain number of back-to-back-to-back shocks, numbness set in. She tried for an inner giggle, silent laughter to signify how ridiculous all of these people were, how impossible their claims were. Kayla couldn't dredge up even one snicker. *I'm in deep trouble.*

"You won't be spending any quality time on *my* property."

The force of Sparkle's anger was a scary thing. Without warning, Kayla stumbled back. So did the wizard and Zane. Someone had *pushed* her. Not possible. She would have seen if . . .

Kayla glanced down. Sparkle's feet were six inches off the floor. *She. Was. Freaking. Floating.* Ohmigod, ohmigod! So much for numbness. Kayla widened her eyes and then looked at the others before staring back down at Sparkle's feet. Zane was the only one who seemed to notice Kayla's expression.

He followed her gaze. "Temper, temper. You're levitating again, Sparkle. Any minute now your customers will notice." His smile was malicious. "Not good for business."

Sparkle dropped to the floor and glanced around to see if anyone was looking—she didn't seem to count Kayla with her mouth hanging open as "anyone"—before she again speared Zane with her you're-dead-to-me stare. "You're through here, Zane. I want you off my property tonight. Be sure to take Eric and Klepoth with you. Go sleep on the vampire's Ferris wheel for all I care."

And as much as Kayla wanted—no *needed*—to keep believing that everyone except her was crazy, she couldn't keep denying what she'd felt, heard, and seen. Nausea made her take a deep breath. She wouldn't humiliate herself by throwing up on Sparkle's shiny boots.

Before anyone could say anything, Sparkle turned to Kayla. "This fantasy is almost done. I'll be playing the wicked dominatrix vampire in the next one. Zane usually acted as my faithful demon sidekick. You'll take his part tonight. Holgarth should be able to scrape up a few new cast members by tomorrow."

"Holgarth?" Hadn't Sparkle said that he was her lawyer? "I haven't met him yet." Kayla should. And soon. When she ditched this job, Sparkle might scream breach of contract.

"That would be me, madam. And even though Sparkle has chosen not to introduce us, I assume that you are Kayla, our newly acquired intrepid spy." The wizard's tone turned "intrepid spy" into an insult. "I truly hope she received a discount for accepting you rather than one of your more qualified brothers."

If steam wasn't billowing out of Kayla's ears and nose, it wasn't for a lack of inner fire. For a moment she forgot that she'd be leaving this madhouse. "And you, sir, are a wart on the nose of wizardry." Kayla didn't know if Holgarth really believed he was a wizard, but if he was part of the Castle of Dark Dreams gang, then he probably did. "You don't even have the power to keep your own son here." Okay, so she probably shouldn't have said that. But it was too late now.

Holgarth paled, but he didn't look away. "You're right, madam. I don't. Perhaps we're both doomed to failure."

Kayla could almost see him wrapping his dignity around him. Fine, so she was sorry she'd lashed out the way she had. Other less personal insults would have made her point.

Zane glared at Kayla. "That wasn't necessary."

Kayla was now in fighting mode. "So it's fine for him to insult me, but I'm not allowed to fight back?"

"Not that way. Besides, my father insults everyone. You just need to ignore it."

"I would appreciate it if you'd desist from fighting over my still-warm body." Holgarth avoided his son's gaze. "I'm quite capable of defending myself."

Kayla ignored Holgarth. "One thing you should know about me, Zane: If someone hits me, I hit them back. Harder. My father taught me that." Kayla wouldn't back down from this man, sorcerer, or whatever he was. Once started, backing down became a habit. She needed to remember that when dealing with Sparkle too. *Isn't quitting the same as backing down?* She tried to ignore the thought.

"Well, well, you *are* a surprise." Sparkle looked gleeful. "I love a woman who won't take crap from anyone." She glanced at her watch. "Let's go. We don't have much time before the next fantasy."

Without sparing another glance at Holgarth or Zane, she disappeared into the crowd, every swing of her hips announcing that no one had better get in her way.

Holgarth took off his hat and ran his fingers through his hair. "I wish you'd spoken to me before making your decision, son."

"It seemed the right thing to do." For just a moment, Zane's eyes showed confusion. Then they cleared. "Look, you're the top dog at this castle. No one needs me here. Thorn will give me a chance to show what I can do."

His father looked troubled. "How? Why would he need a powerful sorcerer for an ordinary amusement park?"

Zane's expression turned cunning. "Maybe it won't be quite as ordinary as Sparkle hopes it will be." He smiled. "I'll be in touch, Dad. Have to go tell the others to forget about their two-week notice." Then he walked away.

Holgarth watched his son leave before putting on his hat again and turning to Kayla. His superior expression was firmly back in place. "If shock hasn't nailed your feet to the floor, follow me so I can show you where to change into your demon costume. We have customers waiting for the next fantasy."

Customers waiting. She hadn't meant to look. But once the memory of the man touched her, she automatically glanced toward the wall. He was gone. Kayla shoved aside her twinge of disappointment. It was for the best. She'd be leaving Galveston anyway. Somehow that thought didn't make her feel better. Distracted, she nodded to Holgarth.

Now Kayla felt as though she were the one floating above the floor, supported by a cloud of panic and disbelief. She had a feeling that when she finally touched down again it would be a hard landing.

She seemed strangely disconnected as Holgarth led her to a small changing room, handed her a costume, then left. Ignoring Sparkle, Kayla pulled on the costume without paying much attention until she reached for the next piece . . . and it wasn't there. She stared at herself in the mirror. Holy hanky. That's about how much she was wearing.

"Are you ready?" Sparkle still sounded mad.

Startled, Kayla looked away from the mirror. "This costume. It only goes from my behind to my boobs." She glanced down. "To the tips of my boobs." What the hell was she doing? "Why am I even here?"

Sparkle looked puzzled. "You're my demon assistant. You don't have much to say, so you have to do something to justify your presence. Don't worry, you'll be a success. Holgarth will make sure to send us only male victims." She seemed to think for a moment. "I'll have to find a male assistant by tomorrow night or the female customers will lose interest."

"You've got to be kidding. I'm not wearing this, and I'm definitely not playing your demon assistant." Kayla started to pull off the costume.

"You will if you want answers from me. I know your father. He'll demand explanations when you run home without doing your job. Besides, deep inside you're wondering if you're going crazy. You *need* to hear what I have to say." Sparkle's smile was mocking. "And you *are* planning to run, aren't you?"

Kayla didn't answer her question because she had one of her own. "Bribery?"

Sparkle widened her eyes. "Of course."

Anger pushed Kayla's inertia away. "So I'm your token sex object?" This was so not in her contract.

"Actually, *I* have the sex star power in our little fantasy. You're my pale and almost insignificant shadow. You have a problem with that?" Sparkle sounded impatient.

"Uh, yes? You said that Zane usually played this part. Where's *his* costume?" Kayla would just bet that Zane's costume was more substantial than the piece of lint Sparkle expected her to wear.

"There." Sparkle pointed and then kept talking.

Kayla walked over to see Zane's costume while Sparkle explained her part.

"All you have to do is hang around me, do what I tell you to do, and try to look sexy. Now, when . . ." Sparkle narrowed her eyes. "What exactly are you looking for?"

"Zane's costume."

Sparkle sighed. "You're standing in front of it."

"This?" Sparkle had to be kidding. "It's a loincloth." A *tiny* loin- cloth. If Zane had any kind of package power, he'd be hanging out all over the place.

Sparkle headed for the door. "The women who signed up for this fantasy liked him in that."

I just bet they did. Kayla now understood why Zane had grabbed the offer to work at Nirvana so quickly.

Okay, she could do this. She really did want to know what was going on before she left, and not only so she could survive Dad's wrath. She didn't want him to be able to accuse her of being delu- sional. Besides, if by chance all of this was real . . . She took a deep breath. She could wear this ridiculous outfit for the one fantasy. Then she'd shed it forever. That wouldn't take much effort. All she'd have to do was exhale. It would split and fall off like a snake's old skin. She sort of liked the comparison.

Sparkle led her back into the great hall and over to a stone stairway that spiraled into darkness. "This stairway leads to the upper floors of the castle and down to the dungeon. Most of our guests use the elevator." She headed down.

Kayla gave silent kudos to whoever had designed the castle. The stone stairway, dimly lit by fake wall sconces, was seriously creepy. Once they reached the bottom, Sparkle led her along a short hall- way to a heavy wooden door with a sign reading DUNGEON above it. Sparkle swung the door open. Kayla thought the creak was per- fect. Someone had paid attention to details.

There were a few other doors along the hallway. Kayla assumed they were storage rooms.

"Guest rooms." Sparkle stepped into the dungeon.

"Really? I mean, they can't have any windows, and the lighting is really bad in the hallway. Who'd want to stay in them?"

"Vampires." Sparkle moved aside so Kayla could see the inside of the dungeon.

Kayla had no response to that, so she looked around her. Stone walls and floor, fireplace with instruments of torture neatly hung beside it, iron maiden, ominous table with restraints, chains attached to the wall with blood smears artistically arranged around them. "I love this."

Sparkle looked pleased. "Well, finally someone who understands the sensual connection between pain and pleasure." She thought about that. "Or at least the promise of pain. The imagination is an erotic conduit to—"

"No, no." Kayla waved her hand frantically. "I didn't mean that. I meant that I loved the concern for detail." She breathed deeply. "Someone even added a scent to make it smell like a real dungeon— damp and musty. I can almost smell the fear."

Sparkle frowned. "That's the way it always smells."

"Oh." Kayla glanced toward the door. "So when are your customers coming?"

"Now." Sparkle walked over to the torture implement wall on her impossibly high heels, turned on the electric fireplace, and took down a whip. She snapped it. "I feel in a snapping mood tonight."

"Why an electric fireplace? The wall sconces give off enough light."

Sparkle didn't stop snapping her whip. "Every dungeon has to have fire. It's a reminder of how much pain a burn can inflict. Everything here is a symbol of suffering, even if I never inflict one moment of pain." She finally glanced at Kayla. "Perception is everything. Remember that." She ran her hand lovingly over the whip's handle.

Kayla decided her client was still thinking about her lost employees. But then she forgot about Sparkle as the role-players shuffled into the room. Or at least three of the four shuffled. The fourth one's movements seemed fluid and confident. He wasn't into his fantasy role yet.

Kayla hadn't raised her eyes above knee level because she needed a moment to let her flush fade. Her costume really was embarrassing her.

"On your knees, blood slaves."

Sparkle didn't sound as though she was having any trouble getting into the spirit of the fantasy. Kayla needed to take Sparkle as her model. She had to wear her costume with confidence. Raising her gaze, she took her first look at the kneeling men.

They were all shirtless. But that's all she noticed before three of them completely disappeared from her radar.

He was here.

3

His body delivered what those wide shoulders had promised—a smooth sculpted chest and a stomach ridged with muscle. But she paused only a moment to admire all that, eager to see what the hoodie had hidden.

His blond hair lay tangled around his face, and strands still fell over his eyes. Brown eyes. Kayla had been right about his face. It was hard, beautiful, and tempting in a way that absolutely terrified her. Because she didn't want to be drawn to what she sensed in him, didn't want to be like her parents—overwhelmed by sexual need that drowned out all common sense.

She'd seen men with great bodies and faces before, but he was different.

Her father had taught her to read people. And growing up surrounded by her father's sometimes shady clients, she'd gotten lots of practice recognizing the darkness some people tried to disguise. His private detective agency flourished because he was willing to sometimes step outside legal lines to get the job done.

But this went beyond ordinary darkness. She felt as though she could almost reach out to turn page after page of a book crowded with secrets stretching back and back and back. Instinct warned her not to open it because there would be shadows, violence, and no promise of a happy ending. The terrifying part? She didn't care. Dad had taught her better than this.

The man met her gaze and then he smiled. It was breathtaking and triumphant.

That triumphant expression restored her common sense. She didn't have time for reading. She had a job to do here. A stranger had no part in it. Kayla forced herself to listen to what Sparkle was saying.

"You are my blood slaves." Sparkle struck a pose—one hand on her hip, the other wielding her whip, head flung back, and chest thrust out. "You will submit to me or . . ."—she slid the tip of her tongue across her bottom lip—"suffer untold agonies."

One of the men on his knees—a balding fiftyish guy—moaned his joy at Sparkle's threat.

"Silence." Sparkle snapped her whip. "No moaning, groaning, or pitiful begging without my permission."

"Yes, mistress," the speaker mumbled.

"Now . . ." Sparkle didn't finish. Instead, she paused to stare at gorgeous-guy. "Do I know you?"

Kayla frowned. She could actually *feel* the tension thrumming through him. What was that about?

He met Sparkle's gaze. Held it. "No. We've never met." He *didn't* smile at her.

Sparkle slowly nodded. "You're right. I don't know you. But still, there's something . . ." Once again her voice faded away. Then she shook her head and shifted her attention to the other men. "You may each crawl to me and then kiss the toe of my boot. If you dare to leave a smudge, I'll be forced to discipline you."

From the expressions on three of their faces, Kayla had the feeling that Sparkle would be wiping at least three smudges from her boot. She glanced at her blond stranger. Total disinterest. Nope, he wouldn't be doing any toe-kissing. If he didn't want to play this role, why had he bothered signing up for it? She shrugged the thought away because Sparkle was looking at her.

"Katnip, you will bind the one to the table who dared meet my gaze." Sparkle allowed her lids to drift almost shut as she smiled a feline smile of anticipation. "And then you will torment him with your sensual power."

Whoa. Torment with *what*? Then Kayla realized what Sparkle had called her. "*Catnip?*"

"With a K." Sparkle's evil smile widened. "The K makes it special."

Why did she have to be Katnip? Okay, so maybe her real name was a little tame, but Katnip? Really? And she had no intention of doing any tormenting. Certainly not to a man who broadcast "predator" on every one of her sensory airwaves. "Umm, my tormenting skills are a little rusty."

Sparkle actually hissed at her. "You are a *succubus*. And as a *succubus*, you can't *wait* to wreak sexual havoc on his body and mind. Do it."

Kayla narrowed her eyes. She didn't like Sparkle's tone of voice. This wasn't why she'd come to the castle. It would serve her client right if she marched out of this dungeon, out of the damn castle, and didn't stop marching until she reached Hobby Airport.

Sparkle must have read her expression, because she glared at Kayla. "Paying customers here. We'll talk later." Then without missing a beat, she continued speaking to the other three men. "If you appear submissive enough, I might allow you to touch my fingertip."

Kayla would have stormed from the dungeon right then if she hadn't seen the weariness in Sparkle's eyes. Her client had gone through a lot tonight. Kayla sighed. She could finish this one fantasy.

Sparkle was busy baring her teeth. "But if you're clumsy or dare look at me without permission, you'll receive the punishment *that* one is about to endure." She sneered at Kayla's victim.

The three men looked envious. Kayla stared them down. *Please, no.* She wasn't succubus enough for four men.

But Sparkle wasn't done. "And if you truly annoy me, I'll spank your bare asses until they're bright red."

The three men's eyes glazed with the glorious possibilities. Kayla decided she was off the hook for the moment—she glanced at the fourth one—except with *him.*

But he wasn't looking at her. He'd dropped his gaze, long dark lashes shielding his expression. Kayla took a deep breath. May as well get this over with. She coughed to clear her suddenly closed throat.

"Rise and spread your disobedient body on the table of pain." Her voice came out raspy. Ohmigod, could she sound any cheesier? She bit her lip to keep from laughing.

He still didn't lift his gaze, but he did obey her. He rose in one lithe motion, strode to the table, and lay down on his back. She sighed her relief.

Kayla secured the cuffs around his ankles and wrists. Each time she accidentally brushed his bare skin she tried to deny a tingle of . . . something. *Forget stupid tingles of unknown origins. What would a sexual demon say?* Kayla pressed her lips together and stared at him. Her head emptied of words.

He looked up at her. "Well, I'm here at your mercy." His unspoken question was, "So what're you going to do about it?"

She doubted this man would ever be at anyone's mercy, and she didn't have a clue what to do about him. Kayla skimmed his body with a gaze she suspected would leave blisters in its wake and watched his stomach muscles clench in response. She didn't want to seem gleeful. It was too close to the look of triumph he'd given her. But she couldn't help it. Her lips tipped up in the beginning of a smile.

"You have plans, I assume." He sounded only mildly interested.

She shifted her attention to his eyes and hoped he couldn't read the panic in hers. Kayla tried to concentrate—on her words not his body, on . . . She blinked. *His eyes.* There was something about those eyes—other than the ridiculously long dark lashes. Something important. If she could just . . .

"I think you should touch my body." He sounded serious.

"No." She swallowed hard. Was her panic showing? Wow, some lawyer she'd make. No eloquent speeches in *her* future. An incredible face and body had reduced her to one-word responses.

He turned his head to stare at her. "Why not? You're a succubus. I might be wrong, but I think a succubus would touch her victim."

He gripped his lower lip between strong white teeth. And when he released it, she could only stare. Kayla half closed her eyes. All she'd have to do is lower her head and slide her tongue across his lip's damp sheen. It would be soft and would taste of him. She caught herself just as she started to lean forward. Kayla gave herself a few mental slaps. She was almost certain he'd done that on purpose.

"Sparkle wants you to torture me with your sensual power. I'm waiting."

She narrowed her eyes. Did his lips twitch? Was he laughing at her? "Actually, a succubus would torture you by *not* touching you." There. Let him argue with that. She desperately tried to listen to Sparkle for hints while she reminded herself that this was just a fantasy, not the real deal.

"No, you may not touch me yet." Sparkle sounded almost prim. "You may *never* be worthy to touch me." The tap, tap of her heels emphasized that point.

"Please, mistress, tell us how to be worthy." The man was ready for prime time, his acting was that good.

But then, Kayla suspected he wasn't really acting. He meant what he said. Stupid man. He wouldn't know what to do with Sparkle if he got her.

"Well . . ." Sparkle seemed to be considering his request. "I love the things that every woman loves—diamonds, shoes . . . But, no, even those things wouldn't make you worthy."

Kayla wondered how Sparkle would keep the men motivated for the rest of the fantasy if she didn't give them a little hope.

"But if you *were* worthy, you'd get to smooth your fingers across my soft skin, kiss my whip, and—"

Jeez, Sparkle was making her ears bleed. Kayla stopped listening. This was too much. She couldn't say things like that to a complete stranger. She stared down at *her* stranger's body and tried to figure out what to do.

Time for the truth. "I'm sorry, I can't do this." Surprisingly, Kayla found that she really *was* sorry. If she could have worked her way past her embarrassment, she would have enjoyed trailing her fingers over that gleaming chest, that hard jaw, and then . . . She took a deep calming breath. "This isn't my thing. I'm just filling in for someone. I'll refund your money. I'll . . ."

Kayla finally worked up the courage to look at his face. His lips were unsmiling, but his eyes gleamed with suppressed laughter.

She huffed her outrage. "Don't you dare laugh at me."

He grinned, and she couldn't help herself. Everything about the moment hit her—her dumb outfit, the three middle-aged men playing out their fantasies, and Sparkle's whole spiel. She started to laugh too. And if she sensed a little hysteria in her giggles, she refused to acknowledge it.

Kayla clapped her hand over her mouth to muffle the sounds,

but it didn't work. Sparkle would hear her. The other men would too, and it would shatter their fantasy.

Ohmigod, she had to stop laughing. Without thinking, she buried her face in his chest. Then froze. It had worked. She wasn't laughing anymore. Because something else altogether had replaced the urge.

Awareness. With a capital A. Her lips were pressed against his warm flesh. Her senses exploded. His scent, his taste, his feel—all essential male. No dilution. No hiding behind chemical camouflage. He was primal, predatory, and in one moment he'd stripped thousands of years of evolution from her. She wanted to bite him.

Had she just thought that? She was too shocked to even raise her head.

"You seem to have thrown your entire being into this punishment, Katnip. Perhaps you can share with the rest of us." Sparkle's voice was an eager purr.

No, no, no. She refused to feed the fantasy for the three men Kayla knew would be staring at her with avid eyes. Besides, her lips seemed to be suction-cupped to his chest.

"The succubus is torturing me with her tongue, mistress, while she whispers promises she'll never keep. I'm bound, so I can't touch her, can't smooth my fingers over her beautiful body. I don't know how much more I can stand." His moan was filled with frustrated agony.

Kayla felt the vibration of that moan, heard the sincerity in his words. Wow, that was disturbing. She prided herself on being able to hear the lie in a person's voice. She couldn't hear it in his. But he *was* lying, because her tongue hadn't touched him—yet—and she hadn't whispered any promises.

"Wonderful." Sparkle sounded thrilled. "Continue, Katnip."

Uh-oh. Kayla finally found her backbone—still way too soft and pliable. She straightened and turned to face Sparkle.

"I want to hear his suffering. His cries must be loud, filled with unbearable pain. They will be a lesson to these others." Sparkle cast a dismissive glance at the three men still on their knees. Their expressions said they'd pay extra to land on that table.

"Uh . . ." Kayla knew her face must be bright red. She opened her mouth to say "no" and damn the consequences.

But she was saved from complete humiliation by a man dressed all in white—white jeans, white T-shirt, and white sneakers. He threw open the dungeon door and stepped inside. Kayla had a brief impression of dark hair and eyes that looked almost black. She didn't have time to notice anything else about him because the sword he carried grabbed her attention.

"I'm Dacian. I've come to destroy the vampire and her demon helper." He glanced at Kayla. "Release your victim."

Kayla didn't move. She couldn't decide if embarrassment had frozen her in place or the memory of her victim's super-sexy chest.

Sparkle turned to the other men. "Once a succubus attaches herself to a man, she loses control, lost in her need to drain every drop of sexual essence from him. She won't release her prey until he passes out from too many orgasms."

The guy in white waved his sword around. "I said to release him, demon."

"What if the victim doesn't want to be released? Hey, I'm fine right here." Her "victim" sounded definite about that.

The White Knight looked exasperated. "Shut up. You don't have a say in this." He looked at Kayla expectantly.

Sparkle had another helpful comment for the three men watching raptly. "Notice how the victim is in thrall to his mistress. He'll crawl through fire on his knees just to feel her hands on his naked flesh, her lips touching his—"

"You're not helping." White Knight guy looked really ticked.

One of the other men spoke. "Do you have this fantasy every

week? Can I be on the table of pain next time? I have to buy my tickets now."

He leaped to his feet and hurried toward the door, followed immediately by the two other men. Kayla watched openmouthed as they shoved the White Knight aside and fought to get out the door first. Then they were gone.

The White Knight put down his sword. "Well, hell. That was an epic fail. Find someone to replace Zane fast because I don't want to do this fantasy again." He turned and left.

Sparkle watched him leave and then turned back to her. Kayla avoided her gaze. She couldn't remember the last time she'd felt this flustered and uncertain. Probably because it had never happened. Dad taught all of them to blend in. The business demanded that they avoid calling attention to themselves. He'd have her on the first flight back to Philly if he found out about this.

That thought perked her up. If Sparkle told him about tonight, she wouldn't have to ask that he replace her with one of her brothers.

Kayla had managed to forget about the one man remaining in the dungeon for about three whole seconds. She refused to meet his gaze as she released him. Staring at her feet, she addressed her shoes. "I hope tonight has taught you the power of Mistress Sparkle. Obey her or you might find yourself bound here again. And next time will be worse."

"Really? Worse?" His voice was deep and filled with laughter.

"*Much* worse."

He swung his feet to the floor. Kayla shifted her attention to the iron maiden. She would *not* look at him.

He took the decision away from her. Placing his finger beneath her chin, he forced her to meet his gaze.

"In that case, I'd better get moving if I want to beat those other guys to the ticket counter." He leaned close. "What's your real name?"

Sparkle reached up to firmly remove his fingers from under Kayla's chin. "The fantasy is ended. Let her always remain as Katnip in your memory."

For just a moment, danger filled the dungeon. It was a suffocating cloud, a warning. Sparkle dropped her hand from him.

He stared at Sparkle. "Don't ever touch me again." Then he turned and left the room, closing the door behind him.

Sparkle looked intrigued. "What a fascinating man."

"Yes." Enough said about him. "You promised me answers."

"Tomorrow. Get a good night's sleep first. You can leave in the morning if that's what you decide you want to do."

Kayla thought about that. "Fine." She *was* exhausted. She needed to be clearheaded when she spoke to Sparkle. Kayla started to step past her.

"Wait." Sparkle moved to block her. "You surprised me tonight. In a good way." She wore a speculative expression. "Meet me in the restaurant tomorrow morning at nine so we can discuss your job."

Kayla nodded and made her escape. She tried to think things through calmly on the way to her room. She'd order room service a little later, but first she had something to do. Kayla pulled out her cell phone. To hell with Sparkle's mysterious "answers". She hated that she'd allowed Sparkle to bribe her into doing that fantasy. *With him.*

She didn't give her father a chance to speak. "Dad, who exactly is Sparkle Stardust?"

"A very important client, sweetie. Treat her with respect."

If Kayla didn't know better, she'd swear she heard a note of uncertainty in her father's voice. Not likely, though. Dad never seemed to have doubts about anything in his life.

This was the man who had seen every gangster movie ever produced. He did homage in his own small way to their awesomeness by modeling his career after them.

"She says a vampire owns the amusement pier across the street, the one I'm supposed to spy on and hopefully destroy."

She hated the family business. Whatever It Takes said it all. Dad took on clients that other private detective agencies wouldn't touch—the ones who wanted someone who would climb over the fence into illegal territory if needed. This was her first and last job for Dad. And if he thought once she got her degree she'd use it to haul his behind out of trouble with the law, he was in for a huge disappointment.

"You'll have to be creative with this one, Kayla. But I taught you, so I'm not worried."

"Hello? Dad, I said a *vampire* owns it."

"Right. Make sure you cover your neck when you're on the job. Do you still have that cross your grandmother gave you?"

Kayla had to be hallucinating. Her father couldn't be giving her hints on how to deal with a vampire. "Vampires don't exist, Dad." As soon as she got home, she'd talk to Mom about getting Dad some help.

"If you say so, sweetie." He sounded distracted. "Whatever you do, keep Sparkle happy."

There was a pause. Kayla could hear him breathing.

"Sparkle can be a dangerous woman. But if you treat her right, she can be very generous. She introduced me to your mom."

"Yes, and that worked out so well." Had she injected the right amount of bitchiness into her voice?

"We were great together while it lasted, Kayla."

Was that nostalgia in his voice? Nah.

"I want to quit, Dad." A *cat talked to me in my head.* Would it matter to him? Not if he didn't find a vampire who owned an amusement park strange.

"No. Don't. Sparkle wants you."

Panicked? Her dad? She sighed. No matter how much he

annoyed her, she still loved him. And this job was evidently a lot more important to him than she'd first thought. At least she wasn't crazy, unless Dad was delusional too. What were the chances? Kayla would probably regret this, but now that she was over her initial horror she was curious enough to consider staying for a while. After all, she could always walk away if things got too intense. Besides, maybe her beautiful victim from the dungeon would show up again. Not that he had anything to do with her decision. Really. Nothing at all.

"Relax. I've decided to stay unless it gets too crazy." It was already too crazy.

"That's my little girl." His relief oozed from the phone.

"Oh, and Dad . . . ?" She paused. "Payback is a bitch."

She hung up to his chuckle. Then she called room service and ordered something to eat. While she waited for it to arrive, she lay on the bed thinking. About *him*, her mystery guy.

Who was he? Was he staying in the castle? And then she remembered his eyes. Something niggled at her. She closed her eyes and pictured them. What was it . . . ?

When she opened her eyes again, she had her answer. He'd been wearing colored contacts. His pupils gave him away. They looked artificial, too perfect. Colored contacts had the center cut out of them. That meant that the pupils never seemed to change size, they always stayed exactly the same. Dad had taught her to notice details like that. Come to think of it, his lashes were way too dark for his hair. A wig?

She smiled. Things were getting interesting. Now she felt energized, because someone who felt the need to wear a disguise at the Castle of Dark Dreams had secrets.

And he was one mystery she wouldn't mind solving.

4

Thorn paused to reclaim his clothes once he reached the great hall. He didn't bother pulling up his hood again. Sparkle hadn't recognized him. Guess he wasn't a memorable kind of guy if she'd forgotten him after a mere thousand years.

He smiled. For the first time, Thorn admitted exactly how forgettable he must have seemed to someone like Sparkle. He'd been a twenty-three-year-old savage who thought he was a mighty Viking. She had probably laughed her ass off behind his back.

He stopped smiling. So she'd dumped him. No big deal, right? Okay, so it *had* been a big deal then. But that's not what had fueled his need for revenge for so many centuries. It was what had come after. *That* he couldn't forget.

Thorn had prepared himself for the bitterness and hate he'd feel when he faced her again. Sure, there had been plenty of that. And he'd handled it. But he hadn't expected someone else to compete for his attention.

Katnip. His grin returned. He'd wanted to laugh out loud at her expression when Sparkle called her by that name. In fact, everything about his beautiful succubus made him feel like smiling. Not the reaction Thorn had expected when he'd descended into the dungeon. Katnip, with her long gold-kissed brown hair and her way-too-serious gray eyes, had captured his interest.

Not a good thing. He had to stay focused on making Nirvana a success and driving Sparkle's theme park out of business. No distractions allowed.

Thorn glanced at his watch. The next fantasy was scheduled to begin in five minutes and would last a half hour. During that time, he'd be busy. He strode out of the great hall and into the hotel lobby right next to it. He was opting for the elevator rather than the stairs.

On the way up he went over the layout of the castle in his mind. Timing would be everything. He'd start with the towers and work his way down.

Twenty minutes later, Thorn was almost ready to head down to the ground floor. He stood in a shadowed corner, about to stick one of his few remaining transparent wafers on the wall. The size of an eraser head, the wafers were almost undetectable.

Suddenly, the elevator doors opened and two people emerged. Crap. He palmed the wafer and pulled out his cell phone. He held it to his ear and didn't glance at the man and woman walking toward him.

Thorn was busy thinking about where he'd stick the last three wafers once he reached the ground floor when he *felt* them. The man and woman weren't human. He glanced up and smiled as they went past before pretending to speak into his phone.

Except for both being so thin he wanted to feed them, they looked human. But there was something *off* about the two. Not vampire, not demon, not fae, not anything he recognized.

They had human features, but there was a strangeness about the male's unblinking stare, the female's sinuous movements that were

definitely *not* human. Shutting his eyes, he reached for their scent.
The sea. Unusual. He opened his eyes. Whatever they were had
nothing to do with him.

He waited a few seconds until he heard the sound of a door
closing before glancing down the hall to make sure they were gone.
Then he finished attaching the wafer to the wall. Before walking
away, he stripped off the clear plastic covering that protected the
potent mixture beneath. A half hour of exposure to air and interesting things would happen.

Thorn was glad that he'd had the foresight to forge strong friend-
ships with humans in the science community. They might not have
the power of a nonhuman, but in many cases they compensated by
being smarter. He owed Dr. Clancy for this amazing gem.

When Thorn had finished sticking all of his little gifts to the
castle walls, he left through the great hall door and waited in the
courtyard. He probably should have just gone home, but what was
the fun in that? He wanted to enjoy his revenge, and that meant
watching what happened when his time-release wafers did their
thing.

He'd worked fast, so that meant once the ones he'd placed in
the towers activated then the rest would follow at about five-minute
intervals. And if his timing was right, the ones in the towers were
about to go off right . . . about . . . now.

Within minutes, he could hear the rise in the level of voices
drifting from the open door. Those voices grew louder and louder
as the minutes passed. People started spilling from the castle. Soon
the courtyard was jammed with pissed-off and complaining guests.

A woman with her hair in rollers leaned close to him. "I was
getting ready for bed. But then this . . . this"—she waved her hands
in the air—"smell oozed under the door and filled my room. I almost
threw up right there. They charge megabucks to stay in this place.
I want my money back."

Thorn smiled into the darkness. "Yeah, it's pretty bad." And it was. Even standing thirty feet from the open door he could smell the raw sewage stench. It made even him want to run to the bushes and heave. He'd have to send Dr. Clancy flowers, candy, or maybe a few air fresheners.

The best part of the whole thing? Sparkle and her crew would find no evidence. The wafers evaporated as they released the odor. And this was the gift that kept on giving. The hotel's staff wouldn't get rid of the smell just by opening a few windows. Any guests who chose to stay would have to sleep with gas masks.

He was chuckling as he turned away. Then he saw her. Katnip. She wore jeans, a red T-shirt, and a light jacket along with a suspicious expression. Interesting. The other people around him assumed the castle just had a plumbing problem. He wondered what *she* thought.

Thorn worked his way to her side. "I've smelled some bad stuff in my time"—piles of burning bodies during the plague, charnel houses—"and this is right up there with the worst of them."

Startled, she turned to look at him. "Are you staying at the castle?"

"No. I hung around to watch the next fantasy." He smiled. "I liked ours better."

She frowned. "Ours was a disaster."

He decided not to comment on that. "What's your real name?"

"Kayla." She raised one expressive brow. "And yours?"

"Will." Centuries of practice had taught him to lie smoothly, without any tells. "So are you going to be able to get back in there to sleep tonight?"

She nodded. "They have people working on it now. Sparkle said the smell would be gone in less than an hour."

Thorn maintained his bland expression. Holgarth and Zane. Damn. He'd hoped it would take longer than that for them to get rid of the stink. Too bad. He would have enjoyed offering Kayla a place to stay for the night. He perked up at the thought that this might be the last night Zane helped save Sparkle's ass. "So I assume you have a job description other than succubus." He waited for details.

"Yes." No details.

Kayla's narrow-eyed gaze made him a little wary. Her expression said she was trying to solve a puzzle. He couldn't afford to be that puzzle. "Guess all the fun is over. I'll head on home. I live here on the island, so maybe I'll see you again." He turned to walk away.

"Oh, Will?"

He paused and glanced over his shoulder.

"Is there a reason you wear colored contacts and a wig for just a night out at the local theme park?" Her expression showed only casual interest, but her eyes said, "Gotcha."

"I work for the dreaded Succubi Seekers. We heard there was a rogue succubus messing with men's dreams in Galveston. I've been working undercover to find her." He made sure his tone sounded lightly teasing. "Mission accomplished."

She wouldn't be able to see his eyes well in the darkness. But if she could, would she read the truth in them, understand the danger? If she didn't fascinate him, and if he hadn't worked for the last two centuries to suppress his vampire responses, she wouldn't survive the night. She'd seen through his disguise, so she was officially a threat to him now.

Thorn didn't give her a chance to reply. He strode from the courtyard and slipped out of the park. He'd take the long way home. He didn't want anyone to notice him entering Nirvana.

He moved silently through the night, staying close to the outside of the park's wall where the shadows were deepest. Two hundred years of perfecting his impersonation of a human hadn't rid him of his predatory instincts. He loved the darkness. And even though his hunts didn't end in death anymore—even vampires evolved—Thorn still loved the pursuit, that electric moment when he finally cornered his prey. Sometimes, on very special nights, his prey would outsmart him. Those were the moments he lived for, when he could match wits with someone who understood a predator's mind.

Speaking of matching wits, two people were following him. He'd picked up their footsteps, their heartbeats, their breathing about a minute ago. To make sure they really were after him, he stopped for a moment and pretended to root around in his pockets. They stopped too. This wouldn't be one of those special nights, because the men stalking him were clumsy and overconfident. They weren't human, but they thought he was. They'd be expecting weak and helpless. They were about to get an unpleasant surprise.

What were they after? Had Sparkle remembered him? Not likely with his different hair and eye color. Besides, as far as she knew, he'd been dead for centuries. And there was no way she'd connect him with the owner of Nirvana.

Time to find out what they wanted. He turned and peered into the darkness. Thorn could see them clearly, but they didn't know that. "Is someone there?" Did he sound like a nervous human?

"Yes." The voice was a low sibilant hiss.

Thorn tensed, a human reaction. He wanted them to keep thinking he was human until it was too late. "What do you want?"

They drew closer and Thorn recognized the same scent of the sea that he'd smelled on the two people in the hotel. Coincidence? He didn't believe in coincidences.

Thorn put his back against the wall. They'd interpret his action as fear. He saw it as a defensive move, which would soon lead to a lot of offensive moves on his part.

Anticipation thrummed through him. He wanted to laugh out

loud. A good fight would rid him of some of the aggression he'd
built up during his first meeting with Sparkle. It might even take
his mind off the mysterious Kayla.

Suddenly they were in front of him. Wow, they were big bastards.
Probably depended on their size and strength to beat the hell out
of opponents. *Not this time, dumbasses.* He waited.

The smaller one—about six-ten—spoke.

"We saw you come out of Nirvana and enter the castle. We
hoped that you would return. Do you work at the pier?"

"Yes." Thorn frowned. Stilted speech, as though he didn't do
much of it. Strange. He wished the guy would talk faster, though.
He wanted to get to the good part where he kicked their stupid butts.

"Then you can take a message to your boss. He must close the
pier down, sell it, and leave Galveston." They edged a little closer.

Thorn narrowed his eyes. Now they were officially in his space.
"Why?" He crouched, ready to make mush of their very ordinary
faces.

"If he does not follow directions, he will die."

Okay, Thorn could accept that as a reason for now. He'd find
out the real reason later, once he'd stomped on their heads a few
times.

"We will give you something to make sure you will remember
our message."

Thorn admitted it, he was a bigot. He didn't trust anyone who
never used contractions. And now they'd try to beat him to a pulp
to make sure he delivered their "message." Well, he was about to
deliver his own message. He smiled.

Kayla saw that smile from where she hid in the shadows and
wondered if he was crazy. He was about to get pulverized by those
men. Jeez, the tall one must be over seven feet and built like a
jumbo jet.

She didn't know what the men wanted with Will. She had

decided to follow him at the last minute and had just caught up. But she didn't have time to figure out what was happening before both men drew back their fists.

Kayla reacted instinctively. No gun. Too loud. She reached down and pulled the knife from her ankle sheath. Then she stepped from the shadows. "Move away from him."

All three men turned to stare at her. The two big men looked shocked. Will just looked disappointed. Maybe he didn't like a woman saving his beautiful ass. Too bad.

Kayla widened her eyes. "What? You've never seen a woman with a knife before?"

"Only in the kitchen." The biggest man smiled. Not a nice smile. "You are small and insignificant. I do not believe you know what to do with your weapon."

He hadn't just said that. No one could be that dumb. She forgot all the snarky comments she could have made and just stared at him.

"Give me that knife, little girl, and then go away so we can finish this." He started toward her.

Two things happened at once. Will leaped into the air and kicked only-in-the-kitchen in his big stupid head, followed immediately by a shot to his gut. Kayla would have liked to stand and enjoy his amazing speed and ferocity, but the shorter man had pulled out his own knife and looked as though he wanted to carve his initials in Will's back.

Kayla shook her head in disgust. See, it was fine for *him* to carry a knife, but not small and insignificant her. With one smooth motion, she threw her knife. The blade sank into his throwing shoulder. He grunted and dropped his weapon.

She didn't give him time to recover. Even as he bent over clutching his shoulder, she ran in and yanked her knife from his flesh before kicking his legs out from under him.

Glancing toward Will, she saw that his opponent had fled the fight. Giant wuss. He was stumbling across Seawall Boulevard. Must have a car parked nearby. Her guy scrambled to his feet and followed at a staggering run. She was surprised how fast he moved with a stab wound. Thinking that was the end of it, she crouched down to wipe her blade on the grass. But she was wrong. Will was racing after them.

Reluctantly, she followed him. She didn't want Sparkle to find out about this. Rescuing random men outside of the park wasn't part of her job description. Kayla was lucky the man she'd stabbed hadn't screamed and brought everyone running.

What did Will hope to accomplish by chasing them down himself? They were still huge, and there were still two of them.

Her conscience bothered her a little. She should call the police, but she didn't need any probing questions about knives and what she was doing at the castle. She needed to keep a low profile.

Damn, Will ran fast. He was closing in on the men by the time she ran across the street and climbed down the steps to the beach. Why the hell had they tried to escape here? She was panting when she caught up with him. And the only reason she *did* catch up was he'd stopped running. What . . . ?

It was dark on the beach, but she could see a little because of the lights on Seawall Boulevard and the moonlight. She stood beside him, staring openmouthed.

Both men had run into the Gulf. She could see them moving farther and farther away from the shore.

"What're they doing? They'll both drown." And if her voice had an edge of hysteria to it, she had good reason. She'd wanted to stop the attack on Will, not see two men die. Kayla pulled her cell phone from her pocket and started to punch in 911.

Will put his hand over hers. "You won't need that."

"What do you mean? They're . . ." She followed his gaze. Kayla could still see them, but something wasn't right. She strained to see in the darkness. It almost looked as though . . . "No. It can't be." But it was. The dark shapes of the men seemed to be melting and flowing into . . . "Fish?" Even saying the word made her question her sanity. "Tell me they didn't just change into big fish." She heard the shrillness in her voice, but she couldn't seem to control it.

They were gone. They'd just walked out into the Gulf, turned into fish, and disappeared. She glanced up at Will. In the darkness his features were harsh, his eyes hard and unreadable. "What just happened?" Kayla's finger still hovered over her phone while confused thoughts scrambled to make meaning of what had no meaning.

"Put the phone away, Kayla." His voice was quiet, devoid of emotion.

"We have to report this. We—"

He turned to look at her. "Reporting it would accomplish nothing."

"I don't believe this." Her voice rose even higher. "They both just walked into the freaking Gulf of Mexico and changed into—"

"Whales, actually. Not one of the large species." Will's expression never changed. "They're shape-shifters. They're sea creatures in their animal forms."

He said this in the same tone of voice he'd use to explain why the sun would come up in the morning.

She started to shake and slowly back away from him. He was crazy. Had to be. "Shape-shifters?" Why not? A cat had spoken in her head and Sparkle had said a vampire owned Nirvana.

Will didn't move, didn't try to stop her. "I'm sorry."

He didn't look sorry, only angry. "You might not want to mention this to Sparkle. Once opened, some doors can never be closed."

"Who are you?" Her question came out in a frightened whisper. "How did you know what they were?"

He shrugged and looked back at the Gulf. "Just someone who knows that things aren't always what they seem."

Kayla turned away then. *Calm down. Breathe deeply. You've made it through talking cats, vampires, sorcerers, and goddesses. What do a few shape-shifters matter? You can handle this.*

Her mind had it all figured out. Unfortunately, her body didn't get the message. Her heart pounded and she fought for each breath while she concentrated on not running back to the castle. *Walk. You are in control.* As she crossed the lobby, Kayla barely noted the lack of any sewage smell. She didn't even wonder how Sparkle had gotten rid of it so quickly.

Once she was back in her room, she'd get a grip. No panic, just rational thoughts. This was just a job. Okay, a really bizarre one.

"I sense a shitload of panic, confusion, and fear. Anything Sparkle or I can help with?"

The voice in her head again. She looked down. The gray cat, no, Ganymede stared up at her from wide amber eyes. Oh, shit. "No."

"Why not? Haven't we welcomed you with open arms? Okay, open paws? Hey, Sparkle hasn't even tried to hook you up with anyone. She usually starts working on that within an hour tops." He padded along beside her. *"What's the problem?"*

She stopped walking. "*You're* the problem. And Sparkle telling me that the owner of Nirvana is a vampire, that's another problem. And . . ." Should she mention the shape-shifters? *Once opened, some doors can never be closed.* No. Not now. "Do I need anything else?" She tried to ignore a nearby couple watching her talk to herself.

"Maybe we should all sit down and have a nice long talk." Ganymede glanced toward the door leading to the great hall as though he expected someone to burst through it at any moment.

Not surprisingly, someone did. Sparkle hurried toward them.

Kayla didn't doubt that the cat who had talked in *her* head had also put out a silent call to Sparkle.

"I hear that you're upset." Sparkle looped her arm through Kayla's and steered her toward a room near the restaurant. "Let's sit for a moment and talk about it." She sighed. "No use putting it off any longer. I suppose it's time for those answers I promised." She opened the door.

It was a conference room. Kayla was more than ready for some answers. She walked in and sat at the long table while Sparkle paused to talk to the cat.

"Order something good for us to nibble on."

Great. The cat was going to order dinner. Her adrenaline rush over, Kayla felt almost too tired to keep her head off the table. But she had to ask the question. "What is Ganymede?"

Sparkle joined her at the table. "Not what, *who.* Mede is one of the most powerful beings in the universe. He's the cosmic troublemaker in charge of planet-changing chaos—volcanic eruptions, earthquakes, meteor strikes, the big stuff." She absolutely glowed with pride. "And he's my fluffy-bunny."

Just kill me now. Kayla didn't know how many more of these . . . revelations she could take. May as well get it all out of the way at once. "And you are?"

"I'm a cosmic troublemaker too. Sexual chaos is my specialty." Her expression said she totally expected Kayla to believe and accept what she said.

Uh-huh. Sure. "So I assume if Ganymede is your . . . fluffy-bunny, then he must change into human form." A shape-shifter.

"Of course." Sparkle widened her eyes as though that must be obvious. "When he's in human form, he's a golden god." Her lips tipped up in a sly smile. "He's a sexual beast in bed."

Didn't need to know that. Kayla closed her eyes. "How can he talk in my head?"

"It's one of his powers."

Well, that cleared things up. Kayla opened her eyes. "Anything else you want to fling my way?"

"Holgarth is a real wizard, and Zane is a real sorcerer. They're the reason why that disgusting smell is gone so quickly. You saw Klepoth and Eric. Klepoth is a demon and Eric is a vampire." Sparkle put her hand on top of Kayla's. "You'll meet a few other nonhumans, but I think that's enough for now."

"Definitely." She wanted to jerk her hand from beneath Sparkle's, but she didn't seem to have the energy. Would this cursed day never end?

"I know you want to run away from us, Kayla." Sparkle's voice softened.

"You think?" She could hardly wrap her mind around the possibility that Sparkle, Ganymede, and Will were telling the truth. *But think about what you've heard and seen. And Dad didn't deny the existence of vampires.* She couldn't explain those things away.

Just then the door swung open and Ganymede padded back into the room. A waiter rolling a cart followed him in. And for the next few minutes she allowed herself not to think as she watched the covered plates being transferred to the table. Finally the waiter left.

Kayla ate her way through two servings of everything while Sparkle watched bemused. Ganymede had his own plate and was having no trouble matching Kayla serving for serving.

Finally, Sparkle didn't seem able to stand it one more minute. She reached out and whipped Kayla's plate out from under her raised fork. "I can't believe you ate that much."

Kayla felt a moment of embarrassment before pushing it aside. "When I'm stressed, I eat. You can tell the level of my stress by how *much* I eat." She'd broken a record at this meal.

"Time to talk." Sparkle ignored the cat who was still stuffing his furry cheeks with food. "What can I do to make you want to stay?"

She paused, her gaze turning thoughtful. "Besides threatening to sue your father for breach of contract." She brightened. "By the time I'm finished, I'll own his company. I've never involved myself in that type of business before. It might be fun. Oh, and of course, I don't think he'll kick in any money for law school if you run home without getting the job done." Sparkle smiled as though everything was very simple.

Food had a calming effect on Kayla, which is why she only called Sparkle a bitch once in her head. She'd save the multiple "bitches" for another time. She decided not to mention that she'd already decided to stay. "Be reasonable, Sparkle. I won't be any good to you. I don't know how to deal with supernatural entities."

"Nonsense." Sparkle stopped long enough to aim a glare at Ganymede, who was trying to lick the garlic mashed potato residue from the serving dish. "What's to know? You just sneak around, do a little spying, a little sabotaging, and once Nirvana folds, you go home and everyone's happy. Besides, if you need any help with the nonhumans, I can loan you some paranormal muscle."

Kayla thought about that. She knew how to do her job, and as long as she kept out of sight, how hard could it be? And if Sparkle could supply her some nonhuman help, she'd feel a lot safer.

Listen to yourself. Do you really believe all this? Kayla closed her eyes, shutting out Sparkle's sly gaze. She had always tried to be practical and a realist. And as much as she'd like to make excuses for everything that was happening, she couldn't. The evidence was mounting that a paranormal world she knew nothing about really did exist.

Kayla opened her eyes. Time to face facts. She'd be going up against a bloodsucking creature that frankly scared the crap out of her.

Ganymede lifted his head to stare at Kayla. Mashed potatoes covered his face and whiskers. *"Yo, Sparkle. Sweeten the pot for her. We need to keep her here."*

Sparkle sighed. "Fine. If you'll stay and do the job, I'll double whatever your father is offering. In fact, if I'm happy with the results, I might give you a job here after you pass the bar exam. Holgarth has been making retirement noises lately. I'll need a new attorney."

Kayla widened her eyes. Work as Sparkle's attorney? That would have to be one of the scariest jobs on the planet. No amount of money could tempt her to accept it. But the extra money that Sparkle had offered for this one-and-done job sounded great. Kayla tried to look as though she was struggling with her decision. "I'll stay. But I want you to get my helper to me as soon as possible. I have a lot to learn about the supernatural realm." Understatement of the year.

Sparkle glowed. "You won't regret this. We'll have fun destroying Thorn Mackenzie."

Kayla frowned. Sparkle sounded as though she meant it. "I have one question. What are cosmic troublemakers?"

Ganymede was washing his face with one gray paw. "*We're incredibly powerful and charismatic beings gifted with the ability to cause chaos in every aspect of human life.*"

Gifted with huge egos as well. "Then why haven't I ever heard of you?" Of course, Kayla's knowledge didn't go beyond the usual—vampires, werewolves, angels, and demons.

Ganymede finished with his face and gave her his full attention. "*Because there aren't that many of us, and we don't have a great PR department.*"

Kayla nodded. That was a good enough explanation for the moment. She started to rise but then sat down again. Earlier, she'd decided not to mention Will or the men who'd walked into the Gulf. But now she needed to know more. Besides, Sparkle was paying her to investigate. She wanted to show her client that she was getting her money's worth.

Kayla gave a brief rundown of events, starting with the attempted mugging and ending with Will and her standing on the beach watching the men run into the Gulf. She had to take a deep breath before telling the last part. "As the men got farther away from shore, they started to . . . change." *Just say it.* "They became some kind of whale." She met Sparkle's gaze. "Was I seeing things or can that really happen?"

Sparkle glanced at Ganymede. Kayla sensed something passing between them.

Then Sparkle shrugged. "There're all kinds of shifters. Some sea creatures have been known to take human shape, but we don't see many around here. Lately though . . ." Abruptly, she stood. "Well, I think we've covered everything for the night. You must be tired, Kayla."

Kayla recognized a dismissal when she heard it. "Right. See you in the morning." She stood and headed for the door.

"*Yo, spy lady.*"

Kayla stopped to glance back at Ganymede.

"*You might want to do some snooping around the castle in the morning.*"

"Why?"

"*Because the crappy smell that drove everyone out of the castle wasn't a plumbing problem. It was sabotage. Probably payback for the refreshment stand I blew up. The war is on.*"

Kayla experienced sudden insight. "I bet that puts you in your happy place, doesn't it?"

Ganymede narrowed his amber eyes and twitched his tail. "*You have no idea.*"

5

Thorn figured he'd exhausted a thousand years of curses in every language he'd ever known. Tonight had pretty much sucked. *Except for meeting Kayla.* But she'd probably be gone from Galveston by morning, so he couldn't even put her in his plus column. He slammed the door in disappointment's face. Nowhere for that relationship to go anyway.

How much would she tell Sparkle before she left? If Sparkle found out that her recent dungeon guest had been wearing a wig and colored contacts, and that said guest had been in the castle right around the time of the Great Stink, it wouldn't take her long to follow the clues. She probably already knew her plumbing was fine and had figured out the attack came from him. But he didn't want her attaching a face to that attack just yet.

He slipped back into Nirvana. Grim had turned off all but a few lights, so no one saw him return. He found Grim standing by the carousel.

His security chief grinned. "Seemed to be lots of excitement going on across the street. Looked like someone stepped on their anthill the way everyone was running out of there."

Thorn forced a smile. "The modern world is soft. A few bad smells and they bail. They should've been around when no one washed for six months at a time. A few whiffs standing in a crowd on a hot day would toughen them up fast."

Grim nodded. "So what went wrong? You're smiling, but I don't sense a lot of happy thoughts."

"Two big guys stopped me on the way back here." Thorn had already decided not to mention Kayla. He quickly told a shortened version of what had happened. "Something's not right. The two I saw in the hotel smelled of the sea. Had to be shifters. And the two who wanted to rearrange my face started their change as soon as they got far enough into the Gulf." Too bad Kayla had seen that. "There aren't a lot of shifters who choose to leave the sea, and now I trip over four in one night. Who're they working for? Why try to drive me from Galveston?"

"Sparkle?" Grim shrugged. "Seems a logical choice."

"Could be. I don't think Sparkle recognized me, but she could've just sent them out to find someone who worked at Nirvana. And they chose me." He stared at the carousel. "But it still doesn't feel right. Ganymede's not subtle. He's a blow-everything-up kind of guy. At least that's what my research showed. I can't see him bothering with muggings and threats."

"At least we'll have security now." Grim sounded . . . grim.

Thorn glanced around. "So where's your team?"

Grim's frown turned to a smile. "You're looking at it."

"The carousel's going to protect Nirvana?" Thorn didn't know what he'd expected, but this wasn't it.

Grim reached back and flipped a switch. The carousel began to turn. No music, so at least Grim had spared him that.

"Look carefully." Grim's voice was tight with anticipation.

Thorn narrowed his eyes. Seemed normal to him, a bunch of horses mixed in with other creatures big enough for people to ride. Then his eyes widened. "Stop."

The carousel slowed as Thorn moved toward a big black horse. He stared. "There's seaweed tangled in its mane." He reached out to touch the seaweed and to smooth his fingers over the mane. "It's wet." He knew his mythology as well as any thousand-year-old vampire. But this seemed beyond belief. "A kelpie?"

Grim nodded. "I met someone centuries ago who had one of the magical bridles that controls a kelpie's shape-shifting power. Now *I* have it. I'm not using it on him, and I promised to give it to him to keep in return for a few favors. He's a freshwater kind of guy, but he'll do his thing in the Gulf for a limited time."

Thorn rocked back on his heels and just stared at the legendary fairy water horse. "And I suppose this man just gave you the bridle."

Grim's smile turned savage. "I took it. Because I could. And because I wasn't as civilized as I am now."

"That's not saying much. I saw you in the wilderness. Grizzlies ran from you."

"As well they should."

Thorn continued pacing around the carousel. He stopped in front of two blue cats as big as ponies. He shook his head. "How?"

"Ah, you recognize them."

"They're hard to miss. As far as I know the only giant blue cats are the ones who pull the goddess Freya's chariot. So once again, how?"

"They're witches in their human forms. I did them a few favors." He shrugged. "Now they owe me a few."

Thorn raised one brow in a silent question.

Grim's grin widened. "Hey, while you were perfecting your imitation of an ordinary human guy, I wasn't. I was busy forging relationships with the most powerful nonhumans I could find." He speared Thorn with a hard gaze. "I don't get you. You could go on TV and convince people to make you king of the universe. Why do things the hard way?"

"I've tried the easy way. It didn't work for me." He'd never make Grim understand his need to actually work for what he got, the sense of accomplishment that had kept him from checking out centuries ago.

Grim didn't look impressed with his excuse. "Fine. Make it tough. Now that you're here, let's have a brief team meeting."

Thorn waited expectantly. He knew Grim's power, but never got used to seeing him wield it.

Grim turned to the carousel. He didn't speak, chant, or do a damn thing that Thorn could see. But suddenly, three people stood in front of them—two women and a man. Thorn glanced at the carousel. The two giant blue cats were still there. He took the time to walk around the carousel. Yep, so was the black horse.

Grim had crazy talent. Who could split one into two? The real horse and cats were held in stasis on the carousel. But at the same time there was a real version of them standing in front of him.

Finally, he returned to the group. He waved at Grim. "Introduce us." He smiled at the women. They didn't smile back.

Grim clapped him on the shoulder. "The lady with the long blond hair is Bygul, and the one with the curly black hair is Trjegul." He smiled at the women. "This is Thorn."

The women ignored Grim.

Bygul cast Thorn an impatient glance. "I have no idea why Grim told you we were here because we owed him favors. We're here because—"

Grim frowned. "I think that's enough for now."

Trjegul's smile was a sly curve of her lips. "You haven't told him, have you?" She gazed at Grim from under long dark lashes. "I think any partnership should be based on truthfulness." She widened her eyes. It didn't make her look innocent. "Don't you?"

Thorn stared at Grim. "What's she talking about?"

Grim glared at the witch before turning to Thorn. "Okay, so they don't owe me favors. They're doing this because my grandfather is Fenrir, the oldest son of the god Loki. The Norse gods and goddesses take care of their own. That's where I get my power to do the two-out-of-one thing."

Wow, some family tree. "Why wouldn't you want me to know that?"

"I don't like to brag about family connections." Grim glanced away. "I bet you feel the same way. I don't hear you saying anything about your relations."

"That's because I don't have any worth talking about." For just a moment, he thought about his father. Then he closed his heart against the old longing. Thorn needed to change the subject. He didn't want Grim asking questions about his family. "You haven't introduced your kelpie friend."

Grim's kelpie friend didn't look particularly friendly. He was tall and lean. A tangled mass of black hair framed his face and fell across his forehead. Bright green eyes glared at them from between the strands of hair.

"He doesn't have to introduce me, and I'm not his damn friend. Kelpies don't have friends. I don't need a name either."

Thorn decided with that crappy attitude it was no wonder the kelpie was friendless. "Maybe you don't need a name, but I need to call you something. So let's compromise. You're now Kel."

The kelpie nodded and sank back into smoldering silence. Thorn ran his fingers through his hair. The perfect end to a rotten night—except for Kayla. He now had a security chief who was related to a bunch of badass Norse gods, and a team that made crappy attitudes into an art form. He focused on Grim. "What will each of them do?"

Grim was glowering at the witches. "Bygul will watch Nirvana during the day, and Trjegul will take over at night. Kel will be on call if trouble comes from the Gulf. When they're not on duty they can do what they please as humans. Their carousel forms will still be here if needed."

"And what will Kel do besides sitting around getting a tan while he watches the waves break?" Yes, Thorn felt cranky.

Kel stared at Thorn from narrowed eyes. "You know my options. In my horse form I can lure the enemy to climb onto my back. Once they're on, they're stuck. Then I dive deep and drown them. And if they're shifters who change into water creatures, I'll just tear them apart." His lips curved up in an anticipatory smile.

Great. Just freaking great. "Murder and mayhem. Can't wait to see *that*. You'll go viral on YouTube within an hour. Nirvana will be a megahit with gawkers and the police."

Kel shrugged. "I can kill quietly. Most attacks will probably happen at night anyway. I'm a black horse. I'll blend. Besides, you guys have the power to make everyone forget what they saw." He allowed himself a small smile. Very small. "And if all you want is to give someone a good scare . . . ? I'm extremely scary."

I bet you are. But he couldn't argue with what Kel had said, although the only time Thorn wiped memories now was after he'd fed. Couldn't have his dinner screaming, "Vampire! Vampire!" from a dark alley. Thorn didn't have to ask what the two witches could do. They'd be lethal in human or cat form. "Well, welcome to Nirvana. We're in great shape. We have a kelpie, two witches, a sorcerer, a vampire, and a demon besides Grim and me. I'll leave you to do your things. I need to make some plans."

Thorn didn't wait to see if Grim had anything else to say. He made it back to his small apartment behind the game stands without having to talk to anyone else. After taking out the contacts and removing the wig, he took a shower then flopped onto his bed and waited.

When the knock came, he glanced at his bedside clock before heading to the door. Sparkle had allowed them to stay longer than he'd expected. He opened the door.

Grim smiled. "Your demon, sorcerer, and vampire are waiting for you at the gate."

Thorn grunted his thanks and walked to meet his new employees. "I see you have your bags with you." Thorn smiled. "Sparkle kicked you out?"

Zane scowled. "She kept me there just long enough to get rid of that god-awful smell you planted in the castle *then* she kicked me out." He glanced at the demon. "Lucky tomorrow is Saturday. Klepoth won't have to go to school."

School? The demon went to *school*? Thorn muffled a laugh. "Too bad about getting thrown out." Not. He'd been counting on it.

Eric looked disgusted. "It's a shitty way to show gratitude. Sparkle has a short memory. I did a lot for her. I won't forget this. My wife's still working in Chicago. I think I'll tell her to hold off moving back here until things are more stable."

Thorn shook his head in mock sympathy. "Good idea." He pulled out his house key and written directions to his place from his pocket and handed them to Zane. "I feel guilty about this. I'm staying here, but you can crash at my beach house. It's a couple of miles down the road." He pointed west. "You can stay there until you get on your feet."

Klepoth grinned. "A beach house? Great. Thanks."

Thorn wondered about the wisdom of turning over his house to a demon. "Eric, I have a safe room set up for vampires. Zane and Klepoth, be here at dawn tomorrow. The day manager will be here to fill you in. You don't have to worry about the running of the pier.

Everything's been taken care of. I'll check in with all of you at sunset."

"One concern." Zane flipped the key into the air and then caught it. "How many hours do you expect us to work? We can't be here every minute that the pier is open."

"Not a problem." Thorn was ready for this night to be over. "Zane, come up with a spell that will make any illusions Eric or Klepoth create automatically repeat with each new customer. Klepoth will control the illusions during the day, and Eric will take the night ones. Once you have things set up, you can kick back and relax. Unless we have an emergency"—like Sparkle mounting an assault on the pier—"you can leave once Grim and I are awake."

The men nodded and left. Thorn closed his eyes for a moment. His revenge had better be worth all this. Then he opened them and headed back to his apartment. He had work to do, castles to destroy and cosmic troublemakers to lay low.

But strangely enough, he spent more time thinking about Kayla—her smile, her voice, her everything—than he did planning.

And as the day sleep finally took him, Thorn regretted that he couldn't dream.

6

Kayla couldn't wait to get out of the castle. She'd spent most of the day dodging Sparkle and Ganymede while she tried to find evidence of what had caused last night's noxious odor. She'd found none.

But Sparkle had managed to find *her* over and over again as she peppered Kayla with ideas for getting rid of Nirvana. Now Kayla waited impatiently by the lobby doors while her client gave her some last-minute advice.

"I don't know why you wanted to wait until night before going over there." Sparkle studied her perfect nails. "Today was their grand opening. You could've done a little of this, a little of that, and then lost yourself in the crowd."

Ganymede sat on Sparkle's foot. He wore his disapproving-cat expression. *"You could've taken me. I would've brought that crappy Ferris wheel down in seconds."*

"Subtle, Mede. We have to be *subtle*. We don't need the police asking questions." Sparkle didn't seem upset by the mass-destruction concept, just its consequences.

"*I don't do subtle.*" He seemed definite about that.

Kayla stared at him. "Doesn't it bother you that innocent people might get hurt?"

"*Collateral damage. It happens.*" He gave the equivalent of a cat shrug.

"Zane is over there." Sparkle glanced down at the cat. "He'll have taken precautions. Besides, do you want to face Holgarth and explain that his son was collateral damage?"

Ganymede looked up at her. "*That'd be ugly, wouldn't it?*"

"Very. And if this Thorn has a bit of sense, he's hired a bunch of nonhumans to help protect his property. We don't want to start a supernatural war. We just got over the last one." Sparkle leaned down to give him a quick scratch behind his ears.

The cat did some low grumbling. "*If he had any sense, he wouldn't have set up shop across the street from us.*"

Kayla had heard enough. "I'm not going over there to do damage. I need to look around, find weaknesses, and then do some planning. I don't intend to get caught by some crazy vampire or go to jail. If I can find a way to put Nirvana out of business without violence, that's what I'll do."

What she really meant was that she'd try to do the job without crossing any legal lines. If not . . . ? She wasn't sure. Her internal battle was epic. Dad never hesitated to embrace illegal if that was the only way to satisfy his clients. Jeez, he'd even named his business Whatever It Takes. He'd been thrilled when she decided to go to law school. If he got in legal trouble—which he did on a regular basis—he was convinced he'd have his very own attorney in the family. But law school had changed her perspective. Soon she'd have to make a choice: do what her father wanted or keep her self-respect.

"*You're a great disappointment.*" Ganymede glared at Kayla before switching his attention to Sparkle. "*You should've asked for one of her brothers.*"

Sparkle sighed. "She's right, Mede. We want Thorn out of business, but we have to keep our own hands clean if we expect to stay
in Galveston."

Ganymede mumbled something about just sinking the whole
pier and being done with it.

"Violence will bring the police. You saw what happened last
night after you blew up that stand. The police came over to find
out what we knew about it. I don't think they believed it was caused
by an electrical problem. I mean, we're Nirvana's competition, so
they'll suspect us first." Sparkle looked thoughtful. "As much as I
hate to admit it, I sort of admire what the vampire did to us. The
stench made some guests leave, but there's no evidence to take to
the police. Smart."

"Dead, if I catch him or his people in the castle." Ganymede wore
a sulky expression. *"Besides, what evidence would he have if I just
made his pier go away? What would he tell the police? The cat did it?"*

Kayla didn't want to listen to any more of this. "So can I leave?"
She wanted to get moving before nerves got the better of her.

Sparkle widened her eyes. "Oh, didn't I tell you? We're waiting
for your partner."

Kayla froze. "My *what?*"

"He's worked for us before. You'll find him perfect for the job."
She frowned at Kayla. "We'll have to get you some new clothes.
The jeans, T-shirt, and jacket make you blend in with the mob of
idiots across the street. Blending is never good for a woman.
Although I suppose a good spy can't look too spectacular." She
seemed to consider the problem. "I'll get back to you about the
clothes."

Kayla was getting used to Sparkle's lightning changes of subjects. She stayed focused on her "partner." Yes, she'd been willing
to accept a nonhuman to watch her back, to protect her from other

nonhumans, but "protector" didn't have the same meaning as "part-ner." Kayla worked alone. "Look, I don't need a partner, I—"

"Here he is now." Sparkle waved at someone behind Kayla.

Kayla turned. She blinked. She sucked in her breath and then exhaled slowly. Were her eyes too wide? Was her mouth hanging open? He was . . .

"This is Banan." Sparkle watched Kayla expectantly.

He was tall. Were all nonhumans tall? Weren't there any short stubby ones floating around? Kayla glanced down at Ganymede. Guess there were.

She forgot about Ganymede, though, as her shock faded and she inventoried her new "partner." Long, pale hair that stopped just short of his butt, sensual mouth, and eyes so dark she couldn't see his pupils. Her gaze slid lower. He was all lean sculpted muscle in his jeans and gray polo shirt. But her gaze kept returning to those dark eyes. She shivered. Surprised, she realized he scared her.

"What are you?" Did she sound a little too breathy?

He smiled. No fangs, just beautiful white teeth. So why did those teeth still make her nervous.

"That info is on a need-to-know basis. You might never have to see the other me." His smile widened. "That would be a good thing."

Kayla nodded. "So what you mean is that if you told me what you are, I might refuse to go into the night with you?"

"Exactly."

"Well, that's comforting."

Banan didn't comment because Sparkle had pulled him close and was talking quietly to him. Kayla was glad she couldn't hear what her client was saying. Probably filling his head with more ideas for how to destroy her competition.

She needed fresh air. Without looking back to see if he was following, she hurried from the castle. Once across Seawall Boulevard, she decided to take a short side trip before buying her ticket into Nirvana.

Kayla glanced behind her. No Banan. Good. She'd have a few minutes of freedom to get a look under the pier. She quickly climbed down the steps to the beach and moved into the shadow of the pilings. Above her, she could hear the shrieks and laughter of the people still crowding the park. The vampire owner was probably lying in his coffin somewhere counting his money.

Down here it was semi-quiet, just the sand along with the soothing murmur of the waves rolling in. For the first time today, she relaxed. No Ganymede shadowing her footsteps doling out apocalyptic ways to end Nirvana's existence, no Sparkle nagging her with questions she couldn't answer yet and making not-so-subtle suggestions about everything from her hair to her shoes, and no snark from a bad-tempered Holgarth who seemed happy to vent his anger at his son on anyone who wandered too near.

Kayla walked along the edge of the pilings, looking for a way down from the pier—steps, a ladder, anything. She'd need an emergency exit in case things ever went south and people were guarding the main entrance.

She didn't worry about anyone seeing her. She could just claim to be taking a walk on the beach before going back to the hotel.

For a moment, she allowed herself to stop and just enjoy the moment. She lifted her face to the cool sea breeze and thought of . . . Will. Okay, she admitted that he'd popped in and out of her mind all day. Kayla wasn't sure why. Banan was just as spectacular as Will, but Banan made her feel uneasy. Will made her feel . . . She wasn't sure. She wanted to see him again to clarify her emotions.

Kayla had a second reason for wanting to meet him again. Why the wig and colored contacts? He'd been inside the castle right before everyone started to smell the odor. A coincidence? And he'd known that his attackers were shape-shifters. She could connect dots. Was he nonhuman? Did he work for this Thorn Mackenzie?

She peered into the darkness. There. At the end of the pier she could see steps that led down to the water. Waves lapped at them. Kayla didn't know anything about how amusement piers were built, so she didn't have a clue about what purpose the steps served. It wasn't as though people could tie up there without the waves slamming their boats into the pilings.

Wait, there was something in the water near the steps. Kayla hated that her first instinct was fear. She pushed it aside. She took a deep breath. *Focus.* What was it? She had to get a closer look. Taking off her boots along with her ankle sheath and knife, she dropped them onto the sand. She still had her switchblade in her pocket. Kayla hesitated before leaving her gun and cell phone with her shoes. But she'd rather not take a chance of getting them wet if she had to wade out farther than expected. She rolled up her pants, and then stepped into the surf. If she soaked her pants, she'd just go back to the castle to change before entering the park.

She moved closer to the object, straining her eyes to identify it. *Please let it be a floating branch.* She'd taken a few more steps before she realized the thing was swimming toward her. Swimming? *Alive.* She stopped.

It looked like the top of a horse's head. Okay, so a horse wasn't that scary. But what was a horse doing out here? Kayla moved a little nearer. The water was now almost to her chest. She hadn't meant to go in this far.

The water chilled her and she had to plant her feet to resist the current's pull. Now she could see it clearly. Definitely a horse. Black. It had raised its head completely above the water and was studying her. Mesmerized, she again moved toward the animal.

She must have stepped off an underwater ledge because suddenly she plunged beneath the surface. Kayla came up sputtering. She lifted her chin to keep the small waves from washing over her head. Damn.

From a distance, she could hear someone yelling. She glanced back to the shore.

Banan was racing toward her, his long pale hair blowing behind him. "Get out of the water!" He waved his arms and shouted again. "Now!"

Puzzled, she turned her attention back to the Gulf. There was nothing near her except the black horse. She could see its beautiful dished face and flared nostrils as it swam closer. Kayla had always loved horses. Its owner would be frantic. Maybe it had escaped from a barn, gone into the water somewhere along the coast, and gotten caught in a riptide. It didn't matter; she had to think of a way to rescue it.

She didn't have anything to use as a halter, but maybe the horse would follow her onto the beach. Then she could call for help.

The horse drew nearer and nearer, almost close enough for her to reach out and grab its mane. She could use the mane to drag herself onto its back. Riding the horse to shore would make things easier.

It was right in front of her now, and Kayla could see its large expressive eyes. Green? Horses didn't have—

She was staring into those green eyes when it happened.

That gorgeous black horse opened its mouth and showed her its teeth. Not big flat horse teeth, but sharp *pointed* teeth. Ohmigod! What the hell—?

Kayla had no time to think. She knew she'd screamed, but all she could hear was the thud of her heart, the rasp of her breaths. She fumbled for her switchblade. Her shaking hand didn't make the search easier. Why had she left her other weapons on the beach?

She looked up, up as the monster reared above her. Kayla didn't have time to process the horror as instinct took over. She threw herself back as those deadly hooves hit the surface right where she'd been. The creature stretched out its neck and snapped at her. She flailed wildly and heard the click of its teeth closing on empty air.

Kayla knew the thing would catch her before she reached shore, but imminent death was a great motivator. She splashed toward safety just as someone wrapped a hand around her waist and yanked her away from the horse.

"Back off, Kel!"

The voice behind her sounded familiar, but she didn't have time to think about it as the person, no, the man dragged her toward shore. And who the hell was Kel?

Kayla turned her head to the side in time to see Banan race past them, shedding clothes as he went. She wanted to shout to him, to warn him not to go near the horse—no, definitely *not* a horse—but he was gone before she could open her mouth. Helplessly, she watched him disappear beneath the waves.

Kayla and her rescuer reached the beach. Her legs wouldn't support her and she sat down hard on the sand. She should turn around to look at the man behind her, but she couldn't look away from what was happening in the Gulf.

A battle? Who? What? The monster horse almost leaped from the water, lashing out with hooves and teeth. Kayla couldn't make out what it was fighting, though. She squinted into the darkness. The water was a white frothing maelstrom. Whatever the horse was battling had to be huge.

"Damn dumbasses. Anyone could see them out there."

What a weird thing to say. Kayla knew she should turn around, look at the man behind her, but she didn't. Because she recognized that voice. Because she knew he was somehow connected to the horse. Now that she had a moment to think, she recalled his command to Kel to back off. The only one in the water at the time that needed to back off was the horse. The *horse?* Who spoke to a horse that way unless the horse was . . . ?

Then she remembered—two men running into the Gulf and becoming something else entirely.

The battle ended suddenly. The horse turned away and disappeared beneath the waves. Kayla kept her attention fixed on the spot where she could just make out the shape of something large in the water. Without warning, the creature the horse had been fighting broke the surface.

"Oh. My. God!" Not *here.* Not in Galveston. Not this close to shore. But she'd seen enough pictures in her lifetime to recognize what she was looking at. "A great white shark." Was this a real shark? How could she tell?

She finally turned to look at the man crouched behind her. He had the same sensual mouth and the same sexy body, clearly exposed by the wet clothes clinging to his body. But his blond hair was now black, damp strands framing his lean beautiful face. And his brown eyes were now blue, muted in the darkness.

Kayla shifted her mental picture of him to fit the real man beneath the wig and colored contacts.

"Will."

But that's all she managed to get out. Panicked, she swung her gaze back to the water. She'd forgotten. Kayla scrambled to her feet. "Banan! We have to save him. He's still out there."

7

Kayla stumbled over to her pile of things. She tossed her phone at Will. "Call 911." Scooping up her gun and knife, she headed back toward the water. Even if the shark was a shape-shifter, it could still kill.

Was she too late? Had the shark found easier prey in Banan? Her father's words played a repeat reel in her mind. "Do not be impulsive. Do not allow emotions to make you stupid. Always think things through."

Dad would give her a failing grade for this night. Too bad. If there was a chance that Banan was still alive, she would go in shooting and slashing. She remembered something she'd read about stopping a shark attack: punch it in the nose. God, she hoped it wouldn't come to that.

"He's safe." Will grabbed her arm. "Look."

She looked. Sure enough, Banan was struggling out of the water. He'd recovered his jeans, because he was trying to pull them on. Not easy when both he and they were soaked.

At another time she would have paused to admire the absolutely amazing body her "partner" had, but right now she was too overcome with joy that said body was still intact. Dropping her weapons, she splashed into the surf and flung her arms around him. "You're alive."

Banan looked puzzled for a moment and then grinned. "Well, yeah. I'm tough to kill." His grin turned just as quickly to a frown. "Never go into the water alone at night."

Kayla finally realized that she was still hugging him, the partner she didn't think she wanted. But he hadn't hesitated to put himself in danger to help her. She stepped away from him. "Thanks."

Banan's smile returned. "Hey, that's what *partners* do."

Kayla didn't miss the emphasis on "partners." Sparkle must have mentioned her lack of enthusiasm for his title.

She wanted to turn to the man who had dragged her to safety, but she hesitated, trying to come up with exactly the right words. "I appreciate that you saved my butt, but who the heck are you?" or "Who is Kel, because the only one out there besides me and thee was the monster horse?"

The silence seemed to stretch on forever. If they were waiting for her to say something brilliant, they'd be waiting a long time. But Kayla's brain finally kicked in. Its short hiatus was understandable. Paralyzing terror could do that.

If she assumed that Banan had run past Will and her to stop the horse from following them, then why was he getting naked as he ran? Where were his weapons, because there was no way he could battle that monster without weapons? And how had he emerged without even a scratch from the exact spot where a great white shark—probably a ticked-off shark because it had lost its horsey meal—had been a moment before? Kayla didn't really buy into nose-punching as a viable defense against Jaws.

Aware of the man who called himself Will standing silently

behind her, she swallowed hard and asked Banan the tough question. "What are you?" She held up her hand to stop a possible lie. "The truth." She thought she knew, but she wanted to hear him say the words.

Banan studied her for a few beats too long before nodding. "My other form is a great white shark. Sparkle and Ganymede thought I'd be the best one to protect you on land and in the water." He shrugged. "After what just almost happened, I agree with them."

She tried to slow her breathing, calm her heartbeat, but none of her body systems seemed to be paying any attention to what she wanted. She was surprised that Banan couldn't hear her pounding heart because she sure could.

Kayla nodded. Right now she didn't think she'd be able to speak to Banan without her voice shaking. She turned to face Will.

He wasn't looking at her. He was glaring at Banan. *What was that about?* When she felt that she had herself under control enough for him not to hear her panic, she spoke. "Well, at least I know what you really look like now, Will." *A beautiful liar.* "So what's your true name? Because if you had fake hair and eyes, I can assume the name is fake too."

"Whatever you want. I'm open to suggestions. Nothing like a new name to wipe the old slate clean." Will's smile never reached his eyes. His *blue* eyes.

"How did you just happen to be here in time to save me?" Kayla couldn't believe how furious she was with him for everything he *hadn't* told her. But that didn't make any sense at all. She had secrets too. Besides, she didn't know him, didn't *want* to know him, so who or what he was didn't matter. *You are such a liar.* "Oh, and who is Kel?"

"I happened to be here because I work at Nirvana. Someone from security reported a woman sneaking around the pilings. I came down to take a look." He held up his hands. "Can I help it if I was in the right place at the right time?" He tried on an innocent expression.

Fake. It didn't work. "Who is Kel?" Her mind was slowing down, clogged with enough freaking-impossible input to bring it to a standstill.

Will smiled, a real smile this time. "The horse."

Kayla had sort of expected that answer, but she knew her mouth was still hanging open. What did you say to that kind of an admission?

Banan moved up beside her. "Kel is a kelpie."

Kayla forced herself not to edge away from the shark. "Explain kelpie and why he was lurking in the dark."

Will glanced up at the pier. "You know Sparkle, you *work* for Sparkle, and so I have to believe you also understand what she and Ganymede are. Ordinary security wouldn't help Nirvana's owner protect his pier from an attack by Ganymede. He decided to bring in a team that could hold its own. Kel is part of that team." He met her gaze. "A kelpie is one of the fae, a shape-shifting water horse. I'm sorry about what happened. He wasn't going to hurt you. Kel just wanted to scare you so you wouldn't come snooping around again."

"Right. Just wanted to scare me. Then why did you race into the water and drag me to shore?"

Will glanced away. "Sometimes Kel gets a little carried away with his job. Better to be safe."

Banan snorted his contempt at Will's explanation. "You just wanted to play the hero."

He glared at Banan. "You overreacted. Anyone glancing down from the pier could've seen you guys. If a crowd had collected, someone would've gotten it on the news. I don't think Nirvana's owner or Sparkle would be happy about that."

Banan narrowed his eyes. "Then maybe your boss should keep his hired help from attacking innocent humans."

Banan reached out to put a protective arm across her shoulders, and Kayla forced herself not to shudder.

Will caught her in his unblinking stare. "Innocent? I'm beginning to wonder." Then he turned away. "I've got to get back to work."

Kayla watched him leave. He'd just disappeared from view when she realized she hadn't thanked him. Whether she'd been in danger or not, Kayla appreciated his effort. She allowed herself a small smile. If he'd wanted to play the hero, he'd done a good job.

After she'd retrieved her boots and other things, Banan guided her back toward the castle. Kayla swallowed her hysterical giggles. She could imagine what they both looked like. He wore only his wet jeans, and his hair hung long and dripping down his back. Okay, it was a great look for him. On the other hand, she was a mess. Her boots were dry, but that was about it. And she was sure her dripping hair didn't look as good as his dripping hair.

Once she reached the hotel lobby, she stopped. "You can take the rest of the night off. I'm going up to my room and staying there. I have a lot to think about."

He nodded. "I have to report to Sparkle. See you tomorrow."

Kayla turned to the elevators. She was lying, of course. She had no intention of staying in her room for the rest of the night. Yes, the thought of crawling under the covers and pulling them over her head held a certain appeal, but Sparkle wasn't paying her to hide in her bed.

Surprisingly, she felt calm. There were just so many times she could freak out before the ohmigods grew redundant. Right now, she had a job to do.

After a hot shower, she dried her hair and reapplied her makeup—Sparkle would expect nothing less. Taking a lesson from he-who-calls-himself-Will, she pulled on a hoodie and headed over to Nirvana for a few hours of entertainment and espionage. She hoped Banan didn't see her leaving the castle. He was way too visible for what she was planning.

As she stood in the long line still waiting to enter Nirvana even at this late hour, she noticed the sign by the gate: NO ONE UNDER 13 ADMITTED. What was that about? Young kids loved thrill rides. An amusement park wouldn't last long if it kept children out. Sparkle had to know that, so why was she worried? Of course, her park didn't allow children either.

Once inside, Kayla looked around. Same rides she'd seen in hundreds of other parks. The amusement pier was huge, which would make it easier to stay off the radar of one über-sexy enemy. Because if Will worked for Nirvana, he *was* her enemy. She just hoped *he* didn't know it yet.

As she started to tune in to those around her, she noticed something a little strange. The crowd was a lot more intense than she'd expected. Crazy screams and whoops of something more than just excitement came from the people on the rides. And the people passing her seemed too enthusiastic for just another amusement park. Weird. The rides looked normal, but the crowd's reaction to them wasn't. It was something Kayla would have to investigate, because she never knew where she'd find ammunition to use against Nirvana's owner.

Kayla tried to make her wandering seem random. She bought some cotton candy to look as though she fit in. Bad idea. She'd forgotten how it stuck to everything. She paused at the carousel and considered climbing aboard. Then she abandoned the idea. The merry-go-round had always made her sick when she was a kid.

Memories of childhood disappeared as the carousel circled around to a large black horse. No, it couldn't be. But it looked like the same horse. It even had green eyes and seaweed in its mane. A woman wearing jeans and an ecstatic expression was riding the horse. Kayla followed the horse as it circled, trying to make up her mind. It couldn't be the kelpie, could it?

"You got me in trouble, sweet thing. But that's fine, because it was worth it to see the expression on your face."

The hard male voice was right next to her. Kayla swallowed a startled yelp. She turned, and her eyes widened. He was tall and lean, with black hair and bright green eyes. He didn't look friendly.

"Excuse me?" She edged away from him.

He smiled. Kayla got the feeling he didn't do it often. No laugh lines anywhere.

"I'm Kel."

Not possible. She glanced at the carousel and then back to the man. "I've heard of split personalities, but this is ridiculous." Was she being a smart-ass? Not a good thing when faced with a mythical monster. The problem? She wasn't mentally or emotionally ready to take on the human incarnation of the kelpie. That's probably why her brain was sputtering and flinging out stupid statements.

"That's it? Nothing else to say?" He looked disappointed.

She took a deep breath. Her brain stopped sputtering. Kayla decided she'd had enough of being scared. It was time she got mad. "Jerk. You saw that I wasn't doing anything. You didn't have to give me a dental close-up. What kind of a-hole gets his thrills by terrifying people?"

"Me?" His smile widened. "Besides, I'm part of the security here. You looked suspicious to me. An ordinary person just out for a stroll on the beach doesn't have an ankle sheath and gun."

Kayla knew she looked startled.

"Yes, my eyesight is that good." He leaned close.

She didn't back up. Kayla figured if she was ever going to stand up to him, it would be here, where there were lots of witnesses and he was out of his water element. "I was raised on the tough side of

Philly." Not true. "When I go anywhere alone at night, I'm prepared." True.

"Then think of what happened tonight as a learning experience.
Around here you don't leave your weapons onshore when you go
into the water." He wasn't smiling anymore. "Because there're more
things below the surface than you could ever imagine. And you
might not always have shark-boy along to watch your back."

She wanted to yell at him for having the nerve to lecture her,
but she didn't. He was right. Kayla had seen his razor-sharp teeth.
She wouldn't go into the water again without all of her weapons.
Maybe she'd invest in a speargun. But before they parted, she had
to ask, "Is that horse really you?" She glanced at the carousel.

"Yes."

"How?" She had a feeling that as long as she stayed at the castle,
"how" would be her favorite word.

He shrugged. "Our security chief has . . . skills."

She frowned. That explained nothing. He started to walk away.

"Oh, one last thing. If I'd been a serious threat, what would you
have done?" Better to know the consequences now than to find out
too late.

"Once I'd lured you onto my back, you wouldn't have been able
to get off. I would've carried you into deep water and drowned you."

She swallowed hard. "And then?" She had to know.

"You saw my teeth. Use your imagination." He walked away.

The true horror of the kelpie washed over her. Not a beautiful
horse. Not a great-looking guy. He was a thing of nightmares.

As laughing crowds broke around her, she was left with her cotton candy and the realization that this job would be a lot tougher
than she'd originally thought. What owner would hire supernatural
entities to guard his park? Then she remembered what Sparkle had
said about Thorn Mackenzie. *Uh, maybe a vampire?* Unlike Nirvana's security chief, she *didn't* have the skills to win this fight.

Sparkle had made a mistake. No human would be qualified for this job.

"Wearing a hoodie as a disguise? Not very creative, Kayla." The deep voice sounded amused, but a thread of danger wove through it.

Oh, crap. Kayla turned to face Will. She blinked. Before this, she'd only seen him in disguise and in the dark. Under the glare of the pier's lighting he was a whole new animal. He'd dried his hair. It was almost as black as Kel's, shaggy with strands framing his face and a few falling over his eyes.

His eyes. Kayla had known they were blue, but it had been too dark to see exactly how blue. Now, though . . . They were a brilliant shade that she'd only seen once before. Where . . . ?

She remembered. Kayla tried not to show her shock. His eyes were the same spectacular shade of blue as Eric's. What were the chances? Those colored contacts. Were they just a random part of his disguise, or did he want to make sure no one saw and recognized their distinctive color?

"I didn't expect to see you here tonight after what happened with Kel." He was doing some eye-narrowing.

She shrugged and hoped it looked casual enough. "I went back to the castle and changed. I didn't feel like sitting around for the rest of the night so I thought I'd come over and have a look. No more playing with horses in the water, though." Kayla cursed her stupid cotton candy. Her hands were sticky and she knew she must have some on her face too. She slid an exploratory tongue across her lips, but that's about as far as she could go right now.

Something hot and primal flared in his eyes. "You left your shark friend behind?"

"He had other things to do." That look shook her. Why hadn't she brought Banan with her? Then she took a deep breath. She didn't need a bodyguard when she was on dry land among crowds of people.

Whom was she kidding? Will could drag her into deep water with just a few more of those sizzling glances. *You'd be in way over your head.* Because despite her suspicions and need for caution, Kayla felt the sexual attraction sliding along every line of communication in her body, from head to heart to . . . Well, to all points south. She was honest enough to acknowledge his pull but not stupid enough to act on it. She closed her eyes for a second to center herself.

Her eyes popped open again when she felt him take the cotton candy from her. She watched him fling it into a nearby trashcan. "Maybe I wasn't finished with that."

"I'll buy you more later. I thought you might like to sample one of our rides, and I didn't want to be wearing sticky candy when you got overexcited."

The sensual suggestion in his husky voice made her feel . . . Made her feel *nothing.* She firmed her resolve. "Why would I want to go on a ride? They're just the same old, same old." She glanced up at the Ferris wheel. Or maybe not. She'd heard the crowd's reaction to the rides. "Why did your boss choose this spot? I mean, there are other amusement parks nearby, so why build one that not only has close-by competition but is across the street from someone who doesn't want him here?"

"So Sparkle told you this, that she doesn't want us here?" He stared down at her, his thick dark lashes hiding some of the intent in his eyes.

Kayla glanced away. Maybe she didn't want him to see her intent either. "She didn't have to tell me. You're blocking the castle's view. You're cluttering up the whole area with hordes of people." She finally stared up at him. "You're ruining the neighborhood."

Time to change the subject. "And what's with the sign at the entrance that says children under thirteen won't be admitted?"

He shrugged. "Some of our amusements are a little too intense for younger children."

Intense? He had to be kidding. She glanced at the carousel. Okay, maybe a little dizziness, a little nausea, but that was the biggest threat she saw here.

Will nodded toward the Ferris wheel. "Are you afraid of heights, Kayla?"

She looked up. "I've ridden a few Ferris wheels in my time. Heights don't bother me."

He put his arm across her shoulders and guided her to the ride. She wanted to shrug off his touch, get rid of the curl of heat in her stomach, reject the desire to slide her fingers under his shirt and touch his bare flesh. Just in time, they reached the Ferris wheel.

While they waited to board the car—the flimsy kind where you sat side by side with only a bar across your body to hold you in and with nothing but empty space in front of you—a man approached them. Will went to meet him.

She couldn't help it. She stared. The man's eyes were the same shade of blue as Will's and Eric's. This was weird to the nth degree. When Will finally turned to walk back to her, she looked away.

Kayla didn't have a chance to ask any questions until after they were seated for their ride, the one that was "too intense for younger children."

Once they were secured in their seat and the Ferris wheel began to move, she asked her question. "Who was the man you were talking to?"

"Grim. He's the security chief for the park." Will realized there was a downside to his impulsive invitation. Now he was trapped with her and her questions.

She shifted in her seat, and her thigh pressed against his. He stopped just short of sucking in his breath. Now he remembered exactly why he'd suggested this ride. Not a good reason. He wasn't exactly sleeping with the enemy, but . . . Fine, so he wanted to do a lot more than have thigh contact. He needed to clear his head and redefine his goals.

Thorn decided to go on the offensive before she could ask another question. "You never told me what you did for Sparkle besides playing the occasional sexual demon role."

She looked away from him, and for a moment he thought she wouldn't answer. "This and that. I don't have a specific job. I do whatever Sparkle needs me to do."

He was starting to think he knew exactly what her job was. Let's see, she had only recently started working at the castle, was proficient with a knife, carried a gun, had been caught sneaking around pilings, and then immediately afterward was discovered wandering around Nirvana. He didn't want to believe it, but it stood to reason that Sparkle would hire someone to spy on him or worse.

"What about you? What do you do here?" She was still looking away from him.

He had to distract her from burrowing into his business. "This and that, with an emphasis on *this*." Thorn slid a little closer and rested his arm across her shoulders. He felt her tense.

"Were you responsible for that odor in the castle?" She finally met his gaze.

"What?" Thorn couldn't decide if she was brave or foolhardy. Shutting her up would be as simple as lifting her over the side of the car and calling it an oops moment when she fell to her death. With the paranormal talent he had working for him, he wouldn't have to worry about witnesses.

But he wouldn't do that. Somewhere during his centuries-old journey to acting human he'd developed a conscience. Besides, he was enjoying her too much. "I hope you have enough sense to keep your weapons with you when you make that kind of accusation."

She blinked. "Of course. So, did you?"

His first instinct was to lie. Admitting to sabotage would pretty much ruin any chance he had to further their relationship. *Relationship? You're kidding, right? You don't need that kind of distraction.*

Thorn shrugged mentally. What did it matter if Kayla knew? Ganymede and Sparkle would've already recognized that the attack came from Nirvana. Besides, it was better for her if she understood what he was and stayed far away from him. *Better for me too.* "Conflicts don't always have to be resolved with violence. There are more subtle methods." Now it was his turn to look away as he waited to field her outrage.

She remained silent for a moment. "It was more effective than blowing up Nirvana's refreshment stand."

He glanced at her. She didn't look outraged, only thoughtful.

"How'd you do it?" She watched him from those expressive gray eyes. "Don't worry, I'll be horrified and angry later. But I want to know how you did it first."

Surprise warred with amusement. She'd managed to surprise him. He started to answer when he noticed she was staring over her side of the car. He watched her eyes widen. He smiled. Now she understood his age limit sign.

"Ohmigod! No Ferris wheel goes this high. This can't be real."

She slid closer until she was pressed against his side. He knew it wasn't because she craved his closeness but because the view had rattled her. He could hear her heart pounding, her breaths coming in shallow gasps, and sense her blood pumping its eternal invitation. He swallowed hard, a remembered reflex from when he was human.

"We're not as high as we'll go yet. Sit back and enjoy the ride." He knew she wouldn't in the same way he knew she'd want to know how and why. Surprisingly, he admired her for that even though the questions would be a pain.

"Why are we getting the satellite view? How did you do it?" She bit her lip as she turned her head to look out at the Gulf.

Thorn took a moment to glance down. His pier seemed a mere speck of light from this height. With his enhanced vision he could see the whole coastline of Galveston Island along with the Causeway and lights from the mainland. Behind him, the Gulf of Mexico stretched to the horizon.

"Magic." He wouldn't get more specific than that. He wouldn't explain that both Eric and Klepoth could create illusions that were for all intents and purposes real.

Kayla now gripped his thigh with one hand and the bar with the other. He could feel the tremble in her. He massaged the back of her neck while he pried her fingers from his thigh and held her hand.

"Stop the magic. I don't want to go any higher." She somehow kept her voice calm and level.

"We're at the top, so we'll start going down now." He hoped he sounded soothing. Thorn didn't want to admit it, but being this high with only a seat and metal bar to keep them from plunging to earth made even him nervous. No matter how often he told himself that this was all an illusion, he still couldn't wait to place both feet on solid ground.

He could almost hear her teeth chatter. It was a lot colder up here, and all she wore was a light jacket. Oh, what the hell. He wrapped his arms around her and pulled her close. "Relax. This is just me keeping you warm."

For a moment, suspicion replaced the horror in her eyes. "Right." She looked down again and then quickly transferred her gaze to the Gulf. "Umm, we don't seem to be moving." Kayla shuddered. "Except for the rocking of this damn car. Did I mention that I get motion sickness? I have to take a pill before I go on a boat."

Great. This high, the wind was pretty strong and the car was swaying back and forth. And she was right, they'd stopped moving. What the hell . . . ?

But before he could reach for his phone, it rang. He pulled it from his pocket. "What's going on down there?" Thorn knew he sounded uneasy, but being stuck up here was bad on all kinds of levels.

Grim sounded tense. "We have a situation here. I'll get back to you in a few minutes." And he hung up.

Possibilities raced through Thorn's mind. Whatever it was must be an emergency if Grim couldn't even take the time to clue him in. But Thorn also figured the other vampire had things under control or else Grim would've called on his crew to start getting customers down from the Ferris wheel.

"What's the matter?" Kayla sounded tense.

"Some kind of mechanical glitch. Nothing serious." *I hope.* "We'll just sit up here and enjoy the view for a little while."

She was quiet for a moment. "This is all an illusion, right?"

He nodded. "The owner wanted a park that offered something new, so he hired Klepoth and Eric away from Sparkle." Thorn figured that Kayla probably already knew this. "Both of them can create powerful illusions, and Zane times the illusions to repeat as needed." He felt her relax a little. "I don't know how they do it, but what you're seeing is the real view from this far up."

"Oh." She frowned.

He loved the way she pursed those sexy lips and got that intense gleam in her eyes when she was thinking up another question.

Just as she opened her mouth to speak, a gust of wind blew his hair into his eyes. Before he could reach up to push it aside, she smoothed her fingers across his forehead, sweeping the strands away.

He held his breath as they locked gazes. Something hot and hungry shone in her eyes. She glided her fingers along his jaw, her gaze never leaving his. Her expression said that her fingers had gone rogue and were taking her hand places it shouldn't go. But the heat in her eyes didn't cool.

"The defendant pleads guilty due to temporary insanity," Kayla murmured. She watched him from beneath half-lowered lids as she traced his bottom lip with one finger.

"Meaning?" He'd never realized that the touch of one finger could heat his whole body, including his cold vampire heart. Amazing, since he'd long ago decided his heart had atrophied. He always pictured a walnut where his heart should be.

"That's legalese for 'I am so screwed.'" She breathed the words out on a soft sigh.

Her finger still rested on his lips, so he didn't even have to exert himself. He drew the end of her finger into his mouth and then swirled his tongue around it. Thorn watched need flare in her eyes. She licked her own lips.

Desire roared to life as he allowed her to reclaim her finger. He closed his eyes for a moment. *Control it.* When he opened them again, he hoped she couldn't see his own need. Vampire hunger looked a lot more dangerous than what burned in her eyes. There were a few things he hadn't been able to humanize.

Without asking permission, he leaned close and slowly licked a spot of cotton candy from beside her mouth. Her skin was warm, smooth, and tasted of sugar along with aroused woman. His favorite blend. "I've never had cotton candy. Now I'll never forget the taste." He hoped she understood the thinly veiled symbolism in those two sentences, because he'd made a decision. He *would* have her, and he was certain he'd never forget it.

Her eyes stayed defiantly open, but her lips parted as he slanted his mouth across hers. He traced her lips with his tongue before deepening the kiss. Kayla's lips were soft, her mouth welcoming. Her tongue met and tangled with his—tasting, challenging, and driving him to the edge of bloodlust.

He was the one to pull away, her heat and taste awakening feelings he'd spent centuries squashing and cramming into a shadowed corner of his mind labeled Dangerous Emotions. Well, damn.

Thorn could see that she was breathing hard, that her face was flushed, but she turned to look out at the Gulf before he could read the expression in her eyes. He allowed himself a small smile of triumph. No need to look away if she didn't have something to hide.

"Is that a ship out there?" Her voice sounded breathy.

Okay, he could play the nothing-really-happened game. For now. He followed her gaze to the ship's lights. "Probably a tanker heading out to sea."

They both sat silently watching the ship's progress as the wind blew and emotions swirled.

Until a massive shape suddenly rose from the water. He swallowed a curse as it rose higher, and higher, and higher, a solid blackness against the night's darkness. The ship looked like a toy beside it. "What the hell is that?"

Kayla didn't answer, but clasped his hand and squeezed. She could see it too.

As they both watched, the tanker's lights blinked off and the dark shape sank back into the Gulf.

She sat silently beside him, but he could feel her horror, her need to scream, to demand that he explain what she'd just seen. A minute later, the waves rose and crashed onshore, signaling that something big had disturbed the tranquility of the sea.

Kayla looked at him and opened her mouth to speak.

His phone rang.

8

Kayla took a deep calming breath. *His kiss.* She commanded that particular thought to sit down and shut up. She didn't have time to think about it now.

Concentrate. No way had she seen a ship disappear. And she definitely hadn't seen something the size of a small island rise from the Gulf and then vanish with the ship.

His kiss. The thought was a persistent devil, waiting to ambush her right in the middle of trying to figure out important things: like how a whole ship could just cease to exist and what the hell the huge black mass had been. Oh, and she couldn't forget to think about how anyone could be powerful enough to create the illusion she was experiencing on this Ferris wheel.

She turned from staring at the waves that were finally calming. Will was still on the phone, and his eyes now had all the warmth of chipped ice as he bit out an occasional yes or no. Something was wrong. Will didn't even mention the ship as he slipped his phone back into his pocket.

He stared at her. "That was Grim."

"And?" This wouldn't be good. His expression was tight and furious.

"Someone planted an explosive device at the base of the Ferris wheel."

Kayla's heart made a mad scramble for her throat. "What? We have to get off this thing." She peered over the side of the car. It still wasn't moving, so they'd have to climb down somehow.

"The security team took care of it." His expression turned colder, if that was possible. "Is this your work?"

"Me? You have to be kidding." She wanted to jump from the car and storm off. Too bad it was such a long way down. "When and how would I have done this dastardly deed? While I was talking to Kel? While I was talking to you? While I was *kissing* you?" Okay, so she hadn't meant to say that last thing. "And why would I plant explosives—even if I knew how—and then go for a carefree ride on your damn Ferris wheel?"

"You could've planted it before you met Kel." Uncertainty warmed his eyes a little.

"No time. Check your security cameras to see when I entered the park." Kayla tried to downplay how angry she really was, because otherwise she'd have to admit how much his suspicions bothered her. But she was having a tough time maintaining her "professional" attitude. She wanted to reach over and slug that perfect jaw.

He remained silent as the Ferris wheel began moving again, taking them down. Kayla could've cried with relief. It was slow going because the car kept stopping to let others get off.

Finally he spoke. "I believe you. I saw what happened to the refreshment stand. Ganymede, I assume. He's good at long-distance destruction. Sparkle wouldn't have to send you over to blow something up." He lapsed back into silence.

This opened a whole new train of thought for her. If Sparkle wasn't responsible, then who? She remembered the shape-shifters who'd attacked Will. Not Sparkle's style either. "Have you considered that your boss might have other enemies out there?" She shrugged. "Just a thought. I mean, it's tough to believe because I know he must be such a lovable guy."

For just a moment, those sensual lips tipped up in a smile, and then it was gone. She glanced away and realized they'd reached the pier. She wasn't going to lie, it felt great to step out onto something firm. Kayla thought of the explosive. If Grim hadn't discovered it, she might have rained down in pieces. Not a comforting thought.

Kayla expected Will to abandon her for Grim, who was standing a short distance away speaking to a woman with curly black hair. From what Kayla could see, the woman was beautiful. "Who's the woman talking to your security chief?"

Will glanced at the woman. "That's Trjegul. She's part of our security team."

That meant Will worked with her nightly. Kayla nodded. Who had a name like that? "Good to know." She refused to acknowledge a small possessive voice whispering, "Mine." Wasn't going to happen. Will was the enemy. And if what she was beginning to suspect was true, he was the enemy with a capital E.

Will looked anxious to join Grim, but Kayla wasn't quite finished with him.

"What should we do about the ship we saw?" She hated her sense of relief when the woman with the unpronounceable name walked away from Grim and disappeared in the crowd.

"I'll call the police, and they'll contact the Coast Guard. But I'd bet they already know." He stared silently at the Gulf for a moment before looking back at her. "If what we saw was real, it means there's something out there we need to pay attention to."

"No kidding." She hesitated. "Who are you?" Kayla shook her head as he opened his mouth to answer her. "Truth. You have the same color eyes as Grim and Eric. I think that's important. If you won't give me an answer then I'll ask Sparkle. I'm betting she'd know. Oh, and I've noticed how much authority you seem to have around here. So . . ."

Kayla hoped she wasn't making a mistake by confronting him. She wouldn't want to take a one-way trip into the Gulf on Kel's back.

He stared at her with those mesmerizing eyes so long that she almost began to fidget. Dad had taught her that showing nervousness in front of a predator could be a death sentence. And she had lots of living to do.

Finally, he nodded. "I'm Thorn Mackenzie. I own this pier."

"A vampire?" Kayla knew she sounded calm, but in her head scenes from every vampire movie she'd ever seen played in gory detail.

He narrowed his eyes. "How'd you know?"

"I was there when Eric told Sparkle he'd be working for you. He said your last name, and I knew it meant something to her. When I asked Sparkle about it, she said you were a vampire." Could things get any worse? Would he drag her into a dark place and drain her dry. *Don't be such a drama queen.* "I appreciate your honesty." Time to make a dignified exit. She glanced at her watch. "Oops, guess I'd better go. Getting late." She knew her grin had Ohmigod-I'm-talking-to-a-freaking-vampire stamped all over it.

"Wait just a minute." He reached out and gripped her hand.

And even knowing what she now knew, Kayla's body reacted with joyous shouts of, "He's touching me." Stupid body.

"I've been honest, so how about a little reciprocity. Who are *you?*"

Her churning thoughts and stomach were in sync. What to tell him?

He looked impatient at her silence. "Are you here to sabotage Nirvana?"

"No." Surprised, Kayla realized she had told him the truth. It would break her father's heart to know she wasn't following in his shady footsteps, but she wouldn't be raining down destruction on Thorn Mackenzie's beautiful head.

"Spying?" He speared her with his hard stare.

"Keeping my eyes open." She needed to elaborate a little on that. "Sparkle wants to know what's going on over here." She shrugged. "So I'll be keeping her in the loop."

Someone bumped into Thorn, and he murmured a curse before guiding Kayla toward the pier's railing. Kayla hesitated.

He smiled. "Don't worry. I won't heave you into the water for Kel." He placed his arm across her shoulders and pulled her close. "I just wanted a little privacy to talk."

She didn't think there was much to say now that they both understood the situation. That didn't stop her from leaning into him, though. Who knew vampires had their own magnetic field?

"Why don't you quit, Kayla?" He kept his gaze on the Gulf as he spoke. "This thing between Sparkle and me will get messy. A human could get hurt."

She stiffened and drew away from him. "Is that a threat?"

He glanced at her. "No. Just a fact. Each of us will be using nonhumans in this war, and they forget that humans are more fragile than them."

"Okay, so you just insulted me. I'm not helpless." Unprepared, yes. Helpless, no. "My father signed a contract with Sparkle, and if I bail, she'll sue Dad."

"Doesn't he have anyone else to send?" He sounded sincerely interested.

"I have two brothers, but Sparkle said she wanted me."

His slow sexy smile said he knew exactly why Sparkle had requested her. "Sparkle plays all the angles."

Kayla made a rude noise. "It won't work. I'm not stupid enough to fraternize with the enemy." Only she was. Stupid. And fraternizing.

His smile widened. "Well, Kayla Stanley, feel free to visit anytime you want. Peek into corners and report back to Sparkle. But while you're here, I'll feel free to . . . fraternize. A lot."

Time to leave. His wicked grin was doing strange things to her equilibrium, and his promise terrified her at the same time it made her feel . . . *No*. It made her feel absolutely nothing.

"But before you go . . ." He pulled her to him.

And she allowed him to. His lips took hers and it was a complete claiming. Or as much of a claiming as he could manage while surrounded by hundreds of people.

His mouth was a contradiction—firm but with a soft lower lip, a tongue that conquered and teased at the same time, and heat, so much heat that he warmed her all the way to her curled toes. And here she'd thought vampires were cold creatures. No, not creatures. Kayla knew she could never again think of them that way because now she had faces to put with a few—Thorn, Eric, Grim.

When he broke the kiss, she was left gasping like a guppy that had flung itself from its fish tank. And like the guppy, she'd never be safe again. Then she looked at him and knew the danger was worth the risk.

"Well, I'll see you. Probably. Soon." She almost ran from him. His soft laughter followed her as she fled the pier.

Kayla managed to pull her tattered dignity around her once she entered the castle. First, she'd report to Sparkle and then she'd go to bed. She forced herself to go up to Sparkle's suite and knock on the door. This meeting wouldn't be pretty.

It wasn't.

"You met Thorn Mackenzie?" Sparkle was in her wicked vampire dominatrix costume. She snapped her whip against the side of her boot.

Kayla eyed the whip warily. "You've met him too. Remember the man on the table from last night?" At least Ganymede wasn't here. She didn't need any input from the cat.

Sparkle's eyes widened. "But he was human."

"He was wearing a blond wig and colored contacts. He has eyes the same shade of blue as Eric and Grim. And he said his name was Thorn Mackenzie." *And he is absolutely the sexiest being I've ever met.*

"Grim?" Sparkle's eyes had grown wider, if possible.

Kayla sighed. Now what had she said? "His chief of security is named Grim. Big guy, dark hair, incredible eyes?"

Sparkle got that fixed look in her eyes, and Kayla wasn't surprised when the door swung open and Ganymede padded into the room. He looked annoyed.

"I was up sharing a pizza with Murmur. I love you, babe, but no one gets between me and my pizza unless there's blood."

Sparkle glared at him and snapped her whip harder. "There soon might be lots of blood."

Ganymede's expression turned cautious. *"Guess I had enough pizza for one night. What's up?"*

"Grim Mackenzie is working as Nirvana's security chief." She looked at Kayla. "What else did you learn?"

"I guess Banan told you about the kelpie."

Sparkle nodded.

"I went on the Ferris wheel." For some reason, Kayla didn't want to admit she'd ridden it with Thorn. She wasn't sure if that was to protect Thorn or her. Maybe both of them. "Talk about amazing. It took me right up into the sky, or at least that's how it seemed. When I looked down, the pier was just a dot of light below. I could see all of Galveston."

"He must be using Eric and Klepoth to create illusions." Ganymede pinned his ears back and hissed.

"Did you manage to do any damage?" Sparkle looked hopeful.

"No, but someone else almost did. One of Nirvana's people discovered an explosive device at the base of the Ferris wheel while I was on it. Luckily, someone was able to disarm it. I . . ." How to explain how she knew this? "I heard a little of what Thorn Mackenzie was saying to his security chief as I got off the ride, so I hung around and listened."

Sparkle's shocked expression convinced Kayla she knew nothing about the attempt.

Kayla glanced at Ganymede. "Thorn doesn't suspect you because he knows you can blow things up without setting foot on the pier."

Ganymede looked like a furry puffer fish. *"This Thorn guy respects my power. Smart. He realizes his existence hinges on keeping me in a good mood. Maybe he can improve my mood by sending me a few cases of chips and dip."*

Since they were already on the subject of sabotage, maybe now was the time for Kayla to define her job description with Sparkle. Yes, Sparkle scared her, but the thought that this assignment could turn her into her father scared Kayla more.

Kayla wasn't going to lie about how she intended to do her job. If she was lucky, maybe Sparkle would fire her. No, that was a selfish wish because Dad would take the brunt of Sparkle's anger.

"Just so we're clear, I've decided that I'm not the kind of person who makes a good saboteur. If that's what you want, you need one of my brothers. I'll spy for you, bring back any information I can get, but I won't destroy property for you. Oh, and Thorn knows I work for you." She held her breath waiting for the explosion.

Sparkle speared her with a hard stare. "Did he catch you listening to his conversation? Did he kick you out and say he'd kill you if you ever came back?"

"No." Kayla decided not to tell Sparkle about Thorn's challenge.

Sparkle nodded. "We're still in business." She dismissed Kayla's admission as she turned to Ganymede. "Grim is a problem. He has connections."

Kayla blinked. What the . . . ? Why wasn't Sparkle yelling, beating Kayla about the head with her whip, or making threats? That had been too easy.

Then Kayla remembered something. "Have you heard anything about a ship disappearing out in the Gulf?"

Sparkle looked annoyed at her interruption. "No. Why?"

Kayla didn't get a chance to explain because Sparkle's cell phone rang. With an impatient huff, Sparkle answered it. A few minutes later, she put it away and stared at Kayla.

"That was Holgarth. The news is spreading that a tanker went down just off the coast. The Coast Guard is on its way out there."

Sparkle picked up Ganymede and hurried to the window. She shut off the lights so they could see outside better. Kayla followed her to the window.

From what they could see past Nirvana, boats and helicopters were headed toward where Kayla and Thorn had seen the boat disappear.

Ganymede turned to look at Kayla from gleaming amber eyes. *"What do you know about this?"*

"I was up at the top of the Ferris wheel when I spotted the lights from the ship. I could just make out its shape in the darkness." Kayla hesitated, but then went on to describe what else she'd seen. "Right before it seemed to disappear, something massive rose up from the water. It looked as big as a small island. Then both the ship and the . . . thing vanished."

Sparkle and Ganymede looked at each other, and Kayla had the feeling they were having their own private conversation. Then Sparkle smiled at Kayla.

"You must be tired. Why don't you call it a night? You'll need to be rested for tomorrow."

Kayla recognized a dismissal when she heard it. She didn't waste any time hurrying to her room. But even after climbing into bed, her mind wouldn't settle.

She tried to focus on how she would spy without being obvious. Thorn didn't seem to think of her as a threat. His mistake. As long as he didn't ban her from his pier, she could get information for Sparkle. And if he did ban her, well, she could whip up a better disguise than his.

What about the ship? Kayla couldn't wrap her mind around that mystery. And she didn't want to even think about the lives lost if it had gone down. *You know it sank because you saw it disappear.*

Then there was Thorn. When she finally managed to fall asleep, it was the memory of his taste, his scent, his feel that she carried with her.

Thorn left Grim debriefing his security team while he walked on the beach. The darkness and the rhythmic swish of the waves calmed him, allowed him to separate his tangled thoughts.

Kayla. She was Sparkle's tool. He should despise her, should make sure she never set foot in Nirvana again. But he didn't, and he wouldn't. Because she'd tugged at something that hadn't felt pull in many years. Maybe he'd allow her to yank whatever it was into the light, dust it off, and see what developed. Dangerous? Yes. But living as a human for centuries had never been safe. He smiled.

His smile faded, though, as he thought about other developments. Thorn was ready to admit that Sparkle and Ganymede hadn't been responsible for the muggers and the explosive device. Then who? He'd better find out before they leveled Nirvana. In the meantime, he'd talk to Grim about some preventive measures.

Finally, he thought about the ship. What the hell had happened out there? It had been real, because even now he could see Coast Guard boats and helicopters heading toward where the ship had disappeared. Something else to worry about, but not right now.

Just as he was about to turn around and head back to his pier, he saw her. A woman sat cross-legged on the beach watching the boats and helicopters. She had long dark hair that shone sleek and damp in the dim light from the street. Not much in the way of clothes, just something short that clung wetly to her. A net lay across her legs.

Strange. And right now Thorn was suspicious of any new weirdness that came even close to Nirvana. He approached her.

Thorn wasn't prepared for what happened next. She turned her head, saw him, and stood in one lithe motion. Without hesitation, she flung her net at him.

For a moment he stood riveted. What the hell . . . ? The net expanded and expanded until it hung above him, ready to drop and imprison him. No way. An ordinary net couldn't do that. He didn't take time to worry about the whys. His vampire reflexes kicked in and he moved. He knew he'd be just a blur to her as he escaped the falling net.

Thorn curled his lip, exposing his fangs. "Who are you? *What* are you?" He kept a wary eye on the net.

It was once more an ordinary net hanging from her fingers. But ordinary would never apply to *her*. Thorn sucked in the breath he no longer needed. She was one of the most beautiful women he'd ever seen, and over the centuries he'd seen a lot. That short little something she wore ended at the tops of her thighs, and her legs went on forever. Her feet were bare, and she watched him from large dark eyes.

Her spectacular beauty wasn't what was giving him a you've-got-to-be-kidding moment, though. She was tall, like *tall*. He was over six feet, and if he were standing facing her, he'd probably be at eye level with her stomach. It was a humbling moment.

Then she smiled, and he forgot about her height. It was slow, sensual, and filled with sly intent.

"Vampire." She offered him a sexy pout. "I wanted you to be human. I love human males." She drew the tip of her tongue across her bottom lip to indicate how much she *really* loved human males.

Thorn was glad he wasn't a human male. "I'll ask again. Who and what are you?"

She ignored his question. "You're breathtaking. That makes up for not being human." She seemed to be turning over something in her mind.

He didn't like the speculative gleam in her eyes. "Glad to hear it. Why were you sitting on the beach?" Thorn decided that maybe he was a dumbshit for sticking around asking questions when he should be running. Because there was something about this woman that chilled him, a hard thing to do to a vampire.

But Thorn was used to thinking like a human. Calmly, he pulled out his cell phone and called Grim. "I've got a situation on the beach." He put the phone away.

She watched him from hooded eyes. "You called for help."

"Yes."

"A vampire should be too proud to admit he needs others."

Thorn sensed that where this woman was concerned, a proud vampire would be a dead one. He showed her his own smile, one he hoped chilled *her* just a little. "I've found that humans are survivors exactly because they understand the power of a pack. Now, before my friends arrive, what were you doing on the beach?"

She didn't seem nervous about the impending arrival of his "friends," and that made *him* nervous.

She turned her head to gaze out at the waves. "I was waiting for my daughters. We were looking forward to a few hours of hunting."

Daughters? "And now?"

She shrugged. "We don't hunt in a crowd." She strolled toward the water. "Some other night perhaps. Besides, my husband's hunting has been fruitful." Glancing back over her shoulder, she stared at him. "I won't forget you." Then she was gone, lost in the waves and the night.

Grim arrived along with Kel just as she disappeared. Thorn briefly told them what had happened.

Grim frowned. "There's something about your description—a very tall woman with a net . . . I can't remember right now, but I will."

Kel looked longingly at the water. "Maybe I should take horse form and follow her."

"Not a bad idea." Thorn balanced the kelpie's safety against learning more about the woman. "Be careful. I didn't sense a shifter. She's something else."

Kel nodded. A momentary blur and he became the black horse. He galloped into the surf and then was lost in the waves.

Thorn and Grim walked back to the pier.

"We have two distinct problems here." Thorn allowed a momentary thought of Kayla to intrude. *All right, so make that three.* "Sparkle and someone else who wants me gone from Galveston. And I'd bet the 'someone else' is out there." He nodded toward the Gulf.

Grim shook his head. "Protecting the pier from an attack might be tough then. We hang over the water. We're vulnerable."

Thorn noticed that Grim didn't feel the need to ask if he was packing to leave Galveston Island. His security chief knew him well enough to understand that running wouldn't be an option.

Once back at the pier, Thorn paced restlessly until Kel returned. The kelpie swept his wet hair from his face and fell into step beside Thorn.

"There's some serious shit going on out there." Kel thrummed with excitement. "The ship definitely went down. It's resting on the bottom."

"Did you see the woman?" Who would want to sink a ship?

The kelpie shook his head. "But I saw other stuff. There were no bodies."

"What?" Of course there were bodies.

"None. I checked. Only the ship." Kel lowered his voice. "There's something else on the bottom of the Gulf, some sort of clear domed building." He paused for a moment. "I don't think humans would see it. I felt strong magic."

Thorn just stared at Kel. "You're sure?"

Kel looked offended. "What? You think I could make that up?"

Thorn shook his head. "We have to figure out what's going on." Whatever it was, he wouldn't allow it to interfere with his plans for Sparkle.

"So what do you have cooked up for the castle?" Kel didn't try to hide his love of evil and chaos.

Thorn smiled. Kel was exactly the kind of employee he needed. "I think one of our lovely witches will pay a visit to the Castle of Dark Dreams tomorrow night."

Kel nodded, satisfied. "I should go someday. A horse in a castle can do lots of damage." He smiled. "And get rid of lots of guests."

Thorn watched him walk away. He stood there for a moment trying to decide what to do next.

Without warning, an explosion rocked the pier. No, *not* the pier. It came from somewhere in or near the castle.

Kayla.

Thorn didn't stop to think of consequences as he raced toward the Castle of Dark Dreams.

9

At least Thorn had proof that he'd internalized his humanity, because the vampire he'd been four or five centuries ago wouldn't have done something this dumb. He would have coldly weighed the rewards versus consequences of running into the castle to save a woman. No contest. He'd have left Kayla to her fate. Who cared about the life of one human?

Well, this version of him cared. That was the scary part. He knew *what* he was risking. It was the *why* that confused him. Hell, he'd only known Kayla for two nights, but still he ran.

He cursed whoever was responsible for this. Thorn should be the only one preying on the Castle of Dark Dreams. At least the person who'd planted the explosives at the base of his Ferris wheel was an equal opportunity bastard. Evidently someone wanted both Sparkle and him out of Galveston.

Thorn's burst of speed took him away from Nirvana and over the wall surrounding Sparkle's park in a nanosecond. Any humans watching him would simply think he'd disappeared. He really hoped no one had noticed.

Once inside the park, he paused to stare at the castle. There was smoke, but none billowing from doors or windows, so the explosion had been outside. Thorn could hear alarms going off in the building along with the shouts of employees guiding people out the lobby doors. They'd be busy making sure guests were safe. No one would notice him.

Thorn calmed down a little. What were the chances that Kayla had been outside? He followed the smoke to the back of the castle with its walled-in courtyard. The blast hadn't been too powerful because there didn't seem to be much damage. It had only blown out the wall at one end. He walked around the outside until he reached the opposite side of the courtyard.

The smoke streaming over the wall was smothering. Good thing he didn't need to breathe to survive. The explosion must've set fire to everything in the courtyard. Strange, though, because Thorn could swear there wasn't enough flammable stuff there to fuel a fire this size.

He closed his eyes, reaching with his senses, searching for Kayla. Relieved, he realized she wasn't there. Thorn opened his eyes. Unfortunately, someone else was.

He could hear gasping coughs from the other side of the wall. Damn. The wind was blowing in Thorn's direction, so that meant the blaze would be closing in on the trapped person. No one would be able to mount a rescue before it was too late. Except him.

No time to think. His leap took him to the walkway atop the wall. He looked down. A woman lay on the ground near what looked like a small greenhouse. He lifted his gaze and cursed. The fire was licking at the greenhouse's far end. With the wind driving the flames, it would take only a few minutes for the fire to reach the woman.

He jumped from the top of the wall and landed running. The smoke burned his eyes and the heat threatened to suck every bit of moisture from his body. Fear battered at him, dragging up images of how fast he'd ignite, how hot he'd burn. Because no matter how long he pretended to be human, in the end he was still vampire, and vampires made excellent kindling.

Thorn had reached the woman before he realized what she was trying to do. Crawling? She was trying to drag herself back to the greenhouse. With a muttered comment about the human capacity for stupidity, he scooped her into his arms.

She stared up at him from glazed and reddened eyes. Her coughs threatened to tear her apart. Finally she managed to croak a few words. "Vince. In greenhouse."

He froze. "Someone's still in there?" Crap. Trying to leap to the top of the wall holding two people would test his strength, but it was doable.

"Plant. Just inside door."

Had he just heard right? "You want me to save a freaking *plant*? Lady, you're crazy."

"Please." She struggled weakly. "Let me down. I'll get him." Her words ended in a paroxysm of coughing.

He tightened his grip on her. "We don't have time to—"

She stared at him from eyes too dry to tear, but he didn't need tears to read their expression—horror, fear, sorrow. He sensed the emotions weren't for her.

He closed his eyes for a moment. Thorn couldn't believe he was going to do it, but he was. Opening his eyes, he set her down and raced for the greenhouse door. The hell with acting human. He ripped the door from its hinges.

Smoke and heat formed a living wall as he tried to shield his face. He peered inside. He blinked. No, he wasn't seeing this. A bunch of potted plants sat on a table close to the door. One of the pots, with some sort of vine in it, was wobbling back and forth on the table. It was the only rocking pot he could see—Thorn leaned closer—and the vine was waving in the air, reaching out to him. He rubbed his burning eyes. Didn't change anything.

If he were sane, he'd say no way was a plant trying to knock itself off that table. And he'd heard of a clinging vine, but this was ridiculous. Thorn decided the plant fit right in with the new kind of crazy his world had become.

That's when he heard the voice in his head. It was only a small voice, but its message was clear. *"Help me."* Okay, he was officially shutting down his imagination.

"I hope you're Vince." He grabbed the pot and almost fell out of the greenhouse. The fire was too close. He staggered to his feet and made it back to the woman.

She raised her hands toward the plant Thorn held. "Thank—"

"We don't have time for talk. Here." He shoved the plant into her hands. "Hold on to it." Then he scooped her up and leaped at the wall.

He landed on the walkway. Thorn could hear people shouting, drawing closer through the smoky haze.

"Where's Cinn? I can't find her." Male voice. Frantic.

"Not the greenhouse. Please, not there." Sparkle. Scared?

Thorn had a moment to think about that. The Sparkle he knew wouldn't allow anything as minor as a human in danger to bother her. Had she mellowed over the years? He didn't like that image of Sparkle. He wanted to hold on to *his* image of a cruel, cold bitch.

Without warning, a drenching rain fell. Within seconds, Thorn and the woman were soaked. Through the downpour, he could see the rain was falling only on the courtyard. The fire burned on.

"It's not working, Mede." Sparkle sounded frantic.

"The fire resists my magic. Someone used dark arts here." Holgarth's voice was tight with worry. "Look. It's still burning even though everything flammable must be gone."

Holgarth would be wondering if his son was involved. For just a moment, Thorn felt sympathy for him.

Then Thorn concentrated on his own safety. He didn't want to land right in front of them. Sparkle and friends would be pissed. Thorn didn't fool himself about who they'd blame for the fire. He'd have a much easier time escaping if he ran along the wall and jumped down somewhere else.

He heard sirens in the distance. Too far away. They wouldn't get here in time to distract Sparkle and the others.

In the end, though, Thorn didn't burn any brain cells making his decision. *He* might not have to breathe, but the woman did. And there wasn't much spare oxygen up here. To hell with Sparkle and everyone else at the Castle of Dark Dreams. He leaped just as four people and a cat emerged from the smoke.

They all froze. Thorn stood with the woman in his arms looking at Kayla. Sparkle, Holgarth, and the man in white from Thorn's succubus fantasy stared blankly at him. Ganymede pinned his ears back and growled.

The fantasy vampire slayer recovered first. "Cinn!" He ran to Thorn and lifted the woman from his arms.

Racking coughs and all, she still clutched the plant.

The guy was a vampire. Not a Mackenzie. Wrong eye color. And he loved the woman. Couldn't miss that emotion. The man's feelings were overflowing and collecting in sticky puddles around him. Thorn moved back so he wouldn't be contaminated. Jeez, he hoped he never got like that.

"Who're *you?*" Holgarth was using his bombastic wizard voice.

Thorn only glanced at Holgarth because that's not where the

real danger lay. "Just someone who happened to hear her coughing on the other side of this wall and figured she needed help."

"*Your eyes.* You're Thorn Mackenzie." Sparkle's shock seemed mixed with something else. "*You* did this." Fury overrode her shock and whatever that something else had been.

"If I was responsible, why would I bother sticking around to get caught?"

He chanced a quick look at Kayla. Horror filled her eyes along with a glimmer of accusation. That hurt. He tried to push the unreasonable emotion away. Of course she'd suspect him. He was the evil owner of Nirvana.

"*I've tried to stay cool, vampire. But when you burn up my backyard, scare the shit out of my guests, and put the people I care about in danger, you've gone too far.*"

Ganymede's voice in his head was a mixture of hisses, growls, and assorted muttered threats, all of which ended with Thorn being dead.

Now *here* was the real danger. Thorn speared the cat with a hard stare. "I didn't do this." He glanced at Sparkle. "Your spy probably told you that someone planted an explosive at the foot of my Ferris wheel. My security team found it before it detonated."

He thought naming Kayla a spy would embarrass her. It didn't. Her gaze hardened.

"He's right." She looked at Sparkle. "Remember? I mentioned it in my report." Kayla didn't glance back at him.

Thorn couldn't decide if her attitude made him sad or glad. Hell, he'd only been here because he was afraid for her. She'd never know that, though.

"*What were you doing here?*" Ganymede sounded as though he wanted an excuse to toast Thorn.

Thorn shrugged. "I heard the explosion. Saw the smoke. I thought someone might need help." He met Ganymede's gaze.

"Guess not." He looked pointedly at the woman still in the vampire's arms. "Better get her away from here. I hear smoke inhalation is a bitch."

As one, they all moved away from the wall. The vampire holding the woman walked around the castle and they followed him. He stopped a short distance from where the guests milled restlessly in front of the lobby doors. Thorn could see the fire trucks being waved through the park's entrance. Made sense. The trucks could reach the courtyard more easily that way.

Thorn watched the vampire gently lay the woman on the ground. He stroked her hair and held her hand. She still didn't put the plant down.

"Shouldn't you get her some oxygen?" Thorn was thankful that at least her coughing had calmed.

The woman looked at Thorn. "I'll be fine." Her voice was raspy. "I'm not as human as you think. I'm feeling better already." She smiled at him. "I'm Cinn, and this is my husband, Dacian." She squeezed the vampire's hand. "I'll never forget that you put yourself in danger to save Vince." Her face crumpled as she looked up at Dacian. "The others. They're gone." She turned her head away to hide her tears.

Thorn didn't know where to look. He wasn't good with the gratitude of others or women's tears. So this was a double dose of discomfort. He said the first thing that came into his mind to end the moment. "What's so special about Vince?" Who named a plant? And had he really seen the vine reaching for him?

Dacian answered for his wife. "Cinn is a demigoddess. She grows sentient plants." He looked at Sparkle. "Can I take her back into the castle? She needs to rest . . . and mourn."

Sparkle never took her gaze from Thorn. "Go in through the food delivery door. The police will stop you if you try to use the main entrance."

Thorn watched Dacian pick up Cinn again and leave before he looked back at the others.

Holgarth made a frustrated sound. "I suppose I'm the most qualified to speak with the authorities. The firefighters won't know that as the magic dies, so will the flames. I have the people skills to make them believe they truly did put out the fire. I'll praise them for their efforts and all will be well in our public relations world. And of course there will be the police." He sighed. "They'll want to conduct an investigation." He looked weary at the thought of answering all those pesky questions.

Thorn watched the collective eye-rolling with the first bit of humor he'd felt since entering Live the Fantasy. At least Ganymede waited until the wizard had left before offering any snark.

"People skills? I've known trolls with more people skills." Ganymede sat down, wrapped his tail around himself, and studied Thorn from unblinking amber eyes. *"You want us to believe you're not responsible for this explosion and fire?"*

Kayla spoke up. "I don't think he is. Someone obviously set explosives at both places. I think you have a mutual enemy." She didn't look at Thorn.

Ganymede wasn't about to be sidetracked. *"What about that god-awful stench?"*

Thorn met his stare. "What about my exploding refreshment stand?"

Ganymede decided to abandon that particular discussion. *"You're trying to ruin us. You fired the first shot by building your crappy park right across the street. People like a great view. You killed the view."* Ganymede paused. *"The word 'killed' just reminded me of what I want to do to you."*

Thorn tensed. He didn't want to drag out his power of persuasion again—he still wasn't comfortable that he'd had to use it on Eric, Klepoth, and Zane—but he wouldn't win a straight-up battle with Ganymede. And he'd decided that maybe life still had some unexplored opportunities for him. He glanced at Kayla and then away. Not now. He'd think about her later.

Sparkle finally spoke. "Do I know you?"

He widened his eyes. Damn. No disguise. But even without one, he hadn't thought she'd remember. "No." Thorn hoped his shock didn't show. "We've never met." If you were going to lie, do it with conviction.

But Sparkle wasn't finished. "Why do you want to ruin my park?"

Thorn had no answer for that. He watched her with what he hoped was a blank expression.

He saw the exact moment when she recognized him. It was in the sudden flare of her eyes, the sharp intake of breath.

Crap. He wasn't ready for this confrontation. Thorn would choose the time and place. This wasn't it.

But he needn't have worried. Sparkle looked away and said nothing. Thorn understood. She wouldn't want Ganymede to witness what they said to each other.

Thorn tried to look casual as he started to turn away. Every one of his instincts screamed for him not to turn his back on the cat. But he was counting on Ganymede choosing not to destroy him in front of so many witnesses.

He smiled at the cat. "If you're not going to fry me tonight, I'll be on my way. Hope you find who did the damage. I'll let you know if my people discover anything." Then he started to walk away.

"Don't set foot in Live the Fantasy again, vampire. The only reason you're leaving here in one piece tonight is because you saved Cinn. I won't be so forgiving next time."

Thorn knew better than to pull this cat's tail, but he couldn't help it. Ganymede's arrogance begged to be deflated. "I don't need to 'set foot' in your crappy park. There's more than one way to skin a cat." He hated clichés, but when he found one that would irritate the hell out of Ganymede, he had to put personal likes aside.

"Are you threatening me, vampire?" The tail in question whipped back and forth. Ganymede was pissed.

Thorn hoped his grin looked insulting enough. "Threatening *you*? Why would I? You're not important to me." He glanced at Sparkle so everyone would know who *was* important to him.

Sparkle paled and looked away.

"Just get your ass off my property." Ganymede puffed himself up, flattened his ears, and growled.

Sparkle glanced at Ganymede. Her glare said she took exception to the cat's use of "my." Good. Thorn loved stirring up dissension.

Deciding that he'd pushed the cat as far as he could for now, Thorn walked away. But he'd only taken a few steps when he heard a different voice in his head, the same small voice he'd heard in the greenhouse. *"Thank you."* Thorn chose not to acknowledge the voice.

All the way back to Nirvana, questions beat at him. Ganymede had banned him from Live the Fantasy. Then shouldn't he demand that Kayla stay away from *his* park? No, because he really wanted to see her again. Often.

Okay, so what he *really* wanted was to get her into his bed. Or her bed. He wasn't picky. Nothing unusual in that. He'd wanted to have sex with a lot of women in his life. *But this is different.* He did some mental eye-rolling before shoving the thought aside. It was *always* about sex.

Back to what was really important. How would he ruin Sparkle's business? It seemed too many variables had popped up suddenly. Thorn couldn't give his revenge his full attention when someone was busy trying to drive him from Galveston. Someone who wasn't Sparkle Stardust. And since it seemed the same person was determined to take out Live the Fantasy too, it spoiled his fun. The bastard who liked to blow things up would get the credit for Thorn's brilliant acts of sabotage. Major buzzkill.

And how would he stave off the inevitable confrontation with Sparkle until her park was in financial shambles? Tonight had helped. No one would be able to stay the night with the smell of smoke. Sparkle would have to relocate her guests to other hotels in the area. And she'd have to close down the Castle of Dark Dreams for at least a few days until they cleaned up the courtyard.

Eric met him inside Nirvana. "Everyone okay over there?" He looked worried.

Why not? Eric had ties to the castle and its people. For just a moment, Thorn felt shame for using his power on the other vampire. But then he shook the feeling off. This was war, and in war you used the weapons you needed to win.

Besides, Thorn was doing penance. He'd used persuasion and woken the need that demanded he do it again and again. When he refused, he suffered. Hence the headache and generally rotten feeling that would take a while to fade.

"Everyone's fine. The fire burned up the courtyard, but the castle wasn't damaged."

Eric nodded. He seemed relieved, but there was accusation in his eyes. "Next time do something that won't hurt people."

"What?" Eric thought *he* set the fire? "I didn't have anything to do with that. But I'd like to know who did."

"Glad to hear it. I like this job. I'd hate to have to quit." Eric didn't smile.

You can't quit until I release you. Thorn wasn't proud of that thought. "Got it."

"So how was your night?" Eric sounded a little more friendly.

"Shitty."

The vampire had enough sense not to ask for details. "Well, tomorrow's another night."

"Right. Look, if anyone needs me, I'll be in my apartment. I have plans to make." Plans for Kayla, for Sparkle, and for whoever the dirtbag was that liked to blow things up. First, though, he had a date with some major painkillers.

Kayla was shaking. Not a reaction her father would applaud. Dad expected his children to sneer in the face of extreme danger and imminent death. But the fear wasn't for her. She'd really believed that Ganymede would kill Thorn.

Standing there, Kayla had *felt* power pouring from the cat. He'd terrified her. If he'd aimed all that aggression at Thorn, the vampire would've been dead. She didn't doubt that for a moment.

How far would she have been willing to go to stop Ganymede? Fine, so she didn't believe anyone could have stopped him if he wanted to destroy Thorn. But she would've tried. And that was a frightening revelation.

"You know him." Ganymede stared at Sparkle.

Startled, Kayla realized she was the only one left standing with Ganymede and Sparkle. She should walk away and allow them their private moment, but she was too hungry to find out whatever she could about Thorn. So until they realized she was still here, she'd stay and listen.

Sparkle wouldn't meet his gaze. "What makes you think—?"

"Don't lie to me." His tail twitched back and forth, growing more agitated with each twitch. *"I've known you for too many years, babe. You recognized him from some other time and place."*

Sparkle sighed and finally looked at him. "Yes. But it was a long time ago, and I don't want to talk about it."

Ganymede stood. *"Well, when you do want to talk about it, you know where I'll be."* He padded away, oozing injured pride.

No matter how much Kayla wanted to hear more, she couldn't justify hanging around any longer. She started to slip away.

"Wait."

It took a moment for Kayla to realize Sparkle was speaking to her. She stopped.

"I've been meaning to work on your image. Come with me."

"Now?" Kayla didn't think this was a good time for a makeover.

"I need a distraction, and you need help."

Kayla considered saying no. She didn't need Sparkle's insults on top of everything else that had happened tonight. But her god-awful curiosity whispered that she might learn more about Thorn from Sparkle. "Sure. Why not?"

Sparkle didn't speak until they were inside her apartment. Ganymede wasn't there.

"Mede won't bother us. He'll spend the night at my candy store. He goes to Sweet Indulgence when he's mad at me. I guess surrounding himself with sweets takes him to his happy place."

She seated Kayla at her dressing table and pulled up a chair beside her. Then she opened a rolling suitcase.

Kayla's jaw dropped open. "Why would anyone need that much makeup and hair stuff?"

Sparkle narrowed her eyes. "I'm an artist. Only a true artist could create a masterpiece given the raw material I have to work with."

She could learn to hate this woman. Kayla stared at her face in the mirror and asked the question that was gnawing at her. "When did you meet Thorn?"

"About a thousand years ago." Sparkle picked the things she wanted from her suitcase.

"How?" Kayla waited for the moment that Sparkle would tell her to mind her own business.

"His name was Brandt back then. He was just out of his teens, still human. So young." Sparkle paused, her gaze fixed on a spot somewhere above Kayla's head. "And so very beautiful."

Kayla waited, holding her breath and hoping Sparkle wouldn't stop.

"Watch every step in my process so you can duplicate it." Sparkle didn't say anything more for a few minutes as she worked on Kayla's face.

"Umm, why are you doing this now?"

"I told you. I need a distraction. When I'm stressed I have to keep my hands busy. And I'm not the only one who needs a distraction. Our angry vampire needs one badly. And what's more distracting than a beautiful woman? One who understands the power of an enhanced face."

Kayla might have argued about the power of cosmetics, but she had something more important on her mind. Finally, she couldn't stand it anymore. "So what happened between you and . . . Brandt?"

Sparkle paused to think. "He fell in love with me, naturally."

Kayla raised one brow. "Naturally?"

"Keep your brows still while I'm shaping them." She continued working. "I'm the queen of sex and sin, the cosmic troublemaker in charge of sexual chaos. He was a child. Of course he fell in love with me."

Kayla tried to keep track of what Sparkle was doing to her face, but it was tough. She kept picturing a young and sexually innocent Thorn falling for the mother of all cougars. It wasn't a pretty picture. *And you're jealous, admit it.* Fine, so maybe she was. A little. "So what happened?"

Sparkle sighed as she rooted for the right lip color. "Things didn't end well. He told me he loved me. I knew I had to end it. Ganymede had popped back into my life, and Brandt couldn't have a part in my future. I didn't know he was a Mackenzie, so I assumed he'd live his short human life and then die." She shrugged.

Kayla bit back her urge to hit Sparkle with a few pointed words, including but not limited to "cruel" and "bitch". She decided it might not be wise to tick Sparkle off when she had a mascara wand in her hand.

"What did he say when you told him you didn't love him?" Kayla had expected to feel sad for Thorn, but the anger surprised her. Why all these emotions? He was a virtual stranger.

Sparkle didn't meet her eyes in the mirror. "I didn't. I was supposed to meet him by the harbor. I think he wanted to talk about us, our future together. I sent a message that I'd met an old friend and was leaving with *him*. I never saw Brandt again until now."

Kayla remained silent, gathering her thoughts, her feelings, into a manageable pile. Her overriding emotion was sorrow for that young Thorn. She couldn't imagine how shattered he'd felt when the woman he loved disappeared without a word. And, yes, some of that sorrow was for herself, because maybe she'd started to like him just a little. "He must've loved you very much to carry your memory for this long." A thousand years. "Must *still* love you."

Sparkle laughed. It was cold and brittle. "Don't fool yourself. Love hasn't brought him here. Try vengeance. He tracked me down so he could destroy my business the same way he feels I destroyed his heart."

Since she put it that way . . . Kayla liked Sparkle's take on the situation better than her own. She found she didn't *want* him to still love Sparkle.

Then something occurred to Kayla. "Why trust me with this story?"

Sparkle's smile held true amusement this time. "It's not a case of trust. I needed to talk about it with someone, and you were there. Besides, I'm positive you won't mention it to anyone because my punishments for blabbing are legendary and infinitely horrible." Her smile widened. "Think about PMS every day, all day, for the rest of your pathetic life. With cramps. Can't forget the cramps."

Kayla thought about it. "I won't say anything."

"I didn't think you would. Mede can never know. Jealousy makes him do crazy things. You wouldn't want to be on the same continent with him if that happened."

Kayla only nodded.

"There. Your face is done, and now I'll do your hair. What do you think?"

"Wow." No other word could express her shock. Her face was . . . She looked up at Sparkle. "Make sure you give me everything you used tonight." Because as shallow as she knew it was, Kayla would be wearing this face the next time she saw Thorn.

And he *was* Thorn to her. Brandt would always belong to Sparkle, but Kayla had hopes that in this time and place Thorn would be hers at least for a little while.

After Sparkle finished her hair and Kayla made the expected sounds of awe and appreciation, she returned to her room and crawled into bed. Kayla didn't remove her makeup. She lay in the darkness and stared at the ceiling. Great makeup and awesome hair and absolutely no one to appreciate it. Some things just weren't fair.

But tomorrow . . . Kayla smiled into the darkness. He thought she was a spy, so she'd live up to her title. She'd put on her makeup, fix her hair, and do the kind of spying that would bring James Bond to tears.

Tomorrow night. She couldn't wait.

10

"You're joking, right?" There were some things so horrific that once seen could never be unseen. Kayla stared. "This is a disguise?"

She had spent all morning creeping over every inch of the castle to make sure no more nasty surprises exploded in everyone's faces. She'd found nothing.

Then Sparkle had ordered Kayla to get ready for her daily visit to Nirvana. Makeup? Check. Sexy outfit straight from Sparkle's wardrobe for wantons? Check. Trusty sidekick to accompany her? Che . . . Wait. No.

So here she was, facing her very own "nasty surprise" while she waited in an endless line to enter Nirvana.

"I don't have a clue why Sparkle felt I needed *you*," Kayla complained to her Sparkle-appointed shadow while the park security guy checked her out with some kind of handheld scanner that clicked and beeped. She noticed that no one else was getting this treatment. Kayla understood. Thorn probably alerted his staff after what happened on the beach. She was the enemy. Surprisingly, the thought bothered her.

Finally done with security-guy, Kayla followed her unwelcome partner into the park. She should have kept Banan.

Wow, the place was packed, more than yesterday if that was even possible. She stopped to study the carousel. If she rode it, would it make her trusty sidekick sick too? The thought tempted. He could ride the kelpie. "No one will believe you're just an ordinary tourist."

Holgarth managed to look supercilious even wearing a wig— long black hair to match his long narrow face. He'd colored his pointy beard a matching black and braided it. Sunglasses along with a sleeveless tee, khaki shorts, and flip-flops completed the transformation. Kayla tried not to stare at his skinny arms and legs, but it was a compulsion.

"Your job is to see what you can see. Mine is to do what I can do. Although I should remind you that I'm not only a wizard, I'm also Sparkle's attorney. And I explored every legal avenue before you arrived. I doubt you'll find anything I missed." Holgarth had perfected the contemptuous sneer. His expression said that since he was an amazing lawyer—and she wasn't—he was *certain* she wouldn't find anything damaging enough to shut down Nirvana.

"Still—"

"You don't have the stomach for the tough stuff, so Sparkle had to send someone who did." He paused to consider the bumper cars. "I'll adjust them on my way out. And of course I don't look like a common tourist. A talented wizard could never disguise his innate brilliance."

"His? Are there any female wizards?" Since she'd have to put up with him, she may as well ask questions. Maybe he'd get tired of listening to them and return to the castle.

"Very few. Women lack the magical sensitivity to excel." He kept walking.

"Sexist slime." She wandered over to examine some machinery tucked behind a small building. Exposed. Sure, there was a keep-out sign that read: THIS AREA OFF-LIMITS. But everyone knew that people never obeyed signs. Besides, the sign was only printed in two languages. Visitors from Russia wouldn't have a clue. They'd trip over the machine or stick a finger where it shouldn't be—not that she could see any place where a finger would fit—and lose said finger. Okay, so she was reaching. Kayla pulled out her phone and took a quick picture. She'd add it to her list of unsafe conditions. She wouldn't guarantee it would fly in court, but it was better than nothing.

"Interesting. Whatever it does, it won't do it much longer." Holgarth stretched his hands toward the machinery and mumbled a few words.

There was a flash of light, a muffled boom, and something flung Holgarth onto his butt. Luckily, Kayla hadn't been standing too close to the wizard.

"I love watching a good ward do its thing."

Kayla gasped. Where had Zane come from?

Holgarth's sorcerer son walked over to his father and helped him up. "Cool disguise, Dad. But if you were going for the braided-beard-of-the-pharaohs look, you didn't quite pull it off. I think they shaved their heads. And they didn't wear khaki shorts."

Holgarth glared at his son. "How did you recognize me?"

Zane's lips tipped up in a crooked smile. "You mean besides the superiority dripping from you with each step? I guess I was pretty sure it was you when you tried to fling a spell at that machine."

Zane glanced at Kayla. "Tell Sparkle to send someone else next time. Someone a lot sneakier."

Holgarth drew himself up to his full height. But it was tough to impress when you were wearing flip-flops.

"Did you ward everything?" Holgarth dusted himself off.

"The important stuff. After what almost happened to the Ferris wheel last night, we're staying alert."

"Aren't you afraid visitors will accidentally bump into the things you've warded and injure themselves?" She'd have to do some research to see if anyone had ever won a personal injury suit claiming a magical attack as the cause.

Zane raised one brow. "You mean the visitors who ignore the very big signs?"

Kayla matched him brow for brow. "The very big signs in only *two* languages?"

"Right." He rubbed his forehead. "I've warded our equipment against a direct assault. The attacker's intent-to-destroy triggers them. An accidental bump does nothing."

Holgarth sniffed. "Wise. But I still think you made a terrible mistake agreeing to work here."

Kayla smiled. Lost dignity and all, Holgarth couldn't hide his pride in his son. He was having a tough time maintaining his angry expression.

Zane slapped his father on the back. "I have some things to do, but I'll send someone to escort you around the park, sort of a tour guide." And he was gone.

Holgarth narrowed his eyes. "He means a guard."

"Well, can you blame him?" Kayla felt weary, and they'd only been in the park a short time. Sparkle expected her to stay here until after dark.

But Kayla perked up a little at the thought that once the sun set she might meet Thorn again. She'd drag Holgarth back to the castle for dinner and then make sure he didn't return with her afterward. Kayla's perkiness wilted a little, though, at the thought that Sparkle would send someone else with her. No alone time in sight.

"I'll be your tour guide for today. You may look, ride, or cast admiring glances at Nirvana's wonders, but spells, charms, or other magical tricks are forbidden."

Kayla hated the sexy snide voice behind her even before she saw who owned it. Holgarth swung to face the woman, and his eyes widened. Kayla sighed. She wasn't looking forward to this. She turned.

The woman was spectacular. Tall and slim, she wore jeans that made her legs go on forever and a skimpy top guaranteed to hold men's interest. Her long blond hair curled over her shoulders.

"And you are?" Kayla kept her voice cool but courteous. She wasn't ready to be banned from the park.

"I'm Bygul. Park security." She watched Kayla from forest green eyes.

By who? Kayla frowned. This woman's name was as bad as the one from last night. Trje something or other. Who named these women?

Holgarth puffed himself up. "Feel free to leave. We don't need your services." He allowed a small shimmer of flame to flicker from his fingertips.

Kayla glanced around quickly. His monstrous ego would attract attention.

Bygosh or whatever the hell her name was didn't look impressed. A flame twice as large as Holgarth's danced across her fingers.

Holgarth sucked in his breath. But his shock didn't last long. He narrowed his eyes, flexed his fingers, and then whipped out flames that made Kayla do some breath-sucking herself. He was well on his way to turning his hands into freaking flamethrowers.

Kayla was having an oh-my-God moment. "Don't make this into a mine-is-bigger-than-yours pissing contest. Put out the fire, wizard. People are staring."

Her angry hiss had the desired effect. The flames disappeared.

Bygone licked her bottom lip, her eyes slits of pleasure. "I can feel your power, wizard. Mmmm."

Oh, jeez. Kayla rolled her eyes. This was *not* happening.

"Witch." Holgarth smiled. *Really* smiled. With teeth and all. "What a pleasant surprise. It's not often I find a rare jewel among all the cheap imitations."

Bygum linked her arm through Holgarth's. "Since the boss wants me to stay with you while you're in the park, we may as well enjoy ourselves. Let's talk shop."

Kayla trailed behind them and thought her own thoughts. Everything had seemed so simple back in Philly—put legal stumbling blocks in the middle of Nirvana's smooth path and do a few harmless this and thats. No real damage. No one would get hurt. Too bad she'd never seen the irony until now of tiptoeing outside the legal lines so she could earn money for law school.

Kayla's first two days here had been a big icy splash of reality. Anything she did to help Sparkle would hurt Thorn. Was that what all this soul-searching was about? Not her conscience, but the fact that she liked Thorn? Kayla wanted to believe her conscience would put up a fight even if Holgarth owned Nirvana. She thought about the wizard's snark. Okay, so maybe not a big fight.

Sighing, she pushed that line of thought from her mind. She had a job to do. Kayla spent the rest of the afternoon thinking about ways to *legally* drive Thorn crazy. There had to be a way to prove that Nirvana's employees weren't safe for visitors to be around. Not an easy sell.

She could just imagine it. "Ladies and gentlemen of the jury, notice the big black horse on this merry-go-round. He's really a mythical monster who will kill your loved ones and enjoy every moment. And you won't even be entitled to a refund. Why not, you ask? Because the sexy owner of this perilous park has posted a tiny notice—barely legible—stating that Nirvana is not responsible for injuries caused by mythical monsters. You are screwed, people."

Kayla finally tired of thinking. Her brain was about to self-combust. Instead, she amused herself by stopping some of the visitors and asking them about their experiences on the different rides. With each telling, her eyes grew wider. No way. She'd have to try all of them. With Thorn? It could happen.

The sun was just dipping below the horizon when Kayla finally dragged Holgarth away from Bypass. "We have to leave. I want to eat dinner and report to Sparkle before coming back here. Too bad you have to get ready for your nightly fantasies. I'll just have to stumble along without you."

"Yes, too bad." Holgarth seemed distracted. "Bygul is quite charming. And her skills are extraordinary."

"I'm sure they are." Kayla wanted to get behind him and push. Could he move any slower? He stopped altogether when he reached the bumper cars.

"Humans have a thirst for violence. Look at them. They get pleasure from slamming those ridiculous little cars into each other." Holgarth smiled. A happy smile. "I neglected my duty today." He spoke a few words while making a small hand gesture. "There. Done. My son warded against destructive impulses, but he forgot to protect against simple performance tweaks." He turned and walked toward the gate, triumph in every step.

Kayla started to follow him but then stopped. Angry cries rose from the cars' drivers. No matter what they did, the cars wouldn't bump into each other anymore. Someone shouted for his money back. She slunk away.

Dinner left a lot to be desired. Oh, the food was great, but the company wasn't. Kayla had never thought of herself as sulky, but she was doing a great imitation right now.

Sparkle sat across from Kayla at the table. They were dining in a small private room off the main restaurant. Her client tapped one perfect crimson nail on the edge of her bread plate. She'd narrowed her amber eyes to ticked-off slits.

"I may as well tear my money into tiny pieces and let it rain down as confetti on that abomination across the street." Sparkle paused to slurp her wine. She was way past the sipping stage. "My wizard spends most of the afternoon drooling over some slutty witch and only manages one small act of sabotage. And my well-paid spy comes back with some dreary plans to *sue* Thorn Mackenzie?" She gulped more wine. "I expected more creativity from you."

"You're right. I'm a failure. Send me home. Dad will get one of my brothers to finish the job." Only Kayla realized she didn't *want* to go home. Not until she worked through the attraction she felt for Thorn Mackenzie.

"This is all a bunch of crap, cuddlebunny. Just turn me loose and by morning there won't even be a piling left standing. I can manifest a wave that'll make Nirvana only a bad memory. The police won't have a clue."

Kayla tried to ignore the whole cat-in-a-restaurant thing. Board of Health? Not her problem. "You can do that? Create a tsunami?" The possibility gave her chills.

He stood with his hind legs on the chair and his front legs on top of the table. His face was buried in a dish of ice cream. *"The big wave is only a thought away. I'm magic, babe."*

Kayla decided not to comment on that.

Sparkle studied her empty glass. "Your big wave would also take out the castle, magic man." She looked at Kayla. "Go back to Nirvana tonight and come up with a few new strategies. Seduce Thorn Mackenzie. I gave you the face and clothes, now use the tools. Find out his weaknesses, things that would make him give up and leave Galveston."

Ganymede tried offering his help again. *"You want him dead? I can make him dead."* He sat down on his chair and cleaned the ice cream from his whiskers and face with one gray paw. *"Or maybe not. Guess I got caught up in the moment. The Big Boss is still stuck in his no-murder-or-mayhem rut."*

"The Big Boss?" Did Kayla need one more person to worry about? Sparkle waved Kayla's question away. Her eyes looked a little glazed. "He's in charge of all cosmic troublemakers. Don't worry, he's not here right now." She smiled at the cat. "Keeps Mede on a short rein." She tilted toward Kayla. "Whoa, I'm a little woozy. Too much wine. Anyway, I don't want to kill Brandt. Woops, forgot. He's Thorn now. Just want him to go away. Forever."

Ganymede growled, a low angry rumble.

Sparkle giggled and slapped at Ganymede. "You're jealous. I like that." She scratched the top of the cat's head. "I'll tell you about him someday. Not now, though. When I'm sober." Her laughter died. "It's a sad story. I hate sad stories." A tear wound a path over her cheek. She swiped it away.

Awkward. Kayla wanted out of there. Now. But she needed something first. "Do you know a cop who isn't afraid to write up citations for . . . minor things?" Very minor.

Ganymede answered. *"No, but I can grab one, do some mental hacking, and make a few subliminal suggestions. How'll that work for you?"*

"Fine." Not really. But she had no choice if she wanted to show Sparkle results. "Will he go back to normal when I'm finished with him?" This could be a deal breaker.

"Sure. No problem." The cat eyed her dessert. *"You going to eat that pie?"*

Kayla shook her head and pushed the plate over to him.

"Thanks." He stood on his hind legs again and buried his face in the pie. *"Too bad it isn't cherry. With ice cream. Don't know how*

you eat pie without it." He raised his head long enough to burp. "*Oh, and it might take a few days to get that cop to you.*"

Kayla took that as a dismissal. "Loved the dinner. I have to get back to work now. I'll report in the morning."

She didn't go directly to Nirvana. Kayla had something to do first. She went up to her room, sat on her bed, and turned on her laptop. Then she did a search for obscure Texas laws.

When she had what she needed, Kayla changed into a top that plunged a little lower and clung a little closer. Tonight wasn't really cool, so she wouldn't need a jacket. Before leaving, she upgraded her makeup to night-glamour status and worked some life into her hair with a brush and dryer.

She wasn't a hypocrite. This makeup wasn't to please Sparkle. Kayla wanted to look good for Thorn, and his sexy witch brigade was tough competition.

Kayla admitted that Thorn drew her in a way she didn't understand, might not be ready for. Sure, other men had attracted her. She'd lusted after some of them, but not this fast, not this powerfully. She wasn't about to analyze her feelings. She'd better jump-start her self-control, though, because a vampire could never fit into her future plans. *Why not?* See, when she started asking questions like that, Kayla knew she was in trouble.

She almost made it out of the castle alone. Almost.

"Kayla! Wait for me."

Sighing, Kayla turned. Cinn, the woman Thorn had rescued last night, hurried toward her. She held a plant, and it was only as she drew closer that Kayla realized it was the same plant Cinn had saved from the fire.

Cinn smiled as she joined Kayla. "I'm your designated destroyer for the night."

"Is the plant your secret weapon?" Kayla returned Cinn's smile. Hey, she was a huge improvement over Holgarth.

A fire engine roared past followed closely by two police cars. Cinn waited until the sirens faded before answering. "No. Vince just wants to visit Thorn. I'm your weapon." She frowned as she stared in the direction the fire engine had gone. "Have you noticed how many times police cars and fire trucks have gone past today?"

Kayla shrugged. She hadn't spent enough time in Galveston to know how often fires or other emergencies cropped up. "I was in Nirvana most of the day. The noise from the park drowns out other sounds."

Once again she had to stand in line. Once again security-guy did his thing with the scanner. He *didn't* scan Cinn. What was that about? Holgarth was the one who'd messed up the bumper cars. Conclusion? This was done to annoy the hell out of her alone.

Cinn didn't say anything else until they were inside the park. Kayla couldn't help searching for Thorn. She didn't see him.

"The tanker that went down is big news. No survivors. No bodies. No reason for it to sink. And two shrimp boats disappeared today. Same thing. No distress signals, no survivors, and no bodies recovered." Cinn stopped talking for a moment. She looked around. "Wow, can you believe the crowd here? Sparkle's going ballistic."

She's also hitting the wine. "What're the authorities doing?" Kayla silently cursed the mob. How would she ever find Thorn among all these people?

Cinn shrugged. "They've told boaters to stay out of the water until they have some answers. Boaters won't like it. They'll just go somewhere else. Lots of bad luck to go around." She shook her head. "Sparkle will be able to open the castle tomorrow, but the last few days are bound to hurt business." She cast a quick glance Kayla's way. "I don't think Thorn had anything to do with the explosion and fire." She didn't mention the Great Stink.

"So what horror are you going to unleash on Thorn?" Kayla didn't want to talk about Thorn's possible guilt.

"I share a part of Airmid, the goddess of healing plants. I've inherited some of her power. But in me, the power took a sharp left turn. I grow sentient plants."

Kayla nodded. *Not believing that for even a second.* "Uh-huh."

Cinn looked away. "I lost a lot of them last night. But Thorn saved Vince, and some of my plants were in the castle, so I'm trying to take care of the ones that survived."

Kayla didn't roll her eyes. Cinn was sincerely devastated, and if believing her plants could think made her happy, more power to her.

"There's Thorn." Cinn waved at him.

Kayla noted that the other woman had avoided answering her question.

Thorn looked their way and then headed over. Kayla was getting used to the breathless sensation whenever she saw him. He was night—darkness, mystery, and danger. And here she'd thought she was so pragmatic. Not after that last thought. "Darkness, mystery, and danger" was romance-novel speak. She didn't read romance novels.

Kayla put on her lawyer face and then smiled at him. It was tough to maintain when he stood so close, looked so good, and smiled back. His smile had definite orgasmic qualities.

Cinn seemed oblivious to the power of smiles. "I'm so grateful for what you did last night. And so is Vince. He wants to spend some time with you."

He looked surprised for a moment but then recovered. "Sure. I'd be honored." Pause. "For how long?"

Kayla almost laughed. She didn't need any magical power to read his thoughts. They went sort of like, "What the hell am I going to do with this plant?"

For a moment, Cinn looked as though she was listening to something. Finally she nodded. "He says as long as it takes." She shrugged. "Sometimes Vince can be cryptic." She held the plant out to him.

Thorn took the plant. He held it gingerly. "If you don't mind waiting here for a few minutes while I put him in my apartment, I can officially show you around." His expression said he didn't want to take *them* to his apartment.

Kayla understood. If they knew where he lived, it would make him vulnerable. "We'll be here."

"Speak for yourself." Cinn stared at the roller coaster. "I want to look around and sample a few rides." She threw Kayla a pointed stare. "You stay here. I'll see you back at the castle."

Kayla couldn't read that stare. She hesitated. On the one hand, she should be cheering Cinn on, hoping the plant lady would smother the pier in a tangle of supersized vines. But on the other hand, she wanted to stay close to Cinn to make sure she didn't go too far, destroy too much. Talk about conflicted loyalties. Dad would say she owed loyalty to the one who paid her. She wasn't sure how much she believed Dad anymore.

And while she was trying to decide, Cinn walked away. Kayla looked back at Thorn. How to handle the moment? She offered him a weak smile. "Well, guess I'll just hang around until you get back." What if he'd only made his offer for Cinn's sake? What if he really didn't want to show Kayla anything except the exit gate?

He bit his lip, and even that looked sexy. She gave herself a mental slap. This had to stop. He was the enemy. But it was getting harder and harder to remember that. She waited patiently while he made up his mind about what he wanted to say.

Finally, he smiled. "Walk to my apartment with me."

Kayla blinked. Not what she'd expected. Unfortunately, when someone caught her by surprise, she tended to blurt out whatever she was thinking. "If I were you, I wouldn't invite me to my apartment."

He laughed. A real laugh with no hidden agendas. "Then I guess

I'm lucky you aren't me." Thorn reached out and clasped her hand. "Let's go."

She allowed her hand to stay in his. Bare skin against bare skin did weird things to her heartbeat. It hopped, skipped, stalled, and then sped up to warp speed. Her heart couldn't make up its mind. But she could. Kayla loved touching him.

He stopped in front of a familiar building. It was the same one she'd visited with Holgarth that morning, the one with the off-limits sign.

"I have a home on the island, but I use this most of the time." He dropped her hand to unlock the door.

She mourned its loss. "Aren't you afraid you'll make an easy target here?"

He stood aside to allow her to go in first. She briefly balanced the possibility that this might be a trap against her overwhelming curiosity. Curiosity won. She stepped into the room.

Not much to see—a bed, a couch, a few chairs, a small kitchenette, and a door she assumed led to a bathroom. No homey touches. No pictures of the grandchildren propped up on his nightstand. No framed Vampire of the Year awards hanging on the wall. "This is . . ."

"Sterile, cold, and empty. I know. It reminds me of my past. I'll have to warm it up when I have time." He followed her inside. "Have a seat."

His comment saddened her, but she wasn't here to offer decorating pointers. She opted for a chair. Safe. "Looks as though business is booming." *Brilliant, Stanley. The queen of obvious strikes again.*

Thorn shrugged as he carefully set Vince on his nightstand. "I give great value."

Kayla's mind took that phrase in a totally different direction. Bad mind. "I heard visitors raving about the rides. I'll have to try a few new ones tonight." *Okay, Mackenzie, your turn to add to the meaningless chatter.*

He dropped into a chair opposite her. "This is probably the safest place I could be. I have round-the-clock security, and this apartment was built to stand up to a supernatural attack." He leaned back in his chair. "Of course, if I invite the enemy inside, then all bets are off. *Are you my enemy, Kayla?*"

She frowned. Hadn't she already answered that question yesterday? But things can change a lot in a few hours. Her head assured her he was, but the rest of her wasn't so sure. "We're still on opposing sides." Was that ambiguous enough?

He nodded as though she'd answered his question. "Zane told me about his father. We're lucky that Bygul managed to distract the wizard or else he would've done more damage." Thorn looked thoughtful. "Why are they sending people with you, Kayla? First Holgarth and now Cinn."

She opened her mouth to defend Cinn, but he waved her words away.

"Cinn is here to booby-trap my business in her own special way. I can't wait to find out what that is. But I have people watching her, so hopefully it won't be catastrophic." He waited a few beats while he studied her. "Why aren't you the one doing the heavy lifting? Isn't that what Sparkle hired you for?"

She wanted to deny what he was saying, shove his words back at him, but she could only look away. Kayla would never work for her father again. She'd tell him that as soon as she got home. "I don't do 'heavy lifting.' I just check to make sure you're not breaking the law."

"Right."

He didn't believe her. No use trying to convince him. Better to put him on the defensive. "What exactly do you want from Sparkle?" *What history do you share?*

"Suffering."

She winced. The one word held a lifetime of rage and need for revenge. It hurt her to think of what could have caused that much hate. "You haven't tried to kill her. Yet."

He leaned forward, bringing all that intensity and disturbing emotion closer to her. She barely resisted the urge to lean back.

"I *can't* kill her. She's immortal, and the king of cosmic chaos has her back."

He smiled, a mere baring of his fangs. "But suffering doesn't have to end in death to be effective. I speak from personal experience. The suffering doesn't even have to be physical. She loves that damn park, so I intend to ruin it."

His emotions battered her. She wanted to leave, to run back to the relative safety of the castle, but pride kept her seated. And something else. She wanted to *know*. "What did she do to you?"

Thorn leaned back and glanced away from her. "It doesn't matter."

It did, to her. But she was smart enough to know it was time to stop pushing. "Sparkle recognized you last night, so I suppose she understands what this is all about."

"Did she tell Ganymede anything?" He tensed.

"No."

"Good." His expression turned calculating. "Work for me, Kayla. I'll pay more than Sparkle, and my benefits package can't be beat."

He lowered his gaze, and his long dark lashes hid anything his eyes might reveal.

Kayla dropped her own gaze to consider his "benefits package." Yes, definitely worth thinking about. She wanted to dismiss his offer. She already had a job. But something . . .

Suddenly, everything was so simple. Of course she'd work for Thorn. Why would she stay with Sparkle? She wanted to be here at Nirvana with him forever. Kayla opened her mouth to tell him that.

She never got the words out. As quickly as the thought had come, it was gone. Kayla frowned. Why had she even for a moment considered his offer? It didn't make sense. She looked up to find him staring at her.

"I'm sorry." Thorn looked furious, but his anger seemed aimed at himself.

"Why?"

She didn't get a chance to say anything else, because in a blur of motion he was kneeling beside her. His inhuman speed took her breath away. Okay, so maybe it wasn't his speed. It seemed that the closer he was, the more breathless she became.

Thorn shook his head. "It's not important. Just know that you have a job here if you ever get sick of working for Sparkle." His smile said that could happen very soon.

"Thanks for the offer. I'll keep it in mind." No, she wouldn't. She couldn't possibly keep anything in her mind when he was so close. Kayla fell into his eyes, so blue, so filled with feelings that hurt—sadness, anger, and something else. She didn't have time to figure out the "something else" because he leaned even closer.

"You make things hard, lawyer lady." He reached up to smooth his fingers along the side of her jaw.

"Ditto." She didn't like the wispy sound of her voice. This was a moment to be strong, to be hard, to be committed, to be . . . Damn, she couldn't concentrate.

He smiled and all she wanted to say was, "Ask me to work for you again." Because his smile destroyed every bit of her resistance.

He was going to kiss her. It was in his eyes—the heated intent— in the wicked slant of his mouth, and the slide of his fingers over her shoulders as he pulled her close. Kayla had never wanted any-thing as much as she wanted this kiss. Wait, wait—

Something shook his apartment, and it wasn't their kiss. The shaking was followed almost immediately by the din of hundreds of screams.

"I don't believe this." Thorn sprang to his feet and was yanking open the door before Kayla could even catch her breath. He glared back at her.

"Were you supposed to keep me busy while Cinn did her thing? Whatever that was."

How could he turn his emotions on and off like that? Outraged, Kayla followed him to the door. "Once you put your brain back in motion you'll realize how stupid that comment was."

They ran around the edge of the building and were met by a solid wall of screaming humanity. Nirvana was a seething mass of panicked people fighting to get off the pier.

"Up here with me."

Kayla didn't have time to process his command before he wrapped his arm around her waist and leaped for the top of the building.

Her scream had barely ended when he set her down on the roof. They both looked to see what everyone was running from.

"Holy hell!"

Kayla couldn't talk past her horror, so she decided that Thorn spoke for both of them.

11

Kayla wasn't in the frozen-with-fear camp. Only cowards used that as an excuse for not taking action. She was fight or flight all the way.

But she remembered reading something somewhere. Scientists claimed that not being able to move in the face of overwhelming danger was hardwired into our DNA. Predators pursued prey that fled, so the prey instinctively froze.

She understood now. The being rising from the water at the end of the pier was beyond any danger she could imagine in her worst nightmare. Human form. Male. Long silver hair and beard. Piercing sea-green eyes. Flowing robes created from streaming water. He kept rising, growing bigger and bigger until she swore he was as massive as . . . a small island.

Her mind flashed back to the tanker, the enormous black shape, the ship disappearing. Oh. My. God. She looked up and up while her heart pounded and her breath caught in her throat.

Her mind went into survival mode. *Run!* But she couldn't move, couldn't rip herself away from Thorn's side. Nausea churned and she hoped she wouldn't embarrass herself. Dad would be calmly assessing the threat and weighing possible responses. But she wasn't her father, and this was a freaking *giant*.

Kayla didn't hear the screams anymore, no sounds of the crowd rushing toward the exit gates. What was that about? Hello, people, there's a supersized person standing in the Gulf watching you!

Thorn didn't release her. "Stay close to me. I'll protect you."

Even as terrified as she felt, she sensed his intensity, his need for her to believe him. And she did. Which was dumb, because anyone could see that no amount of vampire power would bring down something that gigantic.

Kayla couldn't answer him, could barely breathe. No one had told her that frozen with fear also included vocal cords.

He hugged her closer. "Don't go away."

No chance of that. But she didn't feel badly about not being able to tell him, because she sensed he was talking to someone else, someone who *had* gone away. She didn't have time to wonder at the weirdness of that thought.

Thorn said nothing more. Instead, he watched the giant— unblinking, focused. She shivered. No human could be that *still*.

Then the giant began to speak. His voice was as huge as he was, a rumbling roar. Kayla swore the building vibrated with each word. She didn't understand the language he spoke, but she could see he was staring directly at Thorn. Why?

She calmed down a little, enough to actually turn her head and glance at the rest of the pier. The giant probably wouldn't grind Nirvana to dust while he was still talking to Thorn.

Kayla couldn't believe it. The crowd was calm. Some people were glancing back at the giant and laughing as they left the park. No one was running. Then she looked up. Five people stood side by side on the wide flat top of the entrance gate—Eric, Zane, Klepoth, and the two witches. They stared down at the crowd. Kayla could connect dots. She could almost feel the power surge.

Just then the giant stopped talking and Thorn answered him in the same language.

Kayla turned back to Thorn in time to see the giant slowly sink into the Gulf. He was gone. And she was still alive. An event to be celebrated. "Who was that and what did he want?" Her voice shook only a little.

Thorn raked his fingers through his hair. "That was Aegir."

Well, that was helpful. "Who is—?"

She didn't get a chance to finish her question because he wrapped his arm more firmly around her and leaped from the building. Kayla barely squeaked this time. See, she was getting used to this kind of stuff.

He held up his hand to stop any other questions. "I'll explain everything, but not until everyone is together. I need a summit meeting with Sparkle and Ganymede. Now."

By this time all humans had left the park, happy and evidently unaware. Kayla wanted to know how that had happened. The only one remaining who wasn't a Nirvana employee was Cinn. She waited for Kayla and Thorn by the entrance along with the ones who had been standing on top of the gate.

Cinn smiled at her and then looked at Thorn. "That hologram was incredible. I've never seen anything like it. What a clever way to warn visitors that it's almost closing time. It scared the heck out of me at first."

Kayla caught the amused look that passed between the two witches. "Right. Amazing."

From the look on Thorn's face, he was about to charge across the street and search for Ganymede himself. Kayla remembered what the cat had done to the refreshment stand.

She rushed into speech. "Look, how about if I go ahead and ease Ganymede and Sparkle into this meeting?"

Everyone except for Cinn and Thorn seemed to think it was a great idea.

"Why would Thorn have to speak to them?" Cinn looked confused for a moment, and then her eyes narrowed. "That wasn't a hologram?"

Kayla shook her head.

"And why did I think it *was* a hologram?" Cinn scanned those around her. Her gaze settled on Eric and Klepoth. She nodded. "I see."

That was great, because Kayla did *not* see. Sure, she got that all of them had worked together to create some kind of mass illusion, but she didn't understand how. She probably never would.

"I don't know why you have to warn Sparkle and the cat. I can handle anything they throw at me." Thorn started toward the street.

Grim grabbed his arm. "No offense, boss, but you *can't* handle the cat. If he attacked you, you'd be dead before you could use your persuasion on him. If it makes you feel better, I think Sparkle is the only one who can deal with him."

For a moment, Kayla wondered about how Grim had used the word "persuasion" in that sentence. Deciding it was nothing, she concentrated on Thorn. She expected him to throw off Grim's hand and continue on his way, but he didn't. He nodded and then looked at Kayla.

"Go. Tell them what you saw, and say we need to have a meeting with the nonhumans from both parks." Thorn held her gaze, and his expression softened for a moment. "Thanks for trusting me." Then he turned back to his people. "Fast thinking. You saved some lives tonight. People would've trampled each other trying to get out."

Trust? Yes, she'd trusted him to keep her safe. But she'd never trust him with other things that were much more fragile and easily crushed.

Kayla left them and headed for the castle. Cinn walked beside her. "Did you understand anything that just happened?"

Cinn shrugged. "Not all of it. I know that Thorn's people did something to calm visitors and convince them they weren't seeing what they thought they were seeing. Other than that?" She shrugged. "And you?"

"Not a clue." Kayla thought of something else. "Did you get a chance to—?"

"No. I never intended to do anything. Thorn saved Vince. He's a hero to me. Vince would agree."

Cinn left to find her husband once they were inside the castle. Kayla decided to try the great hall first. Even if Sparkle wasn't involved in a fantasy right now, Holgarth would know where she was.

Time was important, so Kayla didn't spend much of it searching. She approached Holgarth.

"Where's Sparkle?" She tried to ignore his supercilious expression.

"Why? Could it be you're bringing glad tidings that you've finally managed to rid us of this Thorn person?" He went from mock surprise to mock sadness. "But no, that would be impossible, because you fear doing what needs doing. You're a talker not a doer. So sad."

"Tonight is not a good night to push me, wizard. Now, where's Sparkle?" She wanted to bring her fist down on top of his pointy hat and flatten his pointy head beneath it.

He must've seen something in her eyes because he just sniffed and answered. "This is her night off. She's in her suite with Ganymede."

Kayla ran up the steps instead of waiting for the elevator. She arrived at Sparkle's door sweating and out of breath. She knocked.

Sparkle answered on the third rap. She wore a long clingy black nightgown cut out in strategic spots. Kayla quickly shifted her gaze beyond her client. She could see Ganymede stretched out on the couch with his paw over the remote and a dish of ice cream in front of him.

What a lazy butt. Kayla wondered what Sparkle saw in him.

Sparkle followed her gaze. "He's a lot different in his golden god form."

Kayla didn't comment on that. "We have a situation." She told Sparkle everything and then waited.

Ganymede leaped from the couch and padded to the door. *"Heard that. We need to meet with the bastard now."*

Sparkle looked as though she wanted to say no, but she finally sighed and nodded. "We'll meet them in the conference room in ten minutes."

"Why not here, sweetbuns?" Ganymede looked longingly at the ice cream.

"I only invite friends into my home." Her expression said that was that.

"I'll go tell them." Kayla started to turn away.

"Won't have to." Ganymede was already hurrying back to the couch. *"I've already messaged Eric. And I told him a half hour, not ten minutes."*

Something in Sparkle's expression said the time change bothered her, but she just nodded. She didn't invite Kayla inside to wait. That was fine, because she had things to do.

Kayla went up to her room and opened her laptop. She did a search for Aegir. A short time later, she shut it down. Then she just sat, eyes wide, thoughts racing. Impossible. But then she remembered where she was and whom she worked for. Maybe not. Damn.

She walked down to the conference room in a disbelieving daze. Kayla was the first one there. She took a seat in the middle of the long table. And then she just thought—about Thorn, about every strange person she'd met so far, and about the giant named Aegir.

Her thoughts always circled back to Thorn, though. She could close her eyes and pull up his exact image—every sculpted line of his face, his eyes, and sensual lips, along with his powerful body. She could hear his voice, soft and husky, murmuring promises. Too bad he would never speak them to her. And she would recognize his scent anywhere, even though she couldn't describe it yet. All she knew was that his scent was sexy and had his picture attached to it.

But she didn't have any idea what went on in his mind. He'd known Sparkle. Her sudden flash of jealousy didn't surprise Kayla. Not really. What powers did he have that she hadn't seen yet? What did he see when he looked at her?

Kayla didn't have time for more questions she couldn't answer, because the door swung open and Thorn strode into the room. Grim and his security team filed in behind him.

Thorn met Kayla's gaze. She stared at him with the innocence of her short human life. He hoped she didn't look too closely at his eyes. They weren't innocent. And if she decided to stroll down the path of his long vampire life, she'd wander into the dark woods and be lost.

He smiled and hoped it distracted her from the truth in his eyes. Thorn went around the table and sat down beside her. He glanced at the wall clock. "They're late. I assume Sparkle and her cat want to make a grand entrance."

Kayla shrugged and then met his gaze. "I looked up Aegir. He's a Norse sea god. Want to tell me more?"

"Patience." He leaned back in his chair and said what needed saying. "You might consider leaving right now. Quit and get on the first plane home. Sparkle will have a lot on her mind. She won't be worrying about you."

"Leave now? That sounds ominous. Let me think." She tipped her head to the side in thought. "Uh, no."

The smooth line of her neck mesmerized him. He imagined sliding his tongue over her warm skin, placing his lips right there where her pulse beat strong, then . . . Thorn gave himself a mental shake. "You might not be safe here." Danger came in many forms. Aegir wasn't the only threat. Thorn knew his interest in her neck and other areas of her body should bump him up closer to the top of her things-to-be-avoided list. Too bad she didn't know that.

"Maybe after I hear all you have to say I'll revisit my answer. But as of right now? No." She seemed to have surprised even herself with that decision.

He felt ridiculously relieved. Thorn didn't like the feeling. Humans had a history of doing stupid things and then dying because of them. Getting involved with individual humans would exhaust a vampire after a few centuries. So far, he'd avoided that particular pitfall. He shrugged. "Your choice. Lots of jobs. One life. Do the math."

Thorn glanced around the table. His people sat on either side of him facing the door. He didn't think that Ganymede would do anything to endanger his precious hotel guests, but you could never tell with the really powerful ones.

Kayla stayed silent beside him, but he was aware of every breath she took, every beat of her heart, every glance she slid his way. He resisted the urge to lean close and whisper all the things he wanted to do to her. Not now. Maybe later. He smiled at the thought of her alarm. She might even try to hit him. The thought entertained him until Sparkle came through the door.

It seemed that she'd brought an army with her. Thorn recognized the wizard, the plant lady and her vampire husband, and the were-shark bodyguard. But who the hell were all these other people? They filled up the seats and then stood against the wall. He hadn't realized how many nonhumans lived here. He'd have a talk with the people he'd hired to scope out the castle ahead of his arrival.

They all stared at him with lethal intent, even the Siamese cat sitting on the shoulder of one of the men. Thorn smiled at them, fangs and deadly warning on full display. And as they watched him, he quietly studied each of them, assessing the threat they posed.

Sparkle was dressed for business, *her* kind of business—skinny jeans, a cling-wrap green top, and heels that no human should be able to even stand on let alone walk in. Her red hair tumbled around her shoulders, and her amber eyes promised death if he was playing her.

Strange that he could coldly recognize her beauty but not care. He'd thought he might still have a few feelings left even after all this time. But Kayla was the only one who stirred him.

Thorn had finished scanning Sparkle's people. He narrowed his eyes. "Where's the cat?" Suspicion flared. At this very minute, Ganymede could be slinking around Nirvana destroying it with every twitch of his tail. He started to rise.

"Sit down, vampire." The man to the right of Sparkle spoke.

Thorn stared at him. He'd overlooked the man as he'd checked out the rest of the room. How the hell had he missed this guy?

The man smiled at him, a smile filled with malice. "You didn't notice me because that's the way I wanted it."

That voice. Thorn kept his eyes from widening, but only just. He was noticing now. The man was big, probably about six-five when he was standing. His tangled blond hair framed his face and almost skimmed his broad shoulders. He looked as though he'd only had time to finger-comb it before he stepped into the room. He could pass for a street-tough fallen angel, with a face that women would call beautiful, but hard enough to cut diamonds. Thorn recognized the look because he'd met a few of the fallen in his time.

"Ganymede." Thorn didn't make it a question.

The man nodded. "It takes a while for me to change, and it's not fun. I left my TV and ice cream to be here. Make it worth my while." He didn't even try to hide the "or else" at the end.

"Why'd you bother?" Thorn thought he knew, but he wanted to keep Ganymede talking while he assessed things.

"I knew you were coming. The cat form is for sneaking. The human form is for other things." His expression said that one of those other things was his desire for his enemies to put a human face to the one who killed them. "Besides, you and Sparkle have some kind of history. I thought we should be on equal footing this time." He didn't smile when he said it.

"Ganymede?" Kayla was an echo beside Thorn. She didn't make any attempt to hide her wide eyes.

Ganymede's smile was slow and meant to impress. "Definitely. You mentioned something about not knowing what Sparkle saw in me. Changed your mind?"

Kayla's eyes weren't wide anymore. She looked ticked. "I *thought* that. You were in my mind without my permission."

"No big deal. I'm in a lot of minds without their permission." He shifted his attention back to Thorn. "Why'd you call this meeting?

Thorn stood. "Aegir came calling a short time ago." A glance told Thorn the others in the room recognized his name.

"He gave his message to me because I was once Viking. I understand the old language. He considers me one of his." Thorn found Eric and Grim. They'd been Vikings too. "Eric or Grim can give you more details if you want them. The bottom line is that Aegir is tired of being an almost-forgotten sea god. Poseidon gets all the press. Aegir is moving his seat of power to the Gulf. More people to recruit. Maybe he's tired of the cold climate, wants to kick back in the sun. Who knows. He wants all humans and nonhumans not of his choosing gone from Galveston so he can bring in those who will worship him."

Sparkle had remained strangely quiet, but she spoke now. "That's what the explosives and sinking ships are about?"

Thorn nodded.

"It's not just that now. There've been fires and explosions all over the island today. Someone is targeting businesses." The speaker leaned forward. He had tawny hair, a grim-reaper tattoo on his arm, and the cosmic troublemaker's amber eyes. "Why would a god try to make this look like a human's work?"

Thorn thought about his answer. "I'd guess he didn't want to alert his enemies in the supernatural community. And the Norse gods and goddesses in Asgard might not be thrilled with what he's doing. But he's grown impatient. So now that he believes he has his operation in place, he's taking off his mask."

"And that means?" The question came from the man with the cat on his shoulder.

"He wants us out of here in three weeks. He'll keep up his attacks on the humans so they'll leave too. At the same time, he's bringing in people who support him to take the place of everyone leaving." Thorn noticed Kayla's horrified expression. The others in the room just looked angry. They understood that gods and goddesses did what they pleased and expected everyone else to fall in line with their plans.

"What did he offer you, vampire?" Ganymede's eyes gleamed.

Thorn tipped an imaginary hat to Ganymede. The cosmic troublemaker had assumed correctly. "If I help him get rid of your park, he'll allow Nirvana to survive with me still in charge."

Ganymede's smile was one of the scariest things Thorn had ever seen. "That would work for you, wouldn't it? Sparkle would be out of business. No more sneak attacks necessary. Problem solved. Maybe you were the one who suggested that Aegir look this way for his new home."

But Thorn had his own scary smile. He used it now. "I don't call in outside help to do my work for me." He glanced at his people. Okay, so maybe he did. "And if I were going to help Aegir, I wouldn't be here now spilling his plans."

Ganymede subsided for the moment, his gaze still drilling holes in vulnerable parts of Thorn's body.

"Anything else we should know?" This was from the woman sitting beside the tawny-haired troublemaker.

"Aegir isn't well liked. He has a rep for sinking ships and taking the crews." He looked around the room, meeting everyone's gaze. "His wife, the goddess Ran, is here too. I met her on the beach. I didn't remember who she was until tonight."

"Damn." Eric breathed the word. "Ran is a cold bitch. She pulls men overboard with her net and drowns them."

"So here's what we have to work with." Thorn had their complete attention. "We have three weeks to get rid of both of them. We know that Aegir isn't beloved. That's probably why he lost his chief-sea-god status. We might try fomenting an uprising in his ranks."

"And we know he has an underwater hall off the coast. Kel has seen it." He nodded at the kelpie before looking back at the others. "Since searchers didn't find any bodies from the sunken ships, Aegir might be holding the crews there to use as hostages if he needs them."

"Some of you may have powerful god or goddess connections." He glanced at Grim. "Use them." Thorn started to sit down and then paused. "Sparkle, you have two guests who probably belong to Aegir." He told her the room number.

She cut him up and scattered his pieces with her stare. "How do you know this?"

He offered her the smile he'd saved just for her, filled with all the promises of retribution he'd planned over the centuries. "I saw them when I was attaching my special air fresheners to your walls."

Her lips tightened, but she said nothing to him. Instead, she looked at two of her people and nodded. They immediately left. "I've sent for the two you mentioned."

"So are we finished here?" Ganymede's expression didn't bode well for Aegir or anyone who worked for him.

Sparkle looked back at Thorn. "I assume you'll still be working to get rid of me even while Aegir tries to take over Galveston."

"Of course." Good. She wouldn't expect a truce while they fought the sea god. If they won, he'd still want her gone. And if they didn't? He wouldn't have much of anything to worry about.

Her smile was sly, wicked, and looked great on her.

"I thought so. I guess you know I'll still try to stop you."

"I'd expect nothing less."

She nodded, satisfied.

Just then the two she'd sent from the room returned shoving a man and woman ahead of them. They pushed their captives into seats and stood behind them waiting.

Ganymede stood for the first time. Thorn felt the troublemaker's power. It hit him and drove him back in his seat. If he'd had to breathe, he'd be gasping for air now. He looked at Kayla to see how she was taking this show of power.

She looked pale, but her gaze met his calmly. He felt a rush of pride in her. Without thinking about it, he reached for her hand beneath the table. She clasped it and hung on.

Ganymede leaned across the table and spoke to the man and woman. "You've stayed in our castle while you worked for a scumbag who's trying to destroy us. That pisses me off."

The walls of the room vibrated while thunder rumbled in the distance. The two captives pressed themselves back in their seats as far as they could to escape him.

"I want you to tell me everything you know about his plans." The ends of Ganymede's hair flickered with blue flames. Suddenly, the electricity went out, leaving his glowing eyes and the flames the only lights in the room. Another crack of thunder that sounded as though it was right over their heads shook the walls.

Thorn grinned. Hey, this was great stuff. Entertainment at its best. Of course, if he'd chosen to use his power of persuasion, he would have had answers from them without all the theatrics.

The lights flickered back on.

Oh, crap. Where the two captives had sat there were now two terrified moray eels. Four-feet long with big teeth. They started to slither off the chairs. Everyone in the room was on their feet and shouting.

Without warning, the eels just disappeared. Everyone sat down and stared at Ganymede. He didn't meet their gazes. "I sent them to the Pacific Ocean. I hate seafood."

"You overplayed your hand." Thorn knew he sounded gleeful. "You scared them into shifting."

"Shut the hell up, vampire." Ganymede's expression said he wouldn't mind sending *him* to the Pacific as well.

Thorn decided the party was over. "Guess we'll get back to Nirvana. I'm keeping my park open until I feel it isn't safe for visitors."

Sparkle stood. "Live the Fantasy will stay open too." The stare she sent Thorn could have stripped the varnish from the floor. "We'll deal with *all* threats."

Thorn didn't feel that needed an answer. He nodded at his people and started for the door.

"Vampire."

Thorn turned slowly to face Ganymede. He readied his persua-sion. He didn't kid himself. He'd need it to survive if Ganymede decided to eliminate a threat right now.

"You knew Sparkle. I want to know about it. Now."

Sparkle reached out to Ganymede. "No. Let it go. We'll talk about it another time."

Ganymede didn't even look at her. "Now."

For a moment, Sparkle looked shocked. That changed quickly to anger. "Bastard."

Thorn wasn't sure if the word was aimed at him or Ganymede. He hadn't planned to confront her now. He'd wanted to save it all up until her business was in ruins around her.

But why not now? He had an interested audience. Besides, his anger was killing off some of his wisest brain cells. He hated Gan-ymede's attitude. This would hurt the troublemaker too. *And then the troublemaker might hurt you.* He'd take the risk.

Thorn stood with his hand on the doorknob. He gathered his revenge into a compact ball and flung it at Sparkle. "He wants to know about us. Let's give him what he wants."

"Please." Only the one word.

Sparkle lifted her chin, letting him know that this was the clos-est she'd ever come to begging.

He just shook his head. Then he faced Ganymede and smiled. "You think you know all about her? Not even a little."

12

Kayla knew she should get up and leave the room. This confrontation had nothing to do with her. But then she'd have to squeeze past Thorn. Besides, this whole thing was like a horror movie. You knew the maniacal laughter rising from the dark cellar couldn't be good. You knew the idiot woman would go down there to see what it was anyway. You knew the laughter would be followed almost immediately by the bloody knife. But you just had to sit and see it happen.

Resigned, she sat back. This would be ugly, and she'd probably find out things about Thorn she didn't want to know. Fine, so that was a lie. She wanted to know everything about him. Kayla cursed whichever of her ancestors had enjoyed suffering and passed the stupid gene on to her.

Thorn spoke directly to Ganymede. He ignored Sparkle. "I met Sparkle a long time ago. I didn't know what she was then, I only knew that I loved her." Thorn's eyes were flat, cold, emotionless. "I was twenty-three and believed her when she said she cared. I never

asked why a woman like her would be interested in me." His lips
tipped up in a humorless smile. "She didn't know I was a member
of the Mackenzie vampire clan. She didn't know that in five years
I'd become vampire."

Thorn had just started talking, and Kayla was already confused.
She glanced at Ganymede. She couldn't see any sign of the snarky
cat in his eyes. A destroyer lived in them now.

Thorn finally shifted his gaze to Sparkle. "You told me to meet
you down by the harbor. My family had come to the village to trade,
and I left them that night to be with you."

Sparkle was pale, but she didn't look away from him. She said
nothing.

"When I reached the place where we were supposed to meet,
you weren't there. A man was there instead. He had a message from
you. He said you'd met an old friend and had decided to leave with
him. I wouldn't be seeing you again. You were sorry." Thorn's eyes
burned with remembered anger and pain. "You. Were. Sorry."

Kayla feared to breathe. It was so silent in the room that a breath
would call attention to her. Sparkle grew even paler, if that was
possible. She started to say something, but Thorn held up his hand
to stop her.

"I'm not finished." Thorn took a step back toward the table. "I
didn't get a chance to return to my family and mourn a love that
was pathetically one-sided." He took another step and Ganymede
tensed. "Because your messenger knocked me out and sold me to a
slaver."

There was a collective gasp from everyone not named Ganymede. Sparkle put her hand over her mouth, and Kayla noticed that
she'd methodically peeled off her nail polish.

Thorn's eyes were narrow slits of fury. "I have lots of sympathy
for demons, because for five years I lived in hell. There were times
when I didn't think I'd see the next sunrise. Most of the time I was

afraid I would. Those years melted me down and reshaped me into someone with lots of sharp edges and a thirst for vengeance."

Then he smiled, a ragged thing that filled Kayla with sorrow, along with pity she suspected he'd hate.

"But guess what happened in five years?" He looked around the room. "I did what every Mackenzie does at that age. I became vampire." His expression turned savage. "And then I killed every one of the bastards who'd tortured me."

Grim put his hand on Thorn's shoulder. "Maybe you shouldn't—"

He shook off the hand. "I should." Thorn stalked all the way to the table and leaned toward Sparkle. "I came home to rejoin my family. You know what I found?" He curled his lip, baring his fangs.

"The night I was taken, only my mother along with my younger sister and brother were in the village. My father was away with his ship. He was due home that week. My father had always told us that when he was away, I was responsible for the family. If I was gone for any reason, they were to stay safe with a cousin who lived in the village."

Kayla knew what was coming, could feel the horror of it creeping up on her, slithering up her backbone and winding around her heart.

"My mother was upset because I'd disappeared. I can only believe she wasn't thinking straight. The next night she told her cousin she had to leave and return to our small farm outside the village. She said she had too much work to do now that I was gone. My mother probably thought they'd only be alone for a few days because my father was returning."

Almost as though Sparkle wasn't aware of her movements, she stood. She gripped the edge of the table so hard that her knuckles turned white.

"She shouldn't have gone home." He closed his eyes for a moment.

Kayla wondered what he saw—his family as they'd once been, his own long path that had led him to this moment, or just his despair.

He opened his eyes. "There hadn't been any raids for a long time. Everyone had grown careless, forgotten how fast death could come. Two days after I disappeared, they attacked our home. My mother, my brother, and my sister died." He was still for a moment. "I sometimes wonder if the raider was the same man who delivered the message from you. The attack seemed too much of a coincidence."

Thorn smiled, and Kayla hoped he never smiled at her like that.

"You know, I only remember one thing about him. He had the same color eyes as you. Does that mean he was a cosmic troublemaker?"

Sparkle only nodded. Ganymede leaned forward and growled low in his throat. It was a warning and threat all rolled into one. Thorn ignored it.

"So now you know. My park isn't blocking your view of the Gulf because you dumped me. I got over that. Nirvana is for the ones I loved who died because I was so stupid. And it's for five years of hell and a thousand regrets."

Sparkle looked lost for a moment, and then she pushed away from the table, straightened, and took a deep breath. "I *did* care for you, Brandt, but we never would've worked. I was a coward for not telling you in person. I didn't know what happened to you after I sent the message. The man who brought it . . ."

"Wasn't Ganymede. I would've remembered him."

Ganymede's eyes burned with his need for violence. "I wouldn't have bothered selling you to slavers. I would've killed you. Dead men don't come back to cause trouble."

"I'm sorry." Sparkle didn't seem to know what to do with her hands.

This from a woman who *always* knew what to do with her hands. The depth of Sparkle's distress shocked Kayla. Thorn's story had stripped away her confident veneer to expose someone Kayla didn't recognize.

"Sorry isn't nearly enough." Thorn looked as though he wanted to tear the castle down around all of them. "I want a name. Who delivered your message that night?"

Sparkle shook her head. "Another cosmic troublemaker who happened to be in the village at the time. I don't remember his name. It was a long time ago."

"You're lying."

Thorn looked ready to explode. Kayla watched him curl his lip away from his fangs and clench his hands into white-knuckled fists. She could almost feel death's cold breath on the back of her neck. Would any of them survive a battle between Thorn and Ganymede in this small enclosed space?

Sparkle looked a little desperate. "Knowing his name wouldn't help you. Going after him would only get you killed."

"My life, my choice." Thorn's eyes had turned black, signaling that he was close to losing control. "One more question. Who was the man you met instead of me? Because I know it was a man. It would always be a man with you."

"She met me, vampire." Ganymede's narrowed eyes suggested that a swift end was the best Thorn could hope for. "She knew me a long time before she knew you."

Ripples of power filled the room. Kayla felt it as pressure building and building until she expected the walls to explode outward. Ganymede's anger terrified her.

"Figures."

Kayla heard nothing but contempt in Thorn's voice.

Grim tried again. He moved up behind Thorn and grabbed his arm. "Enough. Let's get out of here."

Thorn ignored him. "Anything in particular you want to say to me, asshole?" He met Ganymede's gaze.

Grim dropped his hand. "Jeez, next time I take a job I'll make sure my boss doesn't have a death wish."

Kayla started to panic. She didn't think Ganymede would ignore that insult. He might blast Thorn into oblivion.

Without thinking, she jumped to her feet. Making her way around the table, she stopped in front of Thorn. She smiled. *Think before you act.* She could almost hear her father's voice in her head. He'd be disappointed in her.

There were times, though, when everyone had to think on their feet. And the threat of imminent annihilation was a great motivator. "We're all a little tense, but we have to keep our focus on Aegir." She looked away from Thorn's glare. "You left Nirvana unprotected. I mean, Aegir's followers could be doing anything over there." She chanced a quick peek at Ganymede's thunderous expression. "Now might be a good time to go. You remember that stuff about living to fight another day? Well, that might be now."

Thorn blinked and then looked at her as though he was seeing her for the first time. "Yeah, you're right."

"Too late to run back to your little park. I don't allow threats to stick around long. To hell with the Big Boss, I'm going to fix this problem permanently."

Kayla turned at the sound of Ganymede's voice. Great, she was directly in the line of fire. But that was a good thing. She didn't doubt that she was the weakest person in the room. Ganymede would lose face if he used his power on her. At least that's what she hoped.

Except for the major players along with Grim and her, everyone else in the room had stayed frozen in place. Finally, the man with the grim reaper tattoo and cosmic troublemaker eyes stood and walked over to Ganymede. He didn't make the mistake of touching the other man.

Grim-reaper guy made his pitch for sanity. "You don't want to do this, Ganymede. Sure, it would feel good, but you know what'll happen as soon as the Big Boss hears about it. He'll demote you, kick your ass out of the castle, and take away everything you have that makes life worth living."

Kayla figured that "everything" included ice cream, candy, and chips.

"He can try." Ganymede threw grim-reaper guy a murderous glare.

"Shut up, all of you."

Sparkle didn't shout, but there was something in her voice that made them obey.

"You." She pointed at Ganymede.

Ganymede reluctantly turned his attention from Thorn.

"How dare you! This is your fault. You forced him to tell that story in front of everyone. What was between Brandt and me was private."

Ganymede looked surprised. Kayla decided he might be one of the most dangerous creatures in the universe, but he was a zero when it came to understanding women.

"I did this for you, sweetheart."

"Don't you sweetheart me." Sparkle picked up her chair and swung it at his head.

Everyone scrambled out of her way. Ganymede ducked away from the chair.

He tried to explain. "I figured that once the story was out and everyone heard it, the vampire wouldn't have any more leverage. And then I could kill him for threatening you in public."

"Son of a bitch!" Sparkle bent down and grabbed the ultimate

weapon—her shoe. Gripping it by the toe, she leaned toward Ganymede and waved the lethal five-inch heel at him. "I'm going to
punch a hole in your head and then put my ear next to it. I bet I
hear the ocean."

That seemed to be the signal for the rest of the nonhumans to
sneak out. Kayla was amazed at how fast and silently they moved.
Within a few seconds the only ones remaining in the room with
her were Thorn, Ganymede, Sparkle, and her shoe of death. Thorn's
people waited for him outside the room, close enough to come to
his rescue but not close enough to be within reach of Sparkle's shoe.

Ganymede eyed the shoe warily. "We needed to know what his
gripe was. Now we know. We can pay him off, or I'll kill him." His
expression said he had only thrown in the paying-him-off part as
a sop to Sparkle's feminine aversion to violence and other manly
stuff.

Thorn looked outraged. "My dead family doesn't have a
price tag."

Sparkle glared at him. "No one's talking to you." Then for just
a moment she looked regretful. "Sorry. I'll speak to you later." She
turned back to Ganymede. "After I take care of *him*."

Ganymede still seemed puzzled, so he repeated himself. "I did it
for you."

Sparkle's laughter mocked him. "No you didn't. It was all about
your stupid ego. It's always been about your ego. You wanted to force
Brandt to tell his story so you could act the big hero and come to
my rescue. Did you for one minute think about how I'd feel, knowing that everyone in the room was listening and judging?"

"You never cared what people thought before." Now Ganymede
sounded a little mad.

"Maybe I'm changing. Maybe I *do* care about what people I like
think. Now every nonhuman in the castle knows what happened
a thousand freaking years ago." She was breathing hard.

Ganymede narrowed his eyes. "Well, since everyone else is pissed, maybe I have a bitch too. Everyone in the castle also knows you screwed the vampire. Oh, and that you 'cared' for him. How do you think that makes me feel?"

"Who gives a shit? You can go to hell. I don't want you in the castle. Sleep in the candy store for all I care. And don't eat up my inventory." Still gripping the shoe, she stormed from the room.

"Guess she won't be talking to me now. Not that she could say anything that would make a difference." Thorn watched Sparkle go and then turned to Kayla. "That went well." But he looked uncertain about how "well" it had actually gone.

Ganymede ignored both Thorn and Kayla. He pushed past them muttering about women who didn't appreciate what they had.

Without making a conscious decision, Kayla walked with Thorn and the others back to Nirvana. She stopped at the gate. He waited until they were alone to turn to her.

"Thanks for trying to defuse the situation." Thorn raked his fingers through his hair. He looked tired. "I didn't want to do things that way, but Ganymede wouldn't let it go." He smiled. "Would've served me right if he'd ripped off my head. He's capable of it."

Kayla frowned. "I like your head right where it is." She reached up to touch his face. "So how does this Mackenzie vampire stuff work?" She might have imagined it, but he seemed to lean into her touch.

"We're normal humans until our late twenties. We marry and have our children when we're young because after we become vampire we can't reproduce. Then our biological clocks do an automatic reset thing and we change. We don't qualify as the undead because we never really die. Hope you're not disappointed." His smile seemed forced.

One thing puzzled Kayla. "Since you were twenty-three, your mother must have been vampire when the raid took place. The raiders would've had a tough time killing her."

"Whoever murdered them struck around noon. She was lost to

the day sleep. The bastards burned our home down around my family." Old sadness lived in his eyes. "I've often wondered why. They didn't take anything. All they did was kill and leave." He shrugged. "If the raiders were human, then I'll never know the why because they're all long dead."

But if one of them was a cosmic troublemaker? She sighed. "I won't keep you. I know you still have things to do tonight." Kayla started to turn away. She wanted to say something more, but maybe now wasn't the right time.

He reached out and gripped her arm. Startled, she looked up at him. He lowered his head and kissed her.

His mouth was warm and welcoming. She forgot everything in the wonder of it. The touch of his tongue, erotic and tempting, was a sexual invitation. He stirred desires best ignored so soon after what had just happened in the castle. But that didn't mean she couldn't appreciate everything about him—the scent of clean male and that as-yet-indefinable something, the almost-taste of his emotions, and the words he murmured against her mouth in that old language. She might not understand their meaning, but the rhythm and feel of them seemed right.

Thorn moved away from her first. He touched her lips with his finger. "I have lots to think about."

"After tonight, I wouldn't blame you for revoking my visitor's pass." What would she do if he told her to stay away?

He shook his head. "I enjoy your visits. I enjoy *you*. Some of the people you bring with you? Not so much. But my security team can handle anything you throw at them. And since I still intend to make life difficult in the castle, I can't blame you for doing the same to me." He speared her with a hard stare. "I still don't know why you won't accept my offer and work for me. I'm big on benefits." His smile hinted at exactly how big those benefits were. "You don't owe Sparkle any loyalty."

But she did owe loyalty to her father. "Sorry. I signed up for the job and now I have to finish it." She decided to ask one more question. "What about your father? Is he still alive?"

It was as though a curtain fell across Thorn's face. He glanced away. "I don't know. I only saw my father once after I became vampire. He blamed me for everything. If I hadn't gone to meet Sparkle, I would've been at home when the raiders struck. I might've kept my family alive. I failed them."

She wanted to find his father and slap him upside his hard head. Who would condemn the only son he'd ever have because of a series of very human mistakes by his wife as well as his son? She wondered if Thorn's father had ever regretted his words during the last thousand years. Which reminded her . . . "Do you want me to call you Brandt now?"

"I'm Thorn. I haven't been Brandt for a very long time."

Kayla watched him walk away before she returned to the castle and her room. She thought about going to make sure Sparkle was okay, but decided against it. Kayla knew if she were in that situation, she'd want to be alone right now.

And when she finally fell asleep, she dreamed of Thorn and her on that damn Ferris wheel. It took them into the stars before dropping them. She fell a long way, screaming and screaming and screaming.

Thorn watched Kayla enter the park. She had a cop with her. And she was scowling. Thorn smiled. Whoever was manning the entry gate must have given her a hard time. It mystified him how he could be so glad to see her at the same time the sight of her ticked him off.

It had been five nights since his confrontation with Sparkle. Five nights of wondering when Ganymede would lose patience and go for the big kill, but so far nothing. Sure, Kayla had found lots of ways to annoy him, but nothing really serious so far.

Good thing, because he had Aegir to worry about. Thorn still hadn't come up with a plan to stop the sea god. Meanwhile, bad things were happening in Galveston. Killer whales had been seen close to shore. Great whites had attacked a few swimmers. A rash of jellyfish stings had driven people from the water. Some sort of weird seaweed was piling up on the beaches. And more boats had gone down. Galveston was the main topic on every news program.

Kayla reached him. "These searches every time I come into the park are ridiculous. Your people never find anything."

Thorn hoped his expression showed nothing but polite concern. "Sorry. You're still a risk to Nirvana. You either put up with the searches or stay away." He knew she had to come as long as she worked for Sparkle.

She narrowed her eyes. "Don't play the injured party with me." Kayla nodded toward the street where his picketers marched up and down the sidewalk in front of the castle waving their signs.

He shrugged. "Hey, it's a public sidewalk. You can't stop people from expressing themselves."

"This is a new low for you, Mackenzie. 'Sparkle Stardust hunts baby seals for fun'? Really? Who's going to believe that?"

Thorn couldn't control his smile. "The ones who won't visit Live the Fantasy anymore?" He'd sent out a fresh group of picketers every day, each group with a message guaranteed to anger potential customers.

"She's going to sue your ass." Kayla seemed pleased with the thought.

"My amazing ass. You left out the adjective."

Kayla rolled her eyes, but she didn't refute his claim.

He shrugged. "First she has to prove I'm the one doing the instigating. So far she has nothing." Thorn hired different people every day to do the sign-carrying. And they never knew who paid them. Sometimes money was more powerful than magic.

"Right. And I suppose you also had nothing to do with the fire alarm that went off at midnight, the sprinkler system that started raining on guests at two A.M., and the heating system that went berserk and jacked the temperature up to ninety-five degrees at four A.M.?"

"You probably need to get an inspector in to go over the whole place. And Sparkle might consider hiring a more powerful wizard. Just saying." Thorn wondered why the cop was with her. He didn't have a good feeling about this.

She offered him her death stare before turning her back and walking away.

Thorn was a fool for allowing her anywhere near his park. But at some point when he wasn't paying attention, she'd become the high point of each night. He looked forward to their banter, to the way she tilted her head when she was trying to figure him out, to her whole sassy attitude. Of course, the fact that he lusted after her had to be added into the equation.

So that's why he caught up with her instead of talking to Kel as he'd planned. "I couldn't help but notice that you have a representative of the law with you."

The representative of the law glowered at him.

Okay, so not a friendly representative. "I assume there's a reason for that." Thorn waited.

Kayla widened her eyes. "Oh, I don't know. He just happened to be standing outside, and I thought maybe together we might find a few little misdemeanors or possibly even felonies if we looked carefully." She smiled a fake smile. "I'm sure you want to be an upstanding citizen, a pillar of the community, and run a squeaky-clean park. So you could say I was being helpful."

She didn't look helpful. In fact, he didn't like the way she looked at all. Her eyes were a little too bright, her smile a little too wide, and her expression a little too sneaky. He needed to get Grim over here.

"Oh, look, Officer." Kayla pointed.

Thorn groaned. Too late.

"I do believe I see a whole set of the Encyclopaedia Britannica over on that shelf."

What the hell? What was a set of encyclopedias doing sitting next to the stuffed monsters?

The officer cleared his throat. "I'm sorry, sir, but the Encyclopaedia Britannica is banned in Texas. I'll have to write you up."

"Banned? Why?" Thorn hoped his expression said that Kayla was dead once he got rid of the cop.

"It has a formula for making beer at home." The officer did some scribbling and then moved on.

Kayla made a sad face, but her eyes were laughing. "I really don't believe what I'm seeing. Do you see it too, Officer?"

"I most certainly do, Ms. Stanley."

Thorn turned in a slow circle. Crap. At least ten visitors were giving the cop the finger. All at once. Evidently Thorn wasn't the only one who could hire people. Sparkle had been busy.

"I'm afraid, sir, that I'll have to write all those people up for using offensive gestures."

He hurried off to do his duty while crowds of people watched. Some of them headed for the exit.

"I should kick your devious little ass out of my park."

"Oh, but I'm just getting started. And how would that look to the policeman?" She pouted. "In fact, I don't know if it's even legal, since I'm not doing anything wrong."

His response probably sounded more like a growl than human speech.

The policeman returned, and they moved on.

Thorn learned a lot about obscure Texas laws in the next hour. Who knew that you couldn't go barefoot without buying a permit first? The officer was winding up his visit, and Thorn was ready to vent his fury on Kayla.

"Just a little friendly advice, sir." The officer smiled. A shark's smile. "It's not legal to drive a car down Broadway before noon on Sundays."

"What?" Thorn was still thinking about the law that said he couldn't shoot a buffalo from the second story of a hotel. Guess he was lucky he didn't have a hotel, because Kayla would have found a way to get the buffalo.

"You were observed doing just that this past Sunday. I'll let you off with a warning this time." He stopped smiling.

"Wow, thanks." Thorn hoped his sarcasm wasn't too obvious, because there was probably a law against that too.

The cop started to walk away, but he paused to glance back. "Just so you know, people who sit on the sidewalk can be fined. I'm sorry, but you have a whole bunch of them sitting while they wait in line. I'll have to cite them." He looked cheerful as he walked away.

Thorn turned on Kayla. "Is he even a cop?" Unexpected anger exploded. He didn't need this crap.

She opened her mouth to answer, but he didn't give her a chance.

"I want you to leave Nirvana." Even as he said the words, he knew he'd regret them. It was his anger speaking, but he couldn't stop himself.

Kayla paled, but she lifted her chin and glared at him. "Oh, it's fine when you do things to Sparkle, but you don't like it when she hits back. Can't take it, can you?"

"Not *can't*. Try *won't*. Come back when you're not plotting against me." To be honest, he'd known from the beginning what she was doing. But somehow it hadn't felt personal until tonight. What had changed?

You've changed. Before tonight what she did hadn't mattered because she'd just been someone who was sexy and fun to be with. No real threat.

But tonight had been different. She'd enjoyed her triumph too much, he'd gotten used to enjoying *her* too much, and for the first time he realized that he cared. About Kayla Stanley, the woman, not some anonymous employee of Sparkle Stardust.

He'd given her the power to hurt him. His subconscious had recognized the threat before he had. And he'd lashed out to protect himself.

Maybe she needed to remember what he really was. He smiled, allowing just a hint of fang to show. "When you're not working an agenda, come on back. You'd enjoy the roller coaster."

She stared at him for a moment, and then without a word she walked away. He watched her until she left the park.

He sat down on a bench. His anger was already cooling. Well, he'd made a mess of that. But it was for the best. They'd be disastrous together. His dining habits would probably disgust her, and he'd never be able to go anywhere with her during the day. *No, don't go there at all. Stop thinking about her.*

Thorn leaned back and took a deep breath he hadn't needed for a thousand years. Right now he didn't know who posed the greatest danger to him: Sparkle, Aegir, or Kayla.

13

Kayla stormed back to the Castle of Dark Dreams, every step fueled by anger at Thorn Mackenzie. She had right and justice on her side. This was the first time she'd done anything that might actually impact his business, while he had landed quite a few punches in their ongoing battle. How dare he be mad at *her*.

She tried to ignore any twinges of guilt. Kayla couldn't just destroy a person's livelihood and feel nothing. Dad would always see that as a weakness.

She calmed down a little as she went in search of Sparkle. Kayla would make her nightly report and get to bed early. She was tired and, yes, a little depressed. The thought made her furious all over again. Thorn had ruined what should have been a perfect night. For the first time, Kayla had felt as though she was living up to her father's expectations.

Now? If she wanted to get back into Nirvana, she'd have to think up a disguise that would fool not only the people at the gate but everyone else she'd met at the pier. And Thorn hated her.

That really took the joy out of the night. She sighed and admitted the truth. Kayla didn't want him to hate her. She wanted him
to . . .

"We need to talk." Holgarth seemed to pop up out of nowhere.
She looked around. Kayla hadn't even realized she'd reached the
great hall. It was in between fantasies, and the wizard should have
been doing his thing—hassling and intimidating the role-players.
But instead he was leading her to a shadowed corner of the hall.

"Make it quick. I have to find Sparkle."

"Whatever it is, it can wait." Holgarth seemed troubled.

Unease touched her. Her first reaction was fear for Thorn. That
said a lot about her current state of mind. "I'm listening."

"Ganymede and Sparkle have recruited a group of zealot idiots
to demonstrate in front of Nirvana tomorrow night. Sparkle is sup-
plying the buses to bring them in from all over the state."

"Zealots?" That didn't sound good. She pictured a bunch of nuts
dressed in long robes brandishing pitchforks and torches.

He nodded. "They're an Internet group called Humans Against
True Evil. H.A.T.E. Fitting. They've heard about Nirvana's . . .
unusual amusements. And in the time-honored tradition of humans
down through the ages, they've labeled what they don't understand
as evil. They've decided that Nirvana is fueled by demonic power."
Holgarth sighed. "Well, perhaps they're not completely wrong.
There *is* Klepoth."

Kayla didn't like the sound of these whack jobs, but she didn't
see them as much of a danger. "Won't the police be there to make
sure nothing gets out of hand?"

"Usually, but I have a bad feeling about this. And I've learned
to listen to my instincts. Sparkle probably intends this to be a
simple demonstration to discourage Thorn's customers, but Ganymede might have something else in mind. Never underestimate
him." He looked away. "My son is over there. I worry."

"But your son has power to spare. What could a mob do to him?" The word "mob" left a bad taste in her mouth.

Holgarth thought about that for a long time, then shrugged. "Maybe you're right. If Sparkle tells you about this, act surprised. I'm not supposed to know."

"How did you find out?" She was already busy thinking about what she could do to help if things got out of hand.

"I listened at a door." Holgarth didn't look even a little embarrassed. "It's my job to know things."

"Of course." This time Kayla was glad his moral compass didn't point directly north.

"If Sparkle asks your opinion, caution her about the destructive power of fanatics."

Kayla nodded and opened her mouth to ask about Sparkle.

"She's at her club." He turned and walked away.

Wearily, Kayla retraced her steps back to the hotel lobby and entered Wicked Fantasy. She paused for a moment, allowing her eyes to adjust to the dim interior. Finally she spotted Sparkle at a small table tucked into a dark corner. She had a drink in front of her and was doing her nails by candlelight.

Kayla sat across from her and waited.

Sparkle sighed and looked up. "How did things go tonight?"

"Wonderful." Kayla didn't even try to look happy. "Some of his customers left, and he hates Officer . . ." She realized she didn't even remember his name. "He told me not to come back to Nirvana."

"Good." Sparkle went back to doing her nails.

Kayla knew she looked surprised. Sparkle didn't sound any happier than she did. "This is a breakthrough," Kayla said. "I thought you'd be thrilled." *Even if I'm not.*

Sparkle finished her last nail and finally gave Kayla her full attention. "I'm conflicted. My life's calling is not in sync with my business."

"What?"

Sparkle studied her shiny perfect nails. "I'm the cosmic trouble-maker in charge of sexual chaos. I bring together people who lust after each other but have nothing else in common. Then . . ." She took a sip from her drink, making sure her nails didn't touch any part of the glass. "I watch them break each others' hearts. You saw what happened to your parents." She took another sip, a bigger one this time. "I almost got caught in my own trap with Bra . . ."

Sparkle held her glass up and stared into it. Kayla didn't think she'd find the meaning of life there.

"I suppose I should stop using that name. Anyway, I really did care for him, but I *loved* Mede." With the precise motions of the slightly tipsy, she set the glass down. "You care for Thorn, don't you?"

Kayla hadn't seen that question coming. She answered truth-fully. "Yes."

Sparkle smiled as though it should all make perfect sense to her now. "You care for him. And he must care for you or else he never would've allowed you to enter his park night after night knowing that you worked for me." Her smile faded. "Now he's mad at you. You can't go back to Nirvana. You're miserable. I bet he is too." She held her hands out, palms up. "Am I good or what? That's why I had your father send you and not your brothers."

Kayla just stared at her. "Self-satisfied much?" She didn't really believe Thorn cared. He probably only regretted that he hadn't tossed her out sooner.

Sparkle went to sip her drink again and then peered into the glass. "Empty. How did that happen?" She blinked and focused on Kayla. "Remember? I said I was conflicted. So I'm not completely ecstatic. You've finally started to have success, and now you can't go back. Unless . . ." She frowned at her empty glass. "Do I need another one?"

"No." Kayla wanted to mention the demonstration scheduled

for tomorrow night, but she didn't want Sparkle to know that Holgarth had told her about it. "So have you and Ganymede made up?"

Sparkle turned sad eyes her way. "No. What he did was inexcusable. I'll never forgive him."

Kayla didn't sense total conviction in Sparkle's "never."

Sparkle set her glass down carefully. "Think I'll check on the store. He's still holed up in Sweet Indulgence. Have to make sure he hasn't eaten through my supply of chocolate creams. Go with me?"

"Sure." She didn't want to go, but Kayla was still hoping Sparkle would bring up the demonstration. And if Sparkle didn't mention it, maybe Ganymede would. If all else failed, she'd ask some leading questions. "You haven't been taking care of the store?"

"Nope. Mede has. It's only fair, since he's using the apartment there." Sparkle grabbed her purse, climbed out from behind the table, and tottered to the door. "Let's go." She paused. "Should I get one of those drinks to go?"

"No." Kayla was definite about that.

All the way to Sparkle's candy store, she thought about what Holgarth had said. Maybe the wizard's unease was influencing her, but now she *was* worried.

Kayla stopped in front of the door. Uh-oh. There was a closed sign in the window. She glanced at Sparkle.

Fury had burned away some of Sparkle's buzz. "Lazy bastard." She pounded on the door. When no one answered, she whipped a key from her purse and let them in.

All Kayla could do was to stare. The place looked as though an army of rabid candy demons had gone berserk in it. Gumdrops and licorice allsorts were strewn across the floor. Displays had been knocked over. Half-eaten chocolates littered every surface. And then there was Ganymede.

He was still in human form. He'd discarded his shirt. It lay on the floor along with the candy. *He* lay on top of the counter, one knee bent. Ganymede didn't look at them as he stared at the ceiling.

"I should paint your ceiling. Maybe a few cherubs. You could have this naked fat guy stretching out his hand, reaching for the god of soft-centered chocolates." He paused to think. "I was there when Michelangelo did his ceiling. Mine would be better."

Kayla couldn't stop staring. She might have ambivalent feelings for the cosmic troublemaker, but she couldn't ignore his absolutely incredible beauty. His blond hair fanned around his head like an evil angel's slightly tarnished halo. His face was breathtaking. And even though she preferred her ancient vampire with his bad attitude, Kayla could appreciate Ganymede's perfection. She checked out his body. How did he maintain that kind of definition when he was an eating machine?

Sparkle wasn't quite so appreciative. "You've trashed my store." Her voice shook with outrage. "And you've eaten my profits for the next month."

He turned his head to stare at Sparkle. "I had to eat something, sugartart." Ganymede frowned. "I crave something salty now."

His "sugartart" huffed her way across the floor, stepping over and around mashed candy. She stood over Ganymede. "Do you stay awake nights trying to think of ways to hurt me?"

Kayla winced. She could hear the tears in Sparkle's voice. This was personal. She started to back out.

"Please stay, Kayla. I won't be here long." Sparkle didn't turn around to look at her.

Ganymede stared up at Sparkle, and Kayla wondered if her client was blind. Even a stranger would recognize the love in his eyes.

"I've filled my sleepless nights with more entertaining thoughts." He lowered his lids, hiding any message Sparkle might read in them.

Sparkle started to pace, the click, click of her heels on the tile floor beating out an agitated rhythm. Kayla saw tears sliding down her face. She didn't try to wipe them away. "I should give Thorn what he wants. My businesses are going to hell anyway. Some jerk is eating his way through my candy store, and Live the Fantasy will be bankrupt soon if I don't get more visitors."

She turned teary eyes toward Kayla. "To be honest, every business in Galveston is going down the tube except for Nirvana. Too many bad things are happening here. People are afraid to go in the water, and stores are shutting down because Aegir is driving owners away." She threw up her hands. "Every night there're explosions and fires. The police don't have a clue. How could they?"

Sparkle blinked her tears away. Her expression hardened. "But Nirvana is doing fine. He has his demon and vampire whipping up fantasies that keep people coming even if all they do is visit his park and then go home." She drew in a deep breath. "But that won't last long."

"Why not?" Kayla watched Ganymede watch Sparkle. His expression disturbed her.

"I have a plan for tomorrow night."

Kayla listened as Sparkle told her about the demonstration. While Sparkle spoke, Kayla kept her attention on Ganymede. He saw her studying him, and he winked. She looked away.

When Sparkle finished, Kayla made the expected appreciative noises. "Sounds like a great plan. I hope the police can keep control of the crowd, though. You wouldn't want it to get out of hand and spill over into the castle."

Sparkle looked as though she hadn't thought about that. "I'm sure everything will be fine."

"Or not."

Kayla speared Ganymede with a hard stare. "And that means?"

He put on his innocent face. Kayla could've told him that innocence would never work for him.

Ganymede shrugged. "I don't know. Things happen. You can't

predict what a crowd driven by fanatical beliefs will do." He glanced at Sparkle and then looked away.

Sparkle seemed a little troubled. "The police will control the demonstrators. I want his business gone, but I don't want him hurt."

"And why don't you want him hurt? Before you knew who he was, you didn't much care what happened to him. I seem to remember you asking me to incinerate his ass." He sat up in one smooth motion. Ganymede wasn't looking away from her now.

The silence had teeth. Kayla could feel it digging deep and drawing blood from both Ganymede and Sparkle. This could be a bloodbath. She needed out of here.

Sparkle met his gaze. "I cared for him once. Yes, it was a long time ago, but his safety is still important to me."

He swung his feet to the floor and stood. Ganymede towered over Sparkle. The expression on his face reminded Kayla that he was one of the universe's most powerful beings. She backed toward the door.

"Maybe you still care for him. You've allowed your spy lady to fart around for a whole week without doing any real damage." He glared at said spy lady.

Kayla swallowed hard, but then she straightened her backbone and glared right back at him. "If Sparkle had wanted a wrecking ball, she would've hired you. She wanted something a little more subtle. Finesse takes more time."

Ganymede turned the full force of his displeasure on Kayla. "Doesn't seem to me that Mackenzie has cared too much about being subtle. Or maybe that's not it. Maybe he's just smarter."

Kayla wanted to slap his face, but she had enough sense to realize you didn't attack beings of his power without chancing annihilation. Besides, he was right. Thorn *had* been smarter. But that wasn't her fault. Dad hadn't prepared her for this kind of warfare. So she just lifted her chin and glared at him.

"Stop picking on Kayla when I'm the one you're mad at." Sparkle moved closer until only inches separated them. She held him with an unblinking stare.

Uh-oh. The tips of his hair burst into flame and his eyes glowed. The floor beneath Kayla's feet rippled. Gasping, she put her hand on the wall to steady herself. She glanced longingly at the door, but she wouldn't run now. She owed some loyalty to Sparkle, so she'd stay to make sure nothing happened to her client. Not that Kayla would be much of a threat to Ganymede.

He growled deep in his throat. "You had sex with him." His outrage shook the walls. A crack appeared in the ceiling.

"Stop wrecking my store." Sparkle spoke through clenched teeth.

Surprisingly, the rippling and shaking stopped.

Sparkle's cheeks were stained red with rage. "Yes. I made *love* with him. And it was damn good. Deal with it. That was a thousand freaking years ago. And how many women have you had?" That thought seemed to make her even angrier. "We both existed for millennia. What we've done during that time is no one's business except our own."

Personally, Kayla felt that striking at him by using the word "love" had been a mistake.

Ganymede looked stricken. "I thought we were—"

Sparkle had reached the shrieking stage. "We were *nothing*. We *are* nothing. Now get out of my store."

The expression in Ganymede's eyes shocked Kayla. He loved Sparkle, and she'd hurt him. But right now she was too furious to recognize it. The drinks Sparkle had downed before coming here probably weren't helping her make wise choices.

Kayla tried to intervene. "Maybe we should all calm down and—"

Ganymede didn't wait for her to finish. He scooped his shirt from the floor and left. The slamming door shook the store.

Silence settled around them. Sparkle leaned against the counter and then slid slowly to the floor. She sat there looking shattered. "What have I done?"

Kayla couldn't think of one comforting thing to say. *He'll get over it?* From the look on his face, she didn't think that was true. *You'll get over him?* Kayla somehow doubted that.

Sparkle struggled to her feet. "I'll find him. I'll apologize. Things will be fine." She ignored Kayla as she walked unsteadily to the door.

"Give me your key. I'll lock the door." Kayla waited while Sparkle rooted around in her purse.

Once she'd taken care of the door, Kayla followed Sparkle back to the castle. Her thoughts tangled and knotted in her mind. Too much was happening. Aegir was systematically destroying Galveston. The god's three-week deadline was fast approaching, and no one had come up with a plan to stop him. Sparkle and Thorn were still trying to destroy each other's businesses. Which was really dumb, since all they had to do was sit back and wait for Aegir to take care of things.

Kayla considered that. Come to think of it, why *didn't* Aegir just take out Nirvana and Live the Fantasy the same way he was getting rid of everyone else? Why bother with a deadline? He was a god, for heaven's sake. There could only be one answer. Even with all his power, Aegir didn't want to go head-to-head with them in battle. Interesting.

Her thoughts turned to tomorrow's demonstration. Should she warn Thorn? She bit her lip. Sparkle was paying her and deserved some loyalty. Telling Thorn would be a betrayal. She couldn't justify it short of quitting her job. Kayla decided that Thorn and his people were powerful enough to take care of themselves. Still . . .

She suspended her thoughts until she was lying in bed. Kayla stared at the darkened ceiling and thought of Ganymede's cherubs and fat naked man. She smiled, but it faded quickly. What was she going to do with this thing, this *feeling*, she had for Thorn? As she drifted off to sleep, she still didn't have an answer.

Thorn stood on the roof of his apartment, the wind whipping his hair around his face, and stared at the crowd roiling and buzzing like a hive of angry bees outside Nirvana's gate. Grim stood beside him.

"Zane says they've been gathering since this afternoon. Someone's getting booze to them. Don't know how. So far the cops have kept things from turning ugly." Grim watched Nirvana's employees escort visitors out of the park. "The police are keeping the demonstrators far enough away from the entrance so people leaving the park won't be hassled.

"You were right to close down Nirvana until tomorrow. We don't want to take the chance of someone getting hurt." Thorn wondered if Kayla had known this was going to happen. Had she approved? Had she been tempted to warn him? He'd like to think so.

Thorn wasn't so worried that he couldn't think about her. He already regretted last night's words. If he had to apologize, he would. He frowned. Apologies had never been his favorite things to do, so that's why he rarely bothered.

"I called every nonhuman into work. Just in case." Grim glanced to where his supernatural team had gathered right behind the gate.

"Good call." Thorn read some of the signs the demonstrators were carrying. "Death to demons?" He smiled. "I'd like to see them go up against Klepoth. He'd toss them into an illusion that would fry whatever few brain cells they had."

Just then the police controlling the crowd started leaving. Most of them ran to their cars and took off, sirens shrieking. Only a few stayed behind. Too few.

"Where the hell are they going?" Grim sounded worried.

A few minutes later, Eric joined them on the roof. "I jumped into a few of their minds before they left. Dispatch put out a call for as many officers as possible to respond. There's a bunch of stuff happening around the city. Break-ins, people running naked on the beach, fights breaking out everywhere. Even had a report that a parade of elephants was coming across the Galveston Causeway."

A parade of *what?* "Everything's happening at the same time?" Thorn didn't believe in that kind of coincidence.

Eric nodded. "What're the chances?" He looked at the huge screaming crowd. "What'll we do if they get out of hand? Must be hundreds of them out there."

Thorn had a bad feeling about this. The mood of the crowd, the liquor, the cops' sudden abandonment, and . . . He glanced at the TV cameras filming the whole thing. "We can't hit them with anything too obvious. Not if it's going to be on the late news. Use your own judgment, and I'll back you."

The mob got louder even as Thorn stood there. They crowded the police trying to hold them back. There were too few officers for so many. By the time reinforcements came, it might be too late.

You can use your persuasion. The temptation was there. He fought it. He'd come so far in the last two hundred years. He didn't want to start over—fighting the compulsion, spiraling downward again. Besides, this was a large crowd. He remembered trying to persuade a big group right after becoming vampire. It hadn't ended well.

Thorn made his decision. He'd use it as a last resort and just deal with the consequences.

Tense, he watched the crowd pressing against the gate. The police had retreated behind it with Thorn's people. They were calling for backup.

"The other police won't be in time." Grim looked at Thorn. "I'm going down to the gate to see if I can help."

"Only use obvious power to save yourself." Thorn was still staring at the crowd, so he saw the exact moment they tipped over into an outright mob.

Over the next five minutes, demonstrators scaled the gate, climbed up the pilings from the beach, and even managed to swim to the stairs at the end of the pier. They wielded baseball bats— where the hell had they come from—in a frenzy of destruction. They smashed equipment and screamed their rage. He didn't care about the material stuff. It could be replaced. He did care about his people.

Time for him to join the others. He leaped from the roof and fought his way through the mob. Since no one wore Nirvana uniforms, the H.A.T.E. idiots had no one to focus their fury on. Thorn hoped it stayed that way.

He'd just jabbed a big mouthy jerk in his paunchy gut when he saw her. *No.* She couldn't be here. Why would she put herself in the middle of this mess? Thorn got serious about punishing anyone in his way as he cleared a path to reach her.

Meanwhile, Kayla wasn't doing any helpless hand-wringing. Thorn saw her sock a man who shoved her too hard and kick another in the knee as he tried to grab her. She wore an I-am-woman-watch-me-kill expression.

"What the hell are you doing here?" He pushed a screaming woman away from him and listened as the crowd's roar blended with the shriek of the rising wind. Thunder rumbled, sounding closer and closer as lightning played a zigzag pattern across the night sky. What was up with the weather?

For the first time, he felt fear. He had to keep her safe. He could hear the distant sound of sirens. Gunshots made a distinct popping sound. Shit. He only hoped those shots came from the police. He had to make a decision—try to beat the crap out of every H.A.T.E. member in a "human" way or use his power.

"I'm here to help you." She had to scream to be heard above the roar of the mob. Kayla held up her crowd-control weapon of choice—a canister of pepper spray.

The uncontrolled sea of people churned and fought around them, screaming curses and striking out at whatever was nearest them. They were starting to fight with each other.

The Viking in him wanted to leap into the crowd and start slamming heads together. Bloodlust rose on a tide of red. He fought it down. *No killing, no killing, no killing.* His silent mantra helped.

But he had to stop the crazies. Time to use his persuasion. If he was lucky, he wouldn't have to tackle this whole mob. He grabbed Kayla's hand. "Stay with me."

"Where're we going?"

She got a man with her spray as he swung at them with his bat. Kayla ignored his agonized shrieks as she tried to keep up with Thorn.

"I have to find the bastard in charge." *And put an end to this cluster fuck.* He tried to control his fury. Throwing someone the length of the pier would get him noticed.

Jeez, where had they found all of these morons anyway? One big redheaded guy carrying a sign that read ALL PARENTS, TURN IN YOUR DEMON CHILDREN used it to whack another H.A.T.E. member over the head. With a roar, the man he'd attacked gripped his own sign—OUR GOVERNMENT IS RUN BY DEMONS—like a sword and tried to behead his fellow dumbass. Great. Just freaking great.

If he wasn't so pissed, he would've laughed as some of the rioters tried to take their bats to the controls of the carousel and landed on their asses. The wards were keeping the most important equipment in the park safe.

"If you want their leader, I'd follow the megaphone." Kayla sounded a little out of breath as she ducked under the swing of a wild-eyed demonstrator and came up spraying.

She was leaving lots of pain and tears in her wake. He was proud of her. If he could've smiled with clenched teeth, he would have.

"There." He pointed.

A short distance from the entrance gate, a short, skinny guy stood on top of a pickup cab shouting encouragement through his megaphone. Ten big men stood in a circle around the truck. Guards.

Thorn shoved and punched his way out of the park and over to the truck. He squeezed Kayla's hand. "Stay back."

"Not going to happen, vampire, until they pry this pepper spray from my cold dead hands." She sounded committed.

Thorn knew better than to argue with a woman wielding pepper spray. Now, if he could only do this right, she might not realize he was using persuasion.

He shouted at the nearest guard, infusing his words with power. "Yo, I have an important message for him." Thorn pointed. "Let me through."

Only Thorn would have recognized the flash of confusion in the man's eyes before they cleared.

"Sure. Come on." He waved Thorn and Kayla to the truck.

Kayla looked a little puzzled, but she didn't say anything.

Thorn stood in front of the cab and called up to the skinny guy. "I need your megaphone for a minute."

The man blinked at Thorn but handed it down without a word.

Thorn held the megaphone to his mouth and spoke to the mob. "Stop."

The crowd stilled. Everyone turned to look at him. "You'll listen to your leader and do everything he tells you to do."

Thorn handed the megaphone back to its owner. "You have to stop your people. The police are almost here. You're in a world of shit. The owner of this place will sue your ass. Besides that, the cops are going to throw all of you in jail. So *stop them now.*"

The man stared at him blankly for a moment and then nodded. "Have to stop them." He put his megaphone back up to his mouth and started ordering everyone to calm down and leave the park.

Thorn turned to Kayla. She stared at the skinny guy and then at him.

"That was way too easy."

Thorn shrugged. "I just pointed out the downside to what he was doing. When people get caught up in their emotions, they don't think beyond the moment."

Kayla didn't look as though she bought everything he said.

Thorn spoke before she could ask any questions. "Look."

They both watched as the fighting and destruction ended. People milled around with oh-shit-did-I-do-that expressions before wandering out of Nirvana. As soon as police cars arrived and cops spilled out to reinforce the ones already there, Thorn and Kayla walked back into the park.

Once inside the gate, Thorn glanced at the sky. The wind had died, and the brewing storm had disappeared as quickly as it had risen. Thorn found that more than suspicious. He lowered his gaze and searched until he found where Grim and the others stood together. Kayla and he joined them.

Thorn raked his fingers through his hair. "Thanks for trying to hold things together." He scanned the pier and winced at the damage. It was like a rogue wave had rolled over Nirvana and was now flowing back out. Thorn hoped the cops were getting names.

"I think it looks worse than it really is. You'll get everything fixed up in no time."

Kayla's voice was soft beside him. He nodded and looked at her. Something powerful moved in him. She'd braved the mob to come to his rescue. And he had to believe that Sparkle hadn't sent her. She could lose her job over this.

He reached for her hand. "We have to talk."

She nodded as she clasped his hand, her grip warm and firm in his. "Definitely."

Thorn returned his attention to Grim and the others. "That was a big storm brewing. Once the mob calmed down, the thunder and lightning just went away. Anyone find that strange?"

Grim smiled. He nodded at Zane. "Ask him about it."

The sorcerer shrugged. "I have a few untapped talents."

Thorn clapped him on the shoulder. "I just bet you do. Thanks. A good drenching would've cooled them right down." He tucked that information away for future use.

A sudden rise in the sound level jerked Thorn's attention back to the gate. He frowned. The people still milling around the gate broke apart, stumbling to get out of someone's way. A path cleared.

Now what? Whoever was coming had the power to intimidate the crowd.

He stared as the person came into view.

What the hell?

14

Sparkle Stardust sauntered from the human tunnel and set foot on Thorn's pier for the first time. No one challenged her. The mob stopped grumbling and growling to watch. Kayla decided she was well worth watching.

Sparkle spotted them and walked toward them. No, "walked" was the wrong word. What Sparkle had going was a sexual stalk—all swaying hips and smooth, flowing strides. She didn't hurry. She must've decided to give her audience what they craved.

Her black silk dress stopped at the top of her thighs, and her endless legs and four-inch stilettos created a sensual image that would make any man stop, stare, and probably do some heavy breathing. Kayla expected the males in the crowd to liquefy at any moment and drain into the Gulf.

Her long red hair lifted in a nonexistent breeze—Kayla hoped no one noticed that. Sparkle's amber eyes glowed with erotic secrets and her full lips promised acts of incredible pleasure.

Kayla readjusted her previous assumptions. She'd always overlooked Sparkle when she was trying to decide which nonhumans were the most powerful. Now? Sparkle didn't have a blow-everything-up kind of power, but Kayla suspected she could do just as much damage in her own way. Sex had brought down more than one nation.

Kayla heard a collective groan from the men in the crowd and probably some of the women. The groans from the women would be sounds of escaping envy and instinctive hatred.

As Sparkle reached them, her lips lifted in a sexy smile—tempting, teasing, lethal. She looked at Kayla.

"That's the way you win, sister. Practice. It's all about presentation."

Kayla wasn't sure if Sparkle was talking about the presentation H.A.T.E. had produced or her sensual presentation of a minute ago. It seemed everything Sparkle did was a sexual suggestion. Or maybe that was just Sparkle's power.

Sparkle shifted her attention to Thorn. "We need to talk."

Thorn's smile wasn't a smile at all. "Why would you want to talk? Looks to me as though you've won the day. I'll have to shut Nirvana down while I make repairs. When this story hits the news, some people will be afraid to come here. You should be home celebrating by puttering around in someone's sex life."

"I don't putter." Sparkle frowned. "And that wasn't supposed to happen. Things got out of hand. But the riot's not the most important topic of discussion."

"So, talk."

Thorn might sound relaxed, but Kayla could feel his tension. He dropped her hand and instead put his arm around her waist. She leaned into him, sharing her warmth and support. To hell with what Sparkle thought.

"Not here." Sparkle nodded at Thorn's apartment. "I'm getting warm, cozy vibes from that building."

"Someone told you." Thorn sounded resigned.

"Perhaps my demon of music, Murmur, visited Klepoth a few days ago. Klepoth might have told him you had an apartment on the pier. And maybe Murmur mentioned it to me." She shrugged. "I understand. I love living where I work."

Thorn took his arm from around Kayla's waist. She mourned the loss. He pulled a key from his pocket and handed it to her. "I have to talk to Grim. The police will want a statement. I'll be back as fast as I can." He speared Sparkle with a hard stare. "Have something meaningful to say by the time I return."

Sparkle waved him away. "While you're out, send someone to the castle to get Banan. We'll need him at our meeting. And bring your water horse back with you."

Thorn nodded and then he was gone.

Kayla didn't say anything to Sparkle until they were inside the apartment. She collapsed onto the couch while Sparkle wandered into Thorn's kitchen and opened his fridge.

"Blood, blood, blood, and *champagne*. Thank Dionysus. I thought I might have to drink water." Sparkle opened the bottle, poured herself a glass, and then settled onto one of the chairs.

Thorn kept blood in his fridge? Kayla wasn't sure how she felt about that. She'd never asked him about his eating habits. Something else to add to her need-to-know list.

Kayla firmly put thoughts of Thorn aside to focus on how mad she was at Sparkle. "Are you that desperate? People could've died tonight."

Sparkle peered into her champagne. "Sparkly and bubbly, just like me."

Kayla frowned. "You didn't answer my question."

Sparkle stopped staring at the wine. "Are you thinking of quitting, Kayla?"

"I . . . don't know. Maybe." Surprised, she realized that resigning had been hovering in the back of her mind for days. She didn't want to be a party to driving Thorn out of business anymore. Her father would be furious, but it was his own fault. He'd known she didn't want the job. She'd find another way to finance her education.

The thought empowered her. Defying her father had rarely been a viable option. His steamroller personality had flattened all challengers. Maybe she'd found someone important enough for her to refuse to play the part of the pancake anymore.

"You'd resign. Because of Thorn?"

Sparkle sounded sympathetic, but something sly moved in her eyes.

"Yes." Kayla decided to be honest. "And maybe I'm not as committed to my father's business model as I should be." That was an understatement.

"Have you made love yet?"

"Wow, you don't pull any punches, do you?" Kayla prayed that Thorn would get here soon. "I don't think I'll answer that."

Sparkle looked thoughtful. "Probably not. I don't get a satiated sexual buzz from you." She sipped her wine. "I have some information you might find interesting."

"What?" Kayla didn't like Sparkle's small satisfied smile.

"I'd been wondering about Thorn's power. I hadn't seen any sign of it so far, but every Mackenzie vampire has impressive skills. So I did a little research. It was tough, because Thorn changed his name every time he sneezed. But I know lots of people. I finally found someone who knew him about five centuries ago." She set her glass on the coffee table, leaned back, and crossed her legs. All in slow motion.

Sparkle looked at her from under her lashes, waiting for her to ask what his power was. Kayla refused to give her that satisfaction. She remained silent.

Sparkle blinked first. She sighed. "You're no fun. Fine, I'll tell you. It's persuasion." She waited for Kayla's reaction.

"What exactly does that mean?" Foreboding was a black storm cloud building up on her personal horizon. She had a feeling this wasn't going to be good.

"I hate explaining the obvious." Sparkle almost managed to look petulant. "It means he can persuade anyone to believe anything he wants them to believe. For example: I'm sure he used persuasion to steal Eric, Zane, and Klepoth from me."

So what did that have to do with . . . ? Oh. "He could persuade me to care for him." And she wouldn't remember him doing it. Zane, Eric, and Klepoth certainly didn't know he'd used his power on them. She took that thought to its logical conclusion.

Sparkle gave voice to the thought. "And he could make you believe he cared for you." She oozed fake sympathy. "It's a heartbreaking situation. You'll never be able to trust your own feelings or his." Then she smiled, and the ancient cosmic troublemaker shone from those amber eyes.

"This is what you do." Kayla made it a statement.

"Yes. Does it hurt?" She answered her own question. "Of course it does. That's the point of my whole existence—proving that love is painful, messy, and should be avoided." A tear slid down her perfect cheek.

What the . . . ? Kayla leaned forward. "This isn't about me at all, is it?" Well, in a way it was, because Sparkle was taking her down in flames too. But she'd think about that later. "Is Ganymede still gone?"

Sparkle nodded at her wine.

"Where is he?"

Sparkle shrugged.

Frustrated, Kayla spoke louder. "Talk to me."

"I don't know." Sparkle finally met her gaze. "But wherever he is, he's still causing trouble. I brought in the demonstrators, but I didn't cause the distractions that drew most of the police away."

"Ganymede?"

"I spoke to one of the officers. Every one of those reports was real. Who else but Ganymede could get a parade of elephants onto the Causeway?" She looked stricken. "One of the crowd said a big blond guy sneaked the liquor to them." Sparkle glanced away. "The blond man even spoke to the leader of H.A.T.E. and whipped up his anger. That's what Mede can do. He raises aggression levels. He's a destroyer." She looked back at Kayla. "After the Big Boss set boundaries for Mede, I thought he'd settle for only using his power in emergencies, but I have a bad feeling about things."

Kayla remembered the look on Ganymede's face when Sparkle had screamed at him. *We were nothing. We are nothing.* Ouch. "What will he do now?" Did she want to know?

Sparkle shrugged. "Mede is capable of anything when he's in a rage." She looked lost. "We have to pray he'll stick to small stuff: trying to kill Thorn, destroy Nirvana, and hurt me."

"And if he decides to go big?" Kayla thought she knew the answer.

"Everyone and everything on Earth is in danger."

Well, that sort of painted an ominous big picture. They sat in silence. Kayla figured that Sparkle was worrying about Ganymede while she thought about the power of persuasion.

Thorn finally returned. Banan and Kel were with him. He paused in the doorway. "Something happen while I was gone?" Thorn addressed the question to Sparkle.

Kayla and Sparkle just shook their heads.

Thorn walked to the couch and sat down next to Kayla. She edged away. He frowned, but he didn't mention it. Instead he looked at the other two men.

"There're drinks in the fridge. Help yourself." Then he turned his attention back to Sparkle. "Okay, I brought the shark and the water horse. Let's hear it."

Sparkle lifted her chin and showed Thorn attitude. "Stop glaring. I organized the demonstration, but all the bad stuff came from Mede. He's still pissed off, and I don't know where he is. I don't doubt he'll try to cause more trouble for *both* of us."

"Lovely." Thorn leaned back against the cushions. "Just freaking lovely."

"But we have worse problems right now." Sparkle watched Kel and Banan return with their drinks.

"Worse?" As in worse than the destruction of life as Kayla knew it?

"Let me reword that. We have more immediate problems." Sparkle included all of them in that statement. "Aegir's deadline is getting closer, and we don't have a plan to kick his immortal ass out of the Gulf."

"I assume you have something in mind?" Thorn's expression said she *always* had something in mind.

Sparkle seemed uncharacteristically hesitant. "First, we have to stop trying to wreck each others' businesses. Live the Fantasy will go bankrupt no matter what you do if Aegir isn't stopped. No one's staying in the castle because people are afraid of Galveston at night. They might still come to Nirvana, but they scurry right back to the mainland when they leave."

Kayla was on team Sparkle with this one. No matter how many federal agents and local police patrolled the island, Galveston was dying. The cruise ships had shut down operation here yesterday. People were putting their businesses up for sale and hoping someone would buy them. She'd bet that followers of Aegir would be scooping them up for pennies.

Sparkle met Thorn's gaze. "I watched the news right before I came over here. I wanted to see what reporters were saying about the riot. A cargo ship went down about an hour ago. You probably didn't notice because of . . . other things."

"Shit." Kel said it for them all.

Thorn grabbed his remote and turned on the TV. They sat in silence through the announcement that the Port of Houston was closing until further notice. All boats, large and small, were to stay out of the waters near Galveston. Some nearby oil rigs were being evacuated. And since the attacks on businesses were continuing, Galveston officials suggested that those who could should leave the island.

Thorn turned off the TV and pulled out his cell phone. He punched in a number. "Grim, tell everyone we'll be shutting Nirvana until further notice. Don't bother trying to fix anything right now. I'll speak to everyone on the team after I'm finished with this meeting."

Sparkle seemed relieved. "I'll tell Holgarth to shut down Live the Fantasy as of tomorrow."

"Now we deal with Aegir." He looked at Kayla. "You're human."

Kayla heard, "You're fragile."

"You should get a plane home in the morning."

She wanted to believe the pain she saw in his eyes was real. But what did she know about how persuasion worked? If he was using his power now, though, he was doing a crappy job. Because she wasn't listening. "No." No explanation, no begging. Just the one word.

"Fine." But his expression said it was definitely *not* fine.

Thorn spoke to Sparkle. "You had a reason for asking Kel and Banan to sit in at the meeting?"

"No one has found even one body from all of those sunken boats. That makes me believe Aegir is holding them." Sparkle looked as though she was figuring things out as she went along.

Kayla added her thoughts. "Alive, they'd make a great fail-safe in case his plans went south. Hostages are always useful."

"That means we have to get them away from him first, before we hit him." Thorn looked at Kel and Banan.

Sparkle nodded. "Kel and Banan are the only two sea creatures we have. They need to go out and see if they can find a weakness in his headquarters."

Thorn met Kel's and Banan's gazes. "You didn't sign up for this. I'll understand if you walk away from it."

Kel and Banan looked at each other. An understanding seemed to pass between them. Banan spoke for both. "We're in. We'll leave now while it's still dark."

Everyone remained silent until they'd left.

Then Thorn spoke. "Now we plan for war."

Thorn raked his fingers through his hair. He hated that Kayla would be in danger, but he couldn't force her to go. *You can if you persuade her.* No, he wouldn't listen to the part of him he'd rejected so long ago. In fact, the voice wouldn't even be speaking to him if he hadn't used his power twice in the last week. Now it was awake and whispering its small temptations. But he knew small temptations would lead to bigger ones. He also knew the price he'd pay when he kept resisting those temptations.

"I'll speak to Grim. He's related to Loki. I might not trust Loki, but he's a powerful Norse god. And he doesn't have any love for Aegir." Thorn wondered if they might not be creating problems instead of solving them.

Sparkle looked puzzled. "I thought Loki was still bound."

"Don't believe everything you hear." Thorn continued. "I'll meet with my two witches. They pull Freya's chariot in their cat forms. We could do worse than the Norse goddess who leads the Valkyries. What about you?"

While he waited for Sparkle's answer, he glanced at Kayla to see how she was holding up. She might look shocked, but he saw the gleam of determination in her eyes. Pride and something else warmed him.

"Isis is Zane's mother. She's not a Norse goddess, but she controls magic. We need her." She seemed to be going through her mental Rolodex for likely god and goddess connections. "I think we have enough power without calling in any more outside help. The demon of music works in the castle. He's an arch demon, and an arch demon with legions under his command will help level the playing field."

An arch demon? Thorn was impressed. "Then we'll meet again tomorrow night as soon as I rise to hear what Kel and Banan found out. Then we plan our attack." He had to address one more thing. "What about Ganymede?" Left unasked: who will he support or will he support no one at all?

Sparkle shrugged. "He's never been this angry at me before."

"He's jealous." Kayla folded and unfolded her hands in her lap.

Thorn narrowed his eyes. Something was bothering her. He couldn't wait for Sparkle to leave so he could find out what it was.

"You know it's more than that. I can't take back the words I said, but I hope when he calms down he'll realize I was looped." Sparkle stared at her wineglass. "Don't ever believe me when I'm drunk." She stood. "Time to go back to the castle and rally the forces. I hope the police have cleared away the idiots." A small smile touched her lips. "I will admit, though, to a tiny thrill when I saw all of your broken stuff."

"Goodbye, Sparkle." Kayla sounded weary.

Once Sparkle left, silence descended. Thorn could feel it like a blanket soaked in seawater—heavy and smothering. One of them had to speak first. "Something other than possible death bothering you?"

Kayla looked at him then. She was trying to keep her expression neutral, but her eyes gave her away. They looked stricken. He dropped his gaze.

"I know about your power of persuasion. Is that how you stopped the riot? I thought the H.A.T.E. leader caved too easily."

She had the calm and cool tone down, but the slight quaver in her voice ruined the effect.

"Sparkle told you?" Who knew Sparkle would still be destroying things for him a thousand years later? To be honest, though, he was the one who'd invaded her space this time.

Kayla looked as though she wanted to say something, but in the end she only nodded.

"I guess you want to hear all the details?" He didn't wait for an answer. "I can convince anyone to do or believe anything just by talking to them." He shrugged. "Guess that's it. Unless you have questions, you can leave."

She didn't move. "Can you do it mentally, or do you have to stand in front of someone and speak out loud?" Her gaze slid away from his.

"Don't worry, I can't crawl into your mind. I have to speak aloud to the person I want to persuade. Anything else?" He was a vampire. He wasn't supposed to feel weary or depressed. He must be a crappy vampire, because he felt both.

"Did you use persuasion on Eric, Zane, and Klepoth?"

Thorn admired how she was managing to keep her voice steady with just the right amount of casual interest in it. She shouldn't have allowed him to see her eyes, though. They gave too much away.

He thought about lying, but why? It really didn't matter if Kayla ran to the three and they quit. The park was closed. And if they all survived the coming battle, he didn't think he had enough vengeful fires left to fuel his hatred of Sparkle. He'd probably let Grim manage the place and leave.

But she was waiting for an answer. "Yes. I needed them for my park, so I used my power."

Pink tinged her cheeks. Not embarrassment. Anger. He smiled. A little rage would make things interesting. After all, he didn't care what she thought of him. He allowed the lie to grow and take root. Thorn might even believe it in a few hundred years.

"You took their free will from them to suit your own selfish needs."

He tried to look puzzled. "Not selfish. We're talking righteous vengeance here."

Contempt drew her lips into a thin line. "Do you slither through each day using your 'persuasion' to solve every one of life's daily problems?"

Thorn allowed the silence to grow while he seemed to think about her question. Then . . . "Yes, pretty much."

She stood. "One more question. Did you make me . . . care for you?" She seemed to have surprised herself with that question.

She'd sure surprised him. Kayla cared for him? *Don't get too excited. She's well on her way to hating you.* He wanted to lie, to treat this question the same way he'd treated the others. But he couldn't. "No."

Thorn didn't ask if she believed him. He was pretty sure she wouldn't. He was going to leave it at that. He should have. "Aren't you going to ask if I persuaded you to think that I cared for you?"

Now it was her turn to look puzzled. "Why? I never thought you did." She left his apartment.

He sat staring at the closed door for a few minutes. Then he got up and methodically destroyed everything in his apartment—the cheap print above the couch, the ugly dishes with the flower design he'd bought at the nearest store, every impersonal piece of crap in the place. In the end, with broken furniture and glassware piled around him, he still didn't feel any better. See, he was evolving even further. Breaking things used to improve his mood.

Sitting on the floor surrounded by rubble, he called Grim.

Grim opened the door and then froze. He stared at Thorn sitting on the floor and then scanned the apartment again. "That must've been a hell of a party." His words sounded light, but his expression was serious.

"I expressed my displeasure with my shitty night by indulging in a tantrum. It's healthy to channel your inner child once in a while." Thorn pointed to the floor beside him. "Sit."

"What happened?" His security chief lowered himself to the floor.

"Sparkle and I talked. We decided it wouldn't be safe or profitable to keep our parks going. So we're shutting them down. Tomorrow at sunset we'll make plans to get rid of Aegir."

Grim's eyes widened. "You think big. How will you do that?"

"We'll need some help. Aegir doesn't fear humans, so he's been openly destroying their businesses, sinking their ships, and ordering attacks on swimmers. He's made an attempt to be a little more circumspect with us—first trying to make us believe the guilty party was human, and then once he gained some confidence, giving us a three-week window to clear out. I think there's only one group of beings he really wants to keep out of this fight."

"Let me guess, the gods and goddesses." Grim massaged a spot between his eyes.

"We know Loki would be a ticking time bomb. But if you can get him here, I'll take the chance and hope he goes off all over Aegir and not us."

Grim winced. "Right. I'll try. I suppose you'll want Freya's help too."

Thorn nodded. "You're closer to the witches than I am. See if they can convince Freya to help out. And it wouldn't hurt if she brought her Valkyries."

"No problem." His expression said the exact opposite. "Is that all?"

"Almost. Sparkle did some digging into my past. She found out about my power of persuasion. It didn't take her long to connect dots and realize I'd used my power on her three employees. While she and Kayla were here waiting for me today, she told Kayla. I assume Sparkle's next step is to gleefully tell her former employees what she discovered."

"Ouch. How did Kayla take the news?" Grim didn't look hopeful.

"Kayla took it well." Thorn looked around at the wreck of his home. "*I* broke things."

Grim only nodded as he stood. "I'll get working on those immortal connections."

"One more thing."

"There can't be." Grim glared at him. "You've used up your quota of crappy news for the night."

"Ganymede has gone rogue. Sparkle cooked up the basic recipe for tonight's demonstration, but Ganymede added the spices that turned it hot. She thinks he caused all the trouble that drew the police away from Nirvana. She knows he gave the rioters liquor and pumped them up for violence. And he hasn't phoned home."

Grim didn't say anything, just walked out the door and slammed it behind him. Thorn seconded that emotion.

It was still a few hours until dawn, but that didn't stop Thorn from flinging himself onto his bed. He lay there staring at the ceiling. Tomorrow night he'd start paying for using his power. He'd used it twice within the last week, and his addiction was primed and ready to beat on him if he didn't go back to using it on a daily basis.

But he'd whip it the same way he'd whipped it before. He'd suffer a little, but so long as he didn't use it a third time things would calm down in a few days. He hoped Aegir cooperated with that wish.

He'd kept Kayla for last. He wanted some quality brooding time for her. All of his budding hopes for them had been ground back into the dirt by Sparkle. Kayla would never think or feel anything good about him from now on without wondering if he'd made her feel that way. In other words, she'd never trust him again.

Thorn lay there for a long time thinking about Kayla. Funny that all of Sparkle's in-your-face sensuality left him cold. It was Kayla he wanted. Finally, he turned on his side as he felt the first touch of his day sleep. Maybe he could persuade himself that none of it mattered anyhow.

15

Kayla woke and picked right up where her dreams had left off—thinking about Thorn. At least sleep had helped her find a balance between emotion and reason.

The news that he could persuade her to quack like a duck and think it was a great idea had triggered an emotional tsunami. Betrayal, pain, loss, and fury jockeyed for position in her heart.

Then the realization had smacked her. What did her extreme reaction say about how deep her feelings for Thorn ran? Kayla had leaped into denial. Too bad she had hit her head on the way down.

She had known she was supposed to come to Galveston, do her job, and go home. What she hadn't known was that a sexy vampire would stand in her path waving a sign that read HUGE COMPLICATION.

But now she was thinking clearly—or as clearly as she could where Thorn was concerned. If he had used persuasion on her, wouldn't her attraction have been a lot more dramatic? She would have broken her nose when she did a face-plant on the castle floor the first time she met him. She'd have been so obsessed she wouldn't even have noticed some of the negatives about him. None of that had happened.

Her feelings for him? Not that deep. She had overreacted. When she saw him again, she'd laugh at her initial response. Kayla had liked other men just as much and then forgotten them once they left. *Just as much? Really?* She ignored any opposing views.

His amazing hotness had drawn her, but more intense feelings had grown gradually. She winced. No, that was a slip of her mind. There were no intense feelings.

Thorn had said he didn't use persuasion on her, so why not give him the benefit of the doubt? *You know you want to.* She'd think about it.

Kayla thought about it all day until the sun set. And amid news of more destruction in Galveston, she went with Sparkle to meet Thorn. Actually, Kayla was surprised Thorn even wanted her there. But persuasion or not, she wasn't going to miss a chance to be with him.

"So why am I the only one going to the meeting with you?" Kayla asked Sparkle her question as they crossed the eerily empty Seawall Boulevard on the way to Nirvana.

"Banan will already be there. Mede is still in the wind. Thorn removed his persuasion from Eric, Zane, and Klepoth. Then he told them what he'd done. I wanted to be the one to break the news." She looked annoyed at that. "They're somewhere being mad. And I need everyone else as guards or to help close down the park. I'll bring any decisions we make back to everyone. If they approve, they'll stay. If not?" She shrugged. "They'll go."

"Why not leave me back at the castle too? I won't be much help. My father never covered assaults on supernatural forces in his lessons. But if you want me to pick a lock, I'm your woman." Dumb. Why was she giving Sparkle a reason to send her back? *Fear.* She was afraid to face Thorn, to face her feelings. The ones she kept denying.

Sparkle shot her a long, searching look. "He cares for you. I might be able to use that."

"That is so cold." Was Sparkle telling the truth? The thought that he might care warmed Kayla all over. Not that she wanted the other woman to use her as a weapon against Thorn.

"Not cold. Practical. People perform incredible acts for those they love." Sparkle glanced at Kayla. "Not that he's at the love stage yet, but he's close. And he'll probably go to amazing lengths to keep you safe."

Kayla didn't know what to say to that, so she looked away. Then she frowned, really noticing the destruction around her for the first time. The major rides seemed okay, but Thorn would have to replace most of the other things on the pier.

All of the stuffed monsters had disappeared. She'd bet a lot of the demonstrators' children had stuffed monsters sitting on their beds today. Rotten thieves. *Why all the outrage?*

Dad would applaud. He'd say her job was done and she should come home. But Thorn could be back in business within a month once they took care of Aegir. She couldn't leave. Kayla still had work to do. The sense of relief she felt unsettled her.

The mob had shattered all the windows in the restaurant. She didn't want to think about what they'd done to the inside. The idiots were lucky no one had died last night.

Did Thorn even care about Nirvana? Was it just a means to an end? She looked back at Sparkle. "How can someone still want revenge after a thousand years?"

"Sometimes hate becomes a habit. For some of us who exist for centuries, love and hate are often the only emotions that still warm us." Sparkle made her words sound personal.

Kayla glanced down at Sparkle's nails. Chipped and colorless.

She'd learned that as Sparkle's nails went, so went her world. It looked as though love and hate were still warming one cosmic troublemaker. Kayla decided the conversation was taking her down a path she didn't want to explore right now. Besides, they'd reached Thorn's place.

Sparkle knocked. When Thorn answered, his gaze went directly to Kayla. But he didn't say anything, just stepped aside for them to enter.

Kayla walked into the room and then stopped. She scanned it before looking at Thorn. "What happened to your old furniture?"

Thorn dropped onto a new leather couch. "I lost my temper."

"Remind me never to invite you over when you're in a bad mood." Kayla looked at the other people in the room. Grim slouched in a new recliner, Banan didn't seem quite as relaxed in an armchair, and Kel had pulled up a kitchen chair.

Kel gestured to the couch. "We saved the couch for you and Sparkle."

Kayla moved a little too slowly. By the time she reached the couch, Sparkle had already settled herself at the other end from Thorn. If Kayla made a big deal of avoiding the middle of the couch in favor of dragging over another kitchen chair, then Thorn would see it for what it was—cowardice.

Making sure she didn't meet Thorn's gaze, she sat in the middle. He spread his legs so his thigh pressed against hers. She'd have to sit in Sparkle's lap to avoid touching him.

Thorn looked at her and smiled. Filled with wicked intent, that smile was probably the only persuasion he'd ever need with most women. But Kayla was made of sterner stuff. Her stare dared him to move another body part into her personal space.

Finally, he looked away from her. "First, did anyone have luck recruiting help from the gods or goddesses?"

Kayla sighed her relief. While he was concentrating on the others, she studied him. Now that she wasn't focused on herself, she noticed that something didn't seem quite right. Thorn held himself stiffly, as though any sudden movement might shatter him. There was a crease between his brows, and while she watched he massaged his temple.

Was he in pain? Kayla had never asked if vampires could get headaches. She'd add that question to the one about his eating habits.

Sparkle crossed her legs and every male eye followed the motion. Her small smile said she was very aware of how men would react to anything she did. Kayla felt a momentary stab of jealousy. How would it feel to be so assured of your desirability? But then she thought about how Sparkle and Ganymede were hurting each other. Maybe she didn't want to be Sparkle Stardust right now.

"I asked Zane if he'd contact his mother, but he was too busy making threats against you, Thorn, to answer. You might not want to count on Isis showing up." Sparkle stared at the far wall. "That painting is a spectacular failure. Who paints that crap?"

Kayla could get whiplash from trying to follow Sparkle's change of subjects.

Thorn ignored the insult to his artistic taste. "How about you, Grim?"

His security chief looked conflicted. "The good news first. Loki will be here. The bad news? Loki will be here."

Kayla didn't understand the sudden tension filling the room. Shouldn't everyone be thrilled that Loki was coming? She'd seen *The Avengers*. Loki might be cunning, vicious, and ethically challenged, but he was powerful. Everything would be fine as long as he aimed all that evil power at Aegir.

Thorn broke the silence. He stared at Banan and Kel. "What did you find, guys?"

Kel wasn't smiling. "Aegir's hall at the bottom of the Gulf is pretty much impregnable."

"It's a freaking fortress." Banan seemed offended by the idea of someplace he couldn't get into. "Most of it is buried. The part above the sea floor is a clear dome. No way to sneak up without being seen."

"I spoke to some of the sea shifters in the area. They don't like working for Aegir, but since the only other option is death, they're dealing with him. One of them told me the humans from the ships he sank are being kept in his hall. Ran and her daughters are guarding them."

Ran? Then Kayla remembered: Aegir's wife. "If Aegir's stronghold is at the bottom of the Gulf, how do you reach him?"

Thorn looked at Kel and Banan. "Will any of the sea creatures fight with us?"

"And risk losing fins and tentacles? Not likely." Banan bit his lip as he thought. "You might get some of them to agree to stay neutral if they thought you had a chance of winning. That's the best you could hope for."

"Ganymede and the Big Boss are the only ones who might give a damn about us and are powerful enough to blast Aegir from the bottom of the sea. I'm not counting on the gods or goddesses because who the hell knows what they'll do. Ganymede is busy going rogue, and I don't have a clue where the Big Boss is. Ever since he decided that I'd make a great assistant, I haven't seen much of him. He's probably vacationing in some exotic alternate reality." Sparkle looked at the fridge. "I need a glass of wine."

She got up to get her drink, and Kayla welcomed the chance to edge away from Thorn. "You can't blast anything until you get the people out." Kayla noted that Kel's expression said keeping the humans safe wasn't one of his top priorities. She watched gloom settle over the group.

Sparkle didn't return to her seat. She got a glass for her wine and stood sipping it. "So the first thing we do is find a way to free the hostages. Then we decide how to drive Aegir away." She looked a little more decisive. "I'll talk to my people. A few of them have major talents. Some of them might have an idea we didn't explore."

Everyone stood, and Kayla stood with them. She looked at Sparkle. "Well, my presence certainly helped. We accomplished so much." As weapons went, sarcasm wasn't much, but it made her feel better. Kayla didn't look at Thorn as she followed Sparkle to the door.

"Wait."

Thorn was right behind Kayla. How had he moved that fast? He was close enough for her to feel him, that particular awareness she had for him alone.

"I'd like to speak with you for a moment, Kayla."

His voice was husky and soft, a sensual caress that stroked her with invisible fingers. She imagined he'd use that same voice to invite her into his bed. And God help her, she'd go.

Kayla nodded and turned back to the room. This time she took the recliner. His lips lifted, acknowledging her reluctance to sit near him. He returned to his seat on the couch and waited until everyone had left.

The door closed on the last person. To Kayla, it sounded like the boom of a dungeon door shutting, locking her into his personal keep. *Get a grip.* She smiled at him. "You have something to say?"

He met her gaze. "I wanted to clarify some points from last night."

She raised her brows and remained silent. Kayla wouldn't make it easy for him.

Thorn looked grim. She wasn't sure if it was because of what he was about to tell her or because of physical pain. He reached up again to massage his temple.

"I'll repeat what I said from last night just in case you didn't hear it the first time. I never used persuasion on you."

"Just everyone else." Even she could hear the nastiness in her voice. Kayla didn't like the sound of it.

"Not really." He closed his eyes. "During the last two hundred years I've only used persuasion three times—to convince Eric to fly in from Chicago, to make sure Eric, Zane, and Klepoth accepted my job offer, and to force the leader of the mob to calm his followers."

She had an almost irresistible urge to walk over to the couch and smooth that crease away with her fingers. And from there . . . ? Kayla took a deep breath. And from there, nothing. "That's not what you said last night."

"Last night I was angry and figured if you already thought the worst of me, I may as well live down to expectations. I lied to you."

He opened his eyes and speared her with a hard stare. "I stopped using persuasion two hundred years ago because it made life too easy. I could get whatever I wanted, so there were no challenges. Life grew boring. I even thought of ending it." The last was a mere murmur.

Horror so powerful she felt like heaving shook her. What if he had killed himself? She never would have known him.

"So I decided to live the way a mortal would live. Working for what I wanted gave me goals, reasons for living. It's worked for me."

Kayla straightened in her chair. "True?"

He nodded. "True. Anything else you want to know?"

"Sparkle said you had blood in your fridge, but what about your dining-out nights?"

"I don't kill when I feed. And when I'm finished, I wipe the memories of what happened from their minds. So yes, I do still use a few small powers necessary for my survival."

She wasn't sure she believed everything he'd said, but she wanted to. Kayla decided for tonight she'd go with what she wanted. "Fine."

His smile had hard edges. "That seemed too easy."

"Maybe I'm tired tonight. I'll be argumentative and disbelieving again tomorrow."

"Deal." Thorn stood. He looked as though he expected her to leave.

She didn't. "This might be one of my last chances to try another one of Nirvana's rides. How about the roller coaster?"

He seemed surprised. "Sure."

Something moved in his eyes, a challenge. It was warm and curled like a sleeping cat inside her. But she knew the sleeping cat could always waken, teeth and claws ready. The thought was sort of exciting. At least she knew there was no persuasion involved because it had been her idea.

"Let's go." He sounded eager.

Kayla left his apartment with him, wondering if she'd just made a huge mistake.

Thorn stopped beside the roller coaster. Kayla looked around. Other than some workers who were clearing away rubble and boarding up the restaurant windows, the pier was empty.

"You're lucky to be doing this with *me*. Being the owner has perks." He fiddled with the ride's controls and then guided her into the front seat. Thorn slid in beside her. "A regular visitor would zip right through the ride, no pausing."

Puzzled, she glanced at him. "Isn't that the whole purpose of a roller coaster, to careen around curves and plunge into the depths at warp speed? Then when you get off you can throw up. It's a thrill ride."

Thorn shook his head. "Not this one. The joy is in the intentional pause."

"If you say so." Her stomach was in knots. Sitting next to him was its own thrill ride.

He put his arm across her shoulders and pulled her closer to his side. "No matter what happens on the ride, just go with it." Thorn leaned close. "I'll keep you safe." His breath warmed the side of her neck while goose bumps gathered at other more exposed parts of her body.

She could only nod as they began to move. Kayla reached for his hand and he gripped it hard. His warm hand enveloping hers gave her more confidence than the protective bar holding her into the seat.

Her stomach did somersaults as the car laboriously chugged up the first steep incline. She knew what was coming. They'd reach the crest, pause, and then plunge down the other side leaving her stomach at the top still looking around stupidly.

Kayla was tempted to close her eyes. From her experience with the Ferris wheel, she suspected that strange things would happen on this ride too. But Thorn was with her, so she kept them open.

"Umm, haven't we been climbing a long time?" Of course they had. This was a Nirvana experience. She looked down. The pier seemed an impossible distance below them.

"The farther to fall." He sounded energized by the whole thing.

Kayla thought he was crazy. Finally, they reached the top and she looked down the other side. She gulped. "Uh, the tracks drop into the water." Logically, she knew they didn't. This had to be an illusion. But that didn't stop it from looking real.

Thorn just smiled at her. "Go with it."

"Don't have much choice." Those were her last words before they rocketed down the hill into the Gulf.

She was still screaming as the water closed over her head. Then she stopped. So did the coaster. Her brain felt scrambled. She should be holding her breath, fighting to swim to the surface for air to fill her tortured lungs. She wasn't. Kayla was breathing easily as she floated free of the car.

Puzzled, but calming a little, she looked at Thorn. Her eyes widened. He was naked, every beautiful inch of his body bared to her view. She glanced down. She was naked too. They were naked together . . . Kayla stared around her. This wasn't the Gulf.

First of all, it was daytime because she could see sunlight filtering through the surface of the water above her. The water was warm, sliding over her body in a silken flow. *This was an illusion.* But it felt real.

Everything was so gorgeous she wanted to cry from the sheer joy of staring at it. Brilliant coral competed with equally colorful small fish.

She looked at Thorn. He was by far the most spectacular thing in the water right now. He'd given her this moment. With a few strokes he reached her side. He ran his fingers through her hair, which floated around her.

Thorn needed no words. She recognized the desire in his eyes, the flare of excitement and invitation. Illusion or not, Kayla knew she wanted this, wanted *him*.

She couldn't stop her hands from shaking as she cupped his face and drew him close. Words. He might not need them, but she did. She wanted to tell him how right this felt and how wrong. Right for now, for this time cocooned in soft sea currents. But wrong for any tomorrows. The Stanleys didn't love vampires, didn't even date them. And vampires? Why would they bind themselves to humans, puny creatures who died too easily and too soon?

She didn't have time to think more brooding thoughts before he covered her mouth with his. Thorn's lips slanted across hers. They tasted of the sea and hunger. Kayla parted her lips, welcoming him in. His tongue explored, hot with promises. His fangs were down, and she carefully traced them with the tip of her tongue. What if biting completed his sexual experience? Then he deepened the kiss and she forgot about biting.

Thoughts tumbled and tangled with emotions and senses. Happiness exploded like bright flashes behind her eyes. Smooth skin slid over smooth skin. How the heck would they make love floating in the water? She banished the thought. Thorn would find a way.

He finally broke the kiss to nibble a path from the sensitive skin behind her ear to the base of her throat. The only sound she could hear was the mad pounding of her heart, and if pulses turned him on, then hers would drive him into a sexual frenzy. His lips lingered at her throat for what seemed like forever. He *didn't* bite her.

Thorn skimmed his fingers over her shoulders and then lowered his head to her breasts. She arched her back, floating effortlessly as he closed his lips over her nipple. Tangling her legs with his, she gave herself over completely to the sensation of him teasing the nipple with the tip of his tongue and drawing it into his mouth. He sucked, and she felt the pull all the way from low in her belly to the nipple in question.

She wanted to moan, *needed* to moan. Next time they made love there *would* be sound. Next time? Would there be one? This thought was less organized than earlier thoughts. It floated away before she could really consider it.

When he released her nipple, she slid down his slick body and wrapped her arms around him. She dug her fingers into his butt cheeks, felt him clench, and wished she could glide around him and bite that temptingly tight ass. And here she'd worried about him biting her.

And since everything she wanted to touch was within floating distance, she slid lower. She cupped his balls and massaged them gently as she gazed up at him. He'd flung his head back and closed his eyes. His throat was taut, vulnerable. She didn't associate that word with Thorn, so this moment was special.

Was the water getting warmer? Maybe it was just her.

She wanted to hear him groan with pleasure. But in this silent world the only senses remaining were sight, touch, and taste. Right now touch was front and center.

Kayla twirled her fingertip around and around the long hard length of his cock. Then she substituted her mouth. She kissed and nibbled her way from the thick base of him up to the head. Kayla was just about to close her lips around him when she felt his fingers grip her hair. He pulled.

Thinking had finally been removed from the equation. Kayla didn't reason why he'd stopped her, only felt a sense of deprivation and disappointment. But she would get over it. She had other things to do.

She would swear the water was getting warmer.

But it seemed that Thorn had things to do too. He pulled and pulled until most of her body had floated past him. Then he transferred his hands from her hair to her thighs. He nudged them apart and slid his tongue the length of her inner thigh. Then . . . then . . . he flicked his tongue across . . . She screamed in her mind.

Kayla sucked in her breath—amazing that she could do that—and spread her legs farther apart. The sensation . . . Not only the warmth of his tongue but also the ripple of water touching her . . . right *there*.

Damn, the water was hot.

Not as hot as her, though. She bucked and thrashed as his magic tongue tortured, teased, and tore away any preconceived beliefs of what making love with Thorn Mackenzie would feel like.

Finally, she couldn't stand it one more moment. Her body clenched and clenched some more, begging, howling its silent need. Now. Now. Now. She had to get his attention. Leaning over, she clawed at his back and yanked on his hair.

Kayla couldn't hear it, but she'd bet he was growling. He gripped her around the waist and forced her down until she was standing on the sea floor. Then he backed her against a huge boulder she hadn't noticed before.

Inside her head she was now cursing the water that wanted to float her away. Wasn't going to happen. Thorn cupped her bottom with his large hands and lifted her. She wrapped her legs around him and then gripped his shoulders.

Hot water, hot water, hot, hot water.

He slid just the head of his cock into her and paused. What the hell was that about? *More.* She gave him a gentle hint by biting his shoulder.

Then he buried himself inside her. She gasped as he plunged and then moaned as he withdrew. From there everything was a watery blur. Her gasps and moans formed an ever-quickening rhythm. All her senses coalesced into one shiny ball of ecstasy, and she rode it to an alternate universe. One where pleasure went on and on as something hot and explosive built inside her.

Almost. There. Kayla knew she was sobbing, but she couldn't stop. Nothing should feel this good.

He thrust into her one last time.

Kayla froze. That pleasure beyond reason, beyond description expanded and expanded until she thought she couldn't hold it in. But she tried. She clenched her body and didn't breathe, didn't think, even willed her heart to still as wave after wave of spasms shook her.

She felt Thorn shudder against her even as her spasms started to fade. Kayla held on to them as long as she could but finally they were gone. She felt limp and satiated. He *hadn't* bitten her.

Eventually, she grew aware of her surroundings again. Thorn floated beside her, his arm around her waist. He wore a startled expression.

"What?" She celebrated the return of her voice. And then she felt it. "Jeez, this water will boil the flesh from our bones."

Now he looked worried. "Let's get out of here." Thorn dragged her through the water and back onto the roller coaster. He threw a switch and then they were rocketing out of the Gulf and up the last incline. The cool breeze brought reality with it.

Kayla remembered. Naked? She looked down. Relieved, she realized she was dressed. Just an illusion. No, she could never classify what had happened beneath the water as "just" anything.

Strangely shy, she glanced at Thorn. Then she widened her eyes. "Wait. Your hair is wet." Kayla touched her hair. "So is mine."

"Yes." He didn't look surprised.

"I thought that was an illusion."

"Did it feel like an illusion?" He smiled but didn't look at her.

"No." She knew her voice had softened, and Kayla feared her tone would tell him too much. She wasn't ready to put herself out there, to allow him to see all of her.

Thorn nodded. "That's Eric's genius. He has the power to create illusions that are . . . real, even if they feel surreal. I can't explain it. I don't think anyone can. We absolutely experienced everything in that illusion." He paused to study her. "Do you regret the realism?"

"No." She seemed stuck on that word. "What about the heat?"

He laughed. Kayla loved his laughter. She wanted to wrap herself in it and wear it forever. *Now you're wandering into shark-filled waters.*

"I think our combined passions shorted out a magical wire in Eric's underwater fantasy. But even if I'd ended up cooked, it would've been worth it."

Kayla thought that was probably one of the strangest compliments she'd ever received. And she didn't care that she wore an idiotic grin.

When they left the roller coaster, Thorn invited her to stop by his apartment to dry her hair. She welcomed any excuse to stay with him longer.

Kayla was busy thinking about impossible dreams that somehow didn't seem quite so impossible right now when Thorn opened his door and stepped inside. He stopped. She slammed into his back.

"Why did you . . . ?" She peered around him. "Oh. My. God."

A huge gray wolf sprawled on Thorn's couch. Kayla had only seen wolves in the zoo, but they couldn't come close to the size of this monster. The wolf watched them from cold yellow eyes. She resisted the urge to turn and run.

Thorn reached back and clasped her hand, but he didn't take his gaze from the wolf. The air thrummed with tension.

Thorn finally spoke.

"Welcome, Loki."

16

"Loki? I don't—"

Thorn squeezed Kayla's hand. She got his message and stopped talking. But when he tried to keep his body between her and Loki, she moved around him. Her glare said what she thought about his attempt to protect her.

"Loki is a shape-shifter. The wolf is one of his forms." Thorn damned himself for suggesting she return with him. He didn't want her anywhere near this god.

"Oh?" She infused that one word with all the questions she wanted to ask.

Suddenly the image of the wolf shimmered and became a man. Thorn heard Kayla's muffled gasp, but he kept his attention on the god.

Loki stood. He was tall and lean, pale with shaggy black hair and eyes the same yellow as his wolf's eyes. He was into blending. No Viking gear for him. He could've passed for any human on the street with his jeans, boots, and black jacket. Until you looked into his eyes. What he was lived in those eyes.

"Your name, vampire?" Loki's gaze settled on him.

"I'm Thorn Mackenzie. I own Nirvana." Thorn decided to keep his conversation to a minimum. He didn't trust Loki. And his feelings had nothing to do with the fact that Loki had a face women would like or that Kayla was doing lots of looking right now. Okay, so his feelings had a little to do with that.

"You recognized me." Loki made it a statement.

"Grim said you were coming. I'm Viking. I grew up hearing tales of you and the other Norse gods." He shrugged. "Besides, what other wolf would be lying on my couch?"

Loki rewarded him with a nod of approval and shifted his attention to Kayla? "And you?"

Kayla still held Thorn's hand. She gripped it tightly, but that was her only sign of nerves. She met Loki's gaze.

"I'm Kayla. I work for Sparkle Stardust."

She bit her lip, and Thorn knew she wanted to say more, but she didn't. He relaxed a little.

Loki gave her his first smile. It transformed his face. Thorn hated him.

"I'm certain there is more to tell than that, Kayla." Loki lingered on her name.

"Now that you're here, we have to make plans." Thorn knew he sounded abrupt, but he couldn't care less. He didn't like the sudden flare of interest in Loki's yellow eyes when he looked at Kayla.

"What plans? I'll tell Aegir that Asgard is not a happy place right now because the gods and goddesses know what he's doing." His smile turned sly and malevolent. "Aegir is no longer a strong god. He fears the others."

Could've fooled me. Thorn tried to look awed and attentive. Not difficult considering the legend that was Loki. Too bad that every time he saw Loki's glance slip to Kayla, Thorn's fangs grew a little longer.

"After I destroy his hall, he'll leave this place and hide." Loki's expression said getting rid of Aegir would take a half hour tops.

"You have to rescue the humans first." Kayla's grip had loosened.

"Rescue humans?" Loki looked puzzled. "Why would I do that? I only care about Aegir."

"Aegir has to be holding close to a hundred people hostage in his hall. You can't leave them to die." Her expression had turned mutinous. She dropped Thorn's hand.

Loki's stare said clearly that he could.

Thorn tried to block the insistent voice urging him to use persuasion. *It's an addiction. Resist it.* Even if it worked on Loki—and that wasn't a given—the blowback would zap him unless he kept using it.

Instead, Thorn turned to the human skills he'd honed over the centuries. He smiled—not enough to show fang—so Loki would believe he liked him. He didn't. Then Thorn tried on his best obsequious face. "This shouldn't be a problem. Why don't we go over to the castle and talk about it? They have a comfortable conference room. You can eat and drink. Sparkle will have a place where you can relax afterward. She'll have all the nonhumans there." His expression slid into ingratiating. "No one would want to miss meeting one of the world's most famous gods." That much was true.

Loki considered it and then nodded. "We'll talk. But if you want to rescue the humans, you'll have to do it yourself. I agreed only to stop Aegir."

"How can we save the humans? They're underwater."

Kayla said what Thorn was thinking.

Loki shrugged. "That is your problem. Surely with a roomful of nonhumans you can come up with something."

Just freaking great. Thorn pulled out his cell phone and called Sparkle. He didn't wait for her to say anything. "Get all the nonhumans to your conference room. Now."

"Did I imagine the meeting we had about, oh, an hour ago? Talking again won't change anything." She sounded annoyed.

"Loki is here."

"Oh." Silence. "Well, bring him. I'll have everyone there."

"Order food and drinks." Had to keep the god happy.

"Sure." The one word came out on a tired sigh.

As he returned the phone to his pocket, Thorn wondered what other things were happening in Sparkle's life to cause that sigh. Then he remembered Ganymede. Thorn would add cursing and putting his fist through a wall to the sighing.

He spoke to Loki, but watched Kayla from the corner of his eye. "Let's go. Sparkle is rounding up all the nonhumans. Did you see Grim on your way in?"

"I saw no one. I came directly to this room." Loki joined them at the door.

Kayla stared up at the god with wonder in her eyes. "Does that mean you can dematerialize?"

Loki's gaze softened. He smiled again. "Yes. Would you like to try it before I leave?"

"Definitely. What a rush. We . . ." She glanced at Thorn.

Whatever she saw on his face wasn't good.

She looked away. "We'd better get over to the castle."

They walked across the street, Kayla between Thorn and Loki. Thorn's head still hurt from the persuasion he'd used two nights ago. The pain didn't help his mood.

Jealousy was an ugly thing. He didn't try to justify the emotion. Since he couldn't control it, he may as well own it and do it up right. "A lot of people have written about you, Loki. They always depicted you as a trickster and deceiver. Do you think they were fair to you?" Thorn glanced at Kayla to see if she got that Loki was scum.

Kayla's expression said she thought Thorn should keep his mouth shut. Loki could crush him beneath his heel, scrape off Thorn's remains on the curb, and not interrupt his conversation with her.

Now that was just insulting. Thorn curled his lip, exposing his fangs. She'd never really seen what happened when his vampire nature took over completely.

Kayla stared at Thorn from eyes wide with alarm.

Don't. Lose. Your. Temper. Thorn had the sense to lower his head so his fangs were hidden.

Loki didn't look angry, though. He seemed interested. "Trickster? Deceiver?" He remained silent for a moment. "An accurate description. I'm the ultimate con man. I'm successful because I'm smart about what I do, and I hate everyone equally."

Thorn stared at him.

"I'm only joking." Loki didn't look as though he was joking.

Thorn thought that partnering with this god would always be a life-or-death experience, one in which your "partner" could decide to eliminate you along with the enemy.

Loki wore a calculating smile. "I enjoy manipulating events. What's the fun in doing something if you can't tweak noses or pull tails?"

"Sure. Fun is important." Finally, they'd reached the conference room. Thorn held the door for Kayla, and just managed to stop himself from slamming it in Loki's face.

Sparkle was already seated along with the nonhumans from both parks. Thorn and Kayla sat next to her. No one looked at them. They were too busy watching Loki, who had taken the seat at the head of the table. He looked as though he thought it was his rightful place.

Kayla poked Thorn with her elbow. "I can't believe you insulted

Loki. What were you thinking?" Even though she didn't want to admit it, the expression of primal savagery she'd seen on Thorn's face for just those few moments had triggered something primal and savage in her own heart.

He shrugged. "Loki's tough enough to handle the hard questions. Besides, he wasn't insulted. You worry too much."

She settled back into her chair with an irritated huff. Kayla tried to get her mind off Thorn by focusing on the meeting.

Sparkle stood. "Welcome to the Castle of Dark Dreams, Loki. We appreciate that you've agreed to help us. I—"

Loki held up his hand, effectively stopping whatever Sparkle had been about to say. He didn't stand. "I'm here because my great-grandson asked me and because I hate Aegir. Tomorrow night I'll go out to where the sea god has his hall and I'll blow it out of the water. I'll explain the . . . concerns those in Asgard have about what he's done and then I'll return home. You have until then to plan a strategy to save your precious humans." He yawned. "Now, I'll need a place to stay and something to eat." He studied Sparkle. "Do you supply any women to entertain me?"

"No." Sparkle had narrowed her eyes to amber slits.

Loki's lips tipped up in a faint smile. "Too bad. I suppose I'll have to supply my own entertainment."

Kayla decided that smile should worry Sparkle. Loki was a gorgeous man, but he frightened her in the same way Banan had scared her. Loki was a predator. But he was a powerful one. They needed power right now. Lots of it. You took the good with the bad.

Silence enveloped the room as Sparkle called for someone to take Loki to his suite and to make sure he had food and drink along with anything else he wanted, within reason. Then she sat down.

Once he'd left, Grim coughed. "Sorry about Great-granddad. He's a bit of a jerk. But we need him."

Sparkle waved away his apology. "We're just happy to have one of the gods here." She cast a reproachful glance at Zane. "We could've used a few more."

Thorn leaned forward. "So how do we save the people Aegir is holding?"

Kayla waited as the silence dragged on. She didn't know how they'd receive suggestions from a mere human, but she had a skill some of them lacked. Because she didn't have super anything, she had to be able to make plans and organize to assure her success in life. This wasn't much different than putting a case together.

"I have some ideas." She watched as they all turned to stare at her. No pressure. "I don't know if anything I say will be workable, but at least it'll be a start." A lot depended on how powerful they were.

"We'll certainly consider your input."

Holgarth sounded so patronizing that she wanted to smack his stupid wizardy face.

"First we'll need a ship to handle the rescued humans. One of those ships from the cruise terminal on Harborside would work. Someone will have to captain it."

"I can do that." Anticipation gleamed in Sparkle's eyes.

"Oh, God, no." Eric looked truly horrified.

Kayla saw the same horror mirrored on everyone's face. She rushed to fill in details. "We'll need someone to cloak the ship so the Coast Guard can't see it. We'll also need some kind of illusion to convince everyone the ship is still where it should be." She thought for a moment. "There aren't many people left in Galveston, so hopefully no memories will have to be wiped."

"Sparkle can't captain the ship." Zane still hadn't moved on from that detail. "It'll be an instant shipwreck."

Sparkle glared at him. "I've lived for thousands of years. I have more skills than you'd think. Besides, I bet it's all electronics now." She placed a finger over her lips as she thought. "Someone with strong magic could manipulate the controls manually."

Everyone in the room with even a bit of magic suddenly found the ceiling, walls, or floor fascinating. Kayla would have laughed if the situation wasn't so dire.

"Assuming we can get the ship away from land and out to where Aegir's hall is, then we have to save the humans once Loki blows it up." Now things got tough. "The concussion from any explosion will kill them."

Grim spoke up. "I'll talk to Loki. He has enough power to simply rip the hall apart instead of blowing it up."

"Problem. How do we get the people to the surface before they drown?" Thorn looked as though he had his doubts about the whole plan.

A man with long blond hair and brilliant green eyes answered Thorn. "We were never introduced. I'm Murmur, the demon of music. I have the power to create melodies that can take physical forms. I'll have to work quickly, but as long as I have someone down there that I can connect to, I can create huge musical bubbles around groups of about fifty people and float them to the surface."

Kayla jumped in. "Great. Banan and Kel can be there and ready when Loki dismantles the hall. As soon as there's an opening, they go in, find the people, put them into two groups and then wait for Murmur to send down his musical bubbles."

"Not to be the voice of doom, but all of this will take time. People will drown while they're waiting for the bubbles." Thorn looked frustrated.

"Excuse me. I have something to offer."

Startled, Kayla sat up straight. A voice in her head? Feminine. Frantically she scanned the room. Thorn was doing the same.

"The Siamese cat wearing the exquisite diamond collar." The voice sounded impatient.

Kayla looked at the man she'd noticed the first time they'd all met. The one with the cat on his shoulder. He smiled at her. The cat did not.

"I'm Asima, *messenger for the goddess Bast. I didn't offer my goddess's services because she has no affinity for water. But I have amazing powers in my own right.*"

Sparkle made a rude noise.

The cat hissed at Sparkle. "*In spite of the slut queen's disbelief, I think I have a solution for keeping the humans alive.*" She took the time to groom one white paw. "*If Murmur can send me down in my own personal bubble, I can put the humans into a brief stasis. They won't have to breathe until they reach the surface.*"

Thorn looked impressed. "You can do that?"

"*I can do many things that few appreciate.*" Asima threw Sparkle a cat glare.

"Wonderful." Kayla tried to ignore the total weirdness of everything being suggested as she ticked off a list in her mind. Only a few more details. Huge ones. "So how do we keep Aegir and his people from simply sinking our ship before we can do squat?"

Holgarth broke his silence. "We have assorted ways of protecting ourselves. Zane and I can ward the ship. Thorn's two witches can help. Edge, the one with the grim reaper tattoo, was until recently the cosmic troublemaker in charge of death. He has many creative ways to kill. You'll find that all of us have unique battle skills." His sneer said that Kayla should have known this.

Kayla sighed as she mentally checked that off her list. Final detail. "What do we tell the humans? We can't just turn them loose on the world."

Grim broke the silence that followed her question. "It won't be enough to just wipe their memories. We have to give them new memories, ones that won't point the finger at us. Memories that will send the authorities away from Galveston." He looked at Thorn.

Thorn closed his eyes for a moment. When he opened them, his expression was bleak. "I'll use persuasion on them." He didn't wait around to hear any more. Standing, he strode from the room.

Kayla frowned. What was that all about? And he'd left before she could ask what new memories he planned to give them. Well, she could find that out tomorrow night before they left.

When she finally pulled her thoughts from Thorn, she looked at Sparkle to see if she had any final words. But Sparkle wasn't paying attention. She was busy staring at a tablet in her lap. She didn't look happy.

"I think we're finished, Sparkle. Any last thoughts?" Kayla jabbed Sparkle with her elbow.

"What?" Sparkle looked up. "Oh. I guess everything's settled then. We'll all meet at the cruise terminal tomorrow night. I'll have a time for you in the morning. Thanks for meeting on such short notice." She looked distracted. "I won't be available for the rest of the night. I have to do research on captaining a cruise ship."

"We're doomed."

Kayla didn't catch who whispered what she knew everyone was thinking. She watched as they all filed out of the room. She stayed behind with a brooding Sparkle.

Once the door shut behind the last person, Kayla turned to Sparkle. "What's the matter?"

Sparkle put the notebook in front of Kayla. "Look at the headlines."

Puzzled, Kayla looked. Blinked and looked again. "Mutant locusts devour everything in Central Park?"

Sparkle nodded. "This morning locusts descended on the park and ate every plant down to the roots. That included the tree trunks. All that's left of Central Park is a bare piece of land and anything that wasn't a plant."

"What kind of locust could do that?"

Sparkle shrugged. "Scientists don't know. The swarm flew away once it was finished destroying the park. No one can find them now." She motioned for Kayla to go on.

The next headline was just as bizarre. "It says that Old Faithful has stopped erupting and that the caldera beneath Yellowstone National Park is showing unusual activity." Now that was scary.

"If the super-volcano beneath the park erupts . . ." Sparkle couldn't even speak the rest.

Kayla glanced through the other headlines, each one progressively stranger. When she had finished, she looked at Sparkle. "Explain."

"Mede is the cosmic troublemaker in charge of chaos. Chaos on a grand scale." She took back her tablet and sighed as she saw a new headline. "The Big Boss stopped him from doing the mass destruction stuff. He's the only one powerful enough to command Mede's respect. Now Mede has slipped his leash and is reverting to his old self."

"Before you." Kayla kept her voice soft.

"Yes, before me."

Sparkle raked her fingers through her hair, a sign of stress from a woman whose hair was always perfect. "I can't reach Mede. I've called his cell and tried to touch his mind. Nothing." She stared at Kayla, eyes red from lack of sleep. "I'm afraid for him."

I'm afraid for us. Kayla put her arm across Sparkle's shoulders and hugged her tight. "Let's take care of Aegir first. Then we'll concentrate on Ganymede." When had she become so involved with this place, these people, *Thorn*? This was just supposed to be a job that lasted a month or so before she headed back to her real life in Philly. Now? She didn't know. God, she didn't know.

Kayla stood. "Try to get a little sleep. Everything always looks better after some rest. Mede loves you." She'd seen it in his eyes. "He's hurt right now, but he'll calm down and start thinking rationally." She hoped.

When Kayla finally closed the conference door behind her, Sparkle was still staring at the tablet.

Once in her room, Kayla found she couldn't follow her own advice. Everything was a tangled mess in her mind—Ganymede, Loki, Aegir, *Thorn*. Then there was Dad. Kayla hadn't spoken to him in a week.

But she always came back to Thorn. And when she finally did manage to fall asleep, it was to dream of their lovemaking beneath the sea. Waking to reality would be tough.

Thorn stood at the railing on the deck of the *Death Wish*. Fine, so that wasn't the ship's name. He didn't remember the stupid name. He had other things to think about. Like how he would survive the agony tomorrow when he refused to continue using his power. Worse yet, maybe he wouldn't refuse. The temptation would be that strong.

"Why did you agree to use your power? I know how you hate the idea."

Kayla asked the same question he'd asked himself over and over since waking from his day sleep.

"Don't have a clue." *I did it because you'd think it was the right thing to do. And I care what you think.* Maybe *he* even thought it was the right thing to do.

She put her hand over his where it rested on the railing. He absorbed her warmth, her support, her confidence that he'd get the job done. He should warn her not to put any hard bets on that.

"You're worried."

Thorn cursed himself for not hiding his unease better. "Other than the H.A.T.E idiots, I haven't tried to persuade a large group since shortly after I became vampire."

"Reason?" She lifted her face to the breeze blowing over the water.

He'd like to remember her this way. Because after she saw what he became in the next few days, she might never come near him again. "There was a battle. Lots of dead. I thought I could end it by persuading everyone to stop fighting. I only managed to persuade half of them. The other half slaughtered the ones who obeyed me. I swore never to try persuasion on a large group again."

"I understand. But you have a lot more experience now. You'll do fine."

He nodded. Her belief in him gave him the confidence he needed. Thorn smiled. No one had thought to ask him what he intended to make the humans believe. Loki might have it right. It was fun to tweak noses and pull tails. Too bad the one tail he'd enjoy pulling the most wasn't here.

She turned to glance across the deck. He followed her gaze. Banan and Kel weren't here. They'd already be in their other forms and swimming toward Aegir's hall. Most of the others were on deck. Thorn smiled as he spotted the guy with the snooty-sounding messenger of Bast sitting on his shoulder. He didn't look happy. Neither did the cat. Thorn didn't want to think about what would happen if she got her paws wet.

"Where's Sparkle?" Kayla searched the crowd.

Just then Thorn saw a limo pull up to the terminal. Who the hell . . . ? Someone got out. Holgarth? The wizard went back to open the door for . . . ?

Thorn watched two people emerge from the car. Loki? What was he doing here? The god had sort of made it clear that he'd get to Aegir's hall on his own. Thorn glanced at Kayla. She was still oblivious, staring in the opposite direction.

Thorn looked back to the limo. The second person was climbing out. He smiled and the smile turned to laughter.

Startled, Kayla glanced at him. "What?"

Thorn pointed. "Our captain has arrived."

17

Kayla decided that Sparkle had gotten it right. If they were all headed for possible annihilation then why not do it in style?

Silence followed Sparkle's path as she boarded the ship. In the midst of a crowd that featured some of the most bizarre and powerful beings Kayla would ever meet, Sparkle was a star.

"Someone has to get her picture before she goes down with her ship. This moment needs to be preserved for future generations." There was laughter in Thorn's voice.

Kayla glanced at him. How could he find anything funny when they all might die in a short time?

"What?" He met Kayla's gaze. "Come on, laugh. I might not like her, but you have to admit she's good for morale. I mean, who would even think about allowing Aegir to sink this ship and ruin Sparkle's outfit?"

"You're right." She smiled and felt some of her tension ease.

Sparkle stopped in the middle of the deck and spun in a slow circle to view her team. She didn't look happy with what she saw.

"You're pitiful, people. First rule, dress for success. Your clothes should announce that you *will* prevail. Look at you, dressed in dull and dreary colors meant for skulking in the shadows. Do you really think they'll make you invisible to Aegir?" She sniffed her contempt. "No. They tell Aegir you're afraid of him, that you hope he won't notice you."

Kayla looked guiltily down at her own clothes—jeans, black sweater and gray coat. No comparison. Sparkle wore a short white captain's jacket with gold frogs across the front and gold epaulets on her shoulders. A little captain's cap perched at a jaunty angle on her head. She had leggings tucked into gold leather thigh-high boots with the prerequisite four-inch heels. Her gold eye shadow and nail color set the tone for the night.

"Black and gray are sexy. I like the understated look."

Thorn's breath warmed Kayla's neck as well as her heart. She slipped her hand into his. "Thanks." Kayla could have told him that he looked great in black, all dark sensual vampire.

Sparkle interrupted Kayla's thoughts of dark sexy vampires.

"Loki decided to come with us. I'll let him explain." She beckoned their resident god to stand beside her.

Loki had evidently gotten some style pointers from Sparkle. He wore what looked like black body armor and black boots. He'd thrown a purple robe edged in gold over his shoulders. He had a fancy gold helmet tucked under his arm. His black hair blew in the breeze as he stared down his perfect nose at everyone. Loki looked . . . godlike. Thorn's voice startled Kayla from her contemplation of Loki's godliness.

"Great outfit." Thorn grinned.

Loki narrowed his eyes and then shrugged. "I watched *The Avengers* last night. I decided to dress more in keeping with human expectations."

Someone on the other side of the deck called out. "Why'd you change your plans?"

"I'm here tonight to preserve your lives." He scanned his audience, his gaze lingering for a moment on Kayla.

She wanted to shrink behind Thorn, but pride wouldn't allow it. Kayla met Loki's gaze. He smiled.

Next to her, Thorn almost hummed with aggression. That shouldn't make her feel better, but it did. What did that say about her?

Loki continued. "Not from Aegir, but from Sparkle and Holgarth. Fortunately for you, I was present while they made plans to guide this ship out to Aegir's hall. Frankly, they terrified me. So I suggested that I pilot the ship tonight."

Prolonged cheering and clapping met his announcement. Sparkle looked insulted and Holgarth glowered.

"Never thought I'd say this, but thank the gods for Loki." Thorn watched as Loki strode to the bow of the ship.

Within minutes the ship began to edge away from the dock. There was no sound of an engine. It just . . . moved. Kayla shivered. What would it be like to sleep next to a man of power night after night? She glanced at Thorn. She'd like to find out.

The rest of their journey out into the Gulf was silent. The ship moved quietly through the water, and no one had much to say. Dacian and Cinn had joined Kayla and Thorn at the railing.

Dacian looked uneasy. "When the ship gets close to Aegir's hall, Cinn will call on the sea plants to grow over the clear dome. Aegir shouldn't be able to see us coming. She's never tried to use her power on such a large scale, though."

Kayla leaned over to clasp Cinn's hand. "You'll do fine."

Thorn agreed. "If Vince is any example of your power, I'm not worried." He frowned. "I'm afraid I haven't spent much time with the little guy. Too much going on. He just sits on my nightstand."

Cinn smiled. "Vince isn't talkative. But when the game is on the line, he'll come through." Her smile faded. "He helped save my life once."

Kayla wanted to hear her story, but just then Loki beckoned Cinn to his side.

"Looks as though the action will start soon." Thorn sounded eager.

"You're looking forward to this, aren't you?" Kayla didn't know how she felt about that.

He seemed to be giving her question a lot of thought. "Parts of it. I was a Viking. The sea, adventure, and fighting were my life. Living a human life nowadays can be . . ." Thorn shrugged.

Sadness gripped her. "Boring?" She was human. Did he think she was boring too? This was the man who had loved Sparkle Stardust. No way would Kayla ever come close to her on the excitement scale. But as much as she wanted him to be content playing at being human, she wanted his happiness even more. And that sucked lemons for her possible future joy. "Maybe you should allow your true nature to shine through once in a while."

"Not boring. More like lacking in epic battles where one mistake means the final death. But I've enjoyed the mental challenges of being human." His gaze touched her with warmth and something more. "I think during the course of a long life, everyone has to shake things up, try something different. Using my persuasion night after night drove me to want to end my existence. I never want to go back to that."

Kayla brightened a little. "So you might be happy running Nirvana?"

He nodded. "Yes, as long as I have other . . . challenging things to do."

His smile was slow and suggested something she was afraid to believe.

Thorn ended their conversation just when it was getting interesting. Kayla hated being dragged back to the real danger they'd soon face. She didn't need any epic battles to complete her.

Not quite the truth, Stanley. With the darkness, the wind whipping through her hair, the ship rocking beneath her feet, and the strength of Thorn beside her, she felt a certain frenetic adrenaline rush at the thought of facing off against Aegir.

And just for a moment, she thought of her father. Maybe this was what Dad was reaching for when he skirted the law or flirted with the forces of evil—the sense of teetering on the brink of oblivion that day-to-day life never offered.

Loki interrupted her musings.

"We're almost there. The sea creatures might have already alerted Aegir to the ship's approach, but plants now cover every inch of the clear dome, so he'll have no visual confirmation. The unnatural plant growth will have warned him that those aboard the ship have magical powers. Aegir will do one of two things: he'll either leave the safety of his hall to engage us or choose to hunker down inside. Our advantage is that he doesn't know yet that one of the Norse gods is aboard. But our advantage won't last for long. We have to move fast starting now."

Loki's gaze grew distant and then he nodded. "I've connected with the kelpie and shark. They're ready. Now I need the messenger of the goddess Bast and the demon who can create musical bubbles."

The Siamese cat leaped from the shoulder of the man. No, not a man. Kayla had grown sensitive enough to realize he was something else. She hadn't asked about him. But the cat was Asima. She'd called Sparkle a slut queen. So not BFFs.

Kayla heard Thorn's snort of laughter beside her. She threw a questioning glance his way. He pointed at the cat.

"Look."

She looked. And smiled. The cat was wearing a pirate's skull and crossbones medallion on her diamond collar.

Sparkle rolled her eyes. "Oh, please."

The cat ignored Sparkle as she padded to Loki's side. The music demon with the long blond hair joined her.

Loki signaled the demon to do his thing. Everyone grew quiet, watching. Suddenly Kayla could hear music. She looked at Thorn.

"'I'm Forever Blowing Bubbles'?" He shook his head. "That's incredibly cheesy. But I like it. It works."

Riveted, Kayla stared at what the demon was creating. Impossible as it seemed, the notes of the melody seemed to coalesce and gain a physical form. The demon looked as though he was shaping a clear ribbon of sound and then wrapping it around and around the cat until she was enclosed in a transparent bubble of music.

Asima offered the music demon a contemptuous stare. *"You couldn't have chosen an aria from Aida? Of course, demons rarely have well-developed musical tastes."*

Kayla would never get used to hearing voices in her head. She took a deep breath. It was really beginning. She moved closer to Thorn and he wrapped an arm around her.

The blond demon gestured and the bubble-enclosed Asima drifted over the railing and down into the water. She disappeared beneath the waves.

Loki turned to spear everyone still on the deck with a hard stare. "So it begins. I'm leaving now to rip apart Aegir's hall. I assume he'll try to engage me, but you can never predict what the sea god will do. He might choose to attack a weaker foe." His expression said they all came under that weaker category. "I won't be able to help you. Use all of your powers." He glanced at Kayla. "I would suggest the beautiful human stay safe in one of the cabins."

Kayla clenched her hands into fists. Wasn't going to happen. She wanted to stay as near to Thorn as possible in case he needed her. *Oh, come on, how could you help him? He's a freaking vampire.* Yes, there was that. But she wanted to be there just in case. Kayla would make sure to stay out of his way, though. She didn't want to turn into a liability.

Thorn looked at her. "Can I persuade you to leave the deck?"

"No."

"Didn't think so." He raked his fingers through his hair. "Just promise me if the ship comes under attack you'll get to a safe place. Otherwise worrying about you will distract me."

"I promise." She reached up to touch his face, to memorize the shape, the texture of him. "Don't take any risks you don't have to."

He smiled at her. "I should be okay. There's no record of an octopus ever taking a vampire's head." Left unsaid was that Aegir might decide to drag the ship below the waves. "If things get too dangerous and I'm not available, stick with Edge, the guy with the grim reaper tattoo. Next to Ganymede, he's one of the most power-ful cosmic troublemakers. He can get you safely to shore."

"I'll be fine." Kayla had believed that before leaving shore. But in the dark, in the Gulf of Mexico, with an angry sea god lurking below, she wasn't quite so sure. Looking back at him one more time, she walked to a door that led to an enclosed area with observation windows. If things grew too dangerous for a human, she'd step inside.

They had no more time to talk.

Loki disappeared.

Seconds later the Gulf erupted. The surface of the water became a churning maelstrom. Huge swells rocked the boat, and Kayla felt her stomach churn. No, she would *not* get seasick right in the middle of probably the only epic battle of her life. She would *not* live down to the puny-human label some of the nonhumans wanted to stick on her.

Waves washed over the deck and sea spray filled the air. Kayla clung to the door. She could see Zane, Holgarth, and the witches spread around the deck. Kayla assumed they were using their power to protect the ship. The music demon had already shaped one huge musical bubble and sent it over the side. As she watched, he created the second one and sent it after the first. God, she wished she knew what was happening down there. Could the humans survive?

Sparkle stood, feet planted in the middle of the deck, shouting directions and encouragement to everyone. She'd produced a sword and was waving it in the air. "There'll be dangers along the way . . . firstly mermaids, zombies . . . Blackbeard."

Pirates of the Caribbean? Really? Kayla wanted to applaud her.

Cinn joined Kayla. "Let's go inside. Dacian's worrying too much about me out here."

Kayla nodded, and they slipped inside. She glued herself to the window and watched Thorn. He was standing with a group of nonhumans, ready for a possible attack. She knew some of those with him, but not all of them. If she stayed, she'd have to get to know everyone. *If she stayed?* Where had that thought come from? Kayla knew there was only one person she would stay for.

And then it was over. What? That quickly? Why hadn't any monstrous sea creatures attacked them? Where was Aegir rising from the water to smite them? What about Ran and her nine daughters? Kayla couldn't deny a letdown, a sense of anticlimax.

The Gulf calmed and Asima's bubble floated to the surface followed closely by the two large ones filled with inert people. God, were they okay? They couldn't be dead.

Once on deck, the bubbles burst and the music stopped. Good thing. Kayla couldn't have listened to one more second of that damn melody. The cat stood looking at the rescued humans until they slowly started moving. They struggled to their feet, wide-eyed, terrified, and confused.

Kayla rushed back onto the deck. She remained in the shadows, though. Thorn would have to use his power now, and she didn't want to weaken his concentration.

She had a bad feeling about this whole thing—his persuading all these people at once, Aegir's too-easy defeat. Maybe she should just accept things as they were, though. Aegir was gone. And Thorn wouldn't attempt this if he didn't feel he could do it.

Loki suddenly appeared on deck, perfectly dry and without a hair or piece of clothing out of place. How the hell did he do that? He didn't say anything, just stood watching with the other nonhumans as Thorn faced the rescued people.

Thorn began talking. Everyone stilled. "Back on Earth at last. You don't know why the aliens decided to free you. You're just thankful that you'll be able to see friends and family again. The aliens sank your vessel. You lost consciousness. When you woke, you were on their ship high above Earth. It was huge, black, and triangular shaped. You can't remember much that happened to you. They must've wiped most of your memories before returning you to Galveston. You don't even remember what they looked like. They did experiments, but they didn't hurt you. You can't recall what kinds of experiments. Before they sent you from their ship, they told you they were going to Australia next. You were allowed to keep that memory. They weren't worried about you telling the authorities this because humans haven't developed the aircraft capable of catching them. Escaping human detection seemed like a game to them. You're on the beach now waiting to be rescued by the police. You're calm and quiet, thinking about all you've experienced, wondering if anyone will believe you."

The rescued people who had been standing sat down on the deck. All of them remained unmoving, staring at nothing.

Thorn turned from them. "They won't hear anything we say. Once we dock, use the vans we came in to drop them off on the beach. Then someone can make an anonymous call to the police reporting a bunch of people sitting on the sand in the middle of the night.

Zane shook his head. "I might still want to punch you, but that was an awesome display of power."

Sparkle zeroed in on Loki. "What happened? I was prepared for a big battle and nothing happened." Her captain persona looked a little droopy.

"Aegir is more of a coward than I ever imagined." Loki sneered. "As soon as he saw me, he fled with Ran and her daughters. He won't have the courage to ever come back here again." Now that he had routed Aegir, Loki looked as though he wanted to leave as soon as possible.

"Thanks for what you did, Loki. I guess. Since I really don't *know* what you did." Sparkle sighed and motioned for Loki to get the ship moving. "What a waste of an incredible adrenaline high."

Thorn sat on the deck next to Kayla on the way back. Other than his first disastrous foray into mass persuasion, he'd never used this much power at one time before. Tomorrow and the days after it would be hell. He glanced at Kayla. Dangerous too. The compulsion to use his persuasion again combined with the agony of withdrawal could make him a risk to those around him. He'd stay at his beach house until he came out of it. Sparkle would have to make sure Kayla didn't come anywhere near him.

"You're awfully quiet." She reached over and clasped his hand. "Alien abductions?" She shook her head in mock sadness. "That was just plain mean. All of those poor people will have to face the Men in Black. They might even end up at Area 51."

Thorn knew his smile looked anemic. "Yes, well it was better than the alternative. The police would cart them to the nearest mental health facility if they claimed to have been kidnapped by a sea god and kept prisoner in his underwater kingdom."

"You have a point." She remained quiet for a few minutes. "Will anything happen to you because you used your power?"

Thorn didn't even hesitate. He lied. "A headache. That's about it. I'll take a few painkillers, and I'll be fine."

He could feel her relief. Thorn only wished this hadn't come along just when he'd found her. Talk about crappy timing. He wanted to shine in her eyes. By tomorrow night, he'd need a hell of a lot of buffing to get rid of the tarnish. Maybe if he could stay isolated in the beach house she'd never have to know. Nah, his luck didn't run that way.

Once Loki docked the ship, everything moved quickly. The rescued humans were left on the beach and the call to the police was made. Klepoth hung around to make sure they stayed safe until the authorities arrived. And Loki disappeared.

Thorn stood with Kayla while they waited for a car to take them home. He said the words before he could overthink them. "I want you to stay with me at Nirvana for the rest of the night."

There. He couldn't call the words back. A considerate man would have suggested she go back to the castle and get some rest, but he was selfish. He refused to feel guilty. This might be his last chance to be with her. He would've held his breath if he'd had any breath to hold.

"There's nowhere else I want to be." She stood on her toes to kiss his cheek.

"Good." How was that for a romantic statement? One thing was sure, the only time he could create magic with his words was when he was weaving his persuasion.

Once at his pier, he guided her to his apartment. Their footsteps sounded loud in the stillness. He still moved silently when alone, but tonight he wanted to *sound* human. For her.

Grim had left only Kel as security tonight. After all, Galveston was almost deserted except for the police and federal agents, and the threat from the Gulf was over.

He held the door open for her to enter. When he stepped inside behind her, he tried to see his place through her eyes. Pretty pathetic. "Hey, maybe I could take our picture together before we go to sleep." Hah, sleep? Not likely.

She threw him a questioning glance.

"I don't have any pictures on the wall." Was that embarrassment he felt? "I thought I'd put up a few. Make the place feel more homey." Great. A homey vampire lair. Next he'd be crocheting doilies for the place. His friends would laugh their asses off.

Her eyes brightened, and she smiled. "I'd love that. Where's your camera?" Then she seemed to think of something. "I thought you guys didn't show up in pictures?"

"Some do, some don't. I do." He'd never figured that out.

He found the camera, set it up so it would catch both of them, and then took the picture.

"Umm, no one was there to click the camera. How did it take the photo?"

"Since I've already used my major power tonight, I didn't see any reason not to use my other ones." He wouldn't add to his suffering with this little display. "I can manipulate things remotely."

Kayla's eyes grew wide with surprise. Her expression reminded him that he was distancing himself from her with everything he did that emphasized how *not* human he was.

Why hadn't he thought first? Thorn regretted taking the photo.

But she didn't move away from him. She merely looked up and smiled.

"I'm impressed, vampire. And I think you should use every power you can cram into tonight. It's like when I break my diet. Since I've already eaten the pizza, I may as well gorge on the ice cream. I mean, the damage is done. You can start over tomorrow."

He raised one brow. "Well, that's one way of looking at it." He searched his mind for something to distract her from his powers. "Want to take a shower?"

She nodded. "I should've stopped at the castle and picked up a few things."

"You can borrow my robe." What else? "I'll fix something for you to eat while you're in the shower." *And I'll be picturing your bare sexy body with warm water streaming over it with every sandwich I make.*

"That's okay. I can make myself a sandwich. I'm not really that hungry." Her eyes gleamed with curiosity.

Thorn could read all of her expressions. This one said, "I want an excuse to see the blood in your fridge."

He went to the closet near his bed and pulled out the robe. "Feel free to scope out my fridge. Yes, I warm the packets of blood. Yes, I drink from humans for the occasional treat. And, yes, I keep human food in the fridge for visitors." In this case, he'd stocked his fridge in the hope that she'd be spending some time here.

Thorn stood holding the robe as she took him up on his offer. She opened his fridge, stared inside, and then closed the door. He held the robe in a death grip while he waited for her reaction. You never knew what would set humans off.

Kayla walked over and pulled the robe from him. "That was underwhelming. I thought I'd feel horrified shivers when I saw the blood. I didn't. Everything is in nice neat packets." She headed toward his bathroom. "I'll be out in a few minutes. I'd like to try your wine. Sparkle seemed to enjoy it."

He listened to the water running as he made her sandwich. The urge to dump the damn sandwich and join her in the shower almost overwhelmed him. Thorn closed his eyes and imagined.

He'd press himself against her back, feeling every curve of her sweet behind. Wrapping his arms around her, he'd slide his hands over her warm, wet skin. Her nipples would harden as he rolled them between his fingers. She'd spread her legs as his hands moved lower and lower. Then . . .

Then nothing. It had been a rough night for her. She hadn't hinted that she wanted him to share her shower. Maybe she needed a few minutes of alone time. There would be other showers. He smiled at the thought.

He opened his eyes and finished the sandwich. Kayla had said she didn't want him to do this, but making the sandwich was a human act. Thorn needed to regain that feeling after everything he'd done tonight. After he poured her wine, he heated up some blood for himself. He drank it before she came out of the shower.

How many centuries had it been since he'd cared so much about what a woman thought of him? Try never. Sure, he'd wanted Sparkle to love him, but his had been an immature love. He'd equated sex with caring. He also hadn't realized you could lose the ones you loved. All of his hard lessons about love, loss, and betrayal had come at once. He'd remembered them until now. Until Kayla.

He had a feeling he was about to put himself out there in a big way tonight. Thorn had given Kayla power over him. A mistake? He hoped not.

The water stopped running and then he heard the hair dryer. A few minutes later Kayla stepped out of the bathroom wearing his robe. She joined him at the counter.

"Looks good. Thanks." She picked up the plate and glass. "I'll meet you in bed."

She hadn't tied the robe tightly. He could see the swell of her breasts and a glimpse of long bare leg.

He watched her put her plate and glass on the nightstand next to Vince and then climb into bed with her robe still on. She picked up the TV remote.

"I'll watch the news while you're in the shower. Sparkle's worried about Ganymede. He's cutting a swathe through the country. The public is panicked. I'm nervous about what he'll do to the caldera under Yellowstone." She frowned. "I've been so concerned about Aegir that I haven't kept up with him."

Thorn didn't want to think about Ganymede now. He was just thankful the cat wasn't cutting a swathe through him. He'd worry about the chaos maker tomorrow night.

It was tough to leave her looking beautiful and sensual in his bed, but he needed that shower. He kept the temperature cooler than was comfortable, but the water didn't do a thing to cool his fever for Kayla.

When he came out of the bathroom with a towel wrapped around his hips, the TV was off and she was lying with the covers pulled up to her chin. Her robe lay on the floor. The small lamp beside her was still on. For the first time he sensed tension in her.

"Ganymede has taken his act to Egypt. Water geysers are shooting out the top of the three Giza pyramids. Then he must've ambled over to Italy. The Leaning Tower of Pisa collapsed tonight. Scientists are blaming a small earthquake for it. Luckily no one was hurt."

Her tone was light, but he could see the worry in her eyes.

"People are pulling out the old end-times and apocalypse explanations. Scientists are blaming climate change. Sparkle must be terrified."

Everyone should feel terrified. A cosmic troublemaker with Ganymede's power could do a hell of a lot of damage if he lost control. And from what Kayla said, the cat was way beyond out of control.

But why the hell were they talking about Ganymede? Thorn had a whole other subject in mind. He had to put an end to this conversation now.

"Sparkle will calm him down as soon she finds him. From what I saw, he loves her. She has to tell him in person that she loves *him*, make him accept that she didn't mean what she said. He needs to hear the words." He stopped beside the bed and dropped his towel.

He needs to hear the words. Maybe Thorn should take his own advice. He was pretty sure what he felt was love. He'd just have to find the right moment to tell her and hope she didn't splatter his heart all over the pier.

Climbing into bed beside her, he watched while she turned off the light. Then he reached for her.

18

Why had she spent precious minutes with Thorn babbling about Ganymede? From the moment he'd come out of the bathroom with that towel hanging low around his waist, she'd lost control of her mouth.

But while her tongue couldn't keep on task, her eyes had stayed totally focused on the goal. He was hard muscle sheathed in smooth skin. His movements were lithe and all-male swagger. She had lowered her gaze by increments. First, the tousled dark hair, brilliant blue eyes ringed by a thick fringe of lashes, straight nose, and sensual lips. Next, the broad shoulders tapering down to a ridged stomach and even farther to . . . the towel. Below the towel were strong thighs and legs. The scenic tour had exhausted her, so she hadn't spent any time on his feet. Kayla had felt sure they were as spectacular as the rest of him.

Then he'd dropped the towel, and her brain had refused to form any new words.

She had automatically turned off the light. But darkness didn't stop her mouth. It kept right on going. Her brain was still searching for words to describe what she'd seen beneath his towel—the length and breadth of him, the awesome manifestation of his need—so it was no help at all to her mouth. Her mouth didn't do well without direction.

It wasn't as though she hadn't seen his bared body before, made love with him before. What was different tonight? *You've had time to think about who and what he is.* And she'd had time to grow nervous.

Kayla knew he was about to touch her. She *wanted* him to touch her. So why not keep quiet and immerse herself in his amazing tactile talents?

But there was something about the absolute blackness of the room that freed her tongue. Without her permission, it blurted out a random thought that had been hanging around in the back of her mind for a while now.

"I was thinking about why the concept of 'vampire' terrifies people." What the hell had she just said?

Beside her, Thorn stilled. He didn't say anything.

No, no, I didn't mean that it scared me. Even if it did, a little, when she thought hard about it. What if he took what she'd said the wrong way? Of course he would. She had to clarify her thought. And now that she needed her mouth, it failed her.

Kayla lay on her back staring up at where she knew the ceiling was. She couldn't see it. She couldn't see anything. The darkness coiled around her, binding her in ties of primal fear. She had forgotten that Thorn's apartment didn't have windows. She couldn't remember ever being somewhere with a complete absence of light. Then there was the silence. He didn't move, didn't breathe, and if his heart was beating, she couldn't hear it because hers was a drumroll of terror.

She had the childish urge to pull the covers over her head and cocoon herself in warmth and the illusion of safety against . . . Against what?

The man beside her was the same one she'd made love with beneath the sea, the same one she'd kissed on the Ferris wheel, the same one she'd wanted to protect tonight. Then *what*?

"The *concept* of 'vampire'?" His words were clipped, controlled.

His voice was the key. She felt something loosen inside her, and her fear drained away. But he'd asked her a question. "For a moment I couldn't feel you beside me. You were just this big dark word, 'VAMPIRE,' in my mind. It freaked me out." That was a really crappy explanation.

"I'll always be a vampire, Kayla. Is that a problem?" He sounded cool, no emotion in his voice.

But she still sensed hurt. She rushed into another explanation. "No, this had nothing to do with you the real man. It just meant that for a moment, in the dark, I realized that a vampire lay beside me. And the thought scared the heck out of my primitive self because the concept of vampire is—"

"A bloodsucking fiend," he supplied.

"Exactly. But stereotypes are everywhere. I mean, what do you think of when I say 'lawyer'?"

"It's not the same, Kayla."

"Close enough." She knew lots of people who thought lawyers were bloodsucking fiends. He should just ask a few of her father's friends.

"So you were afraid of me?"

"My primitive self feared the *word*. Then you spoke, and everything was fine." More than fine.

"You're sure?" She heard him move, propping himself up on his elbow. "Because we can—"

"We can make love because that's what I want." She reached out and switched on the light. "And I want to see the person I'm with. Besides, I don't like total darkness."

He watched her from eyes that shone with desire and, yes, hunger. That only added to the need clogging her throat and causing her body to feel heavy, empty.

"I don't know what you include in your concept of vampires, but I can go against stereotype." He leaned down to tug on her earlobe with his teeth. "I'll make it slow and gentle."

She widened her eyes. Slow and gentle? No! She was looking forward to fast and *not* gentle. Kayla certainly didn't intend to be gentle. She'd stored up a lot of energy for the battle with Aegir, and she hadn't used any of it. "I—"

"Shh. I have a request before I make mind-numbingly slow and drearily gentle love to you." There was laughter in his voice. "I want you to turn over your concept-of-vampire thought and see what's printed on the other side."

"What?"

"Do it. I'll wait." He shifted beside her.

Thorn obviously wasn't going to make any kind of love with her until she did what he asked. She heaved an exaggerated sigh to let him know how annoying his request was and then she tried to focus.

Kayla closed her eyes, blocked his sensual presence out as much as possible, and pictured a card with her first thought printed on one side. Then she mentally turned it over. There was a question on the other side.

Her eyes popped open. "What does it feel like to *be* a vampire?" The question touched something deep inside her. "Why would I want to know that?"

He curled a lock of her hair around his finger. "Your mind, your question. I suppose you'll have to figure it out yourself."

Thorn leaned even closer until she could feel his lips moving against her ear. Goose bumps popped up along various body parts.

"But I can *tell* you what it's like." His fingers moved down her body, lingering on her breasts, stomach, and skimming up her inner thigh. "If you'll open your mind to me."

She clenched around the promise of those fingers. "How?" Why did she want to know this so badly? But the answer was too new for her to face right now.

"Open your mind to me in the same way you open your body. *Want* me there."

He had no idea the many places he was welcome in—her body, her mind, her life. She nodded. "I'll try. But can't you get into my mind even without my consent?"

"I wouldn't do that to you." He kissed the hollow of her throat. "Do you want to know the *complete* vampire experience?"

Considering where his lips were, Kayla had an idea what the word "complete" referred to. Was she ready? She didn't have to think about it for long. "Yes."

"Focus on your senses. What do they tell you about me?"

Kayla turned onto her side facing him. Exploring her senses with Thorn was foreplay at its best. She smiled.

He reached out to trace the shape of her smile with his fingertip. "If you expect me to maintain my legendary iron control, you'll have to stop doing this."

She pasted on a mock scowl. "Better?" Kayla didn't wait for his answer. She leaned close, breathing him in. "Your scent has eluded me since the day I met you. But that's good, because it belongs only to you. I could close my eyes and recognize you anywhere. I'll always remember it *here*." She drew a line with her finger from the tip of her nose to her heart.

Thorn smoothed her hair away from her face. "So I don't have to worry about you cozying up to a vanilla bean thinking it's me."

She laughed. "No, you'll never be a vanilla bean."

He grew serious. "All of a vampire's senses are enhanced. For example: your scent is layered. Right now you smell of my soap and shampoo. But beneath that . . ." Leaning close, he buried his face in her hair. "You smell of apples and lilacs and arousal."

"Apples? I love them. I had one yesterday." His closeness quickened her breathing. "And lilacs are my favorite flowers. I fill my place with them when they're in bloom. They smell of home." She'd just decided not to touch the arousal part of his scent checklist when she actually smelled the faint scent of lilacs and apples along with that certain something she associated with wanting him. "How did you know about the apples and lilacs? And how did I smell them too?"

Thorn shrugged. "It's as though our sense of smell carries with it a 'knowing.' Your scent tells me not only what you wear on your skin now, but what you've brought with you from other places and times. I simply connected with your mind and shared. Don't ask me how the 'knowing' works. Not a clue."

"Why don't you give me the CliffsNotes versions of sight and hearing? I want to get to the good stuff." Just the words "taste" and "touch" would probably have him fanning away her arousal fumes.

His smile touched every inch of her as he raked his gaze over her body. There was nothing slow or gentle in that look.

"I see all of you, Kayla. This part . . ." He touched the tip of his finger to each nipple. "This part . . ." His finger trailed down her stomach. "And definitely this part . . ." That marauding finger slipped between her legs and touched a part that was all too ready for him. "And even here . . ." He touched her forehead.

Thankfully, he didn't pass on any mental pictures. "Maybe I'm wrong, but I could swear that came under touching." *Please touch me again. Everywhere.*

His smile turned sly. "Touch is a crossover sense." His gaze grew intense. "I see the face you show now and all the faces you keep hidden. I see *you*, Kayla."

She swallowed hard. That couldn't be good. Maybe she didn't want him to have such great eyesight. "What about hearing?"

He shrugged. "I can hear the grass grow."

"Really?" She knew her eyes were wide.

Thorn laughed. "No. Just seeing what you'd believe. But I can hear your heartbeat." His laughter faded. "I'd know your heart. Always." His smile returned. "Now we're ready for the 'good stuff.'"

"Taste first." Once again she was five years old as her mother asked her what flavor ice cream she wanted in her cone. "Chocolate. Rich, creamy, decadent chocolate."

"What? I taste like chocolate?"

She put her hand flat against his chest and pushed. He complied by flopping onto his back.

"Not actually *like* chocolate. You embody the *spirit* of chocolate. Tasting you is that first burst of flavor, the slide of orgasmic pleasure, and then the satisfying afterglow." She held up her hand to keep him from replying. "Wait. I have to refresh my taste just to make sure you're not Rocky Road or butter pecan."

She could see him biting his lip to keep from laughing. And when he released that lip, she swooped down to slide the tip of her tongue across it. Then she covered his mouth with hers and savored his warm richness.

Finally, she abandoned his mouth to test-taste elsewhere. Kayla thought she should explain her method to him. "When I taste for overall flavor, I have to do a lot of samplings from different areas to make sure the quality is consistent throughout."

"Makes sense to me." His voice was low and raspy.

By the time she'd licked her way across his hard male nipples down to where his cock rose thick and long, she was sure he was chocolate. She decided not to tell him, though. "Just one more little nibble and I'll be done."

"Me too."

His pained mutter was tough to understand.

"What?"

"Nothing."

She'd left the best for last. With way too much relish, she slowly licked his staff in a spiral pattern. When Kayla reached the head, she nibbled her way around it until, with a harsh oath, he gripped her hair to pull her away from him.

"I'm not done."

"Yes. You. Are." He bit off every word as though it might be his last.

Kayla tried to look mildly puzzled, but couldn't quite achieve that innocent an expression. Her lips kept tipping up in a wicked grin. "You passed, by the way. So, tell me about how vampires experience taste. I suppose blood figures into this." Somehow the thought didn't horrify her.

"I can't remember. You've erased my mind." His words were almost a groan. "Let's go right to touch."

Suddenly, she found herself on her back while he loomed over her. "And I'll handle this lesson."

"Oh." Well, she supposed it was only fair that he get a turn. Her heart ker-thumped its approval.

"Touch, Ms. Taste-tester, is highly erotic for a vampire. Our fingertips are supersensitized."

He demonstrated by smoothing his fingers over every aroused inch of her body. But when he spread her legs, put his mouth on her *there*, and used his tongue to torture her very own super-sensitized pleasure nub, she had to say something.

Kayla tried twice before her mouth would form any sounds other than moans and cries. "That's not fair. You're using your tongue. That's—" Ohmigod, ohmigod! "That's. *Taste*."

His answer was low and guttural. "It is what I say it is."

She forgot then—what they were talking about, where she was, even *who* she was. Kayla was nothing but one giant nerve ending, and every touch lit her up.

"Quick. Now, before I burn out and you have to change the bulb."

Thorn didn't ask what she meant, but he evidently got the message. He straddled her, slid his hands beneath her and lifted. Kayla wrapped her legs around him. She could feel the nudge as his cock pressed between her legs. Everything inside her opened to him.

Even as the heaviness low in her stomach grew, she knew there was one last thing she had to say. "Remember. Total experience."

He didn't answer. Slowly, he slid into her. She felt herself stretching then tightening around him just in case he was thinking about sneaking away. Kayla gasped as he buried himself completely inside her.

She waited, breathless, for the sexual dance to begin.

He withdrew, leaving only a small part of him in her—what a giant tease—and then thrust into her again. And again, and again, and again. Each time deeper, harder until her cries formed a chain connected only by her pounding heart and tattered breathing. She met him over and over, trying to take him deeper when deeper wasn't possible because he'd already filled her all the way to her heart.

She sobbed, each gasping cry equal parts joy so deep no words would do it credit, frenzy to reach that moment when the idea of "perfect" shone brightest, and a soul-deep yearning for only this man.

Her senses spiraled outward, embracing his heartbeat—yes, she could feel and hear it—and all that surrounded them. The air shimmered with almost a life of its own. Every object in the room stood out in stark detail. And the plant on his nightstand waved its vine in the air. Vine?

Then it was as though someone grabbed her and yanked her backward through a tunnel. Everything disappeared except the sensations he created—friction, filling, completing. The end drew nearer until each thrust threatened to destroy her and then rebuild her in a new form.

She strained. Reaching, reaching. And just as she teetered on the edge, she remembered. Kayla was able to ground out only one word. "Share."

As the storm broke, she felt him kneel up taking her with him. She wrapped her arms around him and he lowered his mouth to the hollow of her neck where her pulse beat its potent invitation.

She felt only a brief sting. And while her orgasm shattered her, she knew he was replacing the life force he took with feelings she'd never experienced before—a physical intensity that burned through her, a pleasure so complete she wanted to . . . Once again, her mind failed her. There were no words.

Her spasms peaked and slowly faded until she realized he'd laid her back on the bed. He rested beside her. She was a glass-eyed rag doll, limp from the tips of her fingers and toes all the way to her brain. No, her brain wasn't limp at all. Now that she really didn't need it, her mind wouldn't stay quiet or peaceful. Distracted, she touched the spot on her neck where . . . Nothing. Her skin was smooth and unbroken.

Tell him, tell him, tell him now. Kayla explained to her brain that telling someone you loved them right after making love could be construed as a sexually generated response and therefore not reliable. She watched his face as he lay beside her. Yes, she loved him. And she *would* tell him. Just not right now. *What if you say the words and he doesn't say them back?* Kayla closed her eyes. No, she wouldn't go there.

"Maybe I don't want your input." Thorn didn't sound as though he was in a post-ecstatic state.

"What?" She opened her eyes.

"I wasn't talking to you." He nodded at the plant on the night-stand beside her. "Vince had a few . . . suggestions."

Kayla sucked in an outraged breath. "He *watched* us with his beady leafy eyes?"

Thorn lay on his back. He flung one arm across his eyes. "No. He can't see. But he sort of knows things." He sounded more tired than he should after cataclysmic sex. "I think he needs to mind his own business."

Kayla relaxed a little. "What did he suggest?"

"It's not important." Thorn finally moved his arm and turned his head to look at her. "What we just shared was—"

She put her finger against his lips to stop him. "Don't. Words would spoil it. Just know that I never . . ." She smiled. "See? No words. But I *will* tell you that your plan for mind-numbingly slow and drearily gentle lovemaking was an epic fail."

He reached over to smooth her hair away from her face. "Sleep. It's been a long night." His incredible lips tipped up in a smile. "You were indescribably delicious."

"Like chocolate?"

"I've never tasted chocolate. It didn't exist in my part of the world when I was human. But yeah, the *concept* of chocolate."

Thorn watched her sleep. Vince's advice bothered him. The little shit had said that Thorn should tell Kayla he loved her because you never knew if you'd have the chance again. Talk about a downer. Of course he'd have the chance again. He'd tell her as soon as he marshaled all his arguments for her loving him. He hoped she wouldn't fight him on this. *Love almost never has a happy ending.*

Thorn tried to shove the thought from his mind. This was the new and more positive Thorn Mackenzie. He had to believe that she'd choose to stay with him.

As dawn drew closer, he lost himself in the memory of their lovemaking. Too bad he couldn't have DVR'd his sensations and emotions for future enjoyment. He was right in the middle of remembering the instant he first tasted her life force when Vince interrupted.

"Aegir is coming. I feel him. Get up!" His small voice in Thorn's head was shrill and panicked. *"Wake everyone!"*

Thorn sat up, instantly alert. "Are you sure? Loki chased him off."

"No, he didn't. Aegir . . ." Vince paused as though he was tuning in to his own personal link to the sea god. *"Aegir just wanted everyone to think he'd run away so that Loki would leave. He's coming here to destroy everyone."*

"Why?" Thorn was already shaking Kayla awake.

"Vengeance. You ruined his setup."

"What?" Kayla sat up groggily.

"Get dressed. Aegir's on his way." He didn't bother with explanations. Thank heaven she didn't ask for any, just jumped from the bed and ran to grab her clothes.

Once dressed, Thorn scooped up Vince and followed Kayla out the door. Once he'd yelled for Kel to get off the pier, he called his beach home. It would only take about ten minutes for the rest of his team to get their butts to the castle. Kayla called Sparkle on her cell.

Kayla raced across Seawall Boulevard beside Thorn. "How do you know he's coming?"

"Vince told me." He knew how that sounded. Kayla had been there when Cinn gave the plant to him. She'd heard what Cinn had said about Vince. But did she believe? Too bad he didn't have more time to ease her into acceptance of all that was Vince.

He needn't have worried. She just nodded and kept running. What a woman. And she was *his*. Thorn didn't make any mental excuses for his caveman mentality. *Possessiveness is not a sign of an evolved vampire*. He didn't give a damn.

As Thorn along with Kayla and Kel burst into the castle's lobby, they were met by Sparkle and the rest of the nonhumans there.

Thorn couldn't believe it. Sparkle wore leather pants, high boots with those damn heels, and some sort of clingy top. "Damn, woman, do you sleep in those outfits? Couldn't you find anything more appropriate for a life-or-death struggle?"

Sparkle raised one brow.

Thorn had never realized how much one raised brow could say. Things like: you're an idiot with the brainpower of a doorstop, I've known earthworms with more sense than you.

"Perception is everything. If we look like a ragtag army, that's what Aegir will believe we are. I've fought barbarian hordes in 'outfits' like this."

Thorn didn't have time to argue. He turned to Kayla. "Stay inside." He realized his mistake the moment the words left his mouth. You'd think he would've learned from their sea adventure on the good ship *Death Wish*.

Kayla lifted her chin and narrowed her eyes. "I feel perfectly capable of making my own decisions."

Every once in a while, even after a thousand years, he'd feel the need to express his emotions with a human action. Right now he felt like heaving a huge frustrated sigh. "Great. Decide on how to keep yourself safe." *And if you set one foot outside the castle, I'll keep you safe.*

Thorn held up his hand to still the babble of voices. "I don't know what you guys think, but I feel we should make our stand in front of the castle. Nirvana sticks out into the Gulf. It's too vulnerable to attack from the sea."

Edge, the cosmic troublemaker with the grim reaper tattoo, nodded. "We have to end this battle fast and cover our butts just as quickly. Once the human authorities get involved, everything will go to hell."

"I'll activate the park's guardian gargoyles immediately." Holgarth didn't waste any more words. He headed toward the great hall.

"Gargoyles?" Thorn looked at Sparkle.

She was busy slipping into a short black leather jacket. "Live the Fantasy has protector gargoyles surrounding the park. The two main ones are on either side of the great hall doors leading into the courtyard." She flipped her hair outside her jacket collar and started walking toward the lobby doors. "Holgarth mumbles some sort of spell and wakes them. Once roused, they'll keep our enemies out." She paused. "Most of the time."

Before Thorn could comment, his team rushed through the doors. Relief flooded him. He hadn't realized how much he was depending on them.

He motioned Zane over. "Your dad is outside waking the gargoyles. Maybe he'll want help."

Zane nodded and was gone.

Sparkle reached the doors and turned to face them. "I'm not as powerful as some of you, but I'm very good at organizing. I feel that our magic-makers should scatter themselves along the front of the building. They'll weave wards to keep Aegir from the castle. If he gets past the wards, the rest of us will use our individual talents to defeat him. Don't stand together in a big group. Too easy to take all of you out at once. Remember that Aegir is a sea god. If we can lure him onto dry land, we'll have an advantage."

Banan spoke. "If Aegir is coming, Ran will be with him along with her nine daughters. Don't underestimate any of them. Ran is very good at ensnaring people in her net and drowning them. Her daughters are waves in their sea forms. Rogue waves can take apart most buildings and wash everyone and everything out to sea."

A sudden roar filled the castle. Startled, Kayla spun in a circle. "Is that Aegir?"

"The gargoyles. They're ready." Sparkle watched as Holgarth and Zane rejoined the group. "If the battle gets too intense—by that I mean we're getting our asses kicked—retreat inside the castle. But I have every confidence that with so many powerful beings here, we'll prevail."

"Prevail?" Someone snickered.

Sparkle did the brow-raising thing. "Big occasions call for big words. Let's go." She strode out of the Castle of Dark Dreams and everyone followed.

Thorn set Vince carefully on the counter of the registration desk before leaving. "Thanks for the heads-up." He still felt dumb talking to a plant. "Stay safe." He walked away.

Everyone stood together for a moment staring out at a tranquil Gulf of Mexico. That's when Murmur—who had already surrounded himself with music that sounded a lot like Metallica—spoke.

"Now that we've worked ourselves into a frenzy of anticipation, will someone tell me how the hell we know Aegir is coming?" The pounding heavy metal rhythm punctuated each of Murmur's words.

Oh shit. Thorn had told Sparkle, and Sparkle believed in Vince's message, but he wasn't sure how some of the others would feel about standing out here because of a plant's warning.

Sparkle put on her superior expression. "I'd rather not reveal my information source, but I assure you it's reliable."

Murmur didn't look all that convinced, but before he could delve deeper, the Gulf exploded.

19

Ohmigod! Kayla watched Aegir erupt from the sea. And erupt was the right word. As he rose, the water fell away from him in churning waves that spewed spray and sea creatures.

Her gaze followed him, up, up, up until she was craning her neck to see his face. The top of his head was level with the top of the castle.

He looked the same as he had the first time she saw him, only madder. His long silver hair and beard were encrusted with sea plants. Guess he hadn't had time to clean up after his escape from Loki. And he still wore streaming water as a unique fashion statement.

Then everything happened at once. Someone shouted, calling her attention to the beach. Ran raced from the foaming waves, a giantess gripping her lethal net. Behind her Kayla could see huge waves rushing toward the shore.

"Nine waves. Those are Ran's daughters."

Startled, she realized that Cinn had joined her by the doors.

Cinn tried to smile, but she didn't quite pull it off. "We're turning into perennial door-flowers. I suppose Thorn wants you 'safe' too."

Kayla nodded, her attention riveted on the unfolding battle. "I feel helpless. I can't just stand here and watch them get hurt." Watch *Thorn* get hurt.

"I know." Cinn lapsed into silence.

Kayla didn't doubt she was worried about Dacian. If things ended well—they would, they *had* to—she'd ask the other woman what it was like to love a vampire when you weren't one yourself. Of course, Cinn was a demigoddess, so she didn't have short-life issues. She could be with Dacian for the next thousand years.

Then Kayla stopped thinking about anything but the battle.

Kel and Banan had already leaped into the water. Zane, Holgarth, and the two witches looked as though they were weaving protective wards in front of the castle. See, she was learning the language of her new world.

Something beyond the breakers caught her attention. She squinted into the darkness. It looked like . . . "Is that a giant squid?" It rose above the waves, tentacles wrapped around some huge sea creature she couldn't identify. Then it took its prey beneath the waves.

"Edge." Cinn pointed to where the tawny-haired cosmic troublemaker stood near Sparkle. "He has crazy skills."

Kayla's respect for grim-reaper guy took a giant leap.

She forgot about Edge, though, as Aegir grabbed her attention. The sea god swept through the waves until he reached the end of Nirvana's pier. He didn't roar or shout or make any noise at all as he reached down and tore away half of it. She clapped her hand over her mouth to muffle her scream. Not satisfied with what he'd done, Aegir smashed his way through the wreckage and swiftly took out the rest of Nirvana.

Gone. Within minutes.

Horrified, Kayla listened to the shriek of tortured metal rising above background sounds of destruction. The roller coaster contorted and then fell over. The Ferris wheel tipped and crashed into the waves. The carousel dropped out of sight into the Gulf. Sparks from electrical equipment lit up the night. And then it was over. Only a tangled pile of wreckage and memories was left.

The nine daughters of Ran in their wave forms rose above the destroyed pier and then crashed down onto it. When the waves receded, they took even the wreckage with them. Nothing was left except a few pilings.

Her gaze found Thorn. His face showed only deadly focus and rigid control. Since he had to be all brave and stoic, Kayla lost it for him. Tears streaked her face, and she rooted around in her pocket for a tissue. After the tears came rage. Aegir might not have hurt Thorn physically, but he'd struck at something her vampire cared for. Something *she* cared for.

"Bastard."

Beside Kayla, Cinn said it for both of them.

Kayla clenched her hands so tightly she could feel a trickle of blood where her nails had bitten into her palm.

The battle escalated.

With a few huge strides, Aegir emerged from the Gulf and stood in the middle of Seawall Boulevard. Coming ashore had to weaken him, didn't it? He was a sea god for heaven's sake.

Please let the magical protections hold. Until this moment, the good guys had been safe behind the wards. But now, Aegir pounded the wards with massive fists. With each impact, flashes of light and explosions shattered the night. Sweat glistening on their faces, the magic-makers struggled to keep the wards up. But Kayla could see their walls flickering.

Sea shifters poured from the Gulf, changing into human forms as they came. She wanted to close her eyes, make it all go away. But she had to watch. If Thorn and the others could battle the monsters then she could bear witness to their courage.

She gasped as a killer whale broke the surface of the water and quickly became a dark-haired man with a white streak in his hair. He charged toward the castle with the rest of them.

Kayla felt the exact moment the wards came down. One moment there was a subtle vibration of power and the next . . . nothing.

Now was the time to retreat into the castle. That's what Thorn wanted her to do. But as she looked at the scope of the attack, she doubted the castle would keep her safe. In fact, nowhere in Galveston would be safe from Aegir and his sea hordes.

The defenders of the castle didn't wait for Aegir to come to them. They charged out to meet the invaders.

Frozen, Kayla watched Thorn struggle with another man. His vampire strength obviously trumped the power of whatever sea creature in human form he fought, because suddenly Thorn struck. Kayla looked away as Thorn tore out the man's throat.

No, she couldn't run inside and be sick. She owed loyalty to the ones battling Aegir. She owed *love* to Thorn.

"I can't watch this anymore. I've got to help." Cinn strode purposefully toward the fighting. In a few moments, Kayla saw thick vines pushing up through the concrete, wrapping around the legs of the enemies, pulling them down.

Even Asima was doing her part. Still wearing her diamond collar, the cat prowled the battlefield searching for prey. Kayla watched as she attacked Ran's net and tore gaping holes in it. Ran howled her fury. Asima answered by leaping onto the goddess's head and digging her claws into Ran's scalp. The goddess stumbled and fell to the ground, frantically trying to yank Asima from her head. Blood streamed down Ran's face, blinding her. Cat and goddess rolled and screamed and scratched.

Meanwhile, the nine waves crested, broke, and reformed again. Waiting for the moment they could help Aegir tear down the castle.

Enough. The longer this went on, the greater the chance one of the people she'd grown to care about would die. She had to do something. She had no powers, only the will to stand by Thorn's side and help take this puffed-up bully down.

She had only one advantage over everyone else out there. She was invisible as far as Aegir was concerned. It would never enter his mind that a human could hurt him. And so she crept toward the sea god, making sure that Thorn didn't see her.

When she'd gotten as close as she dared, Kayla reached down and pulled her knife from its sheath. She couldn't kill Aegir, but that wasn't her goal. Kayla wanted to inflict optimum pain while disabling him in some small way. A distracted god was a vulnerable one.

Straightening, Kayla yelled up at Aegir. "Hey, Mr. Big-and-Ugly! Afraid of Loki, weren't you? That's why you ran."

The god paused to look down. Then he bent over to swat at her. His face would never be closer.

Kayla threw her knife in one smooth motion. Then she turned and ran. She didn't have to look back to see if she'd gotten him. His roar of rage and pain told its own story. Terror bared its teeth, urging her to run even faster as she chanced a quick glance over her shoulder. With her knife buried in his eye, Aegir pursued her. And considering that he took one step to her ten—she knew this because she could feel the earth shake every time his foot hit the ground—it would be a short chase.

Kayla could see Grim racing toward her to help. Too late. The cascade from Aegir's robes was already pouring over her.

Thorn. Kayla wanted to see him one more time before she died.

"Stop!" Thorn's voice carried across the field of battle.

And everyone stopped, even Kayla. She closed her eyes, afraid to hope. Footsteps approached. She opened her eyes. Thorn stood beside her facing Aegir. Kayla turned so she was also facing the god. She winced. Aegir had yanked the knife from his eye. It was pretty gruesome.

Thorn spoke to Aegir. "You're losing, Aegir. A bunch of supernaturals who aren't even gods or goddesses are beating your ass. They're humiliating you. The best thing you can do is to leave now and take all your followers with you. Creep away. Hide somewhere far from here. And hope that no one in Asgard hears about this battle."

Aegir stood staring at Thorn from his one good eye. He looked uncertain.

"*Go. Now.* Never come back. Never try to hurt anyone here again."

Even Kayla, who didn't pretend to be very sensitive to nonhuman power, could feel the incredible force of what Thorn was flinging at Aegir.

With a sigh that would qualify as a wind gust, Aegir turned and retreated into the Gulf without saying a word. His followers trailed after him. No one spoke until the last one disappeared beneath the waves.

Kayla looked at Thorn. "Was he losing?"

"No."

She nodded. "Didn't think so."

"I thought I told you to stay safe. Flinging a knife at a god doesn't qualify as staying safe."

Thorn sounded furious, but the underlying fear she heard in his voice warmed her. And he'd used his persuasion to save her. Which brought up another question.

She didn't have a chance to ask it, though, because his fellow warriors descended on him for some hearty backslapping and congratulations.

And while everyone swirled around him, she stepped back. Looking across to where Nirvana had stood only a short time ago,

Kayla mourned. What would Thorn do now? *What will you do now?* She had no more reason to stay here unless Thorn gave her a reason.

In the distance, she heard the sirens. The battle had seemed to go on forever, while in reality it hadn't lasted very long.

She rejoined the others. "Umm, I don't want to stop the celebration, but you might want to move the bodies and get anyone who's injured into the castle before the police get here." Call her weak, but Kayla couldn't look at the dead.

Sparkle took over. "Kayla's right. Three bodies, none of them ours. Zane and Holgarth, can you get rid of them quickly? We have a few people with injuries. Someone help them into the castle. Hopefully no humans were close enough to see what actually happened. We'll claim the rogue waves destroyed Nirvana."

Within minutes, the only evidence that something big had happened there was the missing pier. Thorn stood across Seawall Boulevard viewing the empty spot with the police.

Inside the lobby, Kayla watched him through the glass doors. Grim stood beside her.

"What will he do now?" Kayla still felt dazed by how quickly everything had ended—Thorn's park, her dreams.

"I don't know." Grim looked troubled. "He has some decisions to make."

Kayla remembered the question she'd wanted to ask Thorn. Grim was close to him. Maybe he would know the answer. "I realize Thorn saved everyone's butt tonight, so don't think I'm ungrateful. But why didn't he use persuasion sooner? Why wait till the last moment?"

"He probably wouldn't have used it at all tonight if you hadn't been in danger."

That didn't make sense. Kayla dug deeper. "You mean he'd have allowed Aegir to destroy everything rather than use his power?"

Grim smiled for the first time. "Aegir might not have been losing, but he wasn't winning either. The more time he spent out of the Gulf, the weaker he would've grown. And the sea shifters aren't half as strong on land as they are in the water. Besides, some of our most powerful friends were just getting started. Edge was Death for thousands of years. Piss him off at your own risk. And Murmur's music is insidious. A little longer and a bunch of them would've dropped dead. That's not even taking Zane, Holgarth, and the witches into account."

"Then why did they seem—?"

"As long as the wards were up, our guys could conserve some of their energy. Once the wards came down, the real dance began."

Something still nagged at Kayla. "What's the big deal about Thorn not wanting to use his power at all? So what if he used persuasion tonight? That doesn't mean he has to use it again. He might not need it for another two hundred years. He can just go back to living his life as a human."

Grim looked as though he was choosing his words carefully. "There are consequences to using his power."

Kayla thought back. "I remember now. He looked as though he had a headache once before. I remember thinking that vampires weren't supposed to get headaches. Is that it? Using persuasion gives him a headache?" Even a migraine didn't seem to be a strong excuse. But who was she to judge.

Grim shrugged. "Look, it's not my place to explain Thorn to you. Maybe you should take your questions to him."

She nodded. "I'll do that. Tomorrow night." Tonight he could stay in her room. She would hold him until the day sleep took him. Then she'd sleep beside him and be there when he woke at sunset.

None of what Kayla had wanted went as planned.

Thorn had chosen to stay at his beach house for a while. Alone. Eric had decided to catch a late-night flight back to Chicago to be with his wife. Zane and Klepoth had moved into the castle for the time being.

She'd waited two nights for Thorn to visit her or at least call. Nothing. By the end of the second night, she was frantic. Ugly possibilities took turns poking at her: he'd lost interest in her, he'd discovered that he still loved Sparkle—and the most outrageous one—he'd died and no one wanted to tell her.

At sunset on the third night, Kayla took action. No more waiting around imagining the worst. If he no longer wanted to see her, he could damn well say it to her face. She climbed into the car she'd borrowed from Cinn, glanced at the directions Zane had given her, and then headed west.

When she pulled into his driveway, Kayla didn't see any other cars. If they were there, they must be parked in the garage.

She reached his front door on adrenaline alone. But by the time she got to the ringing-the-bell part, she'd used her supply for the night. She hesitated. *Don't be such a wuss. Postponing this won't make it better. Ring the damn bell.* She did. And waited. And waited.

Kayla had just reached for the bell again, when Grim opened the door. He stared at her from expressionless eyes.

"Thorn doesn't want to see you now." He looked as though he was about to close the door.

"No. Wait." She took a deep breath of courage. Now was the time to break out her pushy-bitch act. Dad would approve. "I want to know what's going on. I never thought Thorn was a coward, but only a coward would send his friend to the door to get rid of someone he didn't want to see."

Grim shrugged. "Not my problem." He moved back, ready to close the door in her face.

Kayla frowned. Something was wrong. She took a closer look at Grim. His face seemed drawn, and now that she was paying attention, those expressionless eyes looked tired. Who knew that vampires could wear the same stamp of human frailty on their faces as ordinary people?

He started to swing the door closed. Kayla had to make her decision now. But her worry over Thorn won out over being polite. She slipped past Grim into the house. Then she turned to face him.

"I have to warn you that tossing me out will be messy. I'll kick and scream and curse. Loudly." She tried on a winning smile.

He didn't smile back. "Crap. Just what I need."

His disgusted mutter didn't bode well for any extended visits.

"All I want is to make sure he's okay." *And to find out if he's avoiding me.*

Grim stared at the ceiling as if hoping for intervention from a higher power. Didn't happen. He did a great imitation of a human sigh. "Come into the great room. I was watching TV."

She followed him into a large room that ran the length of the house. The wall facing the Gulf was all glass. There was a fireplace and lots of comfortable seating. Kayla could feel at home here. *Like there's a chance.*

Grim motioned for her to take a seat. She sank into a large armchair while he clicked off the muted TV. He didn't offer her a drink.

"Where's Thorn?" No use wasting words on polite conversation.

"In his room."

It was Kayla's turn to sigh. He was going to make her work for this. "Thorn disappeared into this house three nights ago. No one has seen or heard from him since. The police, the media, the insurance companies, his lawyer, along with lots of just plain old nosy people are littering the castle. Sparkle is *not* happy." She raised one brow. "So?"

Grim studied her for a long time. His face gave nothing away. And just when she was about to start squirming, he leaned forward in his chair and spoke.

"Do you love him?"

Kayla blinked. What kind of question was that? She started to say it was none of his business, but then paused. There was something intense in his eyes that suggested she think carefully before she answered.

She considered lying, but in the end she didn't. "Yes."

He nodded. "Okay, here's the situation. For eight hundred years Thorn was a bit of a jerk."

Kayla opened her mouth to defend Thorn, but Grim held up his hand to stop her.

"If you want the story, you need to keep quiet, listen, and not interrupt."

She settled into sullen silence.

"For eight hundred years, Thorn used his power of persuasion every day. His attitude? Why do something for yourself when you can get someone else to do it for you? Why buy that piece of jewelry when you can persuade the seller to give it to you? And before you accuse me of exaggerating or not being fair, know that Thorn told me this himself. He used a lot stronger word than 'jerk' to describe himself."

Kayla tried to see the man Grim described in the man Thorn had become. She couldn't.

"Thorn said he'd told you what happened two hundred years ago." She nodded.

"I'd guess that Thorn never did things halfway." He offered her a weary smile. "When he decided to live like a human, he quit using his power cold turkey."

Kayla tensed. She sensed something coming she wouldn't like.

"And endured the withdrawal symptoms from hell for a month. Migraines that no amount of herbs or potions could stop. Stomach cramps and nausea without the relief vomiting would bring. Joint pain that made it agonizing to even move. Thorn told me he thought he would die, wished he *had* during most of it." He shook his head. "The worst part? He was completely helpless. For a month anyone could've destroyed him. Vulnerability is a terminal disease in vampires."

Horror widened her eyes. "I thought vampires didn't suffer the way humans do." This was so much more than the one headache she'd imagined. Why hadn't he told her the truth?

"Guess whoever said that was wrong." Grim leaned back against his cushion. "He'd developed a true addiction to his power. And like any addiction, when he stopped feeding it, pain followed."

"I don't understand." Kayla didn't want to picture Thorn in agony, unable to stop the pain.

"I can't help you there. I don't know of any other vampires who've gone through what he went through. But maybe most vampires don't use whatever major power they have on a daily basis. Eric is a Mackenzie vampire, and he uses his power to create realistic illusions. But he doesn't create them two or three times a day. Even working for Nirvana, he only did one a week that Zane put on magical repeat."

Kayla swallowed as she tried to control her nausea. Was this why she hadn't seen Thorn for three nights? "Is he going through with-drawal now?" Please, no.

"Yes." Grim stood and paced in front of the windows. "Evidently, the addiction never goes away. Once he went through that first withdrawal and survived, he was fine. Until he used his power again. Even using his persuasion a few times in small doses brought on bad headaches."

"And he used massive amounts of power on the ship and to persuade Aegir." She stood.

"You understand now." He walked over to where she waited. "Why don't you go back to the castle? Once he's feeling better—"

"*Will* he feel better?"

"He's strong, and he's fighting. The biggest danger is that he'll give in and use his power just to ease the pain." Grim's eyes said he couldn't make any promises.

"I'm staying." She looked around. "Where's his room?"

"Are you sure you want this?" He speared her with a hard stare.

"Yes." She thought of something. "Some of the others must've come around asking to see him. Did you let them in?"

"No."

"Then why are you allowing me to stay?"

He smiled. "You're the only one who said she loved him."

"Of course." Kayla rested her hand on Grim's arm. "He has a good friend in you."

His smile widened. "I'll remind him of that when I ask for a raise."

She didn't say it, but she very much doubted that Nirvana would rise again. In silence, he led her up some stairs to the second floor and to what must be the master bedroom.

"I'm sure you want to be alone with him." He handed her earplugs. "So far Thorn has resisted the temptation to use persuasion on me to get rid of his pain. But you never know when it'll become too much for him. Put these in if you have any doubts about his intention. Don't bother knocking because he'll only tell you to go away. Just go right in."

Kayla nodded and watched him return downstairs. Maybe she didn't want to go in by herself. Maybe she *wanted* a buffer between herself and any angry words Thorn might fling at her. *Maybe you need to suck it up.*

She took a deep breath and opened the door. Shock held her motionless with the knob still in her hand.

His wrists were bound to the bedposts. Shirtless, his torso gleamed damply. He wore sweatpants that had ridden low on his hips. And he glared at her from eyes that burned with a blue flame.

"I told Grim not to let you in. I'll fire the bastard."

His voice was raspy as though he'd spent a long time shouting. Or screaming in pain. She ignored the fury in his gaze.

"I didn't know vampires could sweat." Kayla sat on the side of his bed. She kept her voice calm when she felt anything but. "I always had this fantasy about a great-looking guy tied to my bed. Too bad it isn't *my* bed. Did Grim do this?" Kayla clenched her hands in her lap to keep from touching him.

"I told him to do it." He turned his head away. "When the pain gets really bad, I sort of lose it. I don't want to go running into the street looking for someone to persuade. And I'm not dead, so I can sweat. Now will you leave?"

"No." She leaned forward and put her finger over his lips. "Don't shout for Grim. He looks beat. I think he deserves a break."

His glare could've bored holes in her forehead, but he didn't call for Grim. "Did he tell you what's happening to me?"

"Yes."

"Figures." He sounded disgusted.

"Stop whining." It killed Kayla to keep up the pretence that this wasn't devastating her. But she sensed he'd hate having her cry over him. "I'm staying until you're better. Have you been taking anything for the pain?"

For a moment, she didn't think he'd answer. Then he nodded toward his nightstand. "Five of those painkillers help a little."

"Five?" She got up to look at the pills. "God, that's enough to stop an elephant's headache." She pulled a chair up to his bed and sat down. "What should I expect?"

He looked resigned. "The pain comes in waves. And when it hits, it hits everywhere at once—head, stomach, joints. I don't vomit, so you don't have to deal with that." He closed his eyes. "I'm not fun to be around then. You might want to leave for a few hours until the pain eases."

"Not a chance." The savage sound to her voice surprised Kayla. It was all about protecting her mate when he was at his most vulnerable. Who knew the primal part of her still hung around in some corner of her mind?

He lay silent for a few minutes. Then he opened his eyes. So many emotions lived in his gaze that she couldn't begin to separate all of them.

"Why are you here?"

It was a quiet question, but she knew her answer might be the most important of her life. *Be brave.* She shoved aside her fear of rejection, her uncertainty about their future, and told him the truth. "I love you." Then waited.

He never got the chance to reply because the pain chose that moment to strike.

Thorn grew rigid, every muscle in his body locked in agony. He clenched his hands into fists and fought the chains that bound him to the bed.

She leaped to retrieve the pills. Dumping five of them into her hand, she mentally thanked Grim for leaving a glass of some reddish liquid on the nightstand.

As she fought to help Thorn swallow the pills, she decided the liquid was too thin to be blood. Maybe a watered-down version?

Once she'd gotten the pills into him, she didn't know what to do next. Frantic to help, she tried to focus. Joint pains? She began to massage his arms, shoulders, thighs, and legs. And she talked, anything to distract him from the pain.

As the agony escalated, Kayla could see him clenching his teeth, trying not to scream.

Grabbing his shoulders, she held him until his eyes focused on her. "Scream, damn it! Let it go. And I'll scream with you."

And so they both screamed. When Grim raced up the stairs to see what was happening, she waved him away.

Then after what seemed like hours, the pain eased. Thorn looked exhausted. His face was pale, his eyes red-rimmed, and his hair was plastered to his forehead. Kayla went to his attached bathroom and brought back a cool washcloth. She smoothed it over his face and torso.

"I'm going back to the castle to get some of my things. Then I'll be back."

"Don't come back." Each word seemed dragged from him. "Don't want you to see this over and over."

"Shut up, vampire." She mock-punched his chin. "We're in this together."

If she hadn't been watching, she would've missed the slight twitch of his lips. Kayla returned his smile and then left. She waited until she was in the car to cry. And when the tears finally dried, she realized that not once had she worried that he might try to persuade her.

The next few nights passed in a blur of pills, screaming, and massaging. The agony was so bad that it even kept him from his day sleep. And when he grew incoherent with the pain, she stroked his face, his hair, and whispered promises she might never get a chance to keep.

He never mentioned her words of love. Maybe he didn't remember them. The pain had been coming on, so he might not have even heard her. Or he could've decided not to say anything because he simply didn't return her love and didn't want to hurt her feelings. That last possibility ripped at her heart.

It was while she sat in the kitchen during one of those nights gulping down a quick meal that Grim found her. He sat down across the table from her.

"How's he doing?" His eyes were warm and sympathetic.

She looked down at her soup. "The pain isn't lessening."

Grim reached out to put his hand over hers. "It'll take a few weeks for him to start feeling better. Hang in there. His mood has improved since you came."

Kayla nodded even though she wasn't sure how much she was helping. "We were talking about you tonight. Thorn said you found your father after being separated from him for centuries."

"It was a freaking miracle." He smiled. "My father married an investigative reporter. She tracked me down along with my brother and sister. Our family's finally together again."

Kayla held his gaze. "I'd like to do the same for Thorn."

"What?"

"His father was a jerk to him the last time they were together. He hasn't seen him in a thousand years. I'd like you to help me find his father. And if old dad is still alive and has mellowed, I'd like to bring him here to see his son."

"What brought this on?" Grim looked serious. At least he wasn't laughing at her.

"He's going through this because he chose to help others." She leaned forward, trying to make Grim understand. "If his goal was just to bring Sparkle down, he didn't have to persuade those people on the ship, and he didn't have to use his power on Aegir. He could've closed down Nirvana and walked away as soon as he realized the sea god would destroy Sparkle's business for him. But he stayed." She looked down at her soup. "I want to give him this. Can you help?"

Grim nodded. "I'll call my stepmother."

20

Every time Thorn clawed his way out of hell, Kayla was there with a cool cloth and whispered promises. But it was her "I love you" that he carried into the flames each time the pain grabbed him with its bloody talons.

Fevered, semiconscious dreams had blended with his lucid moments for what seemed an eternity. Thorn couldn't feed, couldn't think, couldn't do more than simply endure. He had no idea how long he'd been down. But the very fact that he could wonder meant he was getting better. Not that he had ever thought he would die. What had driven his terror was the possibility that during one of those moments filled with agony he'd grow weak and use his persuasion to stop the hurting. Then he'd be lost forever.

Kayla had been sitting beside him tonight when he woke, just as she had for all the other pain-filled nights. He'd gotten used to waking up to her.

Thorn didn't want to blurt out his love while he still felt weak and probably looked like hell. Yes, he had his pride. But he'd tell her. Soon.

It seemed, though, that tonight would be different.

"Time to rise and shine, slacker." She grinned.

He allowed the warmth of her smile to fill all the cold spots in his heart. "You have something special in mind?"

"I think you're strong enough now to make it to the bathroom. First we'll get you out of those sweatpants and then into a nice hot shower."

Out of pants. Hot shower. That combination of words had possibilities. Something stirred that hadn't done much of anything for a few weeks. "Sounds like a plan." The waves of pain had been coming further and further apart. And when they did come now, he could handle them. He no longer had to be tied to his bed. "Do I get my back scrubbed?"

"That can be arranged."

She smiled, but he could see uncertainty in her eyes.

Grim came upstairs to help him into the shower and then left. Jeez, just walking a few feet and shucking his pants had tired him. Where was all his vaunted vampire strength? Kick him if he ever used persuasion again.

He was considering how long he could stand in the shower before collapsing when Kayla entered the bathroom and closed the door behind her.

"One back scrub coming up." She didn't smile as she slowly stripped off her top, slid her jeans down over her hips, unhooked her bra and dropped it to the floor, and then shimmied out of her panties. He knew there was a reason he loved his clear glass shower.

Thorn glanced down. *Yes,* he was alive.

She padded on bare feet to the shower and slipped in behind him. He turned the spray on with hands that shook, and not from weakness. Thorn had promised himself there'd be other showers, but he hadn't quite had this in mind.

Kayla reached around his body to cup him. "Soon. But not tonight."

Soon. A popular word. Thorn knew she was right, though. Jeez, he could hardly stand up. Sex would kill him. But that didn't stop him from reverting to the six-year-old he'd been a thousand years ago who would cross his arms over his chest, stick out his bottom lip, and shout, "But I *want* to."

He didn't speak as she soaped up the washcloth and smoothed it over his shoulders, his back, his buttocks, and then his legs. Thorn locked his knees in place so they wouldn't shake.

Kayla reached for the handheld shower and quickly rinsed away the soap. After she replaced the handheld, he started to turn so she could do his front. *Eager much?*

"No. Wait." She sank to her knees behind him.

He didn't get a chance to ask what she was doing before he felt her fingers slide over his butt cheek followed almost immediately by a sharp sting. Thorn widened his eyes. "You bit my ass?"

Kayla stood, wrapped both arms around, and molded her body to his back. For a moment he was speechless as he tried to find a coherent thought beyond the sensation of her soft breasts pressed against him. She was shaking. Crying? Panicked, he opened his mouth to ask what was wrong. Then he realized she was laughing. *Laughing?*

"I'm sorry. I couldn't resist. I've wanted to do that for a while."

"But you *bit* me." He couldn't get past that. "Why?" Not that he really cared. He was willing to take any bodily contact she was willing to give.

"Practice."

He just stopped himself from repeating the word out loud. Thorn rolled it around in his mind. Looked at it from all angles. Practice for what? And when the answer came, it struck him speechless. Not an affliction he suffered from often. He'd save the discussion of "practice" for another time and place.

Silently, he watched her wash his chest and arms before moving down to his thighs and legs. The feel of the washcloth moving over his skin soothed him at the same time it annoyed the hell out of a part of him that felt she should be using her hands. He tried to ignore that voice. The one that didn't run its opinions through his brain first.

Finally, she handed him the cloth to complete the job. The fact that she stood watching while he handled himself didn't help matters. And her beautiful breasts gleaming wetly almost brought him to his knees. Not that weakness wasn't close to putting him there anyway.

The last thing she did was wash his hair. He closed his eyes and enjoyed the feel of her fingers massaging his scalp. After the final rinse, she turned off the water.

Thorn was a detail man, so he noticed that one drop still clung stubbornly to her nipple. Before she could step away, he leaned down and licked the drop away.

He heard her gasp and reveled in it. "We'll do this again when I'm stronger." Thorn hoped she read the intent in his eyes, because he sure wasn't trying to hide it.

The next few minutes were filled with bliss as she dried his body with a soft towel. Then she helped him climb into a fresh pair of pants.

"Will you be okay alone to shave and brush your teeth?"

He was a vampire. He was strong. All right, so semi-strong. No way would he admit that teeth-brushing and shaving were in the same category as bench-pressing a thousand pounds right now. "Sure. No problem."

Her smile held a secret. "Great. That'll give me a chance to change your sheets."

Thorn frowned as he watched her leave. He didn't like the idea of her doing stuff like that for him. He wanted to pamper her. Forever. He thought about forever as he dried his hair, brushed his teeth, and shaved.

Grim was the one who came to help him back to his room.

"Where's Kayla?" Did he sound possessive? That's how Thorn felt, but he didn't want to *sound* that way. Women hated possessive men. But it was in his vampire nature to guard and protect what he thought of as his. Of course, she'd gotten in his face more than once when he'd tried to tell her what to do. He smiled at the memories.

"She's downstairs. She'll be up in a few minutes." Grim had settled him back into bed quickly. Then he left without saying anything more.

Strange. Grim liked to talk. But Thorn didn't get a chance to wonder about Grim's quietness before he heard footsteps coming up the stairs. *Two* sets of footsteps. Grim had just left, so he wouldn't be returning with Kayla. Then who? She hadn't mentioned any visitors.

He watched the door, tension filling him even though he had no reason to feel it. One of the guys from Nirvana had probably stopped by, and Kayla had felt Thorn was well enough to see him.

The door opened and Kayla stepped into the room. There was a man behind her. Instead of walking over to Thorn's bed, she simply stepped aside.

Thorn stared at the man filling the doorway. And saw himself.

"Hi, son."

The stranger who wore his face walked over and sat on the chair by his bed. "Hope you're feeling better."

Thorn couldn't stop staring at the man's face. *His* dark hair, *his* eyes, *his* mouth. "Father?"

If Kayla had given him time to prepare, Thorn probably would have rolled out his father's name, Rolf. Because the father he knew had died the night he rejected his son. But shock had crumpled Thorn's defenses, and he spoke the first word that entered his mind.

"It's been a long time." His father folded and unfolded his hands.

Then not as calm as he looked. That made Thorn feel better. He didn't want to be the only one who felt his world had just shattered and left him staring at the pieces.

"Your woman and Grim tracked me down. Don't know how they did it. I'll never be able to repay them. I've searched for you everywhere. Damn, but you change your name a lot." His smile was tentative.

Thorn looked past his father to where "your woman" was glaring at Dad's back. "Kayla is a miracle worker." He hoped she understood that her "miracle" included everything she'd done for him since the moment they'd met.

She met Thorn's gaze and smiled. "I'll leave you and your father alone. Call if you need anything." Then she left.

Thorn fought for control. So many emotions. His first instinct was to lash out at his father. But surprisingly, he realized his anger felt old and tired. Just as his love for Sparkle had faded, his fury at his father had lost its intensity over the centuries. That didn't mean he was ready to forget everything.

"Why did you want to see me? You were pretty clear about your feelings the last time we were together." Thorn didn't try to keep the bitterness from his voice.

His father looked away. "I was dealing with a lot of guilt and denial at the time. I reacted by striking out at you. By the time I realized what I'd said, you were gone."

"Guilt and denial?" This was news to Thorn.

"I caused everything that happened." He raked his fingers

through his hair. "The cosmic troublemaker that sold you into slavery and then killed your mom, sister, and brother came to the village looking for me."

Thorn didn't speak, didn't blink, didn't even try to think. Once again he was back in that small village, the cold biting into him as he wrestled with his own guilt and played the if-I-had-only game.

His father stared at the far wall, avoiding his son's eyes. "The bastard had been after me to capture slaves for him on my raids. Others did it, but I refused. You were his revenge. What better punishment than to know my son was a slave? Your mother, brother, and sister died because they were easy prey."

"Because I wasn't there. Because—"

"Stop." His father leaned toward him. "It wasn't *your* fault. Anymore than it was your mother's fault for not staying in the village. Do you think I haven't looked back and wished that I'd come home a week earlier, given him the damn slaves he wanted, killed the bastard when I first met him? Life happens, and we don't have the luxury of knowing the future." He closed his eyes. "God knows how I've regretted so many things, but probably my greatest regret is how I treated you."

The silence was alive with emotions, too many for Thorn to handle. "Who was he? I want his name."

His father opened his eyes and leaned back in his chair. "Caveen. But he doesn't matter anymore." Something deadly crept into his voice. "I made it my life's mission to make sure he paid for everything. I asked questions until I found out that someone called the Big Boss was in charge of all cosmic troublemakers. For centuries I searched for this guy. Finally I found him." He smiled, but it was a cold smile. "Luckily for me, the Big Boss has dealt with our clan before. He likes us. Unluckily for Caveen, he'd pissed off the Big Boss one too many times."

Thorn propped himself up higher in his bed. He wished he were sitting in a chair. He had enough pride not to want his father to see him weakened. "So what did the Big Boss do?"

"He destroyed him."

"I didn't believe anyone could kill one of them." Thorn thought about Ganymede. If the cat didn't get his head together soon, he might see the end of his long existence.

"The Big Boss did it. I saw the bastard die."

Silence filled the room. Thorn knew what happened next was up to him. He could hold tight to the rage and hurt from so many centuries ago. Or he could allow those emotions to slide back into the past.

Thorn looked away from his father. Who was left to hate? The man who'd destroyed his family was dead. Sparkle was guilty of nothing worse than dumping him. And his father had searched for him, cared about him. And what had Thorn done? He'd nursed his anger and not once had he tried to find his father.

Leaning his head back against his pillow, Thorn mentally dug a deep hole on some barren hillside and buried the past with all its pain. Forever.

"So, Dad. What're you doing with your life?" Yes, his father could be "Dad" to him in this time and place. Thorn smiled and meant it.

His father's expression relaxed into a grin. And if his eyes looked a little damp, neither of them mentioned it.

"I design robots."

"No kidding." Thorn laughed. He couldn't help imagining. Robots for Nirvana. Sure, the pier was gone. But that didn't mean it couldn't rise again. "Ever consider changing jobs? I have an offer you can't turn down." Crap. Wrong wording. "Scratch that. I have an offer you'll love."

"Let's hear it."

• • •

Kayla sat in the kitchen drinking coffee alone. They'd been in Thorn's bedroom for hours and both of them were still alive, so all was good. So many things could've gone wrong. And once again she questioned whether she'd had the right to meddle in Thorn's family business no matter how well-meaning she'd been.

She was setting herself up for heartbreak. Maybe he didn't want her inserting herself into every aspect of his life. Kayla had descended on him when he was at his most vulnerable and maybe now that he was growing stronger he'd want her gone.

Once again she thought about the life-changing decision she'd made once she knew she loved him. No one could ever say she hadn't understood what she'd be losing. She would become vampire and never again walk in the sunlight or eat a pizza. She'd watch her family grow old and die while she remained twenty-seven. But Kayla was willing to accept those sacrifices for the joy of loving him for the next thousand years. *If he loved her.* He hadn't said the words yet.

By the time Rolf walked into the kitchen, Kayla was well on her way to completing her list of the one hundred most likely ways Thorn Mackenzie would break her heart.

Thorn's father didn't sit down. "I'm leaving for now, Kayla." He smiled. "My son warned me that you'd react badly if I continued to refer to you as his woman."

She started to rise. "I'll see you out."

"No, you won't. I'll see myself out. You have somewhere more important to be. Thorn is anxious to see you." He started to turn away and then paused. "Words can never tell you how grateful I am that you gave my son back to me."

Then he was gone in a blur of motion that startled her. Kayla took a deep breath of courage and headed for the stairs. She hesitated at the bottom, though. What would he say? Her stomach churned at all the possibilities. *Calm down.* Why was she so freaking nervous? He'd probably just ask her to heat up some blood for him.

Well, nothing would change just because she couldn't work up the courage to face him. Straightening her back, she climbed the steps and walked into his room. Then she stood there and waited.

He was propped up in bed and looked as breathtaking as the first time she'd seen him. His expression gave nothing away.

"Did everything go okay?" *Don't fidget.* Kayla tried to look calmly interested but not obsessively so.

"Why don't you come over here?" He patted the side of his bed.

The bed not the chair? That was a good sign. Kayla offered him a friendly smile. She made sure it didn't say, "I want to bite your butt."

Kayla perched on the edge of the bed down near his feet. "I saw your father on his way out. He seemed happy."

Thorn cocked his head and studied her. "You know, if I didn't know what a fearless spy you were, I'd say you were nervous."

"Nervous?" Were her eyes too wide? She narrowed them. "Definitely not." She forced herself not to chew on her lower lip.

His smile was crooked and sexy and irresistible. "Come closer, Kayla. I'd say I don't bite, but I do."

She inched her way up the bed until she was next to his stomach. And when he just stared at her, she finally broke.

"This is stupid. Where do you want me to sit? And when I get there will you please tell me what happened? And then—"

"And then . . . ," he mocked.

He grabbed her and tucked her in beside him before she could take her next breath. She'd gotten used to thinking of him as fairly helpless. Her mistake. Kayla had forgotten exactly how strong and fast he could be. He was recovering more quickly than she'd expected, more quickly than she *wanted*. Yes, she'd enjoyed having him need her. Kayla couldn't regret this time with him.

"And then we'll talk about how much I love you." His words were a bare whisper next to her ear.

Everything stopped—her heartbeat, her breathing, her life. Because a moment like this deserved to be savored in complete stillness.

By the time she gasped for that next breath and her heartbeat gave a mighty ker-thump, she realized her cheeks were wet.

"You're crying? Here." He pulled a tissue from the box on the nightstand and shoved it at her. "This would really be tearing up my ego if I hadn't already heard you say you loved me."

Kayla shook her head and sniffled. "Tears of joy."

"Oh." He sounded relieved. And then he chuckled. "A thousand-year-old vampire who's nervous about saying three words. My street cred is shot." He lowered his gaze. "You'll marry me?"

"Marry?" Words tumbled around in her head, but none of them seemed awesome enough for this moment.

Thorn wasn't smiling when he looked up. All the passion and love he felt for her, enough for countless lifetimes, shone in his eyes. "It's a human ritual. Your family will expect it." Finally he smiled. "And surprisingly, I find that even though our love will bind us together without them, I want to hear the words, *say* the words so everyone will know." He raised one brow. "So?"

"Yes, yes, yes!" She didn't give him a chance to say anything more. Gripping his hair, she pulled him to her and kissed him. The kiss was long and deep and arousing. "Are you sure you can't . . . ?"

"I damn well can."

And he did.

It had been one week, two days, and four hours since Thorn had said he loved her. Not that Kayla kept track of that kind of thing. And if Sparkle kept them waiting much longer it would be five hours.

Kayla looked at the clock on the conference room wall. "I wonder why she called this meeting?"

Thorn sat beside her. Beneath the table, his hand rested possessively on her thigh. She placed her hand over his and wished they were home in bed. Or on the couch or the pool table or the fluffy rug in front of the fireplace.

"Did you tell Sparkle about your plans?" She glanced at the door. Still no Sparkle.

"No. I'll try to catch her after this meeting." Thorn looked distracted. "You know, I suddenly recalled something I wanted to talk to you about. Remember when you bit my ass in the shower?"

Beside her, Klepoth showed sudden interest in the conversation.

"Shh. Keep your voice down." Frantically, she searched for a way to detour around this subject. Nothing came to mind. Panic was a great mind eraser. "Yes, I remember." It wasn't something she'd ever forget.

Thorn was looking at her now, eyes narrowed and lips thinned. "You said it was practice. Practice for what?"

Now he was annoying her. "You've already guessed or else you wouldn't be wearing that scowl. Practice for when I'm a vampire."

For once he seemed speechless. Good. Because she had a few things to say before he exploded all over her plans. "We're marrying. And somewhere among all those promises are the words 'until death do us part.' Well, death is going to part us pretty quickly if I stay human. That's not an option for me. I refuse to die and leave you crushed by grief." She thought about that for a moment. "Of course, after spending fifty-plus years with me, you might just throw a party. Anyway, I know you can't make me vampire, but Dacian isn't a Mackenzie and he can. I've asked him."

Thorn's expression was thunderous. "No letch of a night-feeder is going to put his fangs into the throat of the woman I love."

Kayla controlled her eye-rolls. "He's not a letch, and he's married to Cinn. Wrist, not the throat. There will be *no* sexual thoughts on either side. Besides, I'll expect you to be there." She was trying to sound in control and sure of herself, but his anger bothered her. She really wanted this, wanted to share everything in his life.

He closed his eyes and she could almost see him reeling in his anger and storing it under the seat. When he opened his eyes, she almost cried with love and relief.

"Are you sure this is what you want, Kayla? It's not something you can take for a trial run and then return if it doesn't make you happy."

Didn't he know that *he* would always make her happy? And what he was, what she would be, was part of that happiness. "Yes."

He nodded. "We'll talk to Dacian later."

Kayla felt as though she'd climbed Mt. Everest and planted her flag on the summit. All her other problems were little ones. Talking about little problems . . .

"I called my father before you woke tonight. I told him I quit and that I'd never be joining the family business. I also told him I was marrying a wonderful man." She smiled. "He yelled, threatened, and generally blustered a lot. Then he got all emotional about his little girl. I promised to send him a wedding invitation."

Thorn looked thoughtful. "Will he try to recruit me for the family business? If so, you'll have to explain that I drink on the job."

Kayla didn't have a chance to answer, because just then Sparkle entered the room. All conversations stopped.

Sparkle wasn't sparkling tonight. She wore plain jeans stuffed into plain boots topped off by a plain black sweater. Her nails were color free and her hair was pulled back in a ponytail.

This never-before-seen phenomenon caused a rush of whispers. Kayla nudged Thorn. "Look. There's a rolling suitcase by the door."

Sparkle went to the chair at the head of the table but didn't sit. She looked around at all the faces. Then she spoke.

"I'm leaving the Castle of Dark Dreams tonight. I don't know when I'll be back. I might never return. I've arranged for Live the Fantasy to continue on in my absence." She held her hand up to stem the shocked exclamations. "A large section of the Great Wall of China disappeared tonight. I suppose we should be thankful Mede left some of it standing."

Kayla had always thought that Sparkle was the most beautiful woman she'd ever seen. Sparkle was still beautiful, but tonight Kayla could see the millennia she'd existed in her eyes.

"I received a call from the Big Boss tonight. He said he can't ignore the chaos Mede is visiting on Earth any longer. He's decided to destroy him."

No one moved. No one spoke. But disbelief was a sonic boom as her words sank in.

"Mede and I saw the pyramids rise and Rome fall. I've loved him throughout the centuries even though we weren't always together. Now, he needs me." Her lips tipped up in a small smile. "Although he'd be the first one to claim that all he needed was a container of ice cream and his remote."

The silence was a living breathing thing.

"I'm going to search for him and hope that I find him before the Big Boss does. Wish me luck." She didn't stop to talk with anyone as she walked to the door, retrieved her suitcase, and headed for the lobby doors.

Thorn rose to follow her. He glanced at Kayla and she nodded. She understood that this was something he needed to do alone.

He caught Sparkle just as she reached her car. "Have a few minutes?"

"Not if all you intend to do is heap more abuse on my head. I'm already having a bad hair night. I don't need you making it worse." She lifted her chin and glared at him.

"Don't worry. I'm fresh out of abuse." He forced himself to meet her gaze. This needed saying. "I've hated you for almost a thousand years."

She frowned. "Look, this isn't the time—"

He held up his hand to stop her. "I was wrong. You didn't sell me into slavery. Yes, you dumped me, but that didn't deserve the kind of vengeance I wanted to hand out."

Sparkle smiled, and Thorn remembered why he had thought there would never be another woman for him those many centuries ago.

"Well, it took you long enough." Her smile faded. "I'm sorry for what happened to you and your family because of that night. You're not the only one who was wrong. I'm a thousand years older and a little bit wiser. I wouldn't ask someone else to do my dirty work now."

He nodded. "Fair enough. Oh, and I'm rebuilding Nirvana. My father will be my partner in the new park."

Sparkle shrugged. "Guess I'll have to get used to staring at another freaking Ferris wheel." Left unsaid was *if she ever returned.*

Thorn smiled for the first time. "Not really. We're building the new park farther up the beach. You'll have your view back."

She didn't say anything, just stood on her toes and kissed him on the cheek. "I hope that you and Kayla live long and well. And tell her to dress sensually. I expect her to be Asima's new slut queen."

He put her suitcase in the trunk and then held the door as she climbed into the driver's seat. Thorn could see the rest of the castle's nonhumans peering through the glass doors at them and waving.

Just before Thorn closed the car door, Holgarth joined him.

The wizard touched Sparkle's shoulder. "If you should need help from anyone here, just call. We'll come."

For one of the few times that Thorn could remember, there was no snark in Holgarth's voice.

Sparkle reached up and patted the wizard's hand. There was a sheen of tears in her eyes. She said nothing as Thorn shut the door. He watched her drive away from the Castle of Dark Dreams for maybe the last time.

Thorn and Holgarth didn't speak as they entered the castle.

Kayla wrapped her arms around his waist. "That's it?"

He nodded. "Sparkle Stardust has left the house."